Blame It on Cupid

JENNIFER GREENE

HQN™

ISBN-13: 978-0-373-77177-6
ISBN-10:   0-373-77177-0

BLAME IT ON CUPID

Copyright © 2007 by Alison Hart

This edition published by arrangement with Harlequin Books S.A.

® and TM are trademarks of the publisher. Trademarks indicated with ® are registered in the United States Patent and Trademark Office, the Canadian Trade Marks Office and in other countries.

www.HQNBooks.com

Printed in U.S.A.

If you're reading a book you can't put down—blame it on Jennifer Greene!

BLAME IT ON CHOCOLATE

"Written with a deliciously sharp sense of humor and her usual superb sense of characterization, RITA® Award-winning Greene's latest romance is a sweetly sexy, thoroughly satisfying, and simply sublime literary confection."
—*Booklist*

"Ms. Greene is a wonderful story teller who pulls you into the lives of her characters.... *Blame It on Chocolate* is intriguing, engaging and full of drama and wit. You'll have a very hard time putting this story down."
—*CataRomance.com*

"...terrifically likeable hero and heroine. The sexual chemistry between them sizzles, the romantic plot is emotionally compelling and the subject matter at the heart of the story is interesting."
—*Romantic Times BOOKreviews*

"The characters are likable, the plot is realistic, and the book is fantastic. I highly recommend *Blame It on Chocolate*."
—*Romance Reviews Today*

"The characters are truly believable, the dialogue is funny, and the situations this couple find themselves in are ones anyone can relate to."
—*Romance Junkies*

"A warmhearted romance with endearing characters, simmering sensuality, and a very interesting subject matter. A book to curl up with on a cold night."
—*Rendezvous*

LUCKY

"RITA® Award-winning Greene's gift for creating strongly defined, realistically complex characters gives her latest book an emotional complexity and richness readers will find difficult to resist. *Lucky* is destined to become a classic."
—*Booklist*

Other recent works by Jennifer Greene

To: Moose, Brody, Havi, Magic

It's about the unconditional love.
Thanks, guys

Blame It on Cupid

CHAPTER ONE

NORMALLY NOTHING SCARED Merry Olson. People teased her about it all the time. On the same morning, you could throw her a flat tire, bad hair and burned eggs, and she'd still be perky. Her dad claimed she could find the silver lining in a tornado. But man, one look at the house and she felt rattled clear to the bone.

The trip from Minnesota to Oakburg, Virginia, had been tediously long, especially driving alone, so she expected to arrive exhausted. She just never expected to feel culture shock as if she'd landed on a completely alien planet.

Taking a huge, bolstering breath, she climbed from her snow-and-salt-crusted blue Mini Cooper and grabbed her cell phone. At twenty-nine, she was hardly tied by the emotional umbilical cord to her dad, but she knew darn well he'd worry himself crazy until he heard from her. She worried about him the same way when he traveled alone.

Waiting for her dad to answer, she glanced at her car. Merry never doubted that her Cooper could make it through anything—the car was far more reliable than she was—but right now, no question, the baby was sagging in the rear end and heaped to the gills.

Upending her entire life in a week had been a major

challenge, but not impossible. For years friends and family had labeled her ditzy, but where they meant an affectionate insult, Merry secretly took pride in the tag. She lived life loose. That was a deliberate choice, not an accident. She'd never taken a job she couldn't quit, never allowed herself to get so attached to a place that she couldn't leave. She'd never settled long with anyone or for anything.

What other people called flaky, she called freedom. And maybe she had a few personal reasons why she was so zealously footloose, but that wasn't the point. The point was now—when she'd needed to be able to change her whole life quickly, she'd been able to do so.

Her Mini Cooper did look a bit odd. The passenger seat alone was weighted down with two suitcases, a pillow and a jumbled collection of shoes—forty pairs, to be precise. The backseat was completely stuffed with a table-sized Christmas tree, already decked out with pink lights and pink satin ornaments, and a mess of various-sized boxes wrapped in pink and silver and gold.

Considering it was January tenth, a long way past Christmas, the tree especially had to look a little weird to a stranger. But Merry had her priorities, and she hoped to Pete that looking sane to other people was never one of them.

"Dad?" Finally, he answered on the fourth ring. "I got here, safe and sound. A mighty long drive, but really no sweat...."

A zingy ice sleet stung her face, but she didn't mind. The chipper temperature was exhilarating after all those cramped hours in the car. Besides, she'd left two feet of snow in Minneapolis, so if this was the worst Virginia could hand out in the winter, living here was going to be a piece of cake.

When she glanced at the house again, though, she suffered another shiver chasing up her spine.

"No, Dad, I haven't seen the lawyer yet. Or the child. There hasn't been time. I thought I could drive it through, but I had to stop for a few hours sleep last night. So I literally just pulled in the driveway to get a look at the place...."

With the phone still tucked to her ear, she whirled around, hoping the look of the neighborhood would be more reassuring. Instead, she suffered another shudder-sized shiver.

Apparently it wasn't just the one house. There was a whole block of them. They were all minicastles, with sculpted yards and fancy architectural features and three-car garages. The only vehicles in sight were BMWs and Volvos and Lexus SUVs.

Her house wasn't any worse than the rest, but it was pretty darn scary. To begin with, the size alone could have slept a small country. A cathedral ceiling and blue crystal chandelier was visible from a two-story-tall glass window. Carriage lamps graced the double oak doors. The flagstone walkway was landscaped within an inch of its life and the porch had pillars, for Pete's sake.

Merry felt another clutch in her chest. There was just no denying the truth. This was upper-class suburbia. *Desperate Housewives* in the flesh. The land of swing sets and soccer moms and lawn mowers.

Come on, Merry. It's not as if someone dropped you in the Amazon without bug repellent. Common sense rarely influenced her, but in this case, Merry was relieved to have her conscience show up with a little re-assurance—and of course it was true. Maybe the house was a shock, but it wasn't as if she didn't realize the suburb thing existed. It was just so remote from her life.

Naturally she'd thought about marriage now and then, but she couldn't imagine falling for a guy who wanted 2.3 kids and the minivan deal. The only kind of guy who'd likely tempt her would have to be as free-footed as she was. If that never happened, no loss. Life offered no end of adventures and interesting possibilities just as it was.

As happy as she'd been with that philosophy, though, it gave her no clue now what a soccer mom was supposed to do all day. With the cell phone still glued to her ear, she squinted again at the chandelier visible from the tall window, wondering how the Sam Hill anybody cleaned that sucker. A fireman's ladder? Maybe someone sprayed Windex from a helicopter? Maybe someone rented climbing gear and belayed down from the chimney?

"No, no, I was listening, Dad!" Swiftly she concentrated back on the conversation. "It's still two hours before five, so I'm hoping to connect with the lawyer today, get the house key. I only wish I could get her out of that place tonight, but at least this way, I'll have tonight to get some things done—like turning on the heat, bringing in some food, opening the place up and like that. But first thing tomorrow, with any luck...sure, Dad. Of course, I'll call you as soon as I know more... the house? Oh yeah, you'd love the house."

As she clicked off the phone, she thought wryly that her dad would most certainly love the place. She was the only one suffering from "suburb allergy."

Her sisters teased that she was maturity-challenged, but they were all older, had all bought into the myth about adulthood being synonymous with mortgages and appliance ownership.

She'd just shoved the cell phone back in her purse when she heard a truck door slam from the next driveway.

After the last unsettling moments, she appreciated the distraction. Especially a distraction as riveting as this one. It was just a guy—but definitely a long, lanky hunk of a guy, arresting enough to put some *kaboom* back in her tired pulse.

He peeled out of a black pickup and immediately hiked around to the rear. Undoubtedly hustling because of the spitting sleet, he cracked down the tailgate and started hefting some long wooden boards. She didn't think he'd noticed her until he suddenly called out, "You must be lost."

It wasn't the time, the moment, or the guy to murmur the old Campbell's soup refrain—*M'm! M'm! Good!*—but she did think it. Just for a minute. Heaven knew, she had no time for silliness right now, but one good long look wasn't hurting anything. He was so definitely adorable. Dark hair, worn a little roguish-long, dusted with snow. Dark eyes that glistened. A long angular face with a scrape of high cheekbones, a distinctly French nose, a chin carved out of granite. The thin mouth was the only soft thing about him, but she'd bet the ranch those lips knew how to kiss.

Maybe she didn't own a ranch, but she happened to be extremely skilled in certain areas. Just because a woman wasn't rabid about settling down didn't mean she hadn't tested out her share of the male population, particularly in the kissing department.

"No, honestly, I'm not lost," she assured him. "But I did just come a long way to find the place. You knew Charlie Ross?"

"Yup. Neighbors for years." He motioned with his head. "The house is locked up."

She watched him unload several more boards—all gorgeous-looking wood. She didn't know birch from beech, but she could see he was treating the boards as if they were precious cargo. "I know," she said. "About the house being locked up, I mean. I just drove here from Minnesota…"

"Uh-huh." He carted two boards at a time to the inside of his garage, then came back for more.

She realized he was hardly inviting more conversation—nor did she have time for chitchat. But a next-door neighbor was a potential ally. And certainly, someone who had to know Charlie and his daughter, so she offered, "I've never been here before. In fact, the last time I saw Charlie, he was still living in Minneapolis, years ago. I had no idea he'd died until the lawyer contacted me. I'm here about Charlene—"

"Yeah?"

"I have to get the house key from the lawyer. And I guess there's a whole host of complicated issues to settle besides that. But with any luck, I'm really hoping to have Charlene back in her own home by tomorrow."

She definitely caught his attention then. In fact, he suddenly stopped dead. "*What? You're* the guardian?"

Okay, maybe his tone was a little insulting, as if the possibility of her being a guardian was as remote as the sky falling in, but Merry made allowances. He was probably cranky from carrying the weight of all those boards. And she'd been hard-core driving, which meant she wore no makeup and her hair hadn't seen a brush in hours, not to mention that her red flowered slippers lacked a certain cachet. Cripes, she generally got more male attention than she wanted when she dressed up—but undoubtedly to this guy, she looked young. At least compared to him. Living in this neighborhood, he was undoubtedly on the married-with-kids side of the fence.

Not that he was decrepit. Merry had guy-shopped long enough to recognize real diamonds from the faux. He wasn't just cute. He was sexy the way only men with some experience-lines could look. He was past the spoiled-boy stage, past the how-was-it-for-you tedium in the morning. More into the I-Know-How-To-Please-A-Woman era. Close to forty, for sure.

Still, he was definitely off her radar. Not because of his age, but because of the married thing.

She still hoped he'd like her, though. Having a friend next door would be a huge help, so quickly and warmly she produced her biggest smile—the smile that had been known to attract male favor since she was, oh, three and a half.

For a good two seconds, it seemed to work on him, too. Between the shiny sleet, the gloomy afternoon and the distance across the driveway, she couldn't see his expression all that clearly...but he definitely stared back at her intensely for those few moments.

And that was about all the time Merry had to mess around. "I won't bug you any longer—I can see you're busy, and I'm in a real hurry as well. But I'm Merry. Merry Olson. So when you see lights turn on in the house later, you'll know it's me."

"Jack Mackinnon here." Swiftly he added, "Merry... you have actually met Charlene before, right?"

He sounded more incredulous than critical, but Merry didn't figure it was the time or place to get into it. "Not yet," she said cheerfully, and then waved as she climbed back in her car.

The look of him lingered in her mind—but so did his expression.

He wouldn't be the first to call her crazy for taking off cross-country to take on an eleven-year-old girl she'd never even met. Hell's bells, even she admitted it was crazy.

But crazy didn't mean it was wrong.

Merry had long, devastating memories from the year she was eleven—so the little girl's age had hugely, hopelessly touched her. The second factor was the poor kid had lost her dad on Christmas Eve—how impossibly devastating was that? On top of which, there were no relatives who could step in. Charlene was far beyond the usual adoptable age, and in an overcrowded foster-care system, the child was absolutely alone, had no one in her corner.

The way Merry saw it, one of the giant advantages to living footloose and fancy free was exactly an issue like this—she had the flexibility to take off and choose a different life path whenever she wanted to. No, she didn't know the child. No, she didn't have a clue if there were any special problems, but when push came down to shove—which it had—what did anything like that matter? How could she possible leave a lonely, grief-stricken eleven-year-old girl when she had the power to do something about it?

And that was her plan. First, to just open her arms and love the kid. And then, to give her a Christmas—in her own home—to make up for the one she'd just lost. After that, well, she'd figure out what the child needed and wanted. There was no way to cross those bridges until they came to them. Together.

Right now, though, driving demanded all her concentration. Lee Oxford—Charlie's estate lawyer—had an Arlington address. The problem was that maps and Merry didn't get along. And that she was already tired. And that Arlington and D.C. traffic was like a prehistoric reality play about the survival of the fittest.

Nobody wanted to play nice. Minneapolis rush hour was no cupcake, but either the drivers in this neck of the woods all had political agendas or were sociopath-wannabes.

She also had to pop into a gas station—not for gas, but to charge into the restroom for a fast cleanup. A little makeup, a brush and putting on some real shoes was all she had time for. Unfortunately, after that she had trouble finding the attorney's address. Not for the first time, she cursed all her relatives for failing to pass on a direction gene, and after all that fiddle-faddling around, it was fifteen minutes to five before she managed to park and chase up the stairs to Lee Oxford's office.

The receptionist took one look at her and sniffed, the little snot. Maybe receptionists on this side of the Mississippi could afford Ellen Tracy suits, but at least where Merry came from, people were familiar with some friendly manners. "It's late, but I'll see if he can fit you in," was all the receptionist offered.

"I left a message on his cell that I was coming in early, but I don't know if he got it. Please tell him it's about Charlene Ross. I know we didn't plan a meeting until tomorrow, I'm hoping he can still see me today."

"Have a seat."

Yeah, right, like she could relax at this point. She slugged her hands in her pockets and paced from window to window. She'd had mental images in her mind for days of the little girl, so young, alone, no mom, and then losing her daddy right before Christmas. It was easy to picture her. Granted, it had been years since she'd seen Charlie, but his daughter was undoubtedly built short and scrappy, because he'd been. Likely she'd be blond. Hopefully she wouldn't have her daddy's hook nose, but with any luck at all she'd have those wonderfully warm crinkle-in-the-corner blue eyes.

Naturally, without knowing her, Merry had had a hard time picking out Christmas presents—but not totally. Eleven was eleven. Whether Merry wanted to or not, she recalled every detail about that age. It was that era when you had to have a best friend. When you first started to notice boys, even if you were still a little worried they had cooties. It was that age when you first got hard-core interested in makeup and fashion styles, started hearing the appeal of the "in" music, talked on the phone nonstop.

And, yeah, it was an age when losing a parent was the worst thing in the universe—especially if the other parent had already deserted the ship.

Merry's heart had been ripped up since she first heard the story. Still was. Still would be, she suspected, until she'd gotten her arms around the little girl. Whatever happened was going to be challenging, she knew. How could anything about this be easy, for her or for Charlene? But Merry didn't really doubt that she'd get along with the child. Wherever this all ended up, love and caring and attention had to help the little sweetheart, and Merry was more than willing to open her heart to the child.

Finally the receptionist gave her the high sign, and Merry sailed into Oxford's office with an eager smile and her hand outstretched. The terrier-sized, dark-haired man on the other side of the polished onyx desk stood up to return her handshake, but abruptly her optimistic spirits suffered a teensy drop.

Unlike everybody else, she usually liked lawyers. Some of her closest friends were lawyers. But most of them were of that earnest, honest breed fresh from law school, hot to make the world a better place, flag-waving hopeless liberals like…well, like herself. Lee Oxford looked about fifty, had a mega-watt diamond in his tie, elegantly styled brown hair—even for a city guy—and wore alligator shoes. He took one look at her and brightened as if she were the freshest meat on the hoof he'd seen in a long, long time.

It's not as if she'd never had that response from a man before, but she'd really wanted to like this guy. Mentally she reminded herself that Charlie Ross would never have picked a jerk for a lawyer, so to just chill on that first reaction and give him a longer chance.

Still, Oxford held her hand more like a caress instead of a handshake, before slowly sinking back in his chair. He started out with, "I wondered what you'd look like. This is a highly unusual situation."

"Believe me, it is for me, too." She sank into the barrel chair across from his sleek black desk. "This is the fastest I could get here. I didn't expect to be able to connect with Charlene still tonight, but I was hoping to get the key to the house. I'd like to open it up, make sure everything's turned on, get some food in, just get to know the place a little. Try and make some things ready for her."

"A good idea. But there's a lot we have to go over first."

Merry leaned forward. There was a ton she wanted to go over, too. And just because little guys tended to worry her—they always seemed to have a mean streak, need to prove their power and all that—she tried to quit pegging him in the negative. So the guy had looked her over a little close. What man didn't?

"As I hope I explained on the phone…if the child's mother happened to show up, or another blood relative who is capable of taking Charlene, they could make a legal claim. But right now, to the best of our knowledge, there's no one."

Merry nodded. "For her sake, I wish she had some family, too."

"Regardless, you need to fully understand that you have no legal obligation to take her."

"I do understand that. You explained on the phone."

"The document you signed years ago isn't binding."

Again she nodded. She'd gone over that night numerous times in her mind. It was hard to explain to an outsider what a rare and special friendship she'd formed with Charlie. It just wasn't like any other friend relationship.

He'd been newly divorced when she met him, living in Minnesota, not Virginia. There'd never been anything romantic between them. They'd met at some ghastly party that they'd both been conned into attending by friends, started talking and never stopped. He was just a totally great guy who'd needed a friend, and she'd valued being one for him. Over days and weeks of talking together, she shared more about her childhood than she'd ever told anyone. Likewise, he'd revealed his circumstances. The court had given him full custody of his baby daughter, but he'd been frantic about what would happen to Charlene if he died or was hurt. Even before his ex-wife had disappeared from the picture, she'd been attracted to anything she could smoke or sniff.

The two of them had written up an agreement on a legal pad in a restaurant. It wasn't fancy, just said that Merry would take care of his daughter, as he'd take care of hers if she ever had kids who needed help. Even if it was just a pact between friends, she'd meant the words. He had, too. And yeah, unfortunately they'd lost track when he took the job in Virginia. He also must have wildly changed if he'd turned into Mr. Suburbia. But she'd never forgotten him. When the lawyer first called, she'd let out a helpless, keening cry on hearing Charlie was gone.

And that fast, Oxford told her that she was the only one listed as a potential guardian for Charlene. He'd also quickly informed her there was nothing legally binding about such a document, nothing to stop her from backing out.

He repeated the same thing now.

She answered him the same way she had then. "Maybe there's nothing in this situation that's *legally* binding. But morally and ethically is a whole different ball of wax. I have no idea if I can be a good guardian for Charlene. But she can't possibly be better off in foster care, and for sure she needs out of the situation she's stuck in right now. And I'm free. I can at least make sure she's back in her own home, her own school, around her own friends again, before anybody has to make any decisions set in granite."

"It's a monumental thing you're taking on." Oxford picked up a pen, and terrier-fashion, started worrying it, poking it end to end. "If you don't mind my saying, I find it odd if not a little suspicious that you'd be willing to take on a kid out of the blue."

Merry tried not to take offense. He didn't know her from Adam. She tried to answer with the same careful honesty she'd expressed to everyone else. "If you're thinking that I easily said yes, I promise you I didn't. But when you described the situation she was in...I couldn't get it out of my mind. A little girl, right at Christmas, who had everything she knew and loved ripped away from her—"

He cut her short, as if he needed to hear an emotional argument like he needed another head. "Somehow I suspect you know there's a sizable trust."

She frowned. "Yes. You said Charlie had a trust set up for his daughter."

"A sizable trust," he repeated, and looked at her.

She opened her mouth, closed it. She told herself again that Charlie would never have chosen a lawyer who was a creep, but the tone of Oxford's voice still stung. He clearly seemed to think she was motivated by money. Of course, he couldn't possibly know that half the world tagged her Ms. Eternal Sunshine...and the other half accused her of being a hopelessly naive idealist. But greedy—sheesh. Of all the faults she'd picked up and excelled at, greed sure wasn't one of them.

"I don't know what you mean by sizable," she said carefully. "But I admit I was shocked when I saw the house. When I knew Charlie, he was an engineer. A good one, making a decent salary. But when I saw the house, I figured it must have a heckuva mortgage—"

"The house is paid for. When Charlie's dad died, he inherited a bundle. Which I suspect you knew."

"No, I didn't, actually," she said evenly. "I never asked Charlie about money. It was never my business."

"Uh-huh." Oxford put down his pen. "I'm not trying to yank your chain, Merry. I wouldn't take on a kid either, unless there was something in it for me. But if there hadn't been that kind of money, the child would undoubtedly have been popped into foster care from the start. And if blood relatives do show up, you'd better believe they'll fight for a chance at that size of pot."

She felt a little like a goldfish stolen from a tank. Her mouth kept opening. She just couldn't temporarily get any words out. She'd never take on a child for money's sake, couldn't imagine anyone who would. Bruising her even more, though, was that the attorney seemed to believe she was like him, now that they'd put some honesty on the table. At least his version of honesty.

"You need to understand though, Merry, that Charlie made that trust iron-tight. Or I should say *I* made the trust tight. No one gets their hands on that money, without verifying that any and all expenses are for the child."

"Which is the way it should be," Merry got in.

"Yeah, right. Naturally, there's an allowance for the guardian." He named a sum that almost knocked her off her chair. "But typical of such situations, there was an immediate guardian *ad litem* appointed by the court."

"You used that term on the phone, but I don't really know what it means."

"Basically the court appoints a guardian *ad litem*, who functions as an impartial voice in decisions involving a minor or incapacitated person. In this case, obviously, the child. I have control over matters involving the trust and finances—but I have no power over custody details. She'll check on Charlene's progress with you. Evaluate how the relationship is working. She has the right to make home visits, to interview Charlene's doctor or teachers or other people who know the child. And you need to understand that she can petition the court to have you removed from the guardian role if she feels Charlene isn't thriving in your care...but she will have to prove it."

"All that sounds like good sense. Fine." Merry found herself wrapping her arms tight around her chest. A lump kept clogging her throat. These were facts she needed to know, no question. It was just that the attorney hadn't said a single personal thing about the child. There was no hint he'd ever even met her. Maybe she was being oversensitive, but he kept striking her as having a heart colder than the Arctic. "Mr. Oxford—"

"Lee. We'll be seeing a lot of each other. No reason to stand on formality."

How ironic, she thought thickly. Because she never stood on formality with anyone in her life. But this was one person she wished she could. "If you don't mind my asking...how did you happen to be Charlie's attorney?"

He smiled, leaned back and cocked his alligator shoe against a drawer. "Actually, I was originally his father's attorney, not Charlie's. When Bartholomew and his wife died—unexpectedly, in a boating accident—I believe Charlie recognized right off that I'd done a good job of protecting his parents' assets. I think he also readily realized that he wasn't good with money himself. He used to say that he didn't need to have a cutthroat bone because he knew I had plenty of them."

Maybe she was supposed to laugh, but all she could think was that now she got it. How and why Charlie had tied up with such a cold-blooded machine.

"Anyhow…" Lee glanced at his watch and zoomed back to business. "The guardian *ad litem's* name is June Innes. She's already seen Charlene, and will undoubtedly be getting in touch with you shortly." He started feeding her forms and papers far faster than she could possibly read or absorb the details. Maybe he thought she wouldn't care about the information—or else he was just in a hurry to get out of there. Outside, night was falling faster than bad news.

Finally, he handed her the last form…several of which she'd had to sign…and got around to handing her the key to the house. "You've landed yourself a nice setup," he said bluntly. "It's a great house. A lucrative allowance. And for the record, I have no intention of being hard on you. As long as the kid's well taken care of, there's financial room for leniency if you need any kind of…flexibility."

Minutes later, Merry tore out of the office as if being chased by bees, carrying a thick slug of papers and the house key. Her heart was pounding and her stomach roiling with acid. Oxford's personality sure matched his alligator shoes. He was scaly and aggressive.

He hadn't said one personal word about the child! Not one! Her mind was still ranting when she climbed back in her car…until she glanced at the rearview mirror and saw her eyes spitting tears. Okay. So she tended toward overemotional. But that little girl needed someone who *gave* a damn.

Not just someone who wanted to administer her so-called estate from behind a black lacquer desk.

She couldn't *wait* to get her hands on Charlene.

CHAPTER TWO

THE COMBINED ODORS of beer, cold pizza and cigars hovered in the air like nectar. There was a time for women, Jack thought, and a time when a guy just needed to relax.

A man could enjoy a woman, be challenged by a woman, love a woman. But for damn sure, he could never relax with one.

"Sorry," he said, without an ounce of remorse in his voice, as he scooped up the heap of poker chips. The faces around the table reflected various degrees of aggravation.

"You're damned lucky tonight, Mackinnon." Robert, alias Boner to his guy friends, was the investment banker who lived two doors down.

"It's not my fault I'm good."

"You know what they say—lucky at cards, unlucky at love." Macmillan was another neighbor. He worked at Langley, like Jack, and was the toughest poker competitor for the same reason he was great at his job—he knew how to keep his mouth shut and reveal nothing in his expressions.

"Yeah, but Jack here's lucky at love, too. It's not fair. Hell, his back door's a steady stream of women leaving early in the morning. I should know, since I can see his back door from across the street." Steve was his best friend in the neighborhood, and not just because he was suffering male-pattern baldness before the rest of them.

Still, Jack couldn't let that dig pass. "Hey, you're married, so you're free to get it every night. A whole lot easier than being single."

"What? You assume marriage means a guy gets it every night? Whatever gave you wild illusions about marriage like that?"

"I don't have any illusions about marriage. Trust me. If I'm ever inclined to try the institution again, I hope one of you'll be a good friend and give me cyanide." He dealt the next round, already sucking it up because he knew he had to lose this hand. Years ago, he'd realized he had the strange problem of a photographic memory. It was a huge asset in his work, but hell on friends. At least if he was playing poker. Obviously no one would play with him if he won all the time. Jack couldn't shut down his brain, but he did his damnedest to tune it out to make the game fair.

Most of the time, anyway.

He had to admit to a teensy competitive streak. He not only liked to win, but he hated to lose. At anything.

His house line rang. Rather than interrupt the game, he just took his cards with him and hooked the kitchen extension to his ear. The cord extended an ample distance for him to ante at the table. He'd drawn a slim pair of fours.

Steve and Boner, for damn sure, had nothing, because Boner was shooting back another beer and Steve was restlessly shifting his butt. Sometimes people were even easier to read than cards.

"Hey, Dad, how's it going?"

Jack kept playing, but his "dad buttons" went on red

alert. He knew his sons. Kicker, at fifteen, was already three inches taller than Jack, couldn't make it through doors without bumping his head, planned on a football scholarship to get into college and had a theory that he didn't need good grades. Kicker, thank God, put his whole personality out front where anybody could see it. "What's wrong?"

"Nothing. Totally nothing. Mom made me call, but I'm fine."

So it was bad. "What happened?"

"Nothing, really. I'm home."

"Home from…?"

"The emergency room."

"Uh-huh. Break or sprain?" He swiveled the cord, anteed another two bucks, then backed up to the sink counter again.

"Neither one. Mom just insisted I go to the hospital. You know how she is. She freaks every time I play football. And we were just passing a few, you know?"

What Jack knew was that he didn't want to get into another wrangle with his ex-wife. He was tired of losing skin, which was always how he felt after talking to Dianne. Unfortunately, he knew the boys played both parents against each other, so it wasn't as if he could automatically take Kicker's side without knowing more details. "Where exactly are you hurt?"

"Just a bump on the head. Nothing. But Mom's on me again about quitting." Jack heard out the whole tale. Kevin, alias Kicker, was his firstborn—by eleven minutes. Kevin was the jock, where Cooper was the brain, the quiet bookworm, the one who looked at him with those deep brown eyes and always made Jack feel as if he'd failed him as a dad. Girls chased after both boys nonstop. It'd help if the boys weren't so damned good looking. Kicker attracted them with his charm and the sports-star thing, but just as many seemed to fall for Cooper's loner brown eyes.

He could talk to his kid and play poker simultaneously any day of the week, but while he was leaning against the granite counter, he happened to glance next door. Charlie Ross's kitchen window faced his. Actually, since neither man had ever lost a minute's sleep about their lack of curtains, Jack could see in most of Charlie's windows, and that was a vice versa as well.

The house next door, though, had been black as a tomb for two weeks, and suddenly lights blazed in every downstairs room. "Okay, Kicker. I agree, a concussion isn't worth a federal case. It happens. But let's talk in the morning. And try not to bounce any more balls off your head until the noggin heals, okay?"

Instead of hanging up the phone, Jack seemed to forget it for a moment. The view across the yard just… startled him.

He already knew the brunette was over there. He'd seen her zoom in the driveway past dark, slam on the brakes of her toy car, and run for the house. It wasn't like he kept track—the guys had come over; he'd been busy—but as far as he could tell, she only had one speed. A boob-bouncing run. And he had to shake his head.

She was one gorgeous cookie, from those sleek long legs to the lustrous swing of chestnut hair. He had yet to notice a flaw, and Jack was good at noticing women's flaws. In looks, she could make a monk perk up.

In personality, though, she did seem a little…floofy. He leaned closer to the window, disbelieving his own eyes. The view into Charlie's living room wasn't as clear as the kitchen, so maybe he was mistaken— *surely* he was mistaken? Because there seemed to be a table-sized Christmas tree in that living room. A bonbon confection of a *pink* Christmas tree.

It was halfway through January, for Pete's sake.

Not even counting the craziness of a holiday tree being baby-pink.

A shadow streaked past the window again. The brunette. She was charging around too fast for him to see much, but he still caught a delectable glimpse of a heaving upper deck in motion.

Not that looks were everything, but Jack was hard pressed to believe a man would ever need Viagra, even in his nineties, around a woman who looked like that.

"Hey, Jack. You've been called, you hustler. Show 'em."

With a laugh, he hung up the phone and rejoined the game. By that time, he had three of a kind, ace high. The others took one look and made ugly hissing noises. Jack threw up his hands. "I can't help it if I win," he said, and this time it was dead true. He'd barely looked at his cards.

Between hands, he poured another round of beer— since everyone was walking home, no one had to fret intake—and shook out more chips for the salsa dip. They played the Wednesday night game as if it were Vegas. What was said there, stayed there. Not about the game. Whoever won likely broadcast that news through the neighborhood and beyond. But any private news was considered sacred.

"How many times you got laid this week, Jack?"

"More than you, that's for sure." Hoots naturally

followed that insult. Jack folded, had a hand too lousy
to waste a bluff on. Crazy, but he somehow found
himself back at the sink, glancing out the window
again.

And there she was. Not in the living room this time,
but the kitchen.

Her back was to him. Jack could see her refrigerator door was gaping wide open—she was cleaning it
out. Undoubtedly stuff was still in there from before
Charlie died.

She was scrubbing like a fiend. And, God, what a
butt she had.

Not that Jack was a fanny connoisseur, but, well,
actually he was. And hers was whistling cute. Whatever
she was wearing—sweats?—caressed the shape of that
little butt just so. The farther she leaned inside, rubbing
and scrubbing, the more fabric dipped down her spine.
The swell of two fine, *fine* fanny cheeks were revealed.
And…

Jack pressed his nose to the window.

A tattoo. By damn, she had a tattoo on one fanny
cheek. And not a little one either. He—

"Jack, what the *hell* are you doing?"

"Nothing, nothing." He hustled back to the card table
and parked there, but that fanny tattoo was so ingrained
in his head that he lost his entire photographic memory
skill. And all the money that went with it.

Usually the game broke up by eleven—everybody had
work the next morning—but tonight no one wanted to
leave. They were having too much fun watching him lose.

"It does the heart good to see you suck, Jack," Steve
said affectionately.

"Does the heart good, hell. It does the wallet good.

May you have a slump like this that lasts weeks," Boner chortled, as Jack watched the last of his stash get cradled into the banker's big fat hands.

"What is this? Does nobody have any sympathy?"

"For you in life, sure. For you in cards, never."

They always played at his place. After the divorce, Jack told himself he needed this mountain of a house in the suburbs like he needed a spare ear, but he'd never put it on the market. It was so easy to have a guy function here, like the card game, because everybody else was married and the women all hated their messes. The real reason he kept it, though, was for his sons. When Dianne took off on him, she also uprooted the boys, stuffed them all in a city apartment in D.C.

Once the neighbors left, his mood nosedived. It was too darn easy to remember that whole divorce debacle—the custody war, his ex-wife's selfishness, his feeling impotent and frustrated at trying to reason with a court system that catered more to moms than dads. Jack did *not* do helplessness well. And maybe the system should cater more to mothers, most of the time, but not in *their* case. And aw, hell, letting it all ooze back in his mind was like picking at a sore.

With the house yawning empty, the smells of stale beer and cigars weren't quite so appealing as they'd been earlier. He cracked a window, started sweeping dishes into the dishwasher, then found himself stalled at the sink window again.

She was still up.

It was just a pinch away from midnight, but now all the lights were on, both upstairs and down. The preposterously pink Christmas tree had a visible mound of wrapped packages under it. In the kitchen, the fridge door was closed, but he could see heaps of stuff on the counters—fruit, bags, bread and what all.

He could also see the front doors—the double oak doors—gaping open.

In January. With snow drifting down like confetti, testimony to the temperature.

Maybe she wanted to chill the inside? Could she really be that flaky?

When he saw her breeze past another window, he turned off the sink light. Naturally he immediately suffered guilt for spying on her…but he could sure see better without the background light.

God knew what all the woman was doing, but she was sure doing it fast. Running. From room to room. Carrying things. Then vacuuming. And dusting. And then carrying more things.

Midnight passed. Then one.

By that time he'd long finished the cleanup, sanitized the chalk-and-granite kitchen, and was ready to hang it up for the night…but he couldn't seem to resist one last look. She was still up. Still visible. He wasn't sure what room she was in, because he didn't know Charlie's house that well, but she was still on the first floor—which meant she should have noticed the north wind blowing in her front door. She obviously hadn't, though, because at some point she'd stripped off the bulky sweater he'd seen her in earlier. Beneath was a body-hugging tee, red as a raspberry, and a headline announcement that her front side was as exquisite as her damn-fine behind.

The boobs weren't huge. Just perky. Firm. Not round-round, more…well, when it came down to it, nothing else was exactly like a perfect breast shape, so there was no point in trying to compare it to anything.

Jack vaguely realized he'd settled in, resting his elbows on the sink—and damn it, he had to work tomorrow!—but at that precise instant he couldn't possibly move. She was peeling off that raspberry long-sleeved tee. He saw a strip of black bra, but only from the back. Then he lost sight of her—until he picked up her moving around two rooms down, when she turned back into the Vacuum Queen.

Apparently she wasn't stripping down to go to bed, like a normal human being past midnight on a week-night. She was just peeling off clothes because she was hot from all that running.

He was definitely hot from all that watching.

With a sigh, he eased away from the sink, knuckled the sore muscles in his back, and grumped around until he located some shoes, then his jacket.

He hadn't looked at a woman seriously in the last three and a half years.

There was a time he'd believed in honor, fidelity, loyalty and all the rest of that crap. There was also a time he thought he was different than his generation—because he really believed in marriage, in the vows, would never have gotten a divorce because of going through a stretch of trouble.

But that was then.

These days he took credit for being a commitment-phobic, allergic-to-rings kind of guy. If that made him irresponsible and selfish—well, he now wore those labels with pride. He'd done the honor thing and got kicked in the teeth. It was a "screw or be screwed" world. He had no intention of playing nice ever again.

Scowling and ticked off, he yanked open his back door and felt the prompt slap of ice air. Hell and more hell. All this voyeurism was going to completely ruin his workday tomorrow—he could already feel a lack-of-sleep headache coming on—and if he wasn't still up, the hounds of memories wouldn't have had a chance to chase after him.

Most days, he wasn't remotely bitter. He didn't want Dianne back, was long over all that. He had a great time with his female friendships and sleep-mates. So did they. He didn't want to hurt anyone. He just had no intention of putting himself in harm's way ever again. Chivalry was very nice, but somebody else could do it. And if somebody thought that made him a cold, unfeeling creep, well, that was tough.

Still glowering, he crossed the yard, swore when the cold, wet grass sneaked into his shoes, hiked up her driveway and closed her damn front doors.

He didn't do it to be nice.

He didn't have a nice-bone left in him. He'd only done it out of plain old selfishness. He knew damn well he wouldn't have been able to sleep, fretting that anyone in hell could have walked through those wide-open front doors. And if he didn't catch at least *some* sleep, he was going to be completely worthless at work tomorrow.

He might enjoy looking at her delectable fanny, but he sure as hell was *not* going to enjoy living next door to such a witless woman.

MERRY WOKE UP TO the caterwaul of her traveling alarm clock. She slapped it off, then blearily opened one eye. Seven o'clock.

A god-awful hour for a girl who'd only made it to bed at four-thirty.

She stumbled off the couch, stretched, then forced both eyes open. She vaguely remembered trying to decide where to sleep, but then just pulling a blanket over her head in the living room. Everything about the house had seemed overwhelming at that point.

Still did, for that matter. She thought she knew Charlie Ross. And, of course, people changed when they matured. But where Charlie had been so warm and natural and likeable, his house seemed decorated by a robot. Almost all the surfaces were gray or stainless steel. The walls were filled with gargantuan canvases of scary modern art, and every room had technology so ultra-cool that she couldn't even turn on the TV or set a clock on her own.

Okay, cookie, enough griping.

She stumbled toward the bathroom. Never mind all the looming crises ahead of her, she felt darn good about all the chores she'd accomplished last night.

When she'd first walked in the front door and looked around, she darn near panicked, but kept her mind on what mattered. Charlene. Getting the place prepared for the little girl to come home. So Merry's first priority, obviously, was to put up the pink Christmas tree and presents—that little girl was going to get a Christmas come hell or high water!

And after that—well, the house had shaken her up on a zillion emotional levels, but just making it livable was the first challenge. Clearly no one had cleaned the house since Charlie died. There was a sock in the living room, a jacket hanging on a kitchen chair—nothing terrible—but reminders of her dad that Merry didn't want Charlene exposed to the minute she walked in the door.

Once all that tidying was done, she'd recognized the ghastly smell in the kitchen as something rotting in the fridge. Hell's bells, there went the rest of the night. She'd dumped the icky fridge contents, scrubbed and sanitized, chased out to an all-night grocery to bring in some milk and basics, then came back to do a dust and vacuum and bathroom-clean.

In the shower, shampoo streaming down her face, she admitted to herself that in real life, she didn't mind being a slob. Or a relative slob. Far too many things were more interesting and important than dust, but Merry could justify her brief cleaning freak-out. It wasn't about dirt. It was about trying to make Charlene's coming home as painless and nontraumatic as possible.

After a fast blow-dry, Merry shimmied into jeans, a fuzzy yellow mohair sweater, socks. In the kitchen, she stared bleary-eyed at the fancy coffeemaker. It looked pizzazz-y, like something created in 2075. Shinier than lip gloss. And she could turn it on, she'd discovered last night. She just couldn't figure out how to make it produce coffee.

It wasn't fair to make a girl start the day without caffeine.

It wasn't fair to make a girl start such a critical day without sleep, either.

She nabbed an apple—bought fresh last night—and reminded herself of the lawyer's behavior the day before. Lee Oxford still grated on her mind. His mercenary thinking. His coldness. The fact that he'd never once even mentioned Charlene's name.

Her resolve ballooned all over again. No matter how crazy anyone thought she was, there was no way—

none in this universe—that Merry would abandon a kid. Ever.

She knew too well what abandonment felt like.

When it came down to it, maybe it was a good thing the lawyer had been such a barracuda. His attitude had hard-wired her determination. She bit a chunk of apple, grabbed her jacket, the directions to the rest home she'd gotten from the lawyer and then sprinted outside. A fresh skid of snow had fallen in the wee hours. Brushed with dawn light, the whole neighborhood looked pearl-soft.

Her neighbor was up, judging from the lights in his kitchen window, but she didn't catch sight of him. More than once last night, she'd thought it'd be no hardship to have such a good-looking guy next door. So he was likely married. She could still look, couldn't she? And he had a truck. He looked mechanical and handy. More things to love in a neighbor.

It looked as if she had *lots* of neighbors. Other cars were steaming in their driveways, warming up, the lineup resembling the start-up of the Indy 500— although this particular lineup was notably chunky gas guzzlers, suburbia getting ready to join the exodus to the freeways and work. A few waved at her.

She waved back, noting they all seemed to be in pin striped suits—both the men and the women—and doing the wool-coat thing. Worry tried to rag her nerves again. She just felt like such an alien. She'd never owned a pin-striped suit, never wanted one. Still, she reminded herself that there wasn't that big an age difference—she was joining the thirtysomething bracket as of her birthday next month.

She loved new experiences besides, right?

Her spirits zoomed higher as she turned on the

freeway, the map crackled over the steering wheel in front of her. When push came to shove, it didn't really matter whether she fit into the neighborhood or the house or not. Screw all that. This was about a little girl.

And she'd waited as long as she possibly could to get her arms folded around Charlene.

The directions to the place did seem a little tricky. She checked the map again, then eased to the right when another driver honked at her. Naturally she was concentrating on her driving. Mostly. But the appalling image of Charlene's bedroom kept popping into her mind.

Nothing about the inside or outside of that darn house matched anything she ever knew about Charlie Ross, but the worst room—the absolute worst—was Charlene's bedroom.

Another driver honked at her. She shook her apple at him. For Pete's sake, was everybody cranky near D.C.?

Last night, there wasn't anything she could do but put a couple fresh bouquets of flowers in Charlene's bedroom. She couldn't find a vase in the house to save her life, but she'd found big glasses, and the grocery store had thankfully sold cut flowers.

And once Charlene got home, Merry figured they could fix the room. In fact, it'd be a super bonding thing to do together. The poor kid had no spread, no curtains, no rugs. It just didn't make sense. If her dad could afford that ghastly house, don't you think he could have sprung for some nice, soft carpeting and pretty colors and girl stuff for his daughter? Merry pictured some Mary Eddy prints, maybe a canopy bed—the room was huge. They could throw out all that awful dark furniture, put in white. Maybe buy a little vanity.

Charlene had a fab stereo system, no question, ditto for the computer and all. But there were cute desks and centers to contain all that mess of wires these days, something with style and color. Maybe Merry knew zip about parenting—but she knew girls.

Her turnoff led her away from bustling suburbia. The last turn was into a remote old neighborhood with dignified shade trees and cracked sidewalks.

Where she pulled in, the big old frame house had been converted into an assisted-living facility.

Charlene's one living relative was a great grandmother, who lived here—along with a dozen of her cronies over age ninety. It was no place for a child, but the foster-care system was predictably jammed up around the Christmas holiday, and the dietician who ran the home claimed they had a bed for Charlene—but only on an extremely temporary basis. Or that was the story Lee Oxford had told Merry when he'd first called.

The driveway was gravel, the only vehicle in sight an aging van. Merry hiked up the handicapped ramp, trying to rev herself up for this first meeting—not that she needed any revving. From the moment she made the decision to come, she'd been researching everything about eleven-year-olds she could think of. Her own memories of that age were intense, but obviously, trends and styles changed. She'd bought *Bratz* and *Elle Girl* magazines, listened to Ciara and the Click Five and the other groups the music store promised her were the "in" music for 'tweens, hit the library, read some Blume and horse stories and tried to pick up on the writers the 'tweens were into these days.

She rapped on the front door, and when no one immediately answered, rapped again. Abruptly a white-haired charmer with a cane answered the door. The lady was dressed in a pink-and-green dotted sweater with purple pants and a huge red bow sagging over one ear. Lots of positive attitude. Just deaf as a rock.

"Well, aren't you the pretty one, dearie-dear. Come on in...."

One step inside and Merry could smell urine. From the entry, she caught a partial view of a giant living room off to the right, where a wall TV did *The Morning Show* at screaming volume. Chairs and couches and wheelchairs cupped close to the set in a tight semicircle. At a glance, she counted around ten people in the cluster, but then she was distracted by a bony, hairless elderly woman barreling straight for her in a wheelchair, evidently bent on escape.

Quickly she closed the door behind her—which prevented the escape, but didn't stop the wheelchair from clipping her in the knees. She winced, ducked, smiled for the charmer.

"Hi, I'm Merry Olson. I'm here for Charlene Ross. I don't know if she's around here or with her great-grandmother? But I have papers—"

"Hey? You're selling cookies, you say?"

"No, no. I'm not selling cookies. I'm looking for Charlene Ross—"

"Hey, Frank, I think she's selling cookies!" the charmer bellowed and then blessed her with another warm smile. "I hope you've got those mint chocolate ones, honey, those are my very favorite—Wilhemma, quit ramming her with your chair, you old bitch—"

"Now, now." A harried-looking man shot out of the

kitchen, a dish towel over his arm. "We don't use that language, Julia. I've told you that before—" A smile for Merry.

She was pretty sure he identified himself as Frank, and the caretaker of the place, but it was impossible to hear anything clearly over the eardrum-piercing volume on the TV.

She explained why she was here—or tried to—but she was so anxious to find Charlene that her attention kept straying to the living room. She didn't expect to find a little girl in the middle of the geriatric set, but still, she wanted an impression of the place Charlene had been camping out in since the funeral.

Closest to the TV, she saw an old man, then an older man, then a man who'd clearly lived in the 1700s and was just hanging on by a thread...then an old lady, who was holding hands with another old lady, followed by someone sprawled on the couch of indeterminate sex and drool drizzling down his chin....

There was only one face she couldn't catch at all, someone in a big old Morris chair, and when she crooked her head forward she identified a young person. Her heart leaped—but only for a second. It was a boy, not a girl. The kid was bent down, playing some kind of computer game, but the clothes gave away his gender. He was wearing army fatigues—long tee and pants—with big boots, and had a brush cut as if he'd just signed up for the marines.

At least Charlene hadn't been the only soul under ninety in the place. Almost everyone looked gentle and kindly, but still, the more Merry saw, the more she wanted to hustle Charlene out of there and get her home.

"Charlene," she repeated again to the caretaker, worried that he hadn't understood her because of the roaring television. "I have papers giving me permission to take her. Mr. Oxford should have called. The only reason she came here was because her great-grand-mother was the only relative she had, until they found a guardian or—"

"Yes. Absolutely. We've been expecting you, like I keep saying. And she's right there."

He pointed at the kid, the boy.

Merry shook her head. God. In the last ten days, she'd argued with her dad and family and friends, quit a job, upended her whole life, packed up, suffered a god-awful two-day drive, landed in a terrifyingly high-end suburb and then had to clean all last night. She wasn't frayed exactly. She just needed one thing to go smoothly. "No. I mean a girl—"

But finally, over all the noise, the caretaker yelled "Charlene" loud enough to catch the child's attention. When the child responded, Merry started to get it.

The skinny scrap of a kid—the one with the marine brush cut, the he-man fatigue shirt and forearm tattoo and combat boots—was actually *her* kid.

The child obediently put down the computer game, got up and hiked toward her. The caretaker ordered the kid to stick out a hand. The kid did. And though Merry desperately wanted to throw her arms around the child and hug her senseless, she found herself returning the polite, stiff handshake.

"Pleased to meet you," Charlene said.

"I'm thrilled to finally meet you, too," Merry said, but instead of the exuberantly warm, reassuring tone she had in mind, her voice came out faint as a whisper. The child looked like her dad, as far as the skinny build and small bones, the blond hair and blue eyes. But the all-guy outfit and the robotic walk and self-contained expression stunned Merry, and for damn sure, confused her.

This was Charlene?

The sweet young girl she'd bought sparkly bangles and pink socks for?

CHAPTER THREE

IT WASN'T EVEN ten o'clock, yet already the morning had managed to turn into one nonstop nightmare after another.

On the drive home, Merry discovered that Charlene was capable of speech. So far, though, the only words she'd freely offered were— "You're taking me home, right?"

And that was the last sign of animation she'd gotten out of the girl. They'd collected a suitcase of stuff, stashed it in the back of the Mini, had the caretaker sign a form releasing Charlene to her care, and started out.

After that, the kid locked herself in the passenger seat and sat there like an obedient machine. She wasn't rude. She just volunteered no smiles, no conversation. She sat with the literal posture of a marine—boots clomped on the ground, posture straight, eyes focused ahead.

Merry kept glancing over, trying to reconcile that stupid brush cut on the face of a little girl with big blue eyes and fragile features and a tiny rosebud of a mouth. It was like trying to pair peanut butter with pickles. The darn kid was tucked inside that seat belt as if she didn't have a fear or emotion or worry in her life—and for darn sure, wouldn't admit to one.

Merry felt so rattled she forgot what road signs she was supposed to be watching for. In fact, she was pretty sure she'd turned the wrong way out of the driveway from the get-go.

This silent business just couldn't go on. "Charlene—" she started to say.

"If you don't mind, I'd rather be called Charlie."

"Okay. Charlie, then." Merry smiled, thinking, *Oh God, could an eleven-year-old girl be suffering from gender issues?* Or transgender issues? Or whatever it was called when one gender wanted to be another? "Charlie, I don't know if anyone told you who I am."

Well, that at least forced a little more dialogue. "Of course people told me. Mr. Oxford told me I couldn't go home until there was someone to take me. Then Mrs. Innes came to talk to me, and I heard that you were coming. So I could go home for a while."

"More than for a while, Charlene—Charlie." Cripes, she almost zoomed through a red light. And her hands on the wheel were slick as slides. She thought landing in suburbia was confounding, but this...she desperately wanted to help this little girl...only so far she hadn't even caught a glimpse of a little girl inside those big, scruffy combat boots.

"We don't know for how long," Charlene said matter-of-factly. "Things may not work out. You don't know me."

"And you don't know me. But we can both try fixing that, starting right now, okay?"

"Sure." The child said "sure," but her voice and posture said *I don't believe you. I don't believe anyone.*

Merry fumbled. She'd always been so gregarious that she figured she could talk to a wall, but how to get a conversation going with a youngster who didn't seem to want to talk back? She said, "Maybe I can share something about myself, and then you can tell me stuff about you, all right?"

No answer.

"Okay! I'll start!" God, had she ever seen that street corner before? She turned right. "I love dark chocolate. Bubble baths. Can't stand peas. I never wear shoes if I can help it and tend to scream if I see a mouse…."

Okay, no response from the other side of the car, so trying to be cute wasn't working. She tried a different tack. "I grew up in Minnesota, mostly in the country around Rochester—where the Mayo Clinic is. My dad's an anesthesiologist. We never lived in a suburb like you do. We had a place on a lake, lots of woods. I have two sisters, but they're both more than ten years older than me, so growing up, it was pretty much just me and my dad…."

Merry thought it might help for the child to know their circumstances were the same, the daughter-and-dad-living-alone thing, but Charlene showed no response to that either. Merry considered shutting up, but surely the more the child knew about her, the faster she'd start to feeling comfortable, right? So she bumbled on.

"I can't say I was a great student. Mostly got Bs and Cs. Just couldn't seem to stick with the books. Did the cheerleading thing…" Definitely didn't add the prom-queen type of history. Not to a girl wearing army fatigues. "I did a couple years in college, but just didn't really have a career in mind…."

She tried to think, what to say, what not to say. "So I just started working. Worked as an assistant DJ for a radio station—that was fun. Worked in an insurance office—actually, that was kind of interesting, too. A way of helping people, hearing about their lives. Was a management trainee at Ann Taylor for a while...."

Finally, a voice piped up from the passenger seat. "You don't have any idea where you're going, do you?"

"Huh?" How many times had her dad asked her that in real life? Was she ever going to get a clue where she was going, find a job she wanted to stick with, a place she was willing to stay?

But apparently Charlene meant something else entirely. The child said patiently, "You keep driving in the wrong direction. I mean, I don't know where you're trying to go. But you're headed the wrong way if you're trying to drive toward home. My home."

"We *are* headed toward your home. Um, I don't suppose you know the way, do you?"

"Sure." Finally, some conversation. Precise, clear directions.

Well, hell. They were only seven or eight miles out of the way. God knew, Merry had done worse. "You *do* want to go home, right, Charle—Charlie?"

"*Yes.*"

There. The first sign of emotion she'd seen so far. An honest yes. A desperate yes. A yes that captured Merry's heart and made her determined to reach the child no matter what it took. And she reminded herself of the obvious. They were just getting started. No one ever promised her this was going to be easy, and she hadn't expected it to be.

"What was it like," she asked, "being with your great-grandmother this last week?"

Charlene scrunched up her nose. "Is that a trick question?"

"No. You were staying there, so I figured—"

"When we first moved to Virginia, I was really little, but I can remember my dad saying that was why. I mean, why Virginia. Because his grandmother was here and there was no one to take care of her. Only that was ages and ages ago. She doesn't know who I am anymore. She doesn't know who anyone is. Everybody there was nice enough. I just really, really want to be home."

"You missed some school?" Merry already knew the answer to that question, but Charlene had finally started talking; she wanted to keep it going.

"Yeah, I know. That's freaking everybody out. But I think that's pretty stupid. I only missed a week or so, because it was still Christmas vacation before that. And I was already getting all As. And I could keep up just as well from the books as from classes anyway." Her face suddenly turned toward Merry. "I'll bet you're thinking that I'm going to be a big problem. But I won't be. I promise. If you just take me home, I won't bother you. I won't bother anybody. I don't need anybody to take care of me."

"Charlene, I wasn't worried about that at all—"

"*Charlie.*"

"Charlie, then. I—"

"You're lost again, aren't you." This time, the squirt didn't waste time phrasing the comment like a question.

Merry said, "Looks like. Feel like a burger or an ice-cream cone or anything?"

"No."

"Do you, um, know which way to turn from here?"

Merry zealously obeyed the eleven-year-old's instructions. Left at the first light, then four blocks later and so on. It was a new experience, actually paying attention to directions, but it still didn't seem to win her any brownie points.

She rashly assumed it might help warm up the waters if she tried talking about Charles. "I knew your dad back when you were just a toddler, when you two lived in Minnesota. We were really good friends. I thought the world of him."

"Come on."

"Come on?" She heard the disbelief, but had no idea where it was coming from.

"If you were such good friends, how come I never heard your name before? How come we never saw you?"

"We were good friends at the time of your parents' divorce, Charlie. Maybe your dad didn't talk about it because it was such a painful time for him—and it wasn't something he wanted you to remember, either."

Zip. Silence.

She pushed on. "But at the time, your dad talked about you all the time. How much he loved you. All his parenting ideas, how he wanted to raise you, how much he wanted you to be happy...."

When they finally pulled into the driveway, the kid bolted out of the car as if jet-propelled to get away from her. Merry hadn't felt this wrung out since she'd paid for a fitness trainer—a foolish move she'd never repeated.

The culmination of the impossible morning, though, was when she got inside the front door, and found Charlene standing in front of the tree. "What is this?"

"Now I realize it's past Christmas, but I knew you missed out on the holiday. I just thought it might help to try and make up." Hell's bells, back in Minnesota

when she'd thought of this, the idea had seemed brilliant. Only now Merry realized the kid could think she
was trying to buy her. Or trying to imply that a bunch
of silly presents could make up for her dad's death. How
could a nice intention turn out so rotten wrong?

And Charlene kept looking at her as if she were
from another planet. "That's real nice of you," she said
politely. "But...it's pink."

"I know, I know. It was the only tree I could find this
late after Christmas," she lied.

"That's okay," she said.

But obviously nothing was okay. The kid sat down
by the presents as if waiting for a shot at the dentist's.
She gingerly opened each gift and produced an obliga-
tory "thank you" even when she didn't have a clue what
the item was.

Merry knew—*knew*—this was going all wrong, yet
it was like changing your mind about a permanent in
the middle of a hairdresser appointment. It was just too
late, once they got that chemical going.

Charlie wasn't trying to be difficult. She was so
clearly trying to do anything Merry asked her, anything
Merry wanted, whatever it took to be home. But everything Merry had chosen, from the Juicy Couture
purse with the rabbit's foot, to the tweed hat with the
bumblebee pin, to the spangly beads, to the Ashton
Kutcher poster...oh, God. Each thing was worse than
the last.

The rock-bottom worst, though, were the pink
cashmere socks with the butterfly motif.

"*Wow,*" Charlie said. The word hung in the air like
a cooking odor.

When it was over, Merry perked up—because, hey,

there was no place to go from rock-bottom but up, right? How could anything more ghastly happen that day?

GOD KNEW, HE LOVED his job, but as Jack pulled into the driveway, he was hungrier than a bear in spring.

No one had twisted his arm to skip lunch or work late. He just forgot the time. When people asked him what he did, he always responded "desk jockey" because that answer worked like a charm. No one ever asked him further questions. They just assumed he was some kind of bureaucrat—no surprise, since there were a lot of white-collar pencil pushers running around Langley and Arlington.

The label had an element of truth besides. Once he "retired" from the navy—Special Ops—he'd settled into a non-dangerous job. Truth to tell, he thought he made more of a difference now than when he'd fought for his country with a weapon in his hand, but whatever. He loved it.

Right now, though, he was conscious that he'd completely forgotten the clock, and he had one of those stomachs. The kind that went with a six-one, hundred-and-ninety-two-pound man. The kind that needed filling or he got real, real cranky.

Whistling up a storm, he took the porch steps two at a time, grabbed the mail, and shucked off his shoes inside the door. He flipped on lights, shocked to discover no one had done the laundry or picked up after him this morning. Of course, he had Hire-A-Wife coming on Monday, but somehow it always seemed a surprise, what complete chaos the house could turn into before they got here.

After the divorce, he'd changed some things in the

house—like redoing the kitchen in chalk and stone. Maybe it wasn't "decorating" on a woman's terms, but smooth surfaces sure seemed easier to clean up. Still whistling, he flipped on the kitchen light and opened the freezer. Ages ago, he figured he needed both a fridge and freezer in the kitchen, because almost everything he ate came out of the freezer. Today that meant lasagna, garlic bread, and a cherry-berry pie with—he checked—half a container of Cool Whip to put on top.

Of course, it all had to be cooked—but that just meant throwing it all in the oven—except for the Cool Whip. Baking Cool Whip was not a good idea. It was the kind of lesson a guy only had to learn once. He got it all going, then scrounged around for some cashews to stave off imminent starvation. He punched on the kitchen TV and had just popped the lid on a soda—hadn't had a single bite of food or sip yet, not even one!—when he saw her.

It had to be past ten. The night was a pitchy, witchy black, with one of those moaning winds that whispered through the trees. A full moon kept sneaking around the clouds now and then, though, so he could see her clearly enough.

She was sitting on her back porch. On the cold cement. She had her head in her hands, in a posture that sure looked as if she were crying her heart out.

She'd left the back door gaping open behind her. What was *with* that woman and doors?

He chomped down on the salty cashews, chewing furiously. Moonlight shined on her head as if her profile were illuminated with silver dust. Even though she was outside, it was unlikely anyone could see her but him. All the bushes and landscaping around the house sheltered the back porch from view.

But he was stuck being able to see her. Far, far too clearly. None of his business, he told himself, and chewed another handful of cashews even more furiously. He didn't do the white-knight thing, not for anyone, not anymore. How could it possibly be his problem, that a stranger decided to have a boo-hoo fest in his vision?

He grabbed the soda bottle, then chunked it back on the counter. It was colder than ice out there. She didn't even have a hat on, for Pete's sake.

As far as he could tell, she didn't have the sense God gave a goose.

He yanked on a jacket and stomped outside. The closer he got, the more the view deteriorated.

She wasn't a good crier. She was one of those throw-her-whole-self-into-it criers. Yesterday, he'd adjusted to the idea of having a flaky neighbor on the grounds that she was damn beautiful, and a guy was generally willing to tolerate a lot when the view was soothing.

But that deal was off. Her face was all blotchy. She was gasping for air. Eyes getting all swollen.

And that was before he was stuck seeing her up close.

"Hey," he said. And then wanted to wince. Maybe he wasn't feeling particularly happy, but he hadn't meant to sound like a bear growling at her.

Her head jerked up as if someone had slapped her. "Oh. You. Good grief. I didn't realize anyone could see me. I'm fine—"

Yeah, right. She was "fine" like cats flew. He wanted to suggest that she go back inside to cry her eyes out—*after* closing the damn door. But it seemed even he couldn't be quite that coldhearted.

"You sick?" he asked bluntly.

She lifted her hands. Apparently the simple question turned on a new blubbery tears switch, because out they came. "She hates me!"

He could have asked her who in God's name she was talking about, but that was pretty silly, when the only conceivable subject of the problem had to be Charlie's daughter. "I take it you met her today."

"Yes. And I expected it to be tough, but not like this. This is so way beyond a mess. She hated the pink tree—"

"No kidding?"

"Her problems are beyond anything I know how to cope with. I don't even know where to start. She doesn't *want* to start—not with me. She doesn't want to talk to me, doesn't want me around—"

He sank on the cement next to her, not because he wanted to continue this conversation, but because if he was trapped listening, it'd just been too long a day to stand indefinitely in the cold. "You don't think you could be jumping to conclusions? She doesn't even know you, Marta."

"Merry, not Marta. And it's Merry as in *M-e-r-r-y,* not as in *M-a-r-y.*"

He dug in his pocket for Kleenex. Because he often jogged on cold mornings, he tended to carry a bunch. Apparently the last time he'd run out and ripped off some paper towels. Whatever. They enabled her to blow her nose. To give her credit, she didn't waste time apologizing for crying or make it out like it was a big to-do that he'd seen her.

When she quit blowing, she said, "You said you knew Charlie. So you had to know his daughter, right?"

"Well, sure. I mean, she was around all the time, but I can't say how well I knew her. Charlie and I were great buddies, good neighbors together. Shared a beer often enough, bitched about yard work, did some fence talk about raising kids, life, ex-wives. Neither of us pried. We just got along. I liked him."

"I did, too. From the first time I met him, there was just this…click. Not a sexual click. Just a friendly one. He was straightforward and funny and bright. And caring—"

"You liked him so well you never saw him once in the last five years?"

"I take it that's how long he lived here." The faucet had almost quit dripping, but now it gushed again. "No, I never saw him here. And I never imagined that he'd live in a place like this."

"Okay." He washed a hand over his face. "The whole neighborhood's been asking the same questions. You hadn't seen him in years. You never met his daughter. You didn't know anything about his current life, apparently. So how did you end up being Charlene's guardian?"

"Well, I'm not 'the guardian' exactly. More a guardian trainee. And if I can't make this work a lot better than it did today, I'll be flunking the course for sure. Which would be fine, if it was just about *me*. But darn it, it's about what happens to Charlene. And the thing is—"

She seemed to do a lot of emotional talking with her hands, which meant she almost smacked him in the nose. He ducked. "The thing is…what?"

"The thing is that everyone was against my doing this. My dad. My sisters. My friends. They all kept telling me I was being crazy impulsive to just up and quit my job. Sublet my place. Put all my stuff in storage, except for what I could fit in the car, and just move—"

So there were intelligent people in her life, Jack thought, but it was the same old story about being able to lead a horse to water. "And you did all this for a stranger? A girl you didn't know from Adam?" She looked at him, with a fresh bout of diamonds in her eyes. "Hell, I'm not trying to upset you more. I'm trying to understand why you did this."

"I did it because she had no one else!"

"That may be, Merry. But that should have been her father's problem. Not yours."

"Maybe so. But Charlie kind of made it my problem by *not* handling it himself. After his divorce, he went to the trouble of making a will. That was when I knew him, when he was making that first will, trying to plan for Charlene in case something happened to him. I have no idea why he didn't change the will in all this time, but as far as I can tell, there simply was no one else he could leave her with."

"But that doesn't make it your problem, Merry."

"But it *does*. Because I can't imagine abandoning a child to foster care if there's any choice. And I *am* a choice. I'm free, no husband or kids, no ties, no job I couldn't shake loose from. I love people and I love kids. And to tell you the truth, I just assumed that I'd love her, but..." She made an emotional gesture. "I think she sees me as an alien from another planet."

He squinted at her. "Trust me, you don't remotely look like a Klingon."

"I'm not kidding! She thought I was talking a foreign language. I couldn't do anything right, or anything that made any sense to her." Out poured more froth. "She didn't even know what a hair scrunchie was."

"You're kidding." He didn't have a clue what a hair scrunchie was either, but he finished the last of the mop-up with the edge of his glove. Might be a few tears still glistening from those thick, soft eyelashes, but she was definitely starting to dry up.

"I put some fresh flowers in her room. She took them back to the kitchen. I got her to open the other presents, but when she saw the rhinestone tee, she looked at me as if I'd sprouted a third head. Apparently she doesn't listen to music. At least not 'tweenie music. And I happened to get lost driving from the rest home this morning. She thinks I'm dumb. She thinks I'd get lost in a closet. And you know what?"

"What?"

"I do. Get lost in closets. I admit I'm not the most logical card in the deck, but that doesn't make me a cream puff, Jack. She looks like a *marine.*"

The way she said "Jack" triggered a buck in his pulse. A sexual buck.

He felt the first fringe of fear.

She was *not* a woman he wanted to feel that buck for…but he couldn't seem to help it. She was talking to him as if she knew him. As if they were friends. As if she inherently assumed he was someone she could be honest with. He couldn't think of way to respond except straight. "She's grieving."

"Oh, God. I know that. But that's also the terrifying part. Because I want to help her, and I'm afraid if we don't get along, that I could make it worse."

He'd waited as long as he could, but now he motioned to the back door. "You want me to close the door there?".

"No, no. I deliberately left it open. She fell asleep. But I'm afraid she could wake up, think no one was there, that she'd been abandoned. I want to be able to hear her."

So at least this time there was a reason why they were heating the entire outdoors, even if he didn't buy it as a logical choice himself. He cut back to the chase, understanding that she needed direct information. "About the clothes she's wearing...first off, the uniform's army, not marine. But to put a general frame on that picture, when Charles first died, a teacher of hers came over to stay at the house until the funeral. Authorities had already figured out that she had no one, got the lawyer and court system involved. I don't know exactly how it all went down, but when the funeral was over, a social worker had become part of the story, and had decided that she could camp out for another week at the rest home where her great-grandmother is. The idea was to buy enough time for the lawyers to do their thing. Hell, I'm bogging this down with the side details, but I'm just trying to explain the timetable of how things happened—"

"And I want to know. In fact, I'd like to know anything you're willing to tell me. I've really been batting in the dark." The tears had definitely stopped now.

"Well, getting back to the issue of the army uniform business. After the funeral, the social worker went in the house with her, waited while she packed some things. I was at the funeral, although honestly, I don't remember what she wore. I can't say I ever paid any attention to her clothes or things like that. I mean she's just a child, so whatever. But the thing is...when she came back outside, she was wearing her dad's clothes. Not straight army, but army reserves."

Merry brightened up as if a lightbulb dawned in her head. "So," she said thoughtfully, "She's wearing her dad's clothes. Not hers."

"Yeah. At least, that's what it sounds like."

"And the brush cut? Did she always wear her hair in a brush cut?"

"Um, no. Truthfully, I don't remember how she wore her hair. Kind of short, I guess. But not buzz-cut short." He had to think. "But, Charlie—"

"He wore it military short? I never saw it that way."

"Yeah, well, I don't think guys change their hairstyles the way women do. They kind of stay with what they start with. But a few years back—well, I guess he got fed up, was annoyed because his hair tended to curl or something, said it was just easier to shave it off."

"So her hairstyle is mimicking his, too." Merry's mind appeared to be racing now. Jack wasn't sure if that was a good idea—not when her mind was already on the capricious and unpredictable side. "And she wants to be called Charlie. Not Charlene. Like her dad was called Charlie. So...it's all starting to add up. Of course, that doesn't make her behavior any less serious. But at least it's better than worrying the child wants a sex-change operation at age eleven."

He wanted to laugh. "Um, I don't think you'll find she was ever on the girly-girl side."

"That has to be the understatement of the century."

"She adored her dad. They did tons of stuff together. He really enjoyed time with her. And she just loved him from here to hell." With alarm he saw her eyes well again, and chose a different topic at jet speed. "Hey, for the record, I don't know what a scrunchie is, either. Is that some kind of code? Vocab or intel for a specific kind of initiation or something like that?"

She laughed. It wasn't a big laugh, more on the tepid side, but it was obviously a mood changer for her. She was over the crying.

And something else changed at that moment. He didn't know what. But until that instant, he'd just been sitting there, on the cold cement porch step, the heat from the house reaching his back, the streetlights down the neighborhood the only real illumination except for moonlight.

Suddenly, he was conscious of sitting close to her. Not hip-bumping close—not intrusive close, exactly, but close. She suddenly turned, facing him eye to eye, and abrupt as a slap he realized something else.

Possibly he'd recognized there was chemistry before this. Why wouldn't there be? She was gorgeous. And he'd always had a hefty dose of testosterone. It didn't matter if she was on the flaky, ditzy side; his body was always going to respond to a beautiful woman. Still, a guy on the experienced side of thirty-five knew enough to ignore the bulge in his zipper.

Like in her case.

One look and he'd known she was trouble clear through. Nothing he'd seen or heard from her since had changed his mind.

So he wasn't looking at her *that* way. She was the one who was suddenly looking at him. Her expression changed. A quick frown furrowed her brow, almost gone before it started, as if she'd discovered something curious that she wasn't expecting. And then, swift as a spring breeze, she suddenly leaned closer to him.

Suddenly put a hand on his shoulder to brace herself. Suddenly tilted her head.

Suddenly kissed him.

Hell, was a guy ever prepared for Armageddon? Her mouth was satin-soft, the scent of her dizzying. His body perked up as if he hadn't been laid in a blue moon. His heart abruptly remembered that it was lonesome. Beyond lonesome. And she was exactly the one it'd been lonesome for all this time.

More mortifying yet, she wasn't coming onto him. It was just a kiss. A kiss where she touched his shoulder, then cupped his head, then simply laid those irresistible lips on him for a single miraculous second. Maybe two.

Then she eased back, still looking at him. "Thank you, Jack," she said quietly, and then stood up, smiled. And simply went in the house. Even closed the door.

Hokay, he told himself. *Hokay.* But it wasn't okay or hokay. Slowly he lurched to his feet and hiked back to his place. He told himself there was nothing wrong with what just happened, no reason to make more of that kiss than it was. She'd just apparently been trying to express a thank-you for talking to her. And that was just fine.

It was just…he'd never expected to feel anything honest and real with her.

He stomped in through his back door, hung up his jacket and abruptly caught the smell of his burned dinner. His very burned dinner. His inedible—very burned dinner.

Eventually the smoke cleared out, but Jack stayed fuming a while longer.

The new neighbor wasn't working out at all well.

CHAPTER FOUR

THE INSTANT SHE HAD a spare second, Merry wanted to analyze the confounding range of emotions her neighbor had aroused in her. Last night, she'd mused quite a while about that kiss. About the kind of man who went out in the cold to help a stranger. About how honest he'd come across. And, yeah, how sexy.

Merry believed in listening to her instincts. Believed that it wasn't impulsiveness, but natural good sense, to be aware when her body perked up near a certain man. It wasn't as if she'd slept with hordes. But every time her body sent out warning signals—and she'd talked herself out of listening—it turned out that the guy was a dog and her initial instinct had been correct.

Last night there had been none of that dog stuff. It had been all lights-turned-on, whew-where-did-that-heat-come-from, this guy is unbelievably-good-news instinct stuff.

Right now, though, God knows, she had to shake him completely from her mind.

Charlene had just joined her in the kitchen. So far things weren't going too stellar. Partially Merry blamed the gray breakfast counter between them, because the gray counter/black sink kitchen décor was enough to depress anybody. The modern art all over the place was even worse—not just depressing but weird enough to give a girl the willies.

Right now, the chicklet sitting across from her was the scariest problem, though.

Charlene had emerged from the bedroom this morning, ostensibly ready for her first day going back to school, wearing the combat gear again. The newly-waxed brush cut looked awful silly on that tiny, feminine little face. The pants had been cuffed up a half dozen times, but the shirt collar was still buttoned tight enough to choke the throat. The clothes dwarfed her skinny little frame—especially the combat boots—but the saddest part was that closed-in, closed-up expression.

Merry had started out with a bubbly, "Hey, g'morning, cupcake!" But that went over like a double homework assignment, and since then, the silence in the kitchen had built up to deafening proportions.

The differences between them, Merry realized, were a lot more complicated than just combat boots versus rhinestone-studded flip-flops. For breakfast, Charlie had chosen a bowl of Wheaties—no milk, no sugar—and an apple. A tidy paper napkin was folded with the edges just so.

Merry was eating breakfast, too, but she'd chosen a gooey cinnamon roll, tomato juice with a bit of pepper, two Oreos, and a highly sugared cereal with fresh blueberries on it.

It was unnatural to eat that healthily, Merry fretted, and even more frighteningly unnatural to be so damned quiet and obedient. The other differences contrasting them were even more pronounced. She was wearing comfortable old frayed jeans with a hole above the knee. The kid had actually ironed her khakis. Repeat, ironed. Whoever ironed unless threatened at knife-point?

And the child's brush cut might look goofy, but it was certainly ultra tidy compared to her own tumble of dark chestnut hair that hadn't even seen a brush yet.

Charlie looked ready to run the world.

Merry didn't figure anyone should be expected to seriously wake up until midmorning. On the other hand, she might not be thinking clearly yet, but she was definitely cheery enough for two. Good thing, since ole stone-face on the other side of the counter looked as if a smile might crack her cheeks.

"So," Merry said, starting a conversation for maybe the fourth time in the last ten minutes. "You need to be at school by eight-fifteen. How do you usually get there—walk, bus, what?"

Charlie didn't look up from her fascinating bowl of Wheaties, but at least she answered. "My dad drives me. It's on his way to work, so he always said it was no trouble."

"Is there a bus, though?"

"Probably. I don't know. It's like a mile. I could walk it."

"I'll take you, Charlie. I just wondered if there was a regular school bus in case there was a day I was sick or something."

"Yeah, I guess there is. I'll find out. You don't have to do anything about it."

Merry heard the unspoken message. *I won't bother you. Just let me be home. You don't have to even pretend I exist.* Darn kid was breaking her heart even when she said nothing at all. "What time do you want me to pick you up after school?"

"No reason to pick me up. There's a car pool thing. Because my dad worked. So, like there are four moms. He always paid the gas. They rotate who's driving. Mrs. Sheinfeld picks me up today. The phone numbers are all in the Rolodex."

"Okay. And then you get home by what time?"

"Depends on the day. Usually before four. Unless there's soccer practice or something like that. Until I was ten, my dad had, like, a babysitter here until he got home, but that was stupid, I told him. There's always somebody around the neighborhood if I needed something. And he trusts me."

Merry felt her heart lurch. Her heart had been regularly doing that lurching thing since she got here. The military looks and the taciturn expressions were worrying and disconcerting, for damn sure, but somewhere under all that attitude was an awfully miserable kid. Tight as a drum. She sure didn't seem to want nurturing—at least not from Merry—but Merry couldn't help feeling that she'd never met a kid who needed more plain old loving affection.

On the legal pad next to her—and Merry was *not* one into making lists—she was on the third page just this morning. She needed the names of the moms who drove Charlene, besides today's Mrs. Sheinfeld. And they needed to know her. Cripes, maybe she was supposed to be part of that car pool now? How many kids was she supposed to be able to fit in her Mini Cooper? Who was the kid's doctor? Her dentist? Who picked up the trash?

Truth to tell, the list thing was scaring the hell out of her—but at least yesterday's overwhelming panic was gone. She was up and ready to boogie, all renewed and charged to take this on again, all because of Jack, she thought. It helped so much to have another adult to talk to. To vent on.

To kiss.

Between bites of blueberry and cinnamon roll, her mind wrapped around that kiss from last night yet again. She tested her conscience, but nope, there wasn't a lick of guilt. He'd been a brick. There was nothing wrong with expressing thanks and affection. It's not as if she laid up against him in some way he could have construed as a come-on.

Even if she'd thought about doing just that.

Still. She readily recognized that he rang her chimes—and that was the whole scale of chimes. But it was the wrong time in her life to finally find a diamond. She just couldn't be thinking about a man right now, couldn't be curious about one, couldn't allow hormones to color anything about her judgment, either.

She couldn't let anything matter right now but Charlene.

So far she'd carefully refrained from saying anything about how the child was dressed, but it was just too hard not to express a teensy hint of honest worry.

"You'll feel okay going to school in those clothes, right?" she asked casually. "There isn't a dress code in your school?"

"Yeah, there's a code. Girls have to cover their stomachs. And you can't have bra straps showing. Like I'd be worried about that." A noisy snort effectively expressed Charlene's opinion about budding breasts. "Oh. No dirty words on T-shirts. And no face jewelry."

Merry had to translate what face jewelry meant. Nose and lips rings, she assumed. "Those rules don't sound too bad."

"Yeah, well, nobody's gonna tell me what to wear."
It was the first time Charlene had met her eyes—not just
with some life but a full splash of belligerence.

Merry was delighted to see some normal kid rebellion, and warned herself not to blow it. "Hey, if you're
waiting for me to criticize your choice of clothes, it'll
never happen. If you're okay with your choice, then so
am I." Well, she was *almost* okay. Or trying to be okay.
Well, maybe she thought the military thing was over the
top—and worrisome besides—but she was a ton more
concerned about creating some trust than superficial
nonsense like clothes. "Charlie…you haven't said
anything about the classes you're taking. Are there any
subjects you have a hard time with? Or any teachers you
really like?"

"Burkowitz."

Not an answer exactly, but Merry had something.
"Yeah?"

"He teaches math. And computers. He's definitely
frantic."

"Frantic?"

"Frantic. Like, he rocks. He's cool. Frantic," she
repeated, as if the meaning should be obvious.

"Got it. Frantic."

The kid, unlike her, tidily rinsed her bowl and put it
in the dishwasher, then pulled on a jacket and stood at
the door. Merry scrambled after her, searching for shoes
and her own jacket, which seemed to have thrown itself
on a chair in the living room.

"While I'm at school, you're not going in my dad's
room, right?" Charlene reminded her as they walked
outside.

"Right."

"And you're not gonna touch my dad's stuff. Any of it. Nothing in his study either, right?"

"Stop worrying, Charlie. I told you I wouldn't." They'd been through this last night, when Charlene had brought up the issue, her fingers twisting themselves into anxious knots and her mouth all but trembling. She seemed to be a little obsessed about any of her father's things being moved or disappearing. Either way, Merry couldn't think of a reason on the planet not to cater to her. Sooner or later the raw edge of grief had to wear off. And then there'd be plenty of time to figure out what to do with Charlie's stuff.

It took less than ten minutes to be parked at the school. Merry didn't walk in with her—how mortifying would that be? It's not as if she'd forgotten how ghastly it was to be a sixth-grader—the lowest rung on the middle school social ladder. Besides which, girls in that preteen age were meaner than bobcats.

Once Charlene disappeared inside and the school bell rang, though, Merry figured it was safe to go inside. She took a quick look around before aiming for the office. The principal turned out to be a woman, Mrs. Apple, a name that was distractingly appropriate because of the dark red color on her cheeks. Merry couldn't fathom why the woman would have chosen such a wildly bright blusher, when it didn't remotely go with her olive skin.

"I just wanted to meet you." Merry extended a hand, explaining how she'd become Charlene's guardian, how Charlene had just lost her father. The principal swiftly interrupted her.

"We know. Very sad situation."

The whole school was kind of a sad situation, Merry

personally thought. Maybe she'd only walked down one long hall, but that single hall had been telling. There was no graffiti, no banged-up lockers, no noise. The bell had only rung a few minutes before, yet the kids were all sitting in their seats like model children. Not only was it a prep school with a capital *P*, but the classrooms were carpeted—besides which, half the girls she saw were already wearing cashmere sweaters. This was just middle school, for Pete's sake.

"Well, I just wanted you to know I'm here, that you can call me. Charlene and I are just getting to know each other, so I'm afraid that right now I'm just another big change in her life. If there's anything I can do, as far as the school or any activities she's involved in—"

"Oh, yes." Mrs. Apple abruptly perked up. "We're always in need of a field mother. Someone to go with the children on bus trips. Field or sports trips." And then there was the PTO. And the bake sales. And the sports equipment fund-raisers. And Brownies. "We have a middle school dance coming up on Valentine's Day—the first one for the sixth-graders. We'll need parents to chaperone that."

"I'd be happy to," Merry said, but on the inside, she was gulping to beat the band. In principle, she was willing to do anything that would help Charlene, but reality was that it was pretty full scale transition to somehow immediately turn herself into a suburban soccer mom. "I was hoping you would let Charlene's teachers know what she's been going through. I know she missed more than a week of school, for one thing—"

"We're not concerned. Charlene, as you know, is an unusually gifted student. We know she'll catch up quickly."

Well, that had been a little hair-raising but it had basically gone okay, Merry thought as she drove back to the house. Her next priority was conquering the coffee machine. And—after calling her dad to check in—her second priority of the day was finding a place to sleep.

The two obvious choices were the master bedroom or Charlie's study—both of which were nice, big rooms. But the first night, she'd camped on the couch because she'd fallen asleep there from exhaustion, and then last night, she'd just glanced in the master bedroom when Charlene saw her and went into that anxiety attack about her dad's stuff. So those rooms were out, and normally Merry wouldn't mind camping out indefinitely. Half the time she felt as if she were camping out in her own life, always ready to move on and move out…but this situation was different.

This time she had to try to settle down. To stay.

There was no reason she couldn't change. Her life and job hopping had never been about character. It had been about her mother. Which would seem to suggest that this was an ideal time for her to come to grips with that old tediously upsetting history, but right now, she just had too much to do.

Because the coffee machine won the technology battle with her—again—she hauled around a mug of instant. She'd looked around and cleaned the place that first night, but now, she conducted a major search—not just to pin down a place to sleep, but to get a stronger feeling for Charlie and the kind of man and dad he'd been.

The living room, at least, had flashes of the whimsically fun man she'd once known in Charlie. The couch was shaped like a dog bone—a huge, gray dog bone in a swelty-soft suede. And in the entranceway, he'd hung a dartboard—the kind that used felt darts, not the sharp kinds, and it showed signs of wear, so it was obviously something dad and daughter played together. A heap of pillows on the floor indicated they both tended to watch the tube sprawled out.

But the strange modern art all through the house continued to spook her.

A life-sized painting took up one entire wall in the living room. The artist had signed it "Red Dominance," and it looked as if an extremely crabby person had swathed on big, violent slashes of red and black and yellow, let it dry and put it in a frame. Turn the corner toward the kitchen, and there was an oil of a long, surreal naked body. It wasn't a sexy nude, or remotely pornographic, nothing inappropriate for Charlene to see. The figure was all huddled up, showing mostly knees and elbows, its head bent at a crooked angle, leaving Merry the impression of a living skeleton—one that jumped out at her every time she turned the corner.

Another new-age-y nude took up wall space in Charlie's den, but that one happened to be green. The green woman appeared to be screaming, although the only identifiable body part for sure was her mouth. Every time Merry passed by it, she wanted to tiptoe.

Okay, so maybe Merry wasn't precisely a connoisseur of valuable art. Her taste ran more toward big yellow smiley faces. But she couldn't seem to reconcile the Charlie she knew with the one who'd picked out these scary, ugly pictures.

She kept thinking that there had to be an important clue here. Something she needed to know. Something that would help her understand Charlene and her relationship with her dad and their lives together—if she could just grasp it.

Eventually she gave up trying to analyze the impossible and settled down to the plain old chore of picking a room for herself. The upstairs was pretty much a huge, cavernous space that had potential in the long run, but for now, Merry didn't want to be that far removed from Charlene. So she picked the spare room past the master bedroom. It had clearly been used to stash stuff no one knew what to do with, from out-of-season sports equipment to luggage to spare coats. But it had a lumpy couch bed already there. The walls were an ugly muddy taupe, but whatever. There was a bathroom across from Charlie's and a view of Jack's backyard.

Her thoughts strayed back to Jack and the kiss last night, but she ruthlessly reined them in. After she did the fresh-sheet thing, organized her makeup in the back bathroom, and carted the seasonal debris upstairs to an out-of-sight closet, it was already late morning. She still had the long, three-page list of things to tackle—only abruptly, the phone rang.

It was the school calling. The vice principal. The man sounded decent, had one of those patient, gentle voices that made Merry think he was a kid lover, but he sure had nothing but trouble to deliver.

He claimed that Charlene had slugged another kid. Because Charlie was a girl and the boy she'd punched was a foot taller than her—and because she'd never been in trouble before—the school had decided not to punish her with the usual automatic suspension. They'd also taken into account her father's death and how much school she'd already missed. But she *was* being sent home for the day—Merry had to pick her up immediately—and she'd have detention every afternoon for the next two weeks.

So much for calling all the carpool mothers and looking into grief counseling and figuring out the washing machine and checking out what clothes Charlie did and didn't have in her closet and calling the guardian *ad litem* woman to see what she was like and trying to figure out where the house finances stood... the finances especially had her worry beads jiggling, because she didn't have the first clue what it cost to maintain the place, much less how the bills were supposed to work with the estate and all.

But all that was just life crap. Nothing that mattered.

She made it to the school in less than three minutes, charged in the front door, and immediately came to a dead stop. The woebegone figure sitting alone in the hall, head bent, dejection painted in her rounded shoulders and sunk-in posture was unquestionably Charlie. It was all Merry could do not to sweep her into her arms. But then Charlie looked up, and faster than spit, her face took on a cold, defensive expression.

"I suppose you're going to yell."

"Actually, what I'm going to do is tell the principal I'm here, so that we can go home."

"Yeah, right."

The VP was about what Merry had expected from the phone call—a tall reed with a quiet voice, who had a lot of things to say about violence never being an answer, and certain rules and controls being important, and about Charlene needing to rethink her actions and how they affected others.

He was ponderous and wordy, not mean, yet from the way Charlie slammed out of the school and slammed the car door and slammed into the house, you'd think somebody'd whipped her kitten.

Merry said nothing, just aimed for the kitchen, rolled up her sleeves, and faced off with the coffeemaker again. It was such a gorgeous machine. Obviously the crème de la crème. Probably cost more than she had in her savings account. But there had to be some doo-hickey to make the thingamabob come out so you could put the grounds in? And she couldn't find it.

Minutes passed. Then more minutes. Than Charlene said from the doorway, in a voice so disgusted it was amazing she could survive it, "What are you trying to do?"

"Oh, I'm *so* glad you're here. Is there any chance you know how to make this work?"

"Of course." The kid came over, touched something, and the thingamabob opened like magic.

"Thanks," Merry said, and immediately started pouring in fresh grind. It was possible she could survive an hour longer without real coffee, but she wasn't dead sure.

"Aren't you going to say anything?" Ms. Attitude had gone back to the doorway to park, clearly leaving herself an easy exit.

"Say anything about what?"

"Gimme a break. You know about what."

Merry glanced up—once she was positive the machine was going to come through and percolate for her. "Naturally, I want to know what happened. But I figured you're probably still feeling really upset, so you'd tell me about the fight when you felt you could."

Mentally holding her breath, she turned around, dug out the bag of Oreos from the new stash of groceries.

When she turned back, Charlene had moved one foot farther into the room, but no more. More carefully than she'd treat a python, Merry cracked open the package and set it in the middle of the breakfast counter. Then she went searching for a mug. Not that she wasn't willing to guzzle the coffee straight from the machine, lapping it up like a dog if she had to, but a standard mug type container would be nice.

"He's in eighth grade. His name's Dougall. Dougall Whitmore. He asked me what was with the hair."

Aha. Words. Merry was careful not to do any kind of victory dance—but man, it was sure tempting. "And you said…"

"I said nothing."

"Right," Merry murmured, believing *that* like she believed in the tooth fairy. Which, come to think of it, she had believed in until she was past puberty.

"But then he said I looked queer. Then I said if looking queer meant being like my dad, then I was happy to look like this. Then he said, well, maybe I was just a lesbo and trying to be honest about it."

"And then?"

"Then I punched him." It took a moment, but Charlene finally risked putting half of her skinny hip on the stool, getting close enough to reach the Oreos.

"Is your hand okay?" Merry asked.

"Are you kidding? *No.* It hurts really, really bad. I'm never hitting anybody again. It's not worth it. I thought it was broken. My whole fist."

"Let's see… Eek! We'd better get some ice on that." As she scrounged for a plastic bag and ice, she said, "Now, Charlie, you realize the guy's gonna be humiliated because a girl hit him. So you might want to strategize about how you want to handle that before going back to school tomorrow."

"Huh? That's all?"

"What do you mean?" Merry gently put the ice bag on her hand, letting Charlie determine how hard or light she wanted to press it. The brush cut was starting to flop, she noted. It was the first time she'd been close enough to see that under all that wax stuff was a headful of wispy, baby-fine, to-die-for blond hair.

"You're not going to yell at me? Hand out some punishment?"

Merry sucked in a breath. This was a serious test, she knew. Maybe even a make it or break it test. She opened her mouth to respond—but just then, the phone rang.

Could one thing go smoothly today? Even the smallest thing? Was that really asking too much?

JACK PUSHED OPEN the back door, buzzed to beat the band. What a *great* day. He plucked a beer from the fridge, a fork from the drawer and promptly carted two white containers of Chinese to the red leather chair in the living room.

He was starving—seeing as it was past nine. And he'd groused with his colleagues about the mighty long work day, but he didn't mean it.

It always seemed crazy to be paid so much to do something he loved. Back in college, he'd aimed for a degree in Geography because he'd wanted to be a cryptographer. Some idealistic cause had led him into the navy, then Special Ops, but even then the military got the idea that he should get a master's in math. No hardship. Special Ops was for the physically fit youngsters. The master's enabled him to get out and end up working for the government, getting paid lots and lots of money to do puzzles.

Codes. He loved breaking them. Some said he was the most brilliant code breaker around—and that was mighty ironic, considering he'd never decoded the mystery of his own marriage. Sometimes he went to work with two different colored socks on. Sometimes— even though he had plenty of money—he bounced a check because he forgot to add up his checkbook.

But give him a puzzle, and he was over-the-moon happy.

That he was doing something for his country gave him pride, too, but people'd think he was corny if he said that. So he tried to complain about his long hours and the tediousness of his desk job. It was better than his friends thinking he was a dork—even though he was.

Heaving a loud, lazy sigh, he scooped up the remote, cocked his feet on the coffee table and gobbled the first forkful of War Sui Gui. He'd TiVo'd a good old Steven Seagal the night before. It was a perfect end to a perfect day, Chinese takeout and a relaxing couple hours of blood and guts.

Only then his cell rang.

"It's Patty, Jack. I'm back from vacation, had a fabulous time. But I couldn't wait to call you!"

"Um—"

"Paris was incredible. Just incredible. But I have admit, I just kept thinking about how great that night was…"

The more she giggled, the more she talked, the more Jack got a tight feeling in the back of his throat. He couldn't recall anyone named Patty. Had no memory of sleeping with anyone named Patty. For damn sure, he didn't remember any blue scarves tying her up.

Hell.

He couldn't remember tying anyone up with blue scarves. Not that he was unwilling.

He weaseled out of making a date that weekend, claiming he had to work, which wasn't true. But even a casual sexual relationship was a little too weird if he couldn't place the woman.

A little less ferociously, he dove back into his War Sui Gui—only to have the damn cell phone sing again. He glared at the phone, scratched his neck. He really didn't want to risk another call right then. The one had spooked him.

But knowing it could be one of the boys, he had to answer. And he was right, because it was Kev. "Dad!"

"You got me," Jack affirmed.

"Well, hey."

"Hey, back." So it was going to be one of those conversations.

"Cooper thinks we should get a car."

"Your brother thinks that, huh? I always find it amazing, how Cooper's name comes up whenever you want something, but it's never Cooper who calls me about it." Jack heard his son sigh heavily and with great patience.

"Cooper is the one," Kevin reminded him, "who never does anything wrong. Who always gets the grades. Who never causes any trouble. So isn't it obvious why I use him, Dad? He's got pull with you."

"Ah." When Kicker was bored, these conversations could tend to go on forever. Not that Jack minded. He pushed the stop button on the movie and climbed to his feet. Might as well get some nuisance chores done. Still listening to Kicker's exuberant arguments, he wandered into the kitchen, sifted through the day's mail, carted a bag of trash to the garage, then opened the dishwasher. Only, damn. There were clean dishes in there. How come a guy could never open a dishwasher and find the thing empty? Ever?

"Although this time I've got some dirt on Cooper."

"What kind of dirt?"

"Good dirt. My brother," Kevin said dramatically, "has a girl."

"Yeah?" That was interesting enough to make Jack stop with the chores for a minute.

"You know me. I play the field like you do, Dad. Why settle for one when there's no end of women out there? But Coop...I'll tell you, he's just not as smart as you and me. You'd think he'd pick someone shy like him, wouldn't you? That he'd go for a brain like he is? But, no. Instead she's a looker. Boobs out to here. A cheerleader." Kevin sighed again, one of those man-to-man exhausted sighs. "She's *my* kind, not his. And who can figure women? I'm right here. I've got the charm. The moves. The looks—"

"Um, Kev? You're twins, remember? You have the same looks."

"Yeah, but he's a *nerd*. He doesn't dress right, doesn't *move* right. Yet she's all over him. Anyways, back to the car. I was thinking, you know, used. Just not too used. And red..."

"Uh-huh...." Only half-listening, Jack opened the fridge for another beer. Just as he flipped the tab, he caught a flash of color in his kitchen window.

He froze, thinking it couldn't be her. Not again.

"So I said to the guys, I said like..."

"Uh-huh," he said to his son, and bent closer to the window. Damn it and double damn it. It *was* her again. Sitting on the porch again. Her head in her hands again.

This time, though, he was butting out. No discussion, no guilt. If she wanted to sit outside bawling her eyes out, that was her problem.

He'd tried to be nice before, hadn't he? And look where it had gotten him. Kissed within an inch of his life, and by a woman who should have a *T* for Traumatic Trouble inked on her forehead. No one in hell could expect him to get involved again.

He was just going to finish talking to his son, go back to his Steven Seagal movie, put his feet up. Ignore her completely.

CHAPTER FIVE

MERRY MUST HAVE HEARD his back door slam, because he saw her head jerk up before he'd even stepped on the grass.

"God. Don't tell me you're going to make this into a regular thing." He crossed the yard, stomping toward her with all the enthusiasm of a guy facing a root canal.

"Jack, you didn't have to come over. I'm not crying."

He heard her, but he didn't pay any attention. It's not like he was going to believe a ditz like her until he saw for himself. Once he neared close enough to get a bird's-eye of her face, though, he wanted to kick himself. Of course it was dark, but even so there was no hint of puffiness in her face, no sign of recent tears in those big, eloquent eyes.

Now that he'd barged over here, though, he couldn't just take off. God knew, he could do rude. Hell, he *was* rude. But it was too damned awkward to just whip around and disappear back into his own house just because he hadn't caught her crying.

So he hesitated, examining the situation. It was warmer tonight, hardly balmy, but at least it wasn't freezing or windy. She had her hair all piled up on top of her head with one of those clips women used. Not like a hairstyle, more like a way to get it off her face, but unfortunately, it also revealed the long slender line of her neck, her clean profile, the straight nose, the pretty lips, that baby's-butt perfect skin.

She was wearing pink, a thick hooded sweatshirt and sweats, nothing that remotely revealed her figure in any explicit way. Yet she was built so lithe, so soft. So all-woman.

And the last thing in the universe he wanted was to keep noticing things about her, but he couldn't help but recognize the strain around her eyes. Maybe she hadn't been crying—but she wasn't sitting on the porch steps in the dark because she was a happy camper, either.

This time, though, he'd gotten smarter. He unzipped his jacket, handed her a Dixie cup and set one down for himself, then pulled out the Jack Daniels.

"I'd better not. Not in front of Charlie."

"Do we see her anywhere around here?"

"But she's studying in her room. So she could come out any time."

"Well, you go ahead and be a saint. But she's seen me and her dad take a drink now and then before, and I never noticed she suffered any trauma from it, so I don't have the same problem. I take it this wasn't a real easy day."

"She got suspended for fighting."

His jaw dropped. *"Charlene?"*

Merry nodded. "Yeah. Only, as crazy it sounds, that actually turned into the easiest thing I tackled all day." Abruptly she grabbed his flask and tipped it into the Dixie cup, filled it a good halfway, gulped it. Immediately she made like a bloodhound, trying to shake the fire out of her jowls—only she didn't have any jowls—and darn it, but he was forced to laugh.

"Whew. That's a little stronger than a glass of wine," she said wryly.

"Works faster, too. So, about the fighting?" He still couldn't believe the quiet little squirt next door who'd followed her dad like a shadow would have initiated a fight with anyone.

"She got in trouble at school for the fighting. Obviously. But for the first time, we were getting along so well. I didn't scold her. I didn't-see any reason to. She already knew she'd done something wrong. I just said that I'd like to be in her corner, and I'd appreciate it if she gave me a chance by telling me what happened." Merry took another sip, did another jowl-shake as the fire hit her throat. "For a while it was so nice. She started opening up. Talking to me about things. Not a lot, just a little. And we were doing just fine until we started doing some things around the house. Damn it, Jack, the child has guns. *Guns!*"

Okay, obviously this was another conversation he was not going to be able to escape from quickly, but as Jack eased down next to her, he was careful to park a good foot distance away. And on second judgment, he edged even farther away, almost to the flower bed. Eighteen inches separation was safer. "I have a feeling where this is going…but she must have told you that her dad's guns aren't really weapons?"

"Of course they're weapons! What else is a gun but a weapon? And she's eleven years old, for Pete's sake. A baby!" She gulped down some more firewater, handed him the Dixie cup. "They were in his room. And all Charlie's stuff, of course, belongs to his daughter now. But she wanted to take them to her bedroom to keep them there. The last thing in the universe I wanted to do was argue with her when we were finally getting along, but *sheesh*. There's no way I could let her do that."

"Well, I agree with you there. Last I remember, Charlie had them in a locked cabinet in the back of his closet. Where they belonged. But Merry, there's a long history there. They're not contemporary guns."

"Like it matters whether they're old or new? They're *huge*."

"They're called long rifles."

"That's what I said. They're huge."

He sighed. This was gonna be slow going, he feared. "This was all about a hobby Charlie developed with Charlene. It started because she didn't like American history in school. She thought it was boring. You know how it is around D.C.—there are a lot of historical re-enactments and that kind of thing. So he took her to some, and she picked up a fascination for the old-fashioned, custom muzzle-loading rifles. They made two or three of them from scratch. Together. It's the kind of gun the pioneers had in the 1700s—what they called a Kentucky rifle or a Pennsylvania rifle."

"Guns killed Bambi's mother." Her voice was still full out of outrage.

He sighed again. "Look, personally, I don't like the idea of guns in a house with kids, either. But this really was different for them. I don't think the guns actually shoot. They're just replicas—"

"They're still guns!" Suddenly he got a lot of arm waving. Punctuation, he guessed. "And then, you know what's in the garage?"

He wildly guessed. "His car?"

"His car is the least of it—although I sure don't

know what to do with it. I can only drive one car, and I like my Mini. But the thing is—there's crud all over the place. Parts. Power tools. Greasy stuff. Oily stuff."

"Ah. And this is upsetting…why?"

"Do you know what an Akino is? Or the VW Eco-Racer?"

"Yeah, sure."

"Well, I don't. Charlie wants an MX-5. I don't even know what an MX is. Or a TSX. Or how to put together a sound system—which I guess is what some of those parts are. Sound-system components. And then she starts in about dampers and antiroll bars— I suppose you know what those are, too."

"Yeah," he admitted.

"Well, I've never even heard that language before. I finally got her talking to me, for God's sake, and then I can't understand a single word. This whole thing—I feel like I got in a cross between Chaos and Cupid."

"Say what? How did Cupid get into this conversation?"

"Because Cupid and Chaos were two of the oldest gods. You studied mythology back when, didn't you? Chaos was a contemporary of Cupid. Or Eros. I always got the Roman and Greek names mixed up. The point, though—"

"I'll be damned. You have a point?"

"The point is, when you go way back in mythology, Cupid and Chaos pretty much only had each other at the start of the world. So pretty naturally, they were always tangling it up. I'm not saying I believe in mythology, for heaven's sake, but as a metaphor it makes a lot of sense, don't you think? Hormones bring on chaos every time, and circumstances with a lot of chaos tend to bring on hormones. Sex and trouble just go together. Always have. Always will. And normally we think of that applying to adults—"

"Sex and trouble? That's for damn sure."

"But in this case, I was thinking about Charlene. Because she's nearing puberty, so hormones are an issue for her, and because she and I are the same gender, I was so sure we'd be able to relate female to female, you know? Instead, it's just crazy. We can't seem to find any common ground."

Jack lost track of the conversation, partly because initially it seemed like she was talking a bunch of female gobbledegook. And then because she wasn't. Hell, what she said was all too eerily true. There *was* a connection between chaos and hormones. She'd brought nothing but chaos since she arrived here. And he'd felt nothing but hormones.

Like now. He couldn't get a single reasonable thought to stick in his head, yet his concentration was flawless on her eyes. And her mouth. And the curve of her butt.

"Jack?"

Vaguely he realized that she'd gone down another conversational road and he'd completely lost track. Of the road, not of her. The curve of her butt really was damn near perfect. If a guy's mind had to degenerate into complete chaos, at least he had a good excuse.

"Have you ever met Charlene's mother?" Merry asked, apparently for the second time. "I knew when Charlie got divorced that it was a really tense situation. Something had to be really wrong for him to get sole custody. But even in an unfriendly situation, it seems odd that Charlene has yet to even mention her mom. I don't want to bring up another touchy or traumatic situation, but I'd like to know the role her mother has in all this."

Okay, enough playing around. Jack tore his mind off her adorable butt and got serious. "To be honest, I just don't know anything about the mother. I'm pretty sure she never showed up here. I never caught any hint that she was active in Charlene's life in any way." He thought back. "When Charlie first moved next door... well, he was divorced and I was fresh separated myself. We were both pretty raw on the subject of women. We just tended to talk about guy things."

"But he must have said something over the years? To give you a clue what happened?"

"Well, I don't know the whole story, but I believe the breakup of the marriage was about her drug use. One time he mentioned the trigger for the final split—that he'd found her zoned out, alone with the baby, when he got home from work one time, and that was it. He took the kid, hit a lawyer, went for the full custody thing. He really didn't talk about it otherwise. He just wasn't one of those people who wanted to vent a whole blow-by-blow."

"I know. I knew him right at the time of the divorce, but he still didn't fill in many details. I know that whatever made him fight for full custody was the same factor that made him worry what would happen to Charlene if he died. That there was no one he trusted to be guardian. He obviously didn't think of Charlene's mother as a guardian even in an emergency, at least back then. But..." Merry frowned. "That still doesn't answer the question of where *is* Charlene's mother now? I mean, I assume she's still alive somewhere?"

"Beats me. I don't know."

Merry rubbed her forehead. "God. What if the woman suddenly shows up in Charlene's life?"

"Um, I'm not sure you need to borrow trouble, when you've already got a handful. Her suddenly appearing after all these years seems unlikely." He hesitated. "If she did suddenly show up, though—the way Charlie always spoke about her—I'd guess it'd be because she smelled money in the estate."

"That'd be my fear, too." Merry leaned back on her elbows, gazing up at the dusty night sky. "But for right now, I'm just trying to understand Charlene. What feelings she might have stored about her absentee mother. Whether she remembers her. Whether those memories are about loss or fear or love or whatever, especially now that she's lost her dad now, too. I mean... this is the kind of thing I thought I'd be able to talk about with her. For darn sure, we're not going to have too many meaningful conversations about guns and roll bars." She sighed. "You have kids, Jack?"

"Yup. Two. Twins, in fact, both fifteen." He motioned to his place. "They grew up in that house. That's why I keep it, in fact. The place is way too big for one guy, but they still think of it as home. Their mother and I share custody, but that's not so easy to work out in real life. She moved, bought a condo on the other side of D.C., far enough away that they had to change schools. They don't seem to mind it as much as I do. They're here a lot, but the commuting distance is just enough to make getting together a little harder."

"You think your ex-wife did that deliberately? Moved to make it harder for you to see them?"

He said dryly, "I don't believe my opinion or the kids' opinions were anywhere near her radar. She made the move because of her career. That's what she cares about." He added, "Aw hell. I know that sounded like a put-down, and I hate when people talk down their exes. Forget I said anything. Truth is, it doesn't matter that much. The last thing fifteen-year-old boys want is to spend weekends with their parents. They've got their own social lives. So even if they lived closer, it's not as if I'd likely see that much more of them, anyway."

She suddenly smiled at him—a smile that made him think of satin fantasies and sweaty sheets, moonlight and dangerous kisses. The first time he'd laid eyes on her, he'd had that kind of trouble, but what guy wouldn't? She was striking as hell. But where her looks were hopelessly riveting, her smiles were in the downright-lethal class. She invoked every bad idea he'd ever had and some he was just getting around to considering.

She stood up, still smiling. "Jack, I'll bet you're an outstanding dad. And there's no doubt in my mind you'd be an outstanding friend as well."

She bent down and brushed those soft-swollen lips on his brow. "Thanks. For being such a wonderful listener. I hope I can do the same for you sometime."

He sat there after she'd gone in the house, wondering if anyone would see him if he bashed his head against the nearest rock.

Here he was thinking about stripping her naked, and she was thinking of him as a good dad and good friend.

Not that he wanted her to think about him in any other way. For Pete's sake, she was the same as a grenade without the pin. Everything going on next door added up to a headache of migraine proportions. She seemed…too flighty, too young…to suddenly take on parenthood, at least parenthood of a girl as complex as

Charlene. It'd be like a poodle trying to mother a baby Rottweiler. Or a fuzzy, fluffy rabbit trying to nurture a porcupine.

Jack could sympathize. She was in a mess.

It just wasn't his mess.

Yet as he trudged across the yard, he still felt unsettled and…restless. He was used to women coming on to him, thinking he was attractive. It's not as if he were in his dotage, for God's sake. He had all his hair. Kept up his build. Women seemed to sense he had exceptional potential between the sheets—which was the total truth. He took major pride in the skills and experience he brought to a lover.

So it'd been a while since a woman had punched him in the ego teeth.

What itched him most was that Merry apparently thought she was complimenting him. Good friend? Nice dad? What the hell was that? When she'd kissed him the night before, she'd sure yanked all his testosterone chains…but hell, maybe he hadn't aroused any of hers and the chemical combustion between them had been all on his side.

So…*fine,* he thought. And slammed the door on the way in.

MERRY LOOKED AT THE GLUM FACE across the breakfast table on Saturday morning. "You sleep okay?"

"Fine," Charlie said, head down.

"You kept saying it went okay in school…but did something happen with that Dougall boy?"

Charlene shrugged. "He said he was sorry. I'm not sure if he was really sorry or not. I think they made him say something because of, like, implying I was gay. The school always has a cow if somebody does the homophobe thing. But, whatever."

Whatever. The universal answer. But the kid's face still looked clunky-low. "Are you still upset with me about the argument we had about the guns?"

"No."

Merry figured any answer that short was really a *yes,* but getting more information was like pushing a rock uphill. "I got a call last night," she mentioned. "June Innes. Do you remember meeting her?"

Finally, a direct glance. Wary. "Yeah. She was the one who met with me after Dad died. I mean, so did a social worker, but Mrs. Innes was different. It was kind of weird, you know? She said she had the power to say what happened to me. Like that she'd be the one who'd represent me in court."

Merry nodded. "I'm not sure I totally understand the whole guardian *ad litem* role, either, Charl. But you've got it right. She's supposed to be on your side, represent your needs. And she called to say she was coming over Monday, after school. Just to see you." She would have added more details, but Charlie's face lit up with alarm.

"I'm *fine.* Nobody has to 'represent' me. Nobody has to see me. Nothing's wrong. I don't want to talk to her. You're not going to throw me out just because of the trouble in school, are you? I've never been in trouble before. Even once. It was just a bad day!"

Merry felt her heart squeeze tight. "I was never going to throw you out, you silly, whether you're having bad days or good days. But we can't stop Mrs. Innes from visiting, Charl. And she really is on your side. I have to admit, though, when she called, I realized we'd been trashing the house. We should probably do straightening up before she gets here."

"I can clean house. I know how. You don't have to." And then another burst. "I don't want to go anywhere else but home. I don't see why she gets to say what happens to me. She doesn't even *know* me. You're not mad at me, are you, Merry? Because I can be quieter. And I can clean good. You're not going to let her take me away, are you?"

"No one, but no one, is going to take you away, Charlie." Merry kept thinking, *Poor baby.* The crazy brush cut and swagger and guns were just the opposite of the real picture. Under all that was such a vulnerable little girl. "But I am guessing that Mrs. Innes will suggest that you see a counselor."

"I don't need any stupid counselor! *Why?*"

"Because it's so hard to lose someone. Hard to deal with the grieving. People can help you—"

"Like somebody can bring my dad back?" Charlie rolled her eyes. "I'm not talking to some *stranger* about my dad. The whole thing's stupid. It's something grown-ups want to do to make themselves feel better."

Merry said slowly, "You're right."

"I'm *trying* not to cause trouble. To do anything wrong. I know, I messed up in school this week—"

Okay. The kid was breaking her heart. She was just so inhibited, so repressed. So tight. So trying to survive something hugely over her head. "Look, Charlie. We have to see Mrs. Innes. We don't have any choice. It's a court mandate. But that's not happening until Monday. A long time away. Let's work on today."

"Yeah, you said. We gotta clean the house. And I said I would."

"No."

"No?"

"No," Merry said firmly, and swept the breakfast dishes to the counter. "I may not know how to do engine parts and guns, kiddo. But I do know how to have fun. Come on."

"Come on where?"

"Out."

The poor deprived child had never Rollerbladed before. Never gone into a department store and tried on fancy hats. Never driven down the road singing at the top of her lungs.

"You're not normal," Charlie said.

"Oh, thank you."

That won a smile.

By then, Merry gave herself credit for winning quite a few smiles—just no outright natural laughter. Charlie went along with her, didn't argue, didn't complain about anything. But she just couldn't seem to really let loose and relax.

Merry worked harder. The day was only half done. After picking up fast food for lunch, she drove around a while longer, trying to think up fresh ideas at the same time she got a better feeling for the town. It was an old-fashioned New England–looking town, with white spired churches and brick houses and lots of streets named after trees—Oak and Maple, Sassafras and Chestnut. But it was awfully hard to get her bearings when the roads were all so curly, swirling around hills, dipping down into valleys.

Eventually, Charlie said in awe, "You really couldn't find your way out of a parking lot, could you?"

"Hey," Merry said in an injured tone, but on the

inside, she was delighted. It was a real live insult. Surely that meant they were making progress? And just then, as she turned down a street she'd never seen before, she caught the sign for a craft shop.

"I don't do crafts," Charlene insisted.

"We're not going to do *crafts*. We're going to do painting."

"But I don't paint, either."

Neither did Merry, but the idea had sparked a project. Anything would be better than the ghoulish contemporary art in the house, right? So she coaxed Charlene into the store and emerged two hundred bucks poorer—two hundred bucks she couldn't afford, because she doubted anyone'd believe this was a guardian expense—but they had canvases and brushes and a zillion cans of colorful paint.

"I don't get what we're going to do with all this stuff."

"Paint some pictures for the walls."

"But I can't paint. Really."

"Sure you can. I *know* we can paint better than the Green Skeleton Girl."

Charlie knew the painting she meant. "But that's art, Merry. That's why my dad bought all those pictures. He said they'd be worth a bunch of money some day."

"Maybe they will be. And they'd be great. You can consider that 'found money' if those ships ever really come in."

"Ships?"

"Never mind. The point is that there's no reason we can't store those paintings in a nice, safe closet, is there? I mean, if you happened to paint something you liked better and actually wanted to look at every day?"

By midafternoon, the sky suddenly turned darker than a nightmare. When they pulled in the driveway, a howling wind chased them inside. Merry doubted a Virginia winter storm could rival a serious Minnesota blizzard, but either way, it was a good time to hole up inside.

Charlie watched warily while Merry set up. Once she draped newspaper all over the kitchen floor, she pushed kitchen chairs together to work as make-shift easels. The chairs weren't remotely the right height for the big white canvasses, but she couldn't think of another one. Charlie came through with a couple of old T-shirts to wear over their clothes, while Merry organized the brushes and bowls of paint. Last, she flipped on all the lights against the gloomy afternoon and turned up some music—some nice, loud, hip-gyrating rock and roll. "Okay, let it rip!"

"Let what rip?"

Merry showed her, taking a brush dripping with sun-yellow and swathing it across a canvas. "Now, your turn."

"What color am I supposed to use?"

"Any color you love. That's what we're going to build. Canvases that are big splashes of colors we love."

"That's all we're trying to do?"

"That's all," Merry affirmed.

Charlie gingerly brushed on a streak of khaki green.

Merry ran over and put a moosh of cherry red on an edge. At Charlie's shocked look, she said, "Go on. Go put something on mine."

"You mean wreck yours?"

"You won't be *wrecking* anything. We'll just be creating something different than anyone else would create."

"In the entire universe," Charlie agreed dryly. But she went over and dabbed a few spots of orange on Merry's canvas.

Merry responded by dipping her entire hand in the sky blue and putting palm prints all over Charlie's picture. Charlie took off her socks and did feet prints—in dark purple—on hers.

For the first time, the very first time since Merry got here, she could taste just a wee bit of elation. They were having fun together. They were *being* together. And if they could just start *being* together, Merry figured the rest had a prayer of working out. Charlie wasn't going to recover from her dad's loss overnight. Merry wasn't going to turn into a parent overnight.

But hell's bells, at last she had a taste of hope.

The two of them slashed and streaked and stroked until a half dozen canvases were completely dripping in various crazy colors and shapes. At some point Merry realized the two of them were head-to-bare-feet covered in paint as well—but who cared? Finally, though, enough seemed enough. Merry stepped back to give their fancy art a critical eye. "Hot damn. Are we good or are we good?"

Charlie made the strangest sound. "Hogwash."

"Huh? Hogwash? What's hogwash?"

"It's—" Abruptly she made that sound again, as if there was a little choke gurgling at the very back of her throat. Her so-careful expression suddenly seemed to crack.

Merry stared, disbelieving. It wasn't just a smile taking over that face. Charlie actually bent over, clearly in response to how god-awful she thought their artwork was—and let out a laugh. A rusty laugh. A little-girl-not-trying-to-be-brave-right-then laugh. In fact, it was a downright boisterous giggle.

Only then…the lights went out. The lights, the music, the fridge, the furnace, the everything. Whatever cut off the power, the kitchen was abruptly dark as a cellar.

And that one precious moment of silly joyfulness disappeared faster than smoke.

GIVEN THE ICE STORM, Jack was just as glad Heather had opted out of a regular Saturday-night date. The original plan had been a movie, then out for drinks, then back to his place. This way, he thought as he finished shaving his chin, they could skip the movie. Just go straight for the main course.

Not that he presumed they'd be having sex. But they had every other time they'd been together. Heather loved her career, flew all over the world with her job, had no interest in settling down. But when she was in town, she got lonely.

Jack had always willingly offered her a solution for that, at least on the extremely occasional basis she called. Truthfully, he hadn't seen her in months and hadn't exactly planned to—but when he answered a call and heard a woman's voice, his heart leaped to the too-fast conclusion that it was Merry. Merry's voice. Merry's face on the other end of the line. Merry, putting that crazy happy zip in his pulse. And when he realized how insanely and inappropriately he was starting to feel for his worrisome neighbor, he immediately told Heather yes.

The way Jack saw it, nothing in his life had been normal since Merry moved in next door. So it was time he got back in the saddle. Literally. And if Heather's acrobat exploits couldn't get his mind off his next-door neighbor, nothing could.

He was still upstairs, freshly showered and shaved, trying to choose a shirt from his closet, when he heard the excited knocking downstairs. Heather was either extra-eager or extra-early. Maybe he wasn't—but with the wild sleet storm building over the last couple hours, he was relieved she was off the icy roads and here safe.

Swiftly he grabbed a chamois shirt and finished buttoning it as he jogged down the stairs. "Coming," he yelled as he heard the exuberant knocking again. He only wished he felt the same exuberance. He was trying. Damn it, she was a nice woman. Fun. She was the rare kind of woman who openly admitted a need for sex, for just plain wanting to scratch an itch sometimes without a pile of complications. Nothing wrong with that. No one was getting hurt. It was honest. Real.

It was just that sometimes he had the oddest feeling that he was lonelier the next morning than if he'd woken up solo.

Still, he forced a welcoming smile on his face as he crossed the kitchen. He'd never been prone to that kind of crappy introspection before. It was one of the aberrations bugging him since his next door neighbor had moved in. He could shake it. It was just going to take some discipline, some self-control. Some mindless sex.

He swiftly opened the back door with a humorous, "Good grief, where's the fire, Heather—?"

Only to abruptly realize there was no Heather. The two characters on his back porch looked like cartoon caricatures. His heart rate recognized Merry in theory—but reality was that this goofy visitor was wearing no coat, just an oversized T-shirt over her clothes and bare feet in flip-flops—even in the driving sleet—but her clothes weren't the shocker. Her eyes, her gorgeous dark eyes, were the only thing normal about her. The rest of her was blotched with something. Paint? Yellow, orange, purple, green, red. In her hair, on her face, her fingers, the shirt.

The fleeting thought blew through his head that this was exactly why he needed sex. With someone. Anyone. Because if his heartbeat could thump like a puppy's tail at the sight of this woman, he needed help. Soon. Fast.

Naturally he tore his eyes off her immediately. Her sidekick had to be Charlene —who he should have easily recognized, considering he'd known her for a solid handful of years. But he hadn't seen her close-up since she'd chopped off and spiked her hair, and she was as drenched in paint as Merry, except that the kid at least had the brains to drape some towels over her shoulders for warmth.

He could barely phrase a sputter, much less a coherent question. "What on earth—?"

"Jack, I hate to bother you, but we're in a terrible mess! I don't know what happened, but the lights went off. And so did everything else. And—"

"We lost *all* power," Charlene clarified.

"Which wouldn't have been so bad except that we were right in the middle of painting. So we couldn't clean up and we couldn't touch anything and everything's still all wet! We were even afraid to put on coats, for fear of ruining our coats and shoes with paint. And I don't have a clue what's wrong. Or what I should do—"

"I told her where the circuit breaker box was," Charlene interrupted. "But she said she barely knew the difference between a fuse box and a boom box."

"We couldn't see to go downstairs anyway. I hate to bother you! But I just don't know what to do. Who to call, or—"

Jack never got it, why females felt they had to talk nonstop when there was a problem. He did the obvious, grabbed both of them and pulled them in out of the cold. "Okay, you two, one at a time—"

"Jack, the kitchen is a terrible mess. And we can't just leave all the wet paint and paint cans open. But—"

"But when all the power went off so fast, it was too dark to see. I know where Dad kept flashlights. But we'd been painting with our feet. Some. It's hard to explain. But we couldn't just walk across the carpets—"

"Skip all the detail, okay? Where's the breaker box?"

"Huh?" Merry said.

So he redirected the question to Charlene. "In the basement, like I told her. Only it was too dark to see down there without a flashlight, and we had the same problem, not wanting to track paint everywhere we walked—"

Both females lifted their paint-splotched feet to illustrate. He didn't need more information. "First off, I'll go over and figure out what happened—"

"I'll come with you," Merry said immediately.

The sick, wayward side of his mind murmured, *I only wish.* How insane was that, to discover sexual potential in the middle of chaos? He told himself to get a grip and keep it. "Neither of you are going anywhere with no coats and no shoes."

"We put on slippers. Or flops. We just didn't want to wreck a real pair of—"

"I get it, I get it." Possibly his crazy neighbor's behavior was infectious, because he found himself making sweeping gestures with his hands, like she did. Anything to communicate above the din. And then he had another thought. "Water-soluble or oil-based?"

"Huh?"

Again, he redirected the question to the brains of the pair. "Charlene, what kind of paint?"

"Water-based."

"Well, there's one relief." Quick as a flash, he grabbed some towels from the laundry room and dropped them on the floor. "I'm guessing this is going to take me a minute. And you two likely won't want to stand here with paint drying all over you. Charlene, you've been in the house before, so you can show Merry where the showers are, up and down. Just use the dirty towels to keep the paint off the floor, all right? And then Charlene, go in the boys' rooms and grab a couple of sweatshirts to put on."

"But—"

He couldn't imagine a single "but" from Merry that he wanted or needed to hear. "Maybe the problem will be as simple as a blown fuse. One way or another, I'll find out. But I'm bound to be a few minutes, no matter what. So it just makes sense for the two of you to get warm and dry."

"But it's not your problem, Jack. I didn't mean to drop it in your lap—"

Yeah, well, she had. And it was the stupidest thing, but before he headed out the back door with a flashlight...well, the darn woman looked so upset and *stressed* standing there with all that crazy paint on her, her heart in those big eyes. He didn't mean to, but somehow his hand reached up. He cupped her face, the side of her head, paint and all. It was just…he couldn't just disappear with her still looking so damned woebegone and upset.

And her eyes tilted immediately up to his when he touched her. "It'll be all right," he said firmly. "I promise. Just chill."

"Okay," she whispered, but her gaze was still glued on his like something else was happening.

When nothing else was happening, for damn sure, and wasn't about to.

He tromped across the yard, thinking that he might as well pave a cement walkway between their back doors if these disasters were going to be a daily occurrence. He realized in a blink that his right palm was damp—because of paint, from touching her. He realized in another blink that he felt a wild surge of longing and wanting from touching a woman with a yellow-and-purple splotchy cheek.

Icy rain slashed his face as he glanced up, suddenly aware of a giant shadow on her roof. Swiftly he jogged past her back door and hustled into her backyard. He saw the problem immediately. A pair of birch trees framed the deck off the back. Typically everybody loved the white bark of the birches, but Jack knew wood, knew the trees tended to be fragile, never lived long, caught every passing tree virus there was. So maybe the one had been weak. Whatever. Sleet had formed around the limbs, snugger than a condom, and at some point the weight of the ice added up and the big limb had just snapped. The branch had crashed onto the main electric line running into the house and fell on the roof.

Of course, being able to diagnose the problem didn't mean it was solved.

The electric company had to be called. And he needed to get in the girls' house, check out the back rooms, see if the branch had caused enough roof damage to cause a leak. It was damned scary to think of either Merry or Charlene anywhere close to that live wire.

He headed for her back door, tripped on the step in the dark and swore—even though he marveled that she'd at least remembered to close the door for once.

He immediately switched on his flashlight. Crisis or no crisis, he slowed down long enough to take one long, meandering, disbelieving look at the disaster in the kitchen.

He suffered the immediate, sure horror that the girls were spending the night at his place. It wouldn't kill them to sleep without electricity. And they were both bright enough to keep reasonably warm in a house that was warmed up to start with. But...he knew.

Anyone capable of making a mess this big, this monumental, this award-winning, just wasn't in the Girl Scout class.

He got the electric company's emergency number from Information and then wanted to be connected as he hiked toward the back rooms.

It was only then, out of the blue, that he suddenly remembered his date with Heather.

CHAPTER SIX

MERRY TURNED OFF THE faucets in Jack's upstairs bathroom shower and grabbed blindly for a towel. Finally, she was warm again. Unfortunately being warm and clean didn't stop her from feeling lower than sludge.

She was used to people thinking she was a ditz. Used to people thinking she was an unpredictable, impulsive, not-always-responsible free spirit even. She knew her faults. But darn it, she never remembered feeling like such a failure before.

She stepped out of the blue-tiled shower, rubbing hard, and with her skin still damp, pulled on the University of Virginia sweatshirt. Jack said it belonged to one of his sons, which told her clearly that his twins mimicked his tall, lean build, because the sweatshirt reached unglamorously to her knees.

There was no way to shape up the rest of her appearance, either. His boys' bathroom medicine chest had tons of stuff—Band-Aids, first aid cream, rolls of gauze, several varieties of toothpaste and deodorant. Deodorant was good. But she had no comb, no underpants, no lipstick. No nothing—except for a heap of paint-stained clothes. Oh, and the guilt sucking at her conscience.

Finally, *finally,* things had been going great with

Charlene—until the power went out. And now she'd embroiled Jack in their problems, as if she were one of those needy, helpless types. Which, come to think of it, she was, at least near anything mechanical or technical. Now she wished she'd argued louder about their not needing to take advantage of his showers and all—but the truth was, she was totally grateful to get the paint off her face and skin and hair. It'd been starting to dry. And itch.

Tufts of steam escaped when she opened the door to the bathroom. She turned toward the stairs, then spun around, realizing immediately that she had to be heading in the wrong direction. For sure, she hadn't passed that black-and-gray bedroom on her way up—she guessed it was Jack's bedroom, because it was huge, the bed big enough for an orgy or two. She almost paused, because darn it, she was mighty curious…but then she remembered the heap of guilt and chased downstairs in search of Charlene.

In the hallway off the kitchen, the girl was just opening the bathroom door, and the view made Merry stop dead. The U of V sweatshirt fit Charlene just as badly as it did her, but that wasn't the point. It was the first time Merry had seen her without the waxed brush cut. Her face, all pinked and fresh-clean, looked so vulnerable and innocent. Her little frame looked so feminine when it wasn't draped in fatigues and adopting a tough posture. And the fluffy, short mop on her head was paler than wheat, fair as silk.

"Aw, honey," Merry murmured. "You're so beautiful."

Wrong thing to say. Merry wanted to kick herself when she saw the squirt immediately stiffen up.

"I don't want to be beautiful."

Okay, maybe they had a ton of immediate serious

things to concentrate on, but Merry was still taken back
by the comment. "Why?"

Charlene produced an even darker scowl. "My mom.
I guess she was beautiful. I mean like, over the top.
People couldn't stop looking at her. That's what Dad
always said."

"And you think that's bad?" Merry knew they were
both standing in Jack's hallway, wearing nothing but
sweatshirts, and they really needed to figure out their
power crisis, but just then, nothing seemed more immediately important than this.

"I don't know if it's bad. I just know...I don't want
to be like my mom. I want to be like my dad. I don't
want to forget my dad for a minute. He was a hero.
Strong. And safe. And he wasn't afraid of anything."

And suddenly so much made sense to Merry. Charlie
wasn't trying to be a *guy.* She was trying to feel safe.
The way she'd felt when her dad was alive.

The kind of safe she hadn't felt since.

"When you feel like it," Merry said gently, "I'd really
like to hear more about your dad."

Charlene might have answered, but they were both
interrupted by the sound of the back door opening, and
a woman's voice yelling out a cheerful, "Jack? It's me!"

Merry only had to turn the corner into Jack's kitchen
to see the intruder—and, of course, to be seen. Her first
thought was a silent uh-oh. And her second was that as
uh-ohs went, this one was on a par with a zit at a wedding.

Merry might be slow at geography, but she grasped
this situation in a millisecond. Jack had a date tonight.
The woman was groomed to the teeth. She was just
wearing slacks and a sweater, but the fit was Saturday-
night, and Merry knew date makeup when she saw it—

from the sex-red lipstick to the careless toss of curls. She'd also have bet the bank the woman had on lace underwear, likely a thong, likely a peekaboo bra with a front catch. The perfume alone would have clogged a man's good sense. Merry should know. She'd worn it for dates herself—at least when she'd been seriously interested in the guy.

"Who on earth are you?" the woman said, her jaw dropping at the sight of Merry's bare legs and wet hair.

Merry said immediately, "Please don't worry, it's not at all what you think—"

"Yeah, right." The woman straightened like a poker, her pretty face turning cool. "I know Jack's adventurous, but I didn't expect anything like this. No offense. But I don't do threesomes."

"Say what?"

And then the woman spotted Charlie, coming up behind her in a matching sweatshirt.

"Whoa," the woman said. "Like, big whoa. Say hi to Jack when you see him. I'm gone."

She obviously intended an immediate exit, but that plan was thwarted when Jack suddenly barreled in the back door. He looked at his date. He looked at Merry and Charlene in their bare feet and damp hair.

He sighed.

A babble of confusion seemed to follow. Jack tried to take the woman aside and explain, but the woman kept saying, "Look, it's obvious you have your hands full here. We'll just make it another time." Which would have been reasonable except that her tone was as frosty as a north wind, so Merry tried to step forward and help.

"Really, we're just neighbors. We had a power outage. It was just all a mess, so Jack let us come in to take a shower, but we're going right home—"

Jack said, "Merry. Would you please not help?"

And the woman said, "I don't know who you are, but no one's talking to you."

And then Jack said, "Hey. There's no reason to be rude. Plans got interrupted. That's all. No one asked for it, but there it is."

"Damn right *there it is*," the woman echoed, and then clipped out the back door with her spine so sharp it could have cut meat.

And then Jack sighed. Again. Merry immediately started up with, "I am *so, so* sorry—"

But he just looked at Charlene, and said, "What'd you think of that mess?"

Charlene had propped herself on the kitchen counter and seemed to enjoy watching the scene unfold. Now she shrugged and said, "Pretty murky. But I think you can do better than her."

Merry blinked, surprised at both Charlene's intuition and opinion, but then she turned back to Jack. Somehow she had to make amends for causing all this mess. "Look, you can go after her. The lady. I mean, you can call her—"

"Is there anything I said to make you think I needed advice about my love life?"

Okay. He was naturally feeling a little testy. She lifted her hands in the universal make-peace gesture, but then immediately realized that the borrowed sweatshirt—even if it was bigger than a boat—still lifted up considerably when she raised her arms.

And his gaze flew down there faster than a politician could lie—which was considerably fast.

Merry fumbled, "Look, we'll just go home—"

"Afraid that's the one thing that's *not* going to happen. One of the big birch trees in the back fell on an electric line and your roof. I reached the electric company. They'll be out tonight, because the wire's live. So it'll be taken care of pretty quickly, but you won't be sleeping there tonight."

Merry refumbled. "Well, okay. I guess I can just go over there and get my purse. We can drive to a motel. This was all we needed, really, a chance to shower, get the paint off us, but we can't just impose on you—"

"A motel is just plain dumb," Jack said flatly. "The boys aren't here. Their rooms are empty, plenty of space. And then when the electric company's done its thing, you're right next door and can head home."

"I'm just so sorry we're being so much trouble." There was just nothing else to say. He didn't seem angry with her exactly. Just cranky. Naturally. She'd screwed up his date, messed his Saturday night up good.

"Yeah, well, I think Charlene had it right. Maybe you guys saved me from a fate worse than death with my date, right, kid?" He hooked an arm around Charlene's neck, and said, "You hungry?"

"Dying of starvation," she affirmed.

"I've probably got stuff in the fridge. Peanut butter if nothing else. Lots of frozen stuff. Or…"

"Or we could order a pizza?" Charlene asked hopefully.

"That's exactly what I was thinking, short stuff."

So they did a pizza, vegged out in the living room where Charlene and Jack turned on a blood-and-guts flick that they were apparently crazy about. Merry watched the two, slowly feeling herself calm down. The two of them got on like a house afire, maybe because Jack was a similar age to Charlene's dad. He was so good with her.

Because the violence bored her senseless, she had ample time to study his living room. Two couches were the prime pieces of furniture, located to watch a theater-size TV screen. A fireplace jutted in the middle of the room, with a wraparound sit-down hearth, all in a dark brick. One giant easy chair snugged up to a window. The room was spacious and comfortable, but very "guy," no *tchotchkes* that needed dusting, for darn sure.

The first day she met him, he'd been carrying in boards from his truck, and now she discovered what they were for. Past the living room was another room, one step down, where he was building a library of shelves. French doors closed off the construction site, but she could see the sawdust, the power tools, the saw-horses and boards and all.

She wanted to explore more of the house, but at some point she must have fallen dead asleep during the movie, because she woke up to feel Charlene's hand on one shoulder and Jack's hand on the other. It was past midnight. Everyone was voting to cave.

Upstairs, Jack's sons had rooms on the same side of the hall, with a bathroom in between. Charlie took the blue one, and Merry crashed in the gray and white one closest to the stairs. She didn't remember falling asleep, didn't remember another thing until she suddenly woke up, startled to see lights flashing in the window.

The electric company had shown up. Jack appeared at the stair top at the same time she did.

"Not your problem," she said sleepily. "I don't want to cause you any more trouble, Jack—"

But he motioned to her outfit. His look seemed to imply that the sweatshirt wasn't exactly appropriate attire for receiving guests or dealing with repairmen. She couldn't argue with that. She didn't have a clue what to say to the electric company guys anyway.

So he went out alone, and she stumbled back into his son's bed, but she was wide awake now, and getting more wide awake by the minute. Jack had been treating her like an affectionate but annoying little sister. She couldn't fault him, especially after she'd caused him no end of trouble since she got here. If she felt fierce twinges of longing and connection every time they were together, that didn't matter. She didn't expect him to reciprocate. She just wanted to *do* something to establish a more comfortable ground between them.

Minutes crawled by. Finally, the flashing lights of the emergency truck disappeared. She heard the back door open. She waited, thinking that Jack had to be exhausted and would be headed upstairs to bed any second now. But more minutes passed and she still didn't hear his footstep on the stairs.

Don't get up, she told herself...even as she was peeling back the covers and climbing out of bed. At the top of the stairs, she hesitated. She heard no sound below, but could see lights spilling in the hallway.

Don't go down, she told herself. Hadn't she intruded on the guy enough for one day? He likely wanted another encounter with her today like he wanted a hole in the head. But she tiptoed down, arms wrapped tight around her chest, feeling to blame for his not sleeping, wanting to fix it somehow.

The lamplight glowing in the living room revealed no one there.

She found him in the kitchen. A stainless-steel light fixture over the eating counter gave his profile a long shadow. He was splashing scotch in a glass, his dark hair rumpled. Her pulse kicked up an instinct of danger. Pretty silly, when she wasn't remotely physically afraid of Jack, but there was just something about those big, broad shoulders, the intimacy of just the two of them downstairs in the lonely hours of the night, that totally male shadow of his. Her pulse kicked up like her internal music had just switched on.

He dropped a few ice cubes into his drink and suddenly turned, spotting her. That sense of danger multiplied times a dozen. Maybe more. He just looked at her with a flash of something electric and alive in his eyes…yet just that quickly, he ducked his head and took a sip.

"Hell, I'd hoped you were able to sleep, Merry. Want a drink?"

"No, thanks."

Before she could say anything else, he leaned back against the counter and filled her in on the power problem, his flannel voice rough-soft, as natural as always. She'd imagined the danger thing, she thought, must have daydreamed the flash of desire in his eyes.

"Afraid you have a real mess in your backyard. But the electric company moved the branch, fixed the live wire. You've got power again. You'll need to call the insurance company tomorrow, see what Charlie's policy covers, but I'm guessing you've got no sweat. It's just a matter of bringing in a roofer to check for damage, and hiring some tree clean-up people."

"Thanks so much." She hesitated. "I should probably go over there. If the power's on, I should start cleaning up all that paint—"

"At two in the morning? It may be a mess, but it's bound to be easier to take on in the daylight, and after you've had some rest."

That was true. But it didn't seem to dent her guilt feeling. "Look, Jack. I just don't know how to thank you. You've been more than a brick."

"It's nothing, Merry. We're neighbors. No big deal."

Maybe it wasn't, but that odd edgy, itchy tone of his was back. She hated being such a pain in the butt. She edged closer another step, until her shadow joined his on the far kitchen wall. "I just can't tell you how sorry I am to be such a bother. I promise not to make a habit of this. I feel really badly about messing up your Saturday night—"

"It's nothing, Merry. Forget it." He slugged down a good gulp of scotch.

"It's not nothing." Again she took a step forward and a big breath at the same time. "Jack, I can see you're irritated with me. It's in your voice. And I totally don't blame you. I realize I've been a complete imposition. But—"

"It's not about that."

She stopped. He'd the same as admitted he was irritated. "It's about what then?"

He plunked the glass down on the counter. "Nothing."

She cocked her head, confused. "I realize you've kind of been looking after me. I never meant to put you in that position. And I'd like to be a better neighbor, a decent friend—"

That last word alone seemed to set off another scowl.

"Merry, this is just going to work way, way better if I stay irritated with you. Get it?"

"Um…no."

He rolled his eyes. "Maybe you think of *me* as a friend. As a neighbor. As a guy too old to have a hot date on a Saturday night."

She moved from confused to downright flabbergasted. She tried to think of anything she'd said that could have been construed as an insult, because that was how he sounded. Insulted. "I never thought any such thing," she started to say.

"So it'd just be better if I stayed on the miffed side."

And they said women were unfathomable. She peered into his eyes, trying to somehow translate this testosterone-speak. "I don't want you miffed at me," she assured him.

"Yeah, you do."

"No, I really, really don't."

"Damn it, Merry." He reached out and roped her close faster than a cowboy with a lasso.

She saw him lift his arms. Saw his scowl. Felt a wild whoosh of shock when he folded her into him, when his soft, whiskey-sharp mouth took hold of hers.

How could she possibly have guessed this was coming? Yeah, of course she'd kissed him before, but those had been thank-you kisses. Maybe she'd felt more. Maybe she'd felt so thoroughly swept under that her entire body had suffered a *pizzazz* alert. But even if he was a good-looking guy with an unprecedented high-tingle factor, she'd never communicated a come-on. She knew she hadn't. For one thing, she had no business adding a complication to her life right now. And for another, darn it, she needed him to be what he was, a good neighbor next door, and she couldn't afford to mess with that.

Besides which, it hadn't crossed her mind that he felt That Way toward her.

Until now. Now changed things, but this was sure as Sam-Hill a come-on.

And a darn good one.

Slowly she slid her arms around his neck and hung on. She'd been kissing men who were way too young, she realized abruptly. Because there was a world of difference between a man of experience and a guy in his twenties who was just hot to get his rocks off. Not that there was anything wrong with the rocks thing. But she'd never felt remotely in danger with a man before.

She sure did now.

It was the difference between taking a commercial flight and skydiving.

Jack was the skydive. Heaven knew what primed his trigger, but she felt swooshed into his field of gravity at a mighty fast velocity. The scotch on his breath added just enough heat to make his kisses sting. His hands slid down her spine, down to the swell of her bottom, tugged her into him.

Danger whispered through her pulse like a promise. Not "fear" kind of danger, but the other kind. The delicious kind. The kind where a woman felt sucked under by someone stronger than she was, someone who made her feel vulnerable...and vulnerably desired.

He groaned against her lips, a sound that sounded frustrated and hungry both. He went back for another kiss, this one involving tongue and teeth, this one that rocked him back against the counter and laid her against his splayed thighs. Faster than lightning, she felt his rough palms on the backs of her bare thighs, as if his hands had suddenly remembered she was only wearing the giant sized sweatshirt—although that wasn't true.

She'd put on her underpants after the shower. Which he abruptly discovered, because his palms cupped her bare cheeks, his thumb discovering the teensy strip of her thong. Another sound erupted from the way-back of his throat. This one was a sound of suffering. The sound of deep pain from a lost soul. Or a soul that was claiming to be lost.

She almost laughed, and instead just shivered down into the next chain of kisses. There were lots of places she could entice, invite, or just take a bit of initiative herself. Teeth, tongue, throat, ear nips. Then back to the throat. She lifted her hands, slivering her fingers through his thick dark hair, luxuriating in the feel of him, the textures, the sounds, the tastes. She snugged her pelvis in tight, delighted at the hardness she provoked, savoring the feeling of girl power. This was a luge of it. A slick, rich, fast slide into sensation.

He pushed up the sweatshirt, just a little, carving the shape of her hips, the nip of her waist. She didn't fight him.

"You're not," he murmured painfully, "a good girl."

"God, I hope not."

She'd never been shy. But this was different. It was a yearning so fierce it took her breath, a feeling of fragility in a way she'd never felt fragile. Something about Jack's touch, his kisses, made her feel peeled like a grape. It was as if he'd skimmed the skin off her defenses and got straight down to the juice.

Lonely. Who'd guess he was so lonely? He seemed so into his life, so contained, so settled. Yet he seemed to need the nurturing of her kisses, her touch. He seemed to need…connection. She told herself to be careful, that this was crazy and unexpected…but those were just token instincts raising a few feeble objections.

She'd never been one to listen to caution. When something felt right, it usually was. And the rare times she felt drawn—deep-down *really* drawn—to another human being, she couldn't imagine regretting giving in to it.

"Hey," he murmured suddenly. She wasn't sure where the caution in his voice came from. Until that instant, his hand had been sliding up, one rib at a time, aiming to circle and cup her bare breast. Her breast had already tightened in anticipation. Tightened and ached with waiting, wanting.

Her eyes felt narrowed to slits, her body engulfed in the unexpected, intense wave of surrender. The wanting, the needing, to surrender. She'd never experienced an aching this fierce, compelling. It wasn't an easy sensation. She not only felt vulnerable, but too vulnerable, too laid bare.

"Merry," he murmured again, in the same forced-caution tone he'd used before. "I don't know what's going on here—"

"I sure do."

He smiled, but it was a raw smile. Unwilling. A clear struggle for control.

The kitchen came into focus again, the intimacy of their joined shadows against the far wall, the thrum of the refrigerator, the lone sink light. The oven clock claimed the time was nearly three in the morning. As far as she could tell, the two of them were the only ones awake in the universe.

At least in her immediate universe. And Jack looked

so worried, so…guilty. She touched his cheek, easing back. "So…we're calling this off, are we?"

"I'm not sure how things went so far, so fast."

"I'm pretty sure you kissed me. Then A followed B. Although I'm not sure why you started this to begin with. If I remember right, you said something about wanting to stay annoyed with me."

"Because of this. I meant…if we're annoyed with each other, we wouldn't be inclined to—"

"Snuggle up? But I'm not annoyed with you. I've just felt badly to be so much trouble, Jack. You may not believe it, but I've been a good friend to other people."

"Of course I believe it."

"I'm just having a harder time being independent, strong right now. Everything is just so different. Charlie. Trying to climb into her life. Trying to uproot and reinvent mine. I'd be the first to admit I'm over my head right now, but I swear I'm not normally a dependent type. Or one to lean. You've just been…great."

"Merry?"

"What?"

"I'm not great. I'm not even a good guy. It'd be a really good idea if you quit thinking that."

He was so damned adorable that she forgave herself for starting to fall in love with him. "Jack?"

"What?"

"I don't see what's wrong about two people clicking together. Honestly, I'm not looking for trouble—and I'm not looking to cause you any, either. But I liked those kisses of yours. I liked the chemistry. And I just don't see a problem here."

And so she wouldn't stress him out any more, she clipped out of the room and climbed upstairs to bed.

SHE KEPT THINKING ABOUT Jack's words, even midafternoon the next day, as she tackled the horrendous painting mess back at home. Charlene had worked beside her nonstop, but somehow even that didn't clear Jack from her mind—or heart. It seemed so odd, how and why he'd insisted that he wasn't a good guy. How he'd seemed to be warning her away from something. Him? But why?

"I don't think this paint is ever coming out," Charlene announced.

Merry knee-walked over to the spot in question, where an unbelievable blend of colors now stained the grout Charlie was scrubbing. The wax was back in the hair. The ironed fatigues were back on. "Charlie, you've been cleaning with me for two hours."

"Yeah, so?"

"It isn't normal. You should be complaining. You should be calling me names. You shouldn't be volunteering. You should be stomping around, screaming that I'm a creep to make you help." Merry shouldn't have to explain to an eleven-year-old how an eleven-year-old was supposed to behave. Five-year-olds worked at being good. Middle-schoolers practiced the art of back talk and rebellion and incessant complaining. Everyone knew that. "We're both beat, had a short night's sleep. You should be whining big-time."

Charlie had to hear her, but just circled back to the original problem. "What if the paint doesn't come out?"

"Well then, several things could happen. One is that we could have red-and-purple grout in this spot until kingdom come. Another is that somebody at Lowe's or Home Depot will know what product to use to make it come out. Another is that we panic and take out the whole floor and put in a whole new one. Maybe one without grout. Whether we choose A, B, or C, I suspect life'll go on okay."

The kid smiled. "Yeah, I know."

Merry only wished the smile were a real one, but it seemed today they were back to the status quo. Charlie didn't fight her about anything. She was trying hard to be as good as a saint, unless some emotional buttons were unexpectedly pushed—like accidentally bringing up the Dougall boy and the fight in school.

But her niceness was starting to scare Merry. Cripes, with Jack, Charlie'd been natural, babbling on through the blood-and-guts movie, gulping down that pizza, sprawled all over the floor. With her, Charlie acted polite as a duchess. Maybe not that bad. But close.

She couldn't keep it up, Merry thought. You could keep a face on with strangers, or with people you worked with indefinitely. But where you lived, you had to know you could let down your hair. You had to have a place where you felt safe.

Merry understood the problem. She just didn't know how to inspire trust in Charlie, and the worry preyed on her mind the whole next day, as she waited for the arrival of June Innes. While Charlie was in school, she prepped for the meeting as zealously as for a job interview. Vacuumed. Hid their cheerful new paintings in a closet, made socks and smelly shoes disappear from sight, hid the cookies in a tall cupboard and put fresh fruit in sight. Then redid herself, starting with tweezing her eyebrows and shaving her legs, and then getting serious. Using all her makeup pots, she went for the matronly look, no eyes, no shiny lip gloss. She swooshed up her hair and tidied it into a clip, chose a jeans skirt, clunky shoes, a clunky watch.

She was pacing the living room windows by three, waiting for June Innes's car to pull up, fretting her stomach into knots. Four weeks ago, she'd been the Pollyanna of Minnesota, always singing the live-for-today mantra, always ready to take off at a moment's notice for the next interesting adventure. The bank knew she'd occasionally overdraw. The clerks at BCBG knew her by name. She'd never had a job where absenteeism didn't rear its annoying little head. She couldn't remember a Saturday night that didn't include music and going out and a guy.

She'd been happy.

Nonstop happy.

Thoughtlessly, mindlessly, happy. A bopper. Delighted to just bop through every day, wringing every ounce of sunshine, every chuckle, every hug she could.

Now...now Merry caught her pale reflection in the living room window and didn't recognize herself. It was June Cleaver's granddaughter in the window. All the color wiped out of her. Hand-wringing whether the house was clean enough—in a house that felt like an alien cage, besides.

It was tough enough to be living in a stranger's life, but to be flunking the job of guardian was the real killer. A dark blue sedan pulled in the drive behind her Mini, and Merry hurried toward the door with her company smile on. So it was fake, so? What was wrong with being June Cleaver's granddaughter for a few minutes, anyway? Darn it, she needed Mrs. Innes to be a true ally for Charlene, and hopefully a good source of advice for her.

So she answered the door and started bubbling before she'd even had a chance to take a good look. "Mrs. Innes, I'm so glad to meet you! Charlene's due home from school in the next few minutes, but I've got a fresh pot of coffee on. Come on in!"

"I don't do coffee, but thanks. You've got quite a mess outside."

"Yes, we had a tree come down in the storm on Saturday night. Thankfully, the insurance guy was wonderful. A roofer's already been here, and the tree guys came this afternoon with chain saws, but unfortunately, there's no way we could get it all cleaned up quite this fast—"

The woman seemed to pick up that she was capable of babbling on indefinitely. "So you're Merry," she said, and gave her an up-and-down as if examining a bolt of fabric.

Merry gulped. Oh God, oh God. It was a good thing she'd done the JC thing, because June Innes looked like a vintage version of June Cleaver herself. Shoes with a little heel. Hair that didn't move. A knee-covering skirt, with a navy pea coat and navy gloves. A tired smile. One of those you'll-never-know-how-much-I-do martyr smiles—but that was all right with Merry. She knew plenty of martyr types—who didn't? She could get along with a martyr. Cripes, she wanted this meeting to go so well that she'd have tried to get along with Attila the Hun.

She trailed June into the kitchen, since June seemed to naturally lead.

"I met with Charlene after her father died, of course. I'm sure Mr. Oxford explained my role. The court appointed me as Charlene's guardian *ad litem.* I'm an active member of the Virginia State Bar, as well as having met all the other state requirements."

"I never doubted that for a second," Merry said warmly, but apparently her opinion wasn't really required.

"My responsibility is to be the child's advocate. That means I'll regularly be talking to Charlene, and to yourself, and to others in her life, such as teachers and neighbors. I'll also be making some impromptu visits to the home. But this time I wanted to tell you about in advance, because I wanted to see both you and Charlene in her home environment. How are the two of you getting along?"

"Just fine. May I take your coat?"

"You're younger than I expected. Or you look younger."

June pronounced every word crisply, as if she'd studied diction, or as if she'd gotten a degree in spike-up-the-behind stiltedness. By the time Merry had her settled at the kitchen table—which seemed wiser than letting her sit in the living room with the dog-bone-shaped-couch and Red Dominance picture, Merry was trying to keep up a perky conversation about homework and preteen stories and healthy nutrition.

When the back door slammed open, though, she jumped.

Charlie clipped in, plopped her school bag on the counter and then suddenly turned carefully, dead quiet, shooting Merry a stricken look. "Hello, Mrs. Innes," she said.

For several seconds, June seemed to have lost her voice. Apparently she hadn't seen Charlie before in the army fatigues and brush cut. She shot a disapproving look at Merry.

"How's it going?" Charlie said, opening the cupboard—the one that was supposed to have the cookies—and finding nothing. She reached for an apple on the table instead.

"Just fine. How was school today?"

"Frantic," Charlie said, making June Innes blink again. "For a while I wasn't sure if I was going to like the eighth grade math class. I mean, everybody's two grades ahead of me. But it's working out. Of course, I have to put up with Dougall. But the computer work and stuff is effing zingy. Hey. Do I have to sit here with you two, or can I go get my homework done?"

"I need to talk to you for a few minutes alone, Charlene." The older woman promptly stood up. The two went off to Charlie's bedroom. Charlie gave Merry a look, as if to say: how could you make me do this alone?

So Merry went back to pacing by the living room windows, stressed she couldn't save Charlie from the private interview she obviously didn't want, and even more stressed that the woman appointed by the court to be on Charlie's side seemed such a rigid, old-school type.

When June emerged from Charlene's bedroom, she pointedly closed the door. Without a word, she implied that what she wanted to discuss was not meant to be overheard by the child. Merry felt the lead-clunk in her pulse as she led her back into the kitchen. It was impossible not to notice that the older woman's lips looked as if they'd been Miracle-Glued into a thin line.

"You allowed the child to go to school in attire like that?" Disapproval dripped from her voice. "Is that how you see your guardianship? You didn't feel exerting some influence over the child's clothes and behavior and language was part of the job?"

Merry felt the back of her neck prickle. She might

have gone into this meeting petrified, but she'd hoped so much that June Innes would be an ally.

"I admit, I was startled when I first saw her choice in clothes. But I believe she's wearing some of her dad's things to try and feel still close to him. And she is only eleven—"

"Her age is precisely the reason why you should have exerted control."

Merry took a careful breath. "Maybe we just see this differently. I don't see her clothes as an issue about my power or control. I see it as about Charlie's need to feel some power and control."

"When you call the child 'Charlie,' you're encouraging this gender confusion problem. The child's name is Charlene."

Merry never got mad. She was too dad-blamed happy all the time to get mad. But darn it, the woman was starting to push her. "I don't believe she has a gender confusion problem. I believe she has a grief problem. And I understand you might think I'm all wet, but I'm still asking you to leave Charlie completely alone about her clothes and her hair."

"You think you know so much about children, do you?"

"No, I don't. I definitely don't. But I think Charlie's trying to cope her own way with something so overwhelming she's having a hard time."

"And you don't think she'd fit in better at school, wearing normal clothes, behaving normally—"

"I don't know what 'normal' is, when you've had a loss this huge. And I don't see how anyone could get over it quickly. It's going to take her time."

"Of course. But your position should be to make

that go more smoothly, by being a constructive image in the child's life. Letting her dress like that and adopt a boy's version of her name is hardly taking your authoritative role—"

"Mrs. Innes. You want to beat me up, go for it. But leave Charlie alone about her clothes." Neither had sat down at the table. Merry felt as if they were circling the table like jousters. Originally she'd hoped to spill out so much, about how Charlie didn't feel safe, about Charlie's fight with the boy in the eighth grade...but now that all seemed impossible. This woman just wasn't turning out to be anyone she could trust with a vulnerability of Charlie's.

Possibly this morning—possibly even this afternoon—Merry had been increasingly bummed about her failure at this guardian job. Possibly she'd even been considering backing out. But that was before she knew June was a turkey.

Charlie only had two other people in her corner. The lawyer who was a vulture and the court-appointed advocate who was a turkey. So how the Sam Hill could she abandon her?

She couldn't.

"Miss Olson," June said, "I looked into your background. That kind of prying is part of my job. And I have to say, I was singularly unimpressed with your history, as far as giving you any qualifications to parent a youngster. On paper you come across as a quitter."

"A quitter! You don't even know me—"

"I know you've held a half-dozen jobs since leaving school. For that matter, you started college and quit that as well—"

"I tried different things along the way. I hardly think that makes me a quitter—"

"You finished three years of college, but even though your grades were passable, you dropped out, never stayed to complete a degree. You started a cooking course, dropped that. You had jobs as a waitress. An insurance adjuster. A management trainee. Nothing seemed to hold your interest for long. You have no history of knuckling down and sticking to anything. I'd be lying if I didn't say this history looks worrisome to me. You may have been drawn to taking on this guardianship because of the financial circumstances—"

"That's totally untrue. I didn't even know there was any money in her dad's estate when I came here. I haven't even been back to the lawyer to ask for anything—even for money to pay the electric and phone bills yet. The only reason I came here was for Charlie—"

"That sounds very nice. Very idealistic. But talk is cheap. So far I don't see any sign of a background or character. Something that would lead me to believe you can be an appropriate guardian for a young girl."

Just to insure she was hopelessly rattled, the telephone chose that minute to ring. The first interruption was the school, asking Merry to be a chaperone for the sixth-grade Valentine's dance. Almost before she'd had a chance to say yes, the phone rang a second time. Her dad. "How's your day, sweetheart?"

"Just fine, I'll call you back, all right?"

Mrs. Innes hadn't budged from her position in the doorway, just picked up the fight again. "I believe the child needs grief counseling. And possibly a physical is in order as well. I'll be checking with the school on her situation there. And my next visit—" She plucked a leather appointment book from her suitcase-sized purse. "Normally, I'd say a visit every couple weeks was adequate in the beginning. But I believe I'll schedule a visit every Monday afternoon for the immediate future. And then we'll see."

We'll see *what?* Merry thought, as she watched the sedan sedately back out the driveway. If she'd run ten miles in the last hour, she couldn't feel more wiped. And then she turned around, to see Charlie peeking her head around the corner from the far doorway.

"You heard most of that?" Merry asked her.

"No."

"Sure you did. You were eavesdropping. You don't have to deny it. I'd have been eavesdropping in your shoes, too."

"Maybe I listened some," Charlie admitted, and then scratched the bottom of her foot, as if the itch suddenly demanded her whole attention. Until she glanced up again. "You're not going to stay."

"What?"

"I heard what Mrs. Innes said. You're not going to stay with me."

"Charlie, that's so not—" But protesting was a waste of breath, because Charlie had zoomed down the hall to her room and snapped the door closed.

Merry stood there, wondering if Lee could possibly have felt this defeated in 1864.

She was alone in suburbia, in a part of the country where she had no friends, no family. Her charge—Charlie—was fabulous at tearing out *her* heart, but Merry couldn't seem to get through to hers no matter what she tried. The lawyers with all the control in the situation had leaped to negative conclusions about her from the get-go.

And if that wasn't enough, she seemed to be falling,

hard and hopelessly, for the wrong man at the wrong time in the wrong place.

Life had to get better after this, right? It couldn't get any lower?

CHAPTER SEVEN

WHEN JACK HEARD THE knock on the back door, he assumed he'd imagined it. The popcorn in the microwave was making a lot of racket, and he didn't dare leave his position right by the stop button. The last time he'd tried walking away to do something else, the microwave caught on fire. Cooking was tricky. Even for basic food groups. Still, with the boys here—and a B-ball game on the tube—obviously popcorn was mandatory. Kettle corn, tonight, since U Conn was playing.

He rarely had the boys during the week because school was such a long commute, but Dianne was out of town on business. The one and only thing he and his ex-wife always agreed on was that it was never, never smart to leave teenagers alone without an adult. Besides which, he loved having the kids.

Again he heard a rap on the back door, and this time spun toward it. At first glance, he saw no one there, but then he glanced down to the bottom of the door pane and recognized the bitsy body. Quickly he opened the door.

"Hey, honey—"

"Oh, Mr. Mackinnon, can I come in? I really, really, *really* need your help!"

"Of course—come on in."

Charlene shot him a grateful look, then quickly peeled off her jacket and heeled off her shoes. "I'm supposed to be asking you if you have a C battery. But just say no. It'll be okay. I know where the batteries are in the house. But that gave me a minute to come over, you know, and… Oh. You've got the U Conn game on in there?"

She went to the doorway. His boys caught sight of her, said an immediate, "Hey, short stuff," and "Hey, Charl."

"Hey, Kicker and Coop. Who's winning?" she demanded.

"Who do you think? Take a seat."

"Aw man, I wish I could watch," Charlene said, but with a sigh bigger than she was, turned back to Jack. "Could we just sit at the table for a short two secs?"

"Sure." Since she motioned to the kitchen table, Jack assumed the child wanted to ask him something away from the boys—but he was completely mystified as to what. Charlene had been in his house a zillion times, had always been her dad's sidekick. His boys had always been good to her, adopted her like a mascot or an honorary little sister…but she was on the quiet side. Certainly she'd never specifically sought him out about anything.

"Mr. Mackinnon, I'm hoping you can help me understand women," she said miserably.

"Oh. Um…" Hell. He couldn't smile. He didn't dare. But he did have a sudden impulse to take off for Tahiti before this conversation had a chance to go any farther.

"This is about Merry."

"Yeah, somehow I guessed that." And he fully understood the kid's confusion, since he'd been struggling to figure out Merry ever since that fateful near-seduction.

The one he'd started. The one where his brain turned into fuzz.

The one he mulled over and over and over, as if the images were Scotch-taped in his mind, and no matter how zealously he'd avoided her in the last few days, refused to go away.

"Everybody likes her," Charlene said wearily. "She made cookies for three teachers. She's been volunteering for everything at school. She's been to the music store, buying all these CDs of groups that kids are supposed to like. Then she's all about shopping for clothes she thinks girls my age will be into. And then you know what she did Tuesday night?"

"No." And actually, Jack was almost dead positive he didn't want to.

"She put mayonnaise in our hair. And that wasn't all. After that, she used the blender to make this cruddy mix of oatmeal and sour cream and orange juice and put it on our faces. Said it was a mask for our skin. Then she put Crisco all over our hands. And we had to wear gloves for a half hour."

"Um…"

"The thing is, she was trying to do this stuff for *fun*, Mr. Mackinnon. She was going on and on about being able to do all kinds of girl stuff without needing to spend a ton of money, just using things that were already in the kitchen." Charlene dropped her head in her hands. "I can't take much more of this. But the worst, the absolute worst—"

"What?" If the kid was just old enough, he'd have poured her a drink. As it was, the only commiseration he could offer was a bowl of fresh popcorn and popping the lid on a soda for her.

"The worst is that there's this Valentine's dance a week from Friday. It's the first sixth-grade dance. And I don't want to go."

"So…don't go," he suggested carefully.

"Yeah, that's what I said. Only the school called and got Merry to agree to be a chaperone. So now I have to go. Even if I wanted to go—and I'd rather drink vinegar than getting anywhere near that thing—I still wouldn't go if she was the chaperone. I mean, come on. This is beyond horrible."

"Couldn't you just tell her how you feel about this, Charl?"

Charlene dug straight into the kettle corn. Which the boys evidently smelled, because they suddenly loped into the kitchen like ungainly giraffes and took up seats near the bowl— after turning on the game on the kitchen TV.

"You don't get it," Charlene said desperately. "I can't tell her. She's trying to do all this stuff for *me*. Any time I try to tell her I don't like something, she looks like I kicked her. And ever since Mrs. Innes came over—the lady from the court?—it's like Merry's pulling out all the stops. She has girl ideas every second we're awake. Can't you help me?"

Jack looked at his boys. "Honey…I'd be happy to. But what do you want me to do?"

"I don't know. But there has to be some way out of this dance thing. And I was thinking that, you know, you'd know about women and all. So maybe you'd have some ideas for me. I can't go on like this much longer. I wake up every morning and don't know what she's gonna put me through next."

Kicker clapped her on the back in a big-brother move,

which was apparently his way of offering support. Cooper, though—the son he never quite understood, the son who always seemed to do things that threw him for six—said, "You got it rough, shrimp. But I've got an idea."

"What? Anything!"

"Make Dad go with her."

"What?" Jack said.

"What?" Charlene said.

"You know. Go with her. Be a chaperone with her at that dance. That way, he could keep her busy, and you wouldn't feel spied on and watched all the time."

"That's a sick idea," Jack told his son sternly.

Cooper shrugged. "I didn't say it was a *good* idea. But nobody else is coming up with *any* ideas."

"Well, it's lousy," Jack informed him.

Charlene, though, seemed to have perked up some. "It's lousy," she agreed, "but it'd be sure better than her going alone, with nothing to do at the stupid dance but hover over me the whole time."

Kicker munched down another handful of corn, and said, "You could pretend to be sick the day of the dance."

Again Charlene brightened, but Jack said quellingly, "You can dock that idea, Kicker. That'd make Merry worry. And if she even started worrying, she'd probably drag Charlene to a doctor. And the school would lose out on a chaperone they counted on. Lying like that always gets complicated. It never pays."

"Sometimes it does," Kicker said.

Cooper lifted his hands, as if communicating he wasn't going near that argument with a ten-foot pole, and then ambled back to the big screen in the living room. Jack stared after his son with narrowed eyes. Cause all that trouble and then get to walk away? That boy was smarter than the rest of them combined.

"I don't know. I kind of like the lying idea. I'm pretty good at lying," Charlene volunteered. "But if you don't like it, Mr. Mackinnon, what about what Cooper said? Like chaperoning with her, to keep her out of my hair?"

"Wait a minute," Jack said, feeling desperation reduce his vocal cords to a coarse whisper.

"It's too much to ask, isn't it?" Charlene said. "It's okay. I understand. I could just die. But it's not like it's your problem."

When Jack heard another knock on the back door, he thought, *No, no, God wouldn't give me any more trouble to handle tonight.*

That fast, Trouble poked her head in. "Jack? Charlie?"

She spotted him, about the same instant he spotted her.

He'd avoided her so well the last few days that he thought the sting would have worn off, the way eventually, given enough time, a bee sting stopped driving you crazy. And he vaguely remembered feeling a bucket load of guilt for coming on to her...she'd had a terrible night in that storm, and it had clawed at his craw that she'd made that crack about his being a good friend/good dad. De-sexed him, so to speak. As if he couldn't ring her chimes, was past his prime, past the juicy stage of life.

But mostly he'd forgotten that guilt.

Mostly all he remembered was being sucked in by her. By that velvet skin. That soft, small, liquid mouth. That lustrous hair, spilling through his fingers. That surrender in the taste of her, the I'm-yours sway of her body into his, fitting his, igniting his.

Hell. Maybe *he'd* thought he was past his prime—but she'd sure cooked that goose. He'd been hotter, harder, faster than he'd been at fifteen—and God knows at fifteen he could turn on from the mere look of a girl.

There was just something about her. Beyond the trouble. Beyond the pain in the neck stuff. She'd sunk into those kisses as if there was nothing else in the universe right then but enjoying them, enjoying him, sipping in the textures and tastes and moment and to hell with whatever else was happening in life. That kind of sensuality, honest, open, vulnerable…it wasn't real life. It was crazy to be that open in real life.

She'd wanted him. He knew it. Knew he could have taken it the rest of the way. Wanted to.

He looked in her eyes right now and thought she'd known it, too. That they could have finished on a mattress. Her gaze claimed she wouldn't have regretted it. That she'd been asking as much as he'd been offering. That she'd been a little confused at his shutdown.

But for God's sake. One of them had to have some common sense. Didn't they?

"Um, earth to Dad."

He vaguely heard a distant voice, but nothing seemed to break the connection between them until Cooper actually stepped in front of him. His son lifted a hand to Merry.

"I'm Cooper. And I know you're Dad's new neighbor. Miss Olson, right?"

"Merry," she corrected him with a warm smile.

And then Kevin pushed his way toward her too. Nothing wrong with his sons' eyesight. They might be young, but they still recognized a damned pretty woman. "I'm Kevin. Although everybody calls me Kicker."

"Kicker…as in soccer?"

"Actually as in football."

"I knew it was one of those ball sports."

Jack winced, but thankfully his boys didn't. They were clearly in love at first sight. Jack figured it was lucky they weren't drooling. And Merry might not know sports, but she seemed to have the sense not to say "you boys sure look alike" or any of the other adult comments that immediately seemed to distance teenagers.

"We really like your car," Kicker said.

"Yeah," Cooper affirmed. "Ever since we got here, we keep looking in the driveway, checking it out. It's ultra cool."

Jack had a second to catch his breath, which irritated the hell out of him, since he hadn't realized he'd been short of breath. There was something about that woman. Something damned dangerous. Above and beyond her being on the ditzy side.

Charlene popped into sight between the boys, like they were all old friends, chatting about the Mini Cooper as if they were long-term car cronies.

Charlie told the guys, "She's got rear disc brakes. Four wheel abs."

"Five speed?" Kicker asked.

"Yeah. And she's been getting 28 mpg even in the city."

"Performance stats?"

Charlie started pelting out numbers and stats that obviously Merry had never heard of, because she shot the kids a confused look. Eventually, though, she gamely tried to rejoin the conversation. "To tell you the truth, I picked out the car because it was blue and had heated seats."

Charlene shot another look at Jack, as if to say, *See? See what I've been talking about?*

But his boys didn't seem to mind. They commented on the "frantic" blue color and styling, making her feel part of the group. In fact, Cooper seemed to especially hang close, doing the same unconscious big-brother thing he did with Charlene.

Once the group had finished their car rant, Merry glanced up at Jack again—this time with more composure, and thank God, he'd found some of his by that time, too. "I swear, I didn't mean to take up all this time. I just asked Charlie to come over to see if you might have a C battery, but I started to worry when she was gone so long."

Cooper—his shy kid, the one who never volunteered conversation, and certainly not with unfamiliar adults—said immediately, "Charl was going home. But we got to talking about that Valentine dance thing at her school."

Merry immediately brightened up. "Yeah, her school has so many side activities for the kids to be involved in. It's really great—"

Before Charlene could react to that comment with abject horror, Cooper said with more of this newfound smoothness, "So we all got talking about how you and Dad might be able to do it together. The chaperoning thing."

Merry cocked her head. "Your dad? But I can't imagine why he'd want to go."

Yeah, exactly, Jack wanted to say. How could she possibly think he'd want to co-chaperone a middle-school dance? How could anyone?

But Cooper was shrugging in that shy, boyish way of his. "We just all thought...it's got to be weird, coming into a new town. Trying to participate in a new school, where you don't know the parents and all. But Kicker and I both went to that school, so Dad knows all the teachers and people and all. And if he went with you, you wouldn't have to be standing by yourself."

Charlene now looked at Cooper as if he were a divine god.

Jack looked at his son with major parental worry. Possibly Cooper had lost his mind? Kicker was his offspring with the high bullshit meter, not Coop. Coop had never invented fairy tales before. Much less ridiculously unrealistic fairy tales that put his father in an impossibly awkward position.

Merry, thank God, was on his side. "That's really kind thinking of you, Cooper. But I can't imagine your dad wanting to be dragged into something like this. And I can handle it, being alone. Charlie and I'll be fine."

Charlene looked mutely at Jack. Then his sons looked mutely at Jack.

Merry looked at Jack, too, and silently mouthed the words, "Honestly, you don't have to, it's okay."

But the kids kept looking at him. Charlene, with that ridiculous brush cut and those big mournful eyes. And his teenage brats, looking as if they expected something out of him. And damn it, but when you were a divorced parent, you were always stuck with the guilt thing. Even if you weren't the one who demanded the divorce, you still felt like you failed your kids, that you had to make up, try harder.

Still. He didn't remember saying yes to this insane chaperoning plan.

But suddenly Merry shot him a surprised smile, and after that came the exodus. After the door closed, he

watched the squirt and Merry walk across the yard—
with their C battery—before turning back to the boys.

"What? What were you two thinking of, to get me
into something like that?"

Kicker shrugged. "Hey, come on, Dad. It's not like
it's a hardship. She's hot."

"*Hot?* She's a neighbor, for Pete's sake."

"That doesn't mean she isn't hot. Come on. Those
eyes. That butt—"

"Get your eyes and your mind off her figure, Kicker.
She's too old for you and it's not respectful."

"Got it," Kicker said gravely. "I didn't notice her
boobs or her butt. Just her face. But she's still hot. And
the kid was the thing. Charlene was so upset about that
stupid dance. So it just made sense. You could make it
better for her."

"Why does it have to be *me?*"

Kicker shrugged again. "Why not? It's just a couple
hours on a Friday night. With a kick-ass date. How
hard can it be?"

"That's not the point." Jack suddenly realized that
Cooper hadn't said a word. In fact, Cooper had buried
his head in the fridge and wasn't even participating in
the conversation…yet now he remembered, Coop had
been the one to push the co-chaperoning idea. Jack's
gaze narrowed on his eldest son.

"What?"

"What what, Dad?" Coop emerged from the fridge
with a platter of cold cuts. The kid had eaten an hour
ago, polished off the popcorn since then, so no wonder
he was starving again.

"What put the bug up your behind? Why'd you set
me up to do that with her? What were you *thinking?*"

Jack watched as his son slathered mustard and mayonnaise, layered pickles, lettuce, tomatoes, cheese and cold cuts into a sandwich that ended up three, maybe three and a half inches thick. His son didn't choose to respond until he'd taken the first mouthful—which meant that no one could conceivably understand a word he said.

"Say it again after you swallow. I can't understand you."

"We have to get back to the basketball game, dad."

"You thought that up. The chaperoning thing. The going with her. *Why?*"

"Because…" Coop spotted the box of chips on top of the fridge and grabbed those, too. "She's the first woman I've seen you around since the divorce who wasn't like Mom."

Well, if that wasn't the craziest thing Jack had heard in a month of Sundays. Jack trailed his son back to the game in the living room, close enough to clip his heels. "What on earth does that mean? I haven't gone out with anyone like your mom—"

"Yeah, you have. They're all the same."

"They are not. Besides which, I don't know what you mean. Besides which, even if they were like your mom, I don't get what you're saying, what's wrong with that."

Coop plunked down next to Kicker, who was already glued to the tube, both of them eating their seventh or eighth meal of the day, not counting the snacks like popcorn and fast food. U Conn scored. Both boys rose to their feet in unison, shook their jowls, high-fived each other, jogged around the coffee table and then plunked back down on the couch.

Jack wiped a hand over his face. The two of them might be over six feet tall, but they were still both like puppies. Potty trained, but definitely a long way from being completely civilized yet. And since he could remember being fifteen, he knew perfectly well they thought with their hormones ninety-nine percent of the time. No one listened to a fifteen-year-old boy. It would be like trying to make sense of the wind.

"Coop," he said finally, when that particular sports din had quieted down.

"Chill, Dad. I wasn't trying to make a big deal out of this."

"I didn't say you were. I just want to know what you meant. About the women I've been around—at least that you've seen me with—how you think they're like your mother."

Kicker didn't look up. Cooper obviously didn't want to, but he answered the question, but with his gaze glued to the screen. "Because they are. They're all into their jobs. They're, like, competitive. All about their careers. They live the same lifestyle Mom does, filling up every spare second. You fit them in when it's convenient. They fit you in when it's convenient."

"And what's wrong with that?"

"I didn't say anything was wrong. I just said that Merry was different. She's not gonna look at a guy and think, oh, maybe I can see him on the third Friday of every month, let me look at my calendar."

"You're talking Greek. No sense at all. Besides which, no one I've gone out with—no one—was like your mom."

"Okay."

"I have no reason or intention of getting married again. I'm totally happy the way my life is right now."

"Okay."

"There's nothing wrong with a woman being serious about her career. I've never said one word against your mother—"

"I know, Dad." Cooper patted him consolingly on the knee, then shrieked a four letter word at the referee.

It stunned him that his son could be so wrong, where he could conceivably pick up the idea that the women he'd been with since the divorce were like Dianne. Of course, he'd only aimed for lightweight relationships since then. So naturally that meant he'd only played the game with women who wanted to play by those same rules.

But that wasn't the same thing as seeking out women who were like his ex-wife. As far as Jack was concerned, that'd be like a man volunteering to be a target after he'd already been shot. It'd be goofy. Masochistic. Dumb.

No one had hurt him the way Dianne had. In fact it struck his ironic buttons now and then that other men groaned and moaned about women cheating on them. Leaving them for other guys.

Jack wouldn't have minded that half as much as being left for a job. That wasn't exactly how Dianne had put it, but it amounted to the same thing. He wasn't enough for her. His love, all he could offer in the way of a home and marriage and sharing parenting, apparently didn't come close to being important...next to a job she wanted more.

So many jobs in her field had been available around here. He never stood in her way, always applauded her successes. But he also couldn't pick up and move his nature of work, so when she was offered a position that required moving...well, apparently for her, that was enough of an excuse to quit the marriage and take off.

He'd felt like a rug.

A zero.

His life, his love, his *self* were all apparently so forgettable that she could walk out on him without a second glance.

He said to Cooper, "I've never once—once—been with anyone like your mother."

"Okay, Dad, okay. Chill. Forget I said anything. Watch the game."

Yeah, right.

MERRY HAD CHARGED INTO the week with such determination and enthusiasm that she was almost looking forward to June Innes's next visit. This time, the guardian *ad litem* didn't arrive until long after Charlie was home from school. This time, the house was whistle-clean and Merry had the broken nails to prove it. This time, she settled June at the kitchen table with tea and cookies, served with napkins, yet. She was so damned prepared that nothing could possibly go wrong.

Or so she thought. The visit turned out as much fun as being locked in the reptile room at the zoo. June expressed an allergy to ginger cookies and began the conversation with, "The school mentioned that Charlene was in a fight."

"But that was the first day she went back to school after the funeral, so it was a really emotional time. And there've been no problems since."

"That's not what the school administration reported to me." Mrs. Innes was wearing the same outfit as last week, only it was in gray instead of navy blue this time. "I was told that the other children are calling Charlene 'fag' and gay and 'queer.' Yet you've persisted in letting her wear that ridiculous attire."

This time, Merry told herself, she was going to be honest and careful and not lose her temper. "It isn't ridiculous to her, June. I don't know why she's specifically picking the military-look thing. But I think the military aspect makes her feel...strong. And she feels comforted by wearing something of her dad's, close to him."

"They're inappropriate."

When she finally left, Merry couldn't get that strident, authoritative voice out of her head. It was Charlie she needed to win over, not June Innes. Charlie, whose trust mattered, not June's. But darn it, Merry kept hearing the quietly voiced worry that if she didn't show *control* over the situation soon, June would "unfortunately" have to take the matter up with the judge.

Merry laid her head in her hands at the kitchen table, the way she used to as a kid, when she just needed a second to regroup.

"I heard her."

She popped her head back up faster than a jack-in-the-box and produced a soothing smile for Charlene. "Don't worry about it."

"I don't get what she means. About taking 'the matter' to court."

"Honey, it's her job to go back to the court. She's supposed to report to the judge about whether I'm a good guardian."

"Well, you are. I told her. I told her we were doing just fine. So what's her sweat?"

Merry knew perfectly well that Charlie'd say anything to live at home, so that kind of affirmation wasn't exactly, well, an affirmation. When she answered, though, she just tried to be truthful. "Mrs. Innes doesn't think I'm a real strong role model, as far as experience with kids, and she really doesn't think I have 'control.' These are issues she should be worried about, Charlie. But to get specific, this time, she just plain thinks you should be wearing girl clothes instead of your dad's stuff."

Charlie brought the milk from the fridge and poured a glassful. "I'm not hurting anybody with what I'm wearing. I'm not breaking any rules. And my dad always said that nobody really had control over anybody else. That that's just an illusion."

"Sometimes I think you're smarter than all the adults I ever knew."

Charlie slugged down the milk, wiped off the mustache—or most of it—with the side of her hand. When she spoke again, though, her voice was older than the hills. "You're going to leave, Merry. This isn't gonna work for you. I got that right from the first. But please don't go because that dumb woman says you don't have control. That's really bullshit."

"We have to try harder not to say words like bullshit. Because they'll slip out when you're with the wrong people. And besides that, I wish you'd try to believe I'm going to stay."

"I do try to believe."

But once Charlene had overheard Innes spill out Merry's past history of job-hopping and life-hopping, she'd added up one and three and decided it all meant that Merry wasn't going to stay around forever. Another week, no matter how hard Merry had tried, just wasn't enough time to prove to her otherwise.

It wasn't enough time for Merry to prove it to herself, either.

"Look," Merry said, "you didn't tell me before that kids were calling you names in school."

Charlie squinched up her nose. "It's school. Kids call each other names. That's what they do. It's not like I care what creeps call me."

"Okay, but how about if we try to do something to show Mrs. Innes that you're doing okay?"

"Like what?"

"Like…" Merry thought. "Like how about having a sleepover?"

"You're saying I can have a bunch of friends over to spend the night?" Charlie asked in a clearly disbelieving tone.

"Sure, why not? You like the idea?"

"It's okay," Charlie said. "How many can I have?"

"How many do you want?"

"Hmmm…Sandra…and Bo. Robin. Quinn. Jane. Hmm…"

"That's a good number. We can do it."

Charlie said, "Maybe we should forget that dumb Valentine's dance, though."

"Nope. We're doing that."

"But you're going with Mr. Mackinnon, right?"

"Um…I know Jack said yes to that, but I don't know that that's an absolute positive, Charl." An understatement, Merry thought. When it came down to it, there wasn't much she was absolutely positive of these days.

The more she got to know Charlie, the more she got the feeling, deep down in her gut, that there was something huge at stake here. Not just for Charlie but for her. There were things she could screw up and be okay. Things she could fail and move on from.

But she couldn't fail Charlie. Without failing something hugely fragile in herself.

Merry sensed, *knew,* the child still felt abandoned. Charlie was still closed off, not trusting, not taking any risks. She was just coasting. And though Merry had read a ton about kids and grief now, as far as she could tell, Charlie hadn't let it out yet. The loss was still balled up inside of her.

And although Merry had never lost a parent, being around Charlie made her increasingly aware that she had one particular loss still balled up inside of her, even after all these years.

For a woman who'd happily, willfully taken zillions of risks all her life, suddenly she found herself petrifyingly cautious. Not just afraid of making the wrong moves with Charlie…but with Jack.

Jack was raising his sons to be just like him. Adorable. But more than adorable, they were kind and good-hearted and just plain old-fashioned heroes. The kind of guys who watched out for a woman. Who let her be herself, yet still made her feel protected.

And right now, Merry had never felt less protected in her life from the war she really had to win…making a home for Charlie. And for making a place for herself. A place where she didn't have to run anymore—from life, from loss, or from herself.

CHAPTER EIGHT

IT WAS DAYS LATER when Merry heard the unexpected sound of laughter coming from the garage. She cracked open the back door, just far enough to see Jack's sons were the source of all the talking. The two of them were hovered over electronics and car parts with Charlie, all babbling on as if they'd shared a shot of joy juice.

When Merry closed the door, she gulped hard. It was the first time she'd seen Charlie happy since she got here. The boys could guy talk with her. Something Merry was distinctly aware she couldn't do, didn't do and—in this life—was probably never going to be able to do.

Still, she bopped back to the recipe taped to a cupboard door for "steak pinwheels with sun-dried tomato stuffing and rosemary mashed potatoes."

Okay, okay, so maybe it was an excessively ambitious goal for a girl whose specialty was boxed mac and cheese, but Merry wasn't about to give up. So she didn't have the mechanical aptitude of a leaf. She could try other things to win Charlie over, to do the good guardian thing. Like make nutritious meals. Specifically delicious nutritious meals.

Hopefully, anyway.

She stirred the brew of broth and tomatoes and

spices on the stove, still half listening to the kids. The boys sounded so like Jack. If she were Charlie's age, she'd have a serious case of hero worship of both of them. They were so good looking. So gentle with her. So adorable.

Not as adorable as their dad, but right now, Merry was well aware she couldn't imagine anyone more adorable than Jack. Only a man of incomparable courage and character strength would have offered to co-chaperone a sixth-grade dance—and of course she was going to let him off the hook. But that wasn't the point. He'd been so chivalrous to offer. Her heart was still full from their last encounter....

The cell phone rang just as she was reading the next set of instructions in the recipe. The steak had to be laid "flat on a clean work surface." Then it had to be pounded "some." The goal was to roll it into pinwheels, with the stuffing inside.

The phone rang again. She reached for it, but her mind was still trying to decipher the directions. The picture made it look so easy. Only she wasn't exactly sure what a pinwheel was, and what was she supposed to pound the steak with? Hire a hit man? Use her fist? Why was she supposed to hit the poor steak at all?

"Merry? It's me."

"Me!" She'd know Lucy's voice anywhere. They'd been best friends since grade school. Of course Lucy wasn't Lucy Fitzhenry anymore. She'd done the whole fairy-tale thing for real—married Nick Bernard of the Bernard Chocolate empire. But a pile of money hadn't changed her. Just hearing her voice made Merry's spirits lift. She settled in the nearest chair and propped

her feet up on the counter. "God, you don't know how glad I am to talk to you."

"They don't have phones in Virginia? You didn't think I was dying to hear how you were doing?"

"I'd have called. But I didn't want to bug you or Nick. You two are the same as newlyweds. And now you've got the baby. I just hated to call and risk waking either of you up."

"Don't worry about that again. The only one who sleeps in a house with a baby is the baby. And that's whenever the adults can't possibly. It's a trick. It's not in the baby books, but it's still a trick all babies seem to know."

Merry sat back for a bit to hear Lucy gush on about the little one. Sheesh, you could hear the glow in her voice. The love. "Aw, Luce, I'm so happy for you two."

"Yeah, well. Now it's your turn. How on earth is it going?"

Who knew that she'd been holding so much back? But her perky smile slipped. And her eternal optimism suddenly hid under the refrigerator. "Maybe...not so good," she admitted. And out it poured. Sitting in the rain at soccer practice. The painting session. The getting lost trying to find the post office. Charlie's physical appearance. The scary attorney. The scarier guardian *ad litem*. Her making seven dozen cookies last week for the PTO. The dance thing coming up.

She didn't *say* she was feeling inadequate and incompetent and insecure, but if her oldest closest friend couldn't pick up that she was rattled out of her mind, no one could.

Finally Lucy interrupted. "You're turning into a full-time-adult mom."

"I'm sure trying."

Silence for a moment. Merry could hear Lucy clinking ice cubes in a glass, moving around. Then. "You remember when you worked at that insurance company? That horrible guy who had you convinced you must be bipolar? Because you were happy all the time. And he said nobody could be that happy. It just wasn't normal."

"Hey, do we need to bring that up ever again?"

"Not to tease you. I'm just trying to say, Mer, that you do everything whole hog. You always have. You don't put in a hundred percent. You put in five hundred percent. And now you're suddenly trying to turn into a suburban mom, five hundred percent."

"What's wrong with that?"

"Nothing's wrong with it, you doofus. Except that it's all about the child. What about *you?* What about what you want, what you need?"

"What I want is for Charlie to be happy."

"I understand that, Mer. But you haven't said a word about setting up your own life there. I mean, have you been out? Met some guys? Gone dancing anywhere? Shopping? I can't think of a spring you didn't sign up for at least three classes, even if you didn't get around to finishing any of them."

"But I just got here. I haven't had time to think about myself. I'll get selfish again, honest."

"It's not about selfish or unselfish. It's about exhausting yourself."

"Whatever, Lucy. It'll be worth it if Charlie ends up okay. She's just been through a ton."

"This is about your mother, isn't it?"

It was Merry's turn to fall silent. "It's about Charlie."

"I know that. And I know we never talk about your mother. We always act like she never existed. But when you took this on, this whole guardianship thing, without even a second thought—"

"I gave it a ton of thought!"

"Still. It's not the same thing as taking a yoga class or first aid or whatever. You uprooted everything you ever knew to do this. I didn't think it was just about you, being impulsive. This wasn't even remotely a whim—"

"At all. No matter what anyone thinks."

"And your heart's always been as big as the sky. But even so. The way your mother took off…the reasons your mother took off—"

"I'm not like my mother," Merry blurted out. And immediately wanted to bite her tongue. She was too old to be still singing that same old mantra. It hadn't snuck out in years—and neither did that adolescent defensiveness in her tone.

"I know you're not."

"I'd *never* desert a child."

"I know you wouldn't."

"I'd never put money or a lifestyle ahead of what a child needed. And for sure, for *damn* sure, I'd never abandon a kid. If it killed me."

Darn it. When Merry finished the call, she felt itchy-frustrated. Normally talking with Lucy and Nick were a guaranteed day-lifter. Only this time the conversation had made her feel more isolated than ever, as if Virginia were on the other side of the world from everyone she could talk to. Darn it, she needed affirmation from *someone*. Anyone. Any how. She had a dad and sisters and friends who loved her, but it wasn't the same thing as having a live body close by—someone who could see what she was doing, see what she was up against, and help her know if she was on the right track with Charlie.

No matter what Lucy said, this wasn't about her mother. It *wasn't*. It was about the here and now.

The instant she clicked off the receiver, unfortunately she came smack-dab against an immediate here-and-now crisis. Smoke billowed from the pot on the stove.

Charlie walked in, her hands and a cheek shiny with grease. "Whew. What stinks in here?"

Merry thought, my life? Could I just do one thing right?

But she said cheerfully, "You lucked out. I screwed up a big fancy dinner with a lot of vegetables, so now you get mac and cheese."

"Thank you so much," Charlie said fervently.

JACK APPROACHED THE GROCERY store the same way he'd walk into a dark alley at midnight, wary, alert, head down, moving fast.

It was one of those behemoth-sized stores. Had a decent hardware section. Pretty good sporting goods and books. And yeah, of course it had food. It was just…there were so many aisles. So much *shopping*. How was a guy supposed to feel safe?

He grabbed a cart and started out at a fast jog—all the better to get this over with before a panic attack set in. Produce first. The boys couldn't get enough fresh fruit, and that aisle had a lot of stuff he didn't have to cook besides. His mind kept straying to Cooper, because he knew damn well there was something going on with Coop. What, he wasn't sure. But something had the kid distracted and over-quiet for the last couple weeks.

When he spun into the aisle with the oranges and apples, though, he forgot his son. Both sons. And any other rational connection to reality.

Until that moment, he didn't realize how intently he'd made a study of Merry's behind, but facts were facts. He'd have recognized that particular enticing fanny anywhere. She was facing away from him. The waistband on her yoga pants revealed just a hint of the tattoo he had yet to make out, and above that she wore a double layer of long-sleeved tees. She'd thrown her jacket in her grocery cart. The view from behind was as damn close to delectable as anything that was conceivably edible in the store—and then some.

Although that wasn't, Jack told himself sternly, what made him stop.

His neighbor was talking to her. Robert was the one the poker group called Boner whenever the guys were alone together, a natural nickname for a guy who turned on for anything female at the speed of light. There was nothing wrong with Robert exactly. He was a good poker pal. It was just Jack immediately noticed how he'd pushed his cart in a way that blocked Merry's ability to move. He saw Robert's posture. The cocked leg. The bullshit boyish smile.

"I've been wondering how you were doing, knocking around alone in that big house."

"I've got Charlie. I'm not alone. But we're doing just great…"

Jack heard the innocuous dialogue, but he still braced. Boner had been married forever, golfed like it was a religion, had two kids and a wife who brayed when she laughed. But he was a cheater. Jack knew it the way guys just knew that about other guys, didn't need discussion.

He didn't care. Boner's business was Boner's business. And God knew, he didn't need any more involvement in Merry's life. The more he was around her, the more they seemed to "accidentally" touch...but Jack hadn't bought those accidental excuses since he was sixteen.

Nobody touched by accident. A magnet was pulling them together. The same old sexual magnet that always got a guy in trouble—but darn it, this wasn't the normal dig of testosterone. This was more like a plunge into a testosterone lake, unignorable, deep, submerging him in thoughts of her. All of which told him the obvious—he should spin around his grocery cart and gallop in the other direction. It's not as if he feared Boner would try to pull off anything in the middle of a grocery store. It's not as if were worried about her at all.

He didn't worry about anyone but himself and his kids anymore.

But he did accidentally keep listening to the conversation.

"So...Susie sends you to do the grocery shopping?"

There, Jack applauded her. Bring the wife into the conversation. See? She didn't need any help handling a rover.

"Naw," Boner said. "She was under the weather. That time of the month."

Jack mentally winced. Too much information. Inappropriate information. Merry seemed to instinctively back up her cart another step or two. "How're the kids?"

"Same old, same old. Saw you at the kids' volleyball game."

"Yeah, your Samantha did terrific." Jack watched Merry amble back another step, at the same pace Boner was pushing his cart forward. She'd already backed up past the tomatoes. Past the cucumbers and colored peppers.

"She's a trooper, all right. You know…you ever have a leaky faucet or that kind of problem, you know who to call, don't you?"

"Yes. You offered before. Thanks again."

"That Charlene. Can't be easy taking her on out of the blue. She's a different kind of girl, especially since her dad died. You think she's missing a man's influence?"

"I think—" Merry backed up another distance. Cripes, she was about to skid right into the rutabagas. "I just think it's a hard thing she's going through."

"Because I could come over. Just hang with you two sometimes, if you think it'd help—"

Aw, hell. He wasn't exactly saving her. It's just that the damned woman was going to back into a mountain of melons and cause an avalanche if he didn't do something. "Robert. Merry. Amazing who you meet in the grocery store, isn't it?"

Merry spun around, obviously surprised to see him—more than surprised. Her huge, grateful smile could have brought a sixteen-year-old to his knees. It was that stunning.

It was that dead wrong. He was so not a hero, and that was the whole reason he should never have stepped in. Merry kept getting the mistaken idea he was a good guy. She kept giving him those kinds of smiles because she trusted him.

He didn't want her trust. He hadn't earned it, didn't

want to earn it. The truth was, he wanted to lust after her in silent, guilty peace.

Boner, typically, was oblivious to any side undercurrents—or guilt for that matter. They neighbor-talked for a couple more minutes, and then Robert wandered off. When Jack glanced around, he found Merry had stepped over to the apples—not far. At least, not far enough. He could feel her taking in his crew-neck sweater, the old jeans, the scuffed shoes. He had a list in his hand. She had a list in hers. But when he picked up a bag of oranges, she suddenly zoomed back to his side with another big smile.

"I'm guessing you'd like them a little more ripe, wouldn't you?" She replaced his chosen bag of oranges with one she picked.

"How do you tell?"

"No yellow or green tinge. The shape of them." Color bloomed on her cheeks. He hadn't been trying to look her over in an evocative or noticeable way. It was just the way T-shirt material cupped her breasts. How could a guy not notice?

He said casually, "You might want to be a little watchful around Robert."

"Believe me, I watched enough to know he's on the prowl."

"His wife's a prowler, too. A guy isn't safe alone in his own house sometimes," Jack said mournfully. That made her chuckle.

He wanted her to chuckle. Wanted her to feel easy with him—just not too easy, because every instinct warmed him that if a wolf knocked on Merry's door, she'd invite him right on in to dinner.

"The first time Robert stopped over, he seemed so

nice. Welcoming me to the neighborhood, offering to help. Only offering a little too hard," she said wryly.

"I've been known to hide in the basement if Susie knocks," Jack said *sotto voce*.

Again she chuckled. By the time they'd made it back to the apples, she'd taken over as shopping supervisor, didn't even bother asking permission to exchange the bag of apples in his hand for a different one.

"What's wrong with those?" The two bags looked the same to him.

"The ones in the middle were all bruised, started to go soft. You're not much of a grocery shopper, huh?"

He made a face. And she grinned. "Okay, I guess I can trust you on your own with the cherries," she teased. "I have to hustle. Have a sleepover to shop for."

When she ambled away, he told himself that he felt relieved. But the produce section had proven so traumatic that he instinctively pushed his cart toward a guaranteed safe zone. Hardware.

He knew that part of the store. There was no possibility of getting into any trouble there, no anxiety, no threat of harm's way. And the library shelves he'd been building were to the point where he needed to make a decision on stain.

He didn't want too dark a color, but the birch wood was too darn light by itself. So he was thinking maybe maple. Maybe maple blended with some English oak. With maybe a few drops of mahogany to richen it up.

It took a few minutes to make up his mind and choose the staining products. When he turned the corner into the next hardware aisle, though…damn, there she was again. All alone this time. Her cart looked more stuffed than a pregnant whale, rounded with pop

and popcorn, brownie mixes and mounds of chips, all
the major junk-food ingredients for a sleepover. He
was envious of anyone who could finish a cartful of
shopping that fast—yet oddly, her expression appeared
frazzled and frustrated as she studied the shelves of
electrical supplies.

He could hardly duck from sight. What if she'd
turned and seen him?

"I take it it's my turn to save you?" he asked wryly.

She spun around. Immediately her face lit up,
brighter than sunshine. "Oh, God. You can't imagine
how glad I am to run into you again! Charlene said we
needed a three-prong thingie for some electronic whatchamacallit in her room. And she drew me a picture so
I'd know what it looked like. But I can't find it. And
there's no point in asking a clerk because—"

"Because he might not know how to identify it
from the fancy 'thingie' terminology?" How could he
not tease her?

"Give me all the grief you want. As long as you help
me," she teased right back.

He had to come close enough to see the drawing on
her list. "I hate to lose my hero status, but honest to
Pete, this isn't remotely tricky. All you need is an
adaptor."

"Yeah, that's what I thought I needed. Only there
isn't a single package here that spells out a three-prong
whatchamacallit."

"Damn men must have marketed this stuff. What do
they know?"

She chuckled again. Only at that point he couldn't
help but touch her. The part was right over her head.
And he just barely brushed her shoulder, yet damnation,

somehow it was enough to put a velvet ripple up and down his spine.

He was *not* the kind of man who experienced velvet ripples. Up and down the spine or anywhere else. Ever. "Well…"

He didn't have to finish the sentence. She did. "You're off. Me, too. Want to get the rest of this done and get home. But if by some crazy chance we're ever in the store at the same time again, maybe we should just switch lists. I'll do your food. You do my…"

"Whatchamacallits."

Another shared smile—why did it always have to feel as if he'd shared something private with her? But then she took off and so did he. He made a fast trek through frozen foods and was just aiming for the checkout—relieved he hadn't run into her again—when he realized he'd forgotten to make a quick run through the book section. There was a new Iles and Coben out.

He found both books at the end-cap. Discounted, just as he'd hoped. Only he spotted her there again. Apparently she bought books with the same exuberance she bought everything else, because there were tomes heaped on her grocery stack. *Soccer For Dummies. Mechanics For Dummies. Geometry For Dummies. Wicked.* Three Harry Potters. *Talking To Your Preteen About Sex. College Planning. Even You Can Learn Computer Skills.*

He intended to skid right by. Forget the Iles and the Coben, just get the hell out of the store.

But it itched on his heart—how damned hard she was trying with the child. She wasn't just a fish out of water. She didn't seem to have a clue how to swim. And when he wheeled closer this time, she was absorbed in the book about parenting advice on sex, flipping through the pages, a scoop of hair making a comma of dark satin on her cheek .

He said, "They knew more at ten than we knew at twenty-five. It's one of the scarier parenting things."

She glanced up, this time not looking surprised to see him. "I heard her talking to someone on the phone. Another kid. About how some thirteen-year-old had given a blow job to some other thirteen-year-old on the school bus. I almost collapsed on the floor. I'm not that old, but I don't remember kids doing stuff like this. At least not that I knew anything about. She doesn't take the school bus, but my God. I didn't even know what to say, much less what I was supposed to *do* about a story like that."

"You think it's tough raising a new daughter? Try raising sons."

"I don't think it's easy for either gender. But whatever you're doing…it's totally right. Your boys are great."

"That opinion's sure mutual. My boys took one look at you and decided you were cool."

A flush spotted her cheeks. "I really like them both, Jack. They've been over to car-talk with Charlie a couple of times. They're so good with her, treat her like a little sister, but they don't talk down to her. And they just seemed to accept me. The way you have."

His boys had done just that, accepted her, Jack knew. But he hadn't.

And something just snapped in his head. He knew what she'd been doing. Him, too. Both of them had been playing the moth game, maybe not exactly flirting, but still edging closer and closer to the flame. And when Jack stepped forward, he kept thinking that they might as well get the burn over with.

She had to quit looking at him with those idealistic eyes. With that open welcome in her smile. With that you-are-one-sexy-guy posture. Or he was going to get sucked in. So maybe it was an impulse, but it was real enough. Get the burn over with; quit with all that dangerous fluttering toward temptation.

So he grabbed her—with her hand still on the book about sex and adolescence, with the grocery store neon lights as unsexy as knees. And maybe no one else was in the book aisle at that moment, but like any other evening, there were people all over the store. Someone could show up at any second. Maybe a neighbor. Maybe someone at the school. For damn sure, it'd be someone neither wanted to be seen by.

So when he hooked her arms—book and all— around his neck and aimed for a kiss, he was thinking fast and dark. He was thinking, just get this completely over with right now, put the kaputz on her believing him a good guy, on thinking those inviting smiles were okay. He was thinking...

Well, he *was* thinking. But then the whole deal got murky.

Something noisy hit the floor. The book she'd been holding. Then some more books.

He ground his mouth on hers. Nailed her lips good. He was thinking frustrated, annoyed, thoughts, he was sure of it.

Only, for Pete's sake, the taste of her was like some exotic nectar. Wild and sweet. Alluring. Confounding. She arched against his body, leaning into him, her eyes closing as if she were lost in the moment. Lost in him.

Sixteen-year-olds got lost in the moment. Not grown-ups. With grown people it was about sex. Satisfaction. Of course you gave in to the mood when it was appropriate, but that wasn't the same as falling under some immature, amateur, dad-blamed *spell*.

Her naiveté was yet another difference between them.

He shifted a leg. Had to, or risked falling. He hadn't broken off that punishing kiss yet. He was about to. But for that second or so... for that minute or so, he felt stirred into a wicked, forbidden soup, swirling around the taste of her, the wrongness of her, the texture of those plump, firm breasts teasing against his chest, the arch of her back making a meld of her pelvis rocking against his.

Her arms, that had been so tidily lassoed around his neck, suddenly weren't. Her hands were gliding down on his back, pressing, sliding down to his butt. Then pushing in, pushing his groin tighter against her pelvis.

Inviting murder and mayhem. Or worse. Right there in the grocery store. In public. With all those lights.

He couldn't very well end the kiss right then, when it was so completely obvious that she hadn't learned a thing. You don't poke a sleeping bear. You don't go into dark alleys alone. You don't entice a guy unless you're inviting the consequences.

That was the kind of stuff he was trying to make sure she understood. Stuff her mama should have taught her. Or a guy, a lot earlier than this. He didn't want to hurt her feelings, but darn it, get this over with and then she'd know. Then she'd be safer. Then she wouldn't poke any more bears.

Lights blurred. Under that thin shirt of hers, he could feel the suppleness of her skin. Feel the glossy softness of her. The scent of her.

The shape of her mouth, not too big, not too small, just devourably just right.

The tiredness of a long day seemed to float off, forgotten. His irritation with the grocery store, gone. The troubling mystery of Cooper's recent behavior…well, that wasn't gone, his kids never totally disappeared from his mind, but right then the problem had definitely disappeared from the docket. In fact, there was nothing on his immediate docket but—

But that lesson he wanted to teach her.

Right.

A sigh groaned from his mouth to hers.

His hands snaked down her spine, down to her fanny. Lots of clothes between them. Not enough. Too many. Either way, it didn't matter, because any touch was better than none. Any way he could grind against her—and be ground against—was better than not. Any way he could keep their lips glued, her flavor locked against his tongue, was worth fighting for, even if it meant a loss of oxygen, a loss of sanity, a complete loss of lucidity.

Her skin was softer than silver, the heat coming off her more erotic than nakedness—at least almost. Every kiss, every squeeze, made him imagine her naked. Prone. Rolling on the moonlit grass, somewhere in summer, somewhere there was no one and nothing but her. Just her sounds, her textures, her smells. Just that lustrous hair under his fingers, that winsome mouth, that wicked, willing invitation in the rock of her hips against him.

Some thumping noise jolted him, jolted her into opening her eyes. Something seemed to have fallen. Like a major stack of magazines. He noticed, sort of, but mostly he noticed her liquid eyes, her breathlessness. "Are you okay?" he asked in a low voice.

"Um...sort of," she responded with complete honesty, her voice as dusky as a whisper. She seemed to gather herself, realize where they were, see the fallen books and magazines. "Good grief."

Yeah, he thought, she'd finally gotten it. How dangerous they were together. The price you paid for teasing the tiger. Or the bear. Whatever.

He couldn't help feeling a little bad that now she looked so...vulnerable. "I'll take care of all this stuff that fell down," he said firmly.

He bent down, and so did she, but he reached the scatter of magazines and books first. He picked them all up, pushed them back on the shelves.

They all fell down again.

"You're sure you're all right? I could walk you out," he said.

"No, honestly. I'm fine."

"I don't know what to say—"

"You don't have to say anything," she said gently. "I had a feeling that was coming. Maybe not this minute, in this silly store. But that it was going to happen sooner or later."

"I did, too." Well. He took a breath. It felt darn selfish to just leave her in that state of intense arousal, by herself, not do anything to help her get over it. But then that was the point, wasn't it? Teaching her a lesson? Making sure they didn't keep risking this kind of crap. "I have to get home, Merry—"

"Of course you do. Me, too."

So he stumbled away from her—at least until she called him back.

"Jack?"

He turned.

"Don't you want to take your shopping cart?"

"Oh. Yeah."

He got to the front, went through the checkout, forgot his wallet. Then realized it was in his back left pocket. In the parking lot, he momentarily forgot where he'd parked his truck.

He kept thinking, maybe it was cruel to do that to her in a public store like that. She *was* his neighbor, after all. And his hands had been all over her, even if they had been wearing all their clothes. When he was younger—he'd just been nicer, that's all.

He opened the truck door, climbed in, then couldn't fit the key in the lock. A minute later—possibly three— he realized that the black GMC only looked like his. It was someone else's.

He stumbled back out, recarrying all his groceries and swearing at shopping in general. It was definitely a good thing they got that kind of dark, dangerous embrace thing over with, he mused.

She'd really learned a lesson.

He wouldn't have to worry about her so much after this.

CHAPTER NINE

THE CHILLY RECEPTIONIST in Lee Oxford's office had told Merry to have a seat fifteen minutes ago. Normally she'd have minded the wait, especially since she was nervous about the coming conversation with the attorney. But this morning, she was content to just curl up in a chair. Her mind was on Jack, had been since those crazy kisses in the grocery store two nights ago.

He'd been such a basket case, the darling. Who'd ever guess that a few kisses would shake up a sophisticated grown man so much?

Yet she'd seen him falling over his feet, then walking off without his cart. And in the parking lot, she'd watched him climb into the wrong truck—not that she'd ever tell him. It was just so adorable and endearing that a few kisses from her—with her—had affected him so strongly.

Of course, they'd affected her, too.

So much so that she was seriously considering jumping him. It was increasingly obvious—no matter how volatile he was when he responded to her—that he was too chivalrous to initiate an invitation himself. Merry had never experienced chemistry this powerful. She sure as Pete didn't want to waste it. Because she was trying to be more cautious, though, she kept trying to think of reasons why she shouldn't seduce him.

There didn't seem to be any.

He was a good man. A hero. Trustworthy. A great dad. Honest. Helpful. Hot. He seemed lonely—she had the impression from the neighborhood that there were a fair number of women wandering in and out of his Friday nights—but no one who stayed. He was all alone in that big house most of the time.

It wouldn't be a good idea for the kids to find them in bed together, of course, but that was a question of care and logistics, not a deterrent in itself. And she'd given up her entire private life. She had absolutely no private life, come to think of it. But she could hardly give up sex altogether until Charlene was grown up, could she? So a relationship overall seemed a good idea. For him. For her.

Or was she just giving herself an excuse for jumping him?

As much as she loved mulling the problem of Jack, though, the attorney's secretary finally signaled that Lee Oxford was free. She popped to her feet, but dread immediately rolled in her tummy. She'd called Lee for this meeting, but that didn't mean she really wanted to be here. Questions and worries just kept coming up that she couldn't answer on her own.

Mr. Napoleon had shoes that gleamed like mirrors and bling for cuffs this morning. Like before, he had a smile that could charm a snake, and he might have kept her waiting, but now she was barely seated before he handed her a check.

"What's this?" she asked in confusion.

"For the storm damage. The insurance settlement came directly to me." He raised a brow. "Actually, I thought you'd be chafing at the bit to get the money before this. And you don't seem to be drawing on your guardian account, so I assume there was a problem that you needed a fast resolution about there, too."

Truthfully, she'd completely forgotten about all that. Sooner or later, she had to get around to paying some bills and all that, but right now, she had serious questions on her mind, not silly issues like money. "I have four questions," she said.

"Shoot."

"June Innes. Lee, do we have to do what she says?"

Lee poured coffee from a sterling carafe for both of them. "Well, yes and no. She was appointed by the court, so she has the court's ear, and she will be regularly reporting to the judge for at least a year. That doesn't mean you *have* to do anything she says. But she does have the power to haul you in front of the judge, question your fitness, any time she wants."

"That's what I was afraid you'd say," Merry muttered. "I don't think she likes me."

"You're young and pretty. Of course she doesn't like you," Lee said wryly. "But she's been doing the *ad litem* thing for the court for years. Most of her cases are elderly. She pulls a real tiger act for them, so I tend to label her on the good-guy team. But I have to say—I've never seen her in an adolescent case. I can't believe she'd relate too well to today's kids."

"That's my impression."

"I also think she's always on the side of the victim, which means that she'd inherently see you as a potential problem. She's used to protecting old people from others who are trying to swindle or use them— so that's how she'd tend to see you. As the person who'd be involved in this for Charlene's money.

She'd tend to be suspicious of you, even if you weren't damned adorable."

There were times Merry loved a compliment. But not from the attorney, and not now. "She just has very rigid ideas about how Charlene should be raised. And maybe she's right. I've never been a parent. But I can't see why I have to push stuff on Charlene—like discipline—unless there's a reason. And she's really adamant about Charlene seeing a counselor, but Lee, Charlene just as adamantly doesn't want to."

Lee leaned back with his coffee. "I hear you. But overall, I can't make those calls for you, Merry. It's on you."

"Thanks." She should have known, Mr. Armani wouldn't stick his neck out, either to defend her or to offer advice that wasn't related to his financial interests. "Okay. Easier question. What am I supposed to do about Charlie's car?"

"What do you want to do?"

"I don't know. I mean—I already have a car. A good car that I love. And I can't drive two. But Charlie's car would carry around more kids, if and when I do more carpooling. So I just need to clarify—do I have permission to drive Charlie's car? Or to sell it? I mean, what am I supposed to do?"

"God. If clients would just bring me problems this easy to solve," Lee said wryly. "Do whatever the hell you want. If Charlie's car works better for you in the parenting role, you're fully entitled to it. I'll get your name on that insurance if it isn't already. No sweat."

"Okay." She guessed that one, but now she fidgeted in the leather chair. "Lee, I'd like to redecorate Charlie's room."

"And you're telling me this, why?"

"Because I'd need money to do it."

"Merry, we talked about this. You have a whole checking account that regularly refills from Charlie's estate. You don't have to ask permission to use the money. You just have to keep receipts and be able to verify that the use is for the upkeep of the house, the issues related to Charlene's life."

"I know you told me that." She rubbed two fingers on her temples. "But it feels like stealing."

"Huh?"

She should have known Lee wouldn't get it. Stacks of bills had been breeding by the phone in the kitchen. It just felt weird to use money that wasn't hers, even though she knew she was entitled to pay the electric bill—and using the money on something "unnecessary" like redecorating was a lot less practical than electric bills. In principle, she should love living a princess's life. The reality just seemed a little touchier. But she moved on. "Next question. Could I get a job?"

"You don't financially need a job." Lee's tone reflected his opinion that they'd already covered this subject.

"I know I don't. Financially. And I've been filling every hour I can with Charlie's life, doing things at her school, volunteering every place in her life that I can get involved. But there's still a lot of time in a day. Is there something illegal or problematic in my being her guardian if I also had a job?"

"If the job didn't interfere with your full-time care of Charlene, I can't imagine a problem. But you've got a helluva generous living allowance, so I guess my advice is…what's your hurry with working? Hold your horses. Settle in for a few months. You're always going to look better to the court if you look like a devoted full-time mom figure."

"Which brings me to my last question," Merry said slowly. "The real mom figure. Charlene's mother. I keep worrying about her—if she's still alive, where she is, if she could show up in Charlene's life. What I should do if she did show up."

Lee didn't hesitate. "That would be a legal issue, Merry. Basically out of your hands. I don't think you need to borrow trouble. She hasn't been part of Charlene's life in all these years. But if she shows up, just call me. It'll be my problem after that."

"I believe the mother knew Charlie's family in Minnesota, so she could have heard that Charlie died, that her daughter's alone. That's why I keep thinking about it."

"Well, you can think about it until the cows come home, honey. Charlie used to worry that she'd show up, too. But basically there's nothing anyone can do unless the woman actually appears and then tries to make some kind of claim on Charlene. Let's not worry about a cow that hasn't even left the barn, okay?"

Maybe the attorney thought all his folksy cow metaphors were reassuring, but on the drive home, Merry was antsier than ever. At least she'd gotten those issues off her chest, but the meeting hadn't solved anything.

The deeper she got into this guardian business, the more she realized that Lee couldn't give her answers. Neither could any outsider. The only answers that seemed to matter had to come from inside her.

How unfair was that?

Quickly, though, she pushed that annoying thought aside. Charlene was going to be home from school shortly…and then they had a sleepover to prepare for.

If there was one thing Merry was outstanding at, it was parties.

Charlie was going to have a fabulous night tonight with her friends, or Merry was going to die trying.

A hum started in the back of her throat and built to a full-fledged zesty mood. It didn't even bother her when Charlene walked in the door from school, as excited as a sleepy turtle. Charlene was never going to be the kind of kid to dance on the table with joy.

Merry was. In fact, she figured she could do enough boogie-woogie-ing for the two of them.

"Merry, you don't have to *do* all this. You don't have to fuss at all," Charlie kept saying. "It's just some kids coming over."

"We're not fussing. We're just getting stuff ready." Like pushing all the living room furniture against the walls so there'd be room for a half-dozen sleeping bags. Like baking three batches of brownies, four platters of chocolate chip cookies, and a half dozen flavors of chip dip. Like piling up a dozen DVDs to choose from. Like heaping pillows around, and games, and decks of cards.

"What are you wearing?" Merry asked Charlie, who looked down at her khakis with surprise.

"What I've got on. Why not?"

"That's fine, that's fine," Merry assured. "I just thought maybe you'd like something more comfortable…."

"I'm comfortable."

"Okay. No prob." Maybe Merry had sneakily hoped that having a bunch of girls over might coax Charlene to try some different clothes, but one step at a time. Obviously her friends didn't care how she looked, right? Because eight had all accepted invitations to the sleepover.

Merry was just heaping pretzels and chips on a plate with fresh dip when the back door rang.

"I'm in the bathroom," Charlie called out.

"That's okay, I'll get it," Merry called back, and jogged to the door, higher than Charlie was at the idea of company, voices, laughter—a houseful of fun—this evening. But then she opened the door. And said curiously, "Hi. What can I do for you?"

"I'm Robin. I'm here for the sleepover. And you're Charlie's Merry, right?"

For a moment Merry lost her voice, but then she bobbed her head like a wind-up toy. "Of course. Come in, come in, Robin."

He did. And that was just the thing. She'd mentally pictured Robin as a chirpy little preteen, apple-cheeked, kind of plump. Not as a tall skinny reed with gangly arms and a face full of zits. A tall skinny male reed. The word *male* being the operative shock.

"Hey, Charlie?" he yelled out as he traipsed through the kitchen, wearing boots that looked about a size fifteen.

A boy, Merry repeated to herself. Not that sleepovers with boys were that odd. It's just…Charlene was eleven. The best-friends era. The best-*girlfriends* era. Or that's how she remembered it.

She sank against the counter to get a grip—until the doorbell rang a second time. Two fresh-cheeked kids were piling out of a BMW in the driveway—one was a redhead with more freckles than skin. "Sandra," she identified herself. "And you're the cool Merry, right?"

"I'm Merry, for sure—come on in, honey—and you're—" Oh, God, oh God.

"Bo." Bo pumped her hand, as if he'd been taught

manners. She couldn't see the top of his head because he was that much taller than she was. He had young eyes. He was just so football-player-big. And he knocked three things down just trying to walk through the kitchen.

So there'd be two boys, she mentally told herself cheerfully.

Only then came Quinn. And Quinn wasn't a girl, either.

And then came Tanguy, and Merry had expected someone of another culture, but damnation, she'd expected a girl from another culture. Not a four-foot miniature boy with his hair iced with mousse and a diamond in his eyebrow. Not that she had anything against tattoos or piercings. She didn't. But her opinion of body holes had changed since becoming a mom last month.

The last guest showed up five minutes later and took up the entire doorway. The name was Cyr.

Another boy. This one was wearing fatigues like Charlie's. He was blond, blue eyed, and carrying a suitcase big enough to survive in Europe for six months.

The next big question in her life, Merry thought, was whether to have a heart attack immediately or wait a half hour. Maybe it'd be easier to just get it over with….

JACK ALMOST NEVER GOT the kids on a Friday night. Kicker invariably had a date and Cooper got something going with this guy friends. This time, though, Dianne had something she needed to do, so he'd picked up the boys. Coop just had a three-cavity trip to the dentist, so the only one whining too loud about the Friday confinement with Dad was Kicker.

He'd brought home soup for Coop, and Po'Boys for

him and Kicker, rented some classic guy flicks. The three of them were settled in the dark living room, chilling with some good blood and guts when the phone rang.

Kicker—it was a knee-jerk reaction for him to gallop at the sound of a phone, any phone—bounded over the back of the couch to reach it.

"Considering it's the house land line, I'd think the call would be for me," Jack said dryly. "Not like it's your cell."

"I know, I know," Kicker said, but he still smashed it to his ear as if hoping the latest female sex symbol in his class had located him here. Which, as far as Jack could tell, it might very well be. Girls seemed to find Kicker everywhere. They all sounded giggly and breathless.

Jack zoned back on the movie, kicking off his shoes. It had been a long work week. Good one, but he was more than ready for a weekend. Still…another minute passed and Kicker was still on the phone. Kicker could talk for hours that way, but something cocked Jack's parenting trigger, even though all he caught were bits and pieces of Kicker's side of the conversation. At least initially.

"Hey, it's okay. I could come right over, if you want. In fact, Cooper and I could both come over…."

Jack pushed up to a sitting position.

"…or my dad. We could make Dad come over…."

Jack stood up, quick as a spring.

"Naw, I don't blame you for having an edge on. So maybe it's cool, you know. But I totally get it, why you're freaked. You know what? Coop and I could just come over and—"

Jack shook his head at his son. Kicker motioned to the phone. Jack motioned to the phone, too. The sign language was exuberantly physical but didn't seem to communicate a damn thing to each other.

"Naw," Kicker said, "I'm telling you, my dad wouldn't mind at all. In fact, he'll probably be the one to come over. That's what friends are for, you know? Calling when shit goes on. I mean, when stuff goes on. I didn't mean to say shit. I mean…"

Jack made a firm motion, clearly indicating—in sign or verbal language—to fork over the telephone. Now.

"Okay, Merry, one of us'll be over. Just detox until then, okay? Yeah, stay cool." Finally Kicker hung up.

"What?" Jack demanded. The single word communicated enough. He didn't need a full sentence.

"It's Merry—"

"I realized that when you used her name," Jack said wryly.

"You know, for a woman her age, she is so cute."

"Skip the detail. Get to the grit, Kicker. Now."

"She thinks she's got a big problem. I don't think she does, but anyway. The deal is, the squirt's having a sleepover. No sweat, right? Only it turns out there's a houseful of boys."

"Boys?"

"Yeah. She thought they'd be all girls. And instead Charlene asked a bunch of guys in her class. One girl, I guess. But the rest guys. And maybe they're just eleven and twelve, but they're all set up to sleep on the living room floor together. She said she called a few parents. They already knew, didn't seem to care at all."

"But…"

"Merry probably wouldn't have, either. She said. If it was up to her. But it's not that simple anymore now, because she suddenly turned into a mom. So now she thinks she's supposed to protect the squirt. I loved it, her asking my opinion. She actually listens, you know, Dad? God, she's so cute."

"Would you skip the *cute,* Kicker! Fill in the rest of the blank—"

"She's upset. So I said I'd come sleep over. Me and Coop. Like no biggie, right? Nothing to walk next door. She has a tube, or we could take the belly telly. I think she's tight about nothing, but who cares? Easy enough to go help her."

"Let's see," Jack said. "You think it'd logically help her to have two more boys sleep over there?"

"Well, I did think there might be a little ironic problem there," Kicker said ingeniously. "That's why I brought up your name. I knew you'd be willing to go over, be another parent helping her. It was never like it *had* to be Coop and me."

Jack scowled at his son, feeling pressured and antsy. "It's not a good time for me to go anywhere. Cooper feels rotten—"

"That's not a headliner. But he's just gonna lay there and watch vids. And you don't mind going over—"

"What makes you think you know that?" Jack asked.

"Dad. You just pulled on your jacket."

Damn kid. See a pretty face and that's it, out went the common sense, offering to do anything and everything without a second thought. And because Kicker had been hot to play White Knight, Jack was stuck tromping across the cold yard.

He thumped on her back door, but no one answered for obvious reasons. Music was playing so loud inside that there was an imminent threat of shattering glass.

He thumped again, then turned the knob and poked his head in. "Merry?"

She didn't need him. He knew what she'd volunteered for. Sleepovers were torture for parents, but primarily because they involved noise all night and a god-awful mess. In that age-eleven bracket, though, at least in their neighborhood, there was little worry about drinking or drugs or big-ticket trouble threats. He got it, though. Her fret was the boys and girls sleeping in the same room.

"Merry?" He stomped through the kitchen—although "waded" was probably the more accurate term. Overhead lights blazed on the carnage. Cans and paper plates overflowed from two bags of trash. Spilled pop made several puddles on the floor and counters. Open plates of brownies looked as if mad dogs had made a run on them.

"Mer—?" He sampled one as he tromped through, and then almost had to stop dead. Man. Maybe there were better foods than brownies, but offhand he couldn't think of any. And hers were nectar for the gods. "Melt in your mouth" didn't begin to cut it.

He whipped back to the counter just to sneak one more, and then, of course, couldn't talk straight. "Mryth?"

The body who barreled into him almost ousted his mouthful of brownie—which would have been a criminal loss. On the other hand—hell times three—she was beyond criminally appealing.

"Oh, Jack," Merry said fervently, "I'm *so, so, so* glad you're here."

Cripes, back when, even his dog hadn't been that glad to see him. No one had been. Besides which, she snared his damn heart, just looking at her—the wide eyes, all distraught. She was wearing a big old sweatshirt, so loose in the neck that the slim slope of one gorgeous shoulder peeked through. Her hair was all glossy and loose and tumbled all over the place. She belonged in bed. Right now. His bed. With him.

But then he remembered—he wasn't here for that. "Okay, just tell me what the deal is."

"All the boys—I called their parents. One after the other. I just couldn't believe they wouldn't care their kids were sleeping over at a girl's house—"

"But they were okay with it."

"Yes."

"But you're not."

"Damn straight I'm not!"

"Then just send 'em home, Mer."

She peeled off his jacket, which could have been an aggressive seduction invitation—God knew, it made Wilbur rise at the speed of sound—but he suspected it was just that she was trying to keep him from leaving. "You don't understand. I can't let Charlene down. And the boys coming are really my fault."

"Your fault how?"

"My fault because I should have asked her. But since I didn't, and since I okayed this, now I can't embarrass her in front of her friends. For Pete's sake, Jack, it's the first fun thing she's wanted to do since her dad died. She's as serious as a saint most of the time."

"So they're likely good kids if they're her friends, because she's as straight as an arrow to start with...so maybe they're a little young to worry they're into orgies quite yet?"

"I played strip poker when I was eleven."

So much for thinking about Charlene and her friends. "You did?"

"And the same year raided Mrs. Simpson's liquor cabinet. Got drunk in Bobby Smith's tree house. Damned near killed ourselves, falling out. We did that at ten."

"You did?"

"And my girlfriends all got into this thing, worrying they were gay, how'd anybody know? So we had a sleepover, asked over Joey Meyers, who was two years older than us and the heartthrob of the eighth grade. We asked him to kiss us all so he could get a reaction."

"God. Where were you when I was eleven? All I remember is camping in the woods with my parents."

"What I did isn't the *point,* Jack. The point is that I thought I'd be great for her, great with her. Because I wouldn't be judgmental, it'd be easy for me to be understanding because I'm not that far from her age. I *know* kids do things. I know they survive them. I know they're stupid sometimes. So I could naturally be someone she could really talk to—"

He opened his mouth to sneak a word in, but should have known Merry hadn't worn down yet.

"Only now, I suddenly turned into a parent. Before this, I had no idea that being a parent could be this terrorizing. Especially because she's a girl. You *know* it's worse for a girl. Boys can't get pregnant."

Jack peered around the corner, just trying to see where the bodies were stacked. As it happened, none of them appeared within listening range, even if they could hear over the movie and music. "Not that I've paid any attention, but I'm pretty sure she's a long way from being able to get pregnant, either. I mean, aren't you talking flat as a board—?"

"She's getting bumps! And besides, it's not that far

down the pike when she could! And the one boy—the big one, the older one—he took off his shirt, said he was hot. What am I supposed to do? Walk out of the room? Leave them all alone in there?" She shook her head wildly. "I don't think so."

"Okay, okay. But maybe we could ratchet the terror level down a couple of degrees, you think?"

"It *is* racheted down. Because you're here. In fact, just being able to talk to another parent, an adult... you..."

A couple bodies suddenly stumbled through the doorway—Charlene and a crony. Both of them had empty bowls and were clearly looking for a refill. Charlene beamed a smile when she saw him. "Hey, Mr. Mackinnon. How's it going?"

"Not bad. I hear a movie in there   "

"Yeah." She named an action flick. "The first version. The good one."

God knew what made him say it, but he offered, "A classic already."

"Yeah, I think so, too. Although if they keep doing sequels, maybe they can come up to that level."

The idiot in his head came out with more malarkey. "Mind if I watch for a minute?"

"'Course not."

The kids disappeared. Merry looked at him.

"So we'll just go see the lay of the land, all right? Get an impression from some inside reconnaissance."

She looked at him as if he were brilliant. Which, of course, he actually was—but his IQ wasn't usually what women found appealing about him—and that was wildly assuming they found him appealing to begin with.

As far as inside reconnaissance, though, he couldn't

help but notice the changes she'd made in the house. Candles. A bunch of fresh flowers. And there were piles of fluffy rugs—the kind guys hated; all you ever did was trip on the darn things—but they were in rich reds and blues and greens.

But more than that, the change in artwork startled him. Maybe Jack had always thought Charlie's taste in art was a little gruesome, but that was generally a what-the-hey. Charlie was into art for investments. Besides, one man's art was always another man's trash.

The huge, wild canvases of crazy colors all over the place were definitely trash. But they were…fun. Sensuous. Interesting. Different from anything he'd seen before.

Exactly like Merry, he mused, but that was the last chance he had to notice the artwork. The kids vacated the couch the instant he walked into the living room. He never asked them to move; it just seemed an automatic kid-presumption that an adult wouldn't want to sit on the floor. The kids had sleeping bags spread out all over the living room anyway.

The room looked like an army bivouac, with sleeping bags all fanned out from the center, set up for the best viewing on the big screen. Food supplies surrounded them, somewhat comparable to an arsenal in case of a siege. Screams of annoyance resulted when a body had to walk over the other bodies to get to the bathroom.

Jack looked at the scrubbed faces, and was hard pressed to imagine anything dangerous or immoral going on. But he wasn't Merry. And although he'd suffered every growing-up stage with his boys, he couldn't swear that the same experiences and fears and hormonal upsets were the same for girls.

So he hunkered down on the couch for a minute, just figuring he'd watch the flick for a bit, get a feel for the personalities.

The next thing he knew—who would have thought it—Merry's head was in his lap!

CHAPTER TEN

JACK WOKE UP SUDDENLY, only to discover that the wildly erotic dream he'd been enjoying in Technicolor and surround sound wasn't a dream after all.

Merry's face really was in his lap.

He rubbed a hand over his face, willing the groggy sleepiness to disappear, waiting for some common sense to slap him upside the head. Fast.

He wasn't sure what time it was. Well past 2:00 a.m. Maybe past three? The living room was dark, except for a movie playing on the tube—not the movie he remembered watching, but something similar. The old cartoon-characters-come-to-life scenario.

Bodies were strewn all over the living room, a few sprawled like abandoned puppies, but most scrunched up tight in their sleeping bags. The one little girl—not Charlene—was snoring like a real honker. One boy's feet were in another boy's face. Potato chip crumbs dotted the room like confetti, and in the corner by the hearth, a pop had spilled.

Actually, at least one pop had spilled.

Lights seemed to be blazing from every other room in the house—kitchen, bathrooms, back bedrooms. It was just the living room that was movie-dark.

Good thing. Since the Arbiter of Children's Morality—

alias Merry, the hopelessly overprotective new mom—had her nose and mouth damn near smothered in his crotch.

He had a vague memory of plopping down on the couch with the kids, and then a few minutes later, Merry coming in, taking the far corner of the same couch, murmuring that she couldn't watch these kinds of movies so she was only going to stay there a minute. He remembered talking with the kids, cheering and groaning when they did over some particularly poignant violent scenes. He remembered food coming and going. He remembered a kid curling up, obviously giving up the ghost and falling asleep. Then another.

He remembered seeing Merry yawn, guessed that she was really wiped after getting ready for this madhouse all day.

He remembered thinking that the kids were positively all settled down and he could go home. His sons had to be long crashed by now, and Merry didn't need him—really, she hadn't to begin with. She'd just seemed to need some temporary emotional reinforcement for a short stretch there.

His eyes focused. Refocused. Or tried to. No matter how completely he woke up, his mind kept coming to the same conclusion. If anyone took a picture of them, no one—no one, even a saint—could blame him for the current physical condition he was in.

Apparently he'd nodded off with his arms making a T across the back of the couch, his stocking feet cocked on the coffee table. He wasn't touching Mer. He wasn't touching anything.

Likely Merry had originally fallen asleep in an innocent enough position, but right now she was all curled up, one sock on, one sock off, facing the back of the couch. Somehow, at some time, she'd chosen to use his lap for a pillow, and then turned toward his stomach and scooped an arm around his back. Her cheek was nestled tight in the crease of his thigh—so tight he had no idea how she could breathe.

And that was interesting. And relevant. And arousing. But not as critically or immediately fascinating as the way her lips...as in, Merry's uniquely luscious, soft lips...were pressed right into his crotch. Heaven knew, Wilbur had risen to the occasion. Wilbur probably hadn't experienced this level of hardness in several years. Sure, he was always happy near a woman and had personally pleasured more than a few in recent times.

Hardness had never been a problem.

Getting enough, since the divorce, had occasionally been a problem. But that was just frustration. This was frustration, too, but at a whole new level. A fascinating level.

If he got any harder, he was going to break the zipper from strain.

Jack carefully, slowly, quietly reached over to scratch his chin. Broken zippers seemed the least of his problems. If Merry woke up and realized the position she was in, she was undoubtedly going to have a cow and a half.

If any of the kids woke up and saw her in this position, that wouldn't be too cool, either.

Jack told himself that this dilemma had one and only one cause. He'd mistakenly tried to be a nice guy. If he hadn't come over to help her, nothing like this could have happened. Now the situation had a lot of potential for becoming a downright mess. And who was to blame? Himself. For trying to help her to begin with.

On the other hand...he closed his eyes momentarily...there did seem to be an undeniable positive repercussion to all this messy chaos. Because the feeling of her face snuggled in his lap was damned close to ecstasy. Startling the holy hell out of him, though, was that even though the sensation was sexual—even ninety-five percent sexual—an eensy part of his response was simply...warm. The other kind of warm. The kind where it felt good to be in a protective role with a woman, to have a woman trust you enough to curl up all over you.

Not that he was falling for her.

That petrifying thought was so unsettling that he resolved to immediately get up and go home. That was the only conceivable resolution for this. Get the Sam Hill out of there. Quickly. Very quickly. At least any minute now...

OH GOD. WHEN MERRY OPENED one eye, pale predawn light silvered through a slit in the blinds. TiVo was playing yet another one of those beat-'em-up flicks where someone was hitting someone else every two minutes. In the meantime, bodies carpeted the entire breadth of the living room. No one looked alive, much less awake.

She checked the bodies to make sure the boys weren't too close to the girls, but it was okay. All of them were snuggled tight in their own sleeping bags in the cool of the early morning.

Which left her completely free to concentrate on Jack. Poor baby. He was going to be beyond embarrassed if he woke up and realized where—and how—he'd fallen asleep.

She had no memory of dozing off herself. She remembered his coming over, and what a mountainous relief she'd felt to have another adult there—particularly when the other adult was Jack. She knew she could immediately stop worrying, that he'd speak up and step in if he felt the mixed-sexes sleeping arrangement needed a fix. Heaven knew, the parents had been no help. They not only hadn't cared, they'd tended to laugh—either that or express complete confusion why she was calling. As if *she* were the old fogey and they were the with-it age.

But never mind that now.

Thankfully the couch was unusually wide, because otherwise two people couldn't possibly have stretched out without one ending up on the floor—like herself, since she was the one lying on the outside. Somehow Jack, even sound asleep, must have realized she could have fallen, because he'd pulled her into the spoon of his body, with one arm securing her tight.

All their clothes were on.

Except for her one sock.

But Jack's one arm had scooped beneath her side and come up to shape her breast. In fact, too exactly. Shape. Her. Breast. And his other arm was just kind of hanging over her, the weight of his wrist on her hip. Behind, she could feel the distinct shape of a hammer against the small of her back.

Well, perhaps it wasn't a hammer. But it was certainly hard enough to pound nails.

It wasn't his fault, she mentally told herself. Not that there was any fault or blame involved in this. It wasn't as if either of them had planned to fall asleep,

An Important Message from the Editors

Dear Reader,

Because you've chosen to read one of our fine novels, we'd like to say "thank you!" And, as a **special** way to thank you, we're offering you a choice of <u>two more</u> of the books you love so well **plus** an exciting Mystery Gift to send you — absolutely <u>FREE!</u>

Please enjoy them with our compliments...

Pam Powers

Lift here

The Editor's "Thank You" Free Gifts Include:

- **2 Romance OR 2 Suspense books!**
- **An exciting mystery gift!**

Yes! I have placed my

Editor's "Thank You" seal in the space provided at right. Please send me 2 free books, which I have selected, and a fabulous mystery gift. I understand I am under no obligation to purchase any books, as explained on the back of this card.

PLACE FREE GIFT SEAL HERE

ROMANCE
193 MDL EE3N   393 MDL EE4C

SUSPENSE
192 MDL EE3Y   392 MDL EE4N

FIRST NAME	LAST NAME

ADDRESS

APT.#	CITY

STATE/PROV.	ZIP/POSTAL CODE

Thank You!

The Reader Service — Here's How It Works:

Accepting your 2 free books and gift places you under no obligation to buy anything. You may keep the books and gift and return the shipping statement marked "cancel." If you do not cancel, about a month later we'll send you 3 additional books and bill you just $5.24 each in the U.S., or $5.74 each in Canada, plus 25¢ shipping & handling per book and applicable taxes if any.* That's the complete price and — compared to cover prices starting from $5.99 each in the U.S. and $6.99 each in Canada — it's quite a bargain! You may cancel at any time, but if you choose to continue, every month we'll send you 3 more books, which you may either purchase at the discount price or return to us and cancel your subscription.

*Terms and prices subject to change without notice. Sales tax applicable in N.Y. Canadian residents will be charged applicable provincial taxes and GST.

much less together on the couch. The question was simply what to do about it now.

If she could just get off the couch without waking him, he'd never have to know how intimately he was curled around her.

Not that she minded the curl. Or the hammer. Or the feel of him possessively cupping her breast like a lover. Or the smell of him, warm and male and sleepy. She was, she admitted to herself, slightly inclined to turn around and make the embrace become something actively invitational. The V between her thighs was damp and warm, her breasts tight, her pulse doing the manic dance. Oh yeah, she was totally in the mood.

For him.

Not for any guy. Just for Jack.

It was a relief to admit it, a little like sneezing for days in a row and finally accepting that this wasn't some little allergy but a serious cold. Maybe it wasn't all easy, good news. Still, her attraction to Jack from the beginning had seeds of more than just noticing he was one hot guy.

She wasn't about to use a four-letter word in front of the children—even if they were asleep, even if the word started with L. Still. She thought it as she slowly, carefully put one bare foot on the carpet. Then waited. Then slowly, carefully rolled down to the ground, letting his two hands drift loose, fall gently back to the couch.

Crouched on the carpet, she waited again. He hadn't wakened. Neither had the kids. She wanted to let out a noisy sigh of relief, but didn't dare. Instead, she crept out of the room, and then skedaddled down the hall to the far bedroom.

She had to scrounge to find fresh clothes. Her dad

had shipped more of her stuff from home, but she still hadn't found time to paint the walls or add her own furniture or organize. Shoes still spilled from boxes. Books still toppled from cartons. Spare-room stuff still hadn't found a place in the rest of the house.

For once in her life, she intended to settle. But it just seemed to take so much time, turning herself into the full-time mom of an eleven-year-old.

For now, though, she grabbed clean clothes and zoomed for the shower.

The hot spray helped wake her up, but even with soap in her hair and stinging her eyes, she remembered the feeling of Jack's hand on her breast, the weight and warmth of him snugged to her backside.

He'd come through for her yet again. Yeah, she'd been freaked at the boys who'd showed up for the sleep-over. And yeah, she'd really wanted his advice and perspective. But he never had to actually come over, sit there, spend the time to *be* there for her.

Moments later, wearing snug jeans and a tee and a towel wrapped on her head, she tiptoed back to the living room. One kid was staring bleary-eyed at the tube. The rest were still sleeping. The couch, though, was as empty as silence.

So he'd woken up and split fast, she mused.

But one of these days, Jack, you're not going to be able to escape fast enough.

The thought made her grin—even as she reconnoitered the devastation in the living room and wasn't sure if it could all get cleaned up in a month of Sundays. But post-party messes were just post-party messes. Nothing new. Houses survived them. If Charlene had had fun, it was worth the cleanup.

Jack was a different issue altogether.

That man, she thought, needed someone to love him. Not someone who'd use him or run roughshod over his giving nature, but a woman who'd strip off his cute, tidy button-downs and give him the motivation to really, really let go.

"Hey, Merry." The sleepy boy with fifty cowlicks finally registered that someone else was awake in the room.

"Hey, Quinn." But she was thinking: like *her*. Just maybe she was the ideal motivation to throw that man on a bed and really, really take him down....

As Merry pushed open the door to the mall, she wondered what she'd ever done to the Fate Gods to tick them off this badly. Lately nothing, but nothing, seemed to work out as planned. "Now, come on," she coaxed Charlene, who shot her a look as if crossing the mall threshold was as appealing as a case of malaria.

"I hate shopping. I don't want to shop. I don't need anything. I don't want anything." Charlie hesitated. "Unless we're going to the music store."

"And we are. As a reward for you—*after* we finish this."

Charlie made a sound, mimicking the moan of an animal in dire pain, but limped on through.

Merry recalled the week before, when she'd had such fabulous plans to jump Jack. Great plans. Big plans. Plans she'd expanded in her dreams, daydreams and the night version, all of which had added detail, action, and various imaginative variations that should certainly add something to the seduction.

But suburban Mom Life was more deleterious to

sexual adventure than anything she'd ever imagined. It had to be easier to seduce a guy on top of K-2. Or simultaneously while white-water rafting in a thunderstorm. Or in the freeway in broad daylight.

Moms had no privacy. No time in the day or night when either the kid or a call couldn't suddenly interrupt. There was ample free time, only none of it was *really* free. If she wasn't getting ready for another meeting with June Innes, then she was washing stinky soccer clothes and car pooling a group of preteens to the movies or chaperoning a field trip on a school bus. Every single activity related to mom-ming, as far as Merry could tell, seemed doomed to douse a girl's sexual drive.

On the other hand, this particular adventure wasn't so bad.

Shopping wasn't as good as sex. Or love. Or time for herself, or with an adult she cared about. But it was one thing that she most definitely knew how to do—and that meant, for once, feeling darn sure of herself for a change.

"Did Mrs. Innes say I had to do this? When she came over on Monday?"

"Nope." The meeting with June Innes had gone as well as the other ones.

The guardian *ad litem* had unshakeable ideas about what an eleven-year-old girl should and should not do. Nothing Merry said was right or valid or worth a jalapeño pepper. Anything Merry did was a ditto. Worthless. And yeah, those meetings kept weighing on Merry's mind—but this afternoon, that was all a "to hell with it."

She steered the reluctant turtle—the one all hunched over, illustrating severe depression and horror at being in the mall—toward the escalator.

"Look, Merry. There's a reason why I don't want to go to this dance. Maybe I forgot to tell you. I don't dance."

"Uh-huh. I know you think that sounds logical. But you haven't even tried dancing yet. For all you know, you could love it. It's very…athletic."

"But there's another reason."

"Uh-huh." At the top of the escalator, she herded Charlie toward the young teen section.

"This is the deal, Mer. The real deal. I like boys more than girls."

Merry lifted an eyebrow. "Join the club. Me, too. I'm pretty sure that's the way Nature set it up." There, she'd managed to startle Charlie. But only for a second or two.

"I don't mean *that* kind of liking. I mean there's a reason I don't like being around girls. It's because they're mean. They whisper and laugh behind your back. And they don't *do* anything. They talk about *jewelry*. And clothes. But it's not like they ever *do* anything, like, say, fix a carburetor. Or beat each other at World Triumph. And I don't take Trig yet, you know? Because I'm too young. But I think Trig problems are *interesting*. Not whether some girl ran up and kissed a guy after class. That's just such a yuck."

"Well," Merry said, "I admit I was one of those girls who obsessed all day long about movie stars and nail color and who kissed who. But that doesn't mean you have to like that or be like that." With an eagle eye, she scanned the racks. Then attacked.

Charlie wasn't the only one who could get into military terms. Merry understood missions just fine. The hunt, the recon, the attack, the never leaving a bad sale behind.

"Mer?"

"What, honey?"

"All the girls are *obsessing* about this dance. They're all so stupid. They're driving me crazy. And all they're talking about all the time is what they're going to wear. The dress. How much the stupid dress costs. Bras. Heels. I am *never* wearing bras or heels."

Merry tactfully didn't mention that especially one side of Charlene's chest was developing a noticeable bump. They'd handle the bra crisis when they came to it, and thankfully, that wasn't today. "Now, Charlie, try to trust me, just a little. I was never going to force you into stilettos. Clothes are the one thing I know. And we're going to find something that you really, really want to wear."

"Yeah. Like that'll happen." Charlie found a corner to heave herself into. "I don't see anything wrong with wearing my dad's old stuff. I'm proud of my dad—"

"I know you are. And I'm glad you are." But Merry was also conscious that June Innes was trying to draw a line in the sand about Charlene's attire, so it seemed as if this upcoming dance was the ideal opportunity to…well, to introduce something different. She *had* to find a way to get Charlene out of those clothes, or at least to wean her away from wearing the military things all the time.

Her theory was to give Charlene a sense of her own personal style. "In the dressing room, you," Merry ordered.

Charlie's jaw dropped when she saw the heap of clothes on Merry's arm. "You wouldn't make me try on all that stuff. I thought we were friends. I thought you liked me okay."

"Nah. I like torturing kids. It's my favorite thing. And I'm going to sit right outside, let you try these on yourself. But if you find anything—*anything*—you like, you can just open the door and let me see."

"I won't," Charlie assured her.

But just once in a rare while, life turned out the way it needed to.

For the first five minutes, all Merry heard from the other side of the dressing room door was a bunch of rustling and grumping. Then, more rustling—but without the grumping. Then—complete silence.

And then the door opened a crack, and Charlene's head peeked out, making sure no one was in sight before talking to Merry.

"All right," the kid said irritably, "maybe a couple of these clothes are okay. A little okay."

The look of her almost brought tears to Merry's eyes. Beneath the stupid brush cut and taciturn-neutral expression was such an adorable girl. Merry had easily found some military styles, because that look was in for the preteens—but these khaki pants actually fit Charlene's cute little butt. The cami, naturally, was already completely covered up by the pale green canvas shirt, so no hint of a developing figure was remotely revealed. But it still looked military. It had the brass buttons on the shoulders and pockets and all.

Merry stepped in, immediately turning into serious mode, perking up the collar, checking the length of the sleeves, thinking Charlie could wear variations of this to school and look *so, so, so* much more normal. But for now she just said, "The shirt kind of needs your dad's belt."

"His belts are too big," Charlie said.

Merry shook her head. "Not to wear at your waist. To wear on your hips at an angle." She looked into

Charlie's shy eyes. "I know you don't want to hear this, but you look really great."

There. A smile. One of those desperately unsure, desperately yearning, desperately vulnerable preteen smiles.

"Really, Charlie," Merry said. "I wouldn't tell you if it weren't true."

"Okay. I guess I could wear this stuff." God, the stress. Charlene sighed as if the weight of the world was pressed on her shoulders. "But that still doesn't mean I want to go to the stupid dance."

"Charlie." Merry crouched down, to be on eye level. "Listen to me. If you're telling me it's life and death, I won't make you go. But this is just a couple of hours. No biggie. I get it, that you think you're not going to like it—and maybe you won't. But how bad can a couple hours be?"

Charlene hesitated.

"Did you try on the dark green pants?"

"Yeah, they were okay, too. And that shirt—" She motioned to the off-white one. "That isn't too sucky, either."

Merry still hadn't heard an answer to the real question, though. "I'm serious, Charl. If this is that traumatic for you, I'll back off. I want you to go, but nothing's worth your being heart-and-soul miserable. If you tell me it's that bad, I'll shut up. I promise."

"For Pete's sake, you can detox," Charlene said sourly. "It's not *that* bad. I guess I could go. If I can leave *immediately* after two hours. No more. Not even a minute more."

They weren't, of course, done. Now that Merry had her size—and her number—she heaped items on the sales counter, paid for those, and then herded Charlene into just a couple more departments. Combat boots just wouldn't do. Neither would heels—not for Charlie— or even dress-up girl shoes. But the shoe department had to have something with a rounded toe that wouldn't look too bad under the pants.

And then, of course, came the hair crisis. The waxed brush cut looked terrible, Merry felt, but Charlene was hopelessly touchy about it, so she'd shut up. Now, though, she was determined to find some little magnet earrings in the shape of stars—like a general's brass stars. With a little jewelry, the hair could look a little punky, more like a style instead of so in-your-face-*guy*.

She found the earrings, but she had to pick them out herself, because Charlie balked at going inside the trendy kid jewelry store.

By the time they were done, Merry was yawning, ready for a good hour's nap, and her shoulders were creaking from the weight of all the packages. But man, had they done good.

Charlene was still arguing on the drive home. But not as much.

"Charlie, it's just not that bad." Merry, stopped at a red light, obeyed the kid's subtle directive to turn right. Who knew? "A dance is just an excuse for a group to be together, do something together. Everybody likes music, right? So. You go, you listen to some music, you drink some of the stupid punch or pop, and you stand around with your friends and watch everybody else. That doesn't sound so torturous, does it?"

"But I don't *have* a bunch of girlfriends to stand around with. And I don't want to stand by myself."

"Well, of course you don't. But what about all those

guys who came over for the sleepover? Can't you hang with some of them? They're probably worried about standing alone, too."

Charlie didn't say anything else until they pulled in the drive. "I didn't think about that. That I could, like, hang with Quinn. Or Bo."

"See? You'd be helping them, too, so they didn't have to worry about being alone."

"And Jack'll be there, right? So if anything happened, he could take me home. Even if you had to stay there because of being a chaperone and all."

As Merry scooped up all the packages, she glanced next door. There was no truck in the drive, so Jack wasn't likely home. She hadn't forgotten about Jack being conned into chaperoning with her, that she'd had every intention of letting him off the hook. The whole thing was crazy, his feeling obligated to attend a darn fool thing like this, but now…now, it seemed her thinking had changed.

Certainly there was no seducing a guy in front of a hundred eleven- and twelve-year-olds. In fact, there was nothing remotely suggestive or sexual she could imagine in those ghastly circumstances.

But they *would* be in the same place.

Desire was the creator of invention, wasn't it? Or maybe the quote didn't go quite like that. But close enough, Merry thought. If there was a way to get that man in trouble, she figured she could find it….

CHAPTER ELEVEN

JACK'S CELL BEEPED just as he was grabbing the keys to the truck. Because he was already running late, he wasn't inclined to answer it—until the caller ID identified Cooper. He most definitely wanted to talk to his son.

"Tell me again why the *hell* you think I should have to do this," he barked into the receiver.

"Now, Dad. That's exactly why I called, to coach you through this."

"I do not need coaching, you—" His son's sass damn-near made Jack chuckle. For a second. "Don't mess with me. Somehow you suckered me into going to a dance for a bunch of squirts. I did this when you and Kicker were this age, because that was the parenting thing to do. But this is not my child. Not my problem. And I can't remember why the hell you even wanted me to do this."

"Because Charlene's a good kid. Only she's kind of been lost since her dad died. And for this particular problem, you're really the only one who can help her."

"Yeah, like I believe that." Jack stomped out the back door and aimed for his truck. The night was blacker than tar and colder than a scorned woman, mimicking his mood to a *T*.

"Dad. From Charlene's point of view, she's gonna be embarrassed to death if Merry watches her every second. So you can help that, by diverting Merry's attention from watching her all the time. And Merry... she's just too young for this crowd, you know?"

"Too young for eleven- and twelve-year-olds?"

His son sighed, as if exhausted from the effort of communicating with him. "No. Too young for the parent crowd. The golf groupies. The fund-raisers. The Scout dads. Lots of the parents are okay, but she's still *single,* for Pete's sake. She's going to feel like a red flag in a forest. It'd help if she had someone to talk to, someone who didn't make her feel like she was the only lonely flag."

Damn kid. Jack was all calmed down even before he'd started the truck engine. "When did you get so damned smart, anyway?" he demanded, but the irritation was out of his voice. Coop knew it, too. But instead of his son responding, suddenly there was silence.

"I'm not smart," his son said.

As if someone punched paternal radar, Jack forgot his annoyance and honed straight on his son. "What's wrong?"

"Nothing. I hope," Cooper said. There was a sick note in his voice. Jack heard it.

"Hey," Jack said sharply, but his son signed off with the usual line about stuff to do/people to see. That was okay, but Jack clicked off the phone, determined this wasn't going to happen another time. The next time he could corner Cooper, he was going to sit on the boy if he had to, but one way or another he had to ferret out whatever was bothering him.

Right now, though, he had other crises on his table.

A sixth-grade dance. Holy hell. But he got it, why his sons wanted him to do this now. Damn good hearts, those boys. Kicker was a little irrepressible and impulsive, Coop too damned self-contained, and both of them total rock heads sometimes. But they did have good hearts.

Besides, he was stuck.

And it wasn't the worst thing he'd ever had to do... spend a couple hours near Merry.

As he walked in the school a few minutes later, he tugged the collar of his shirt, trying to breathe. The kids had tried to disguise the gym, which of course didn't work. A gym was always going to be a gym. But red lights flashed on the dark ceiling, red for Valentine's Day. Some dad had volunteered to be DJ and was choosing discs with a nice, solid, pounding beat. A table was set up with a punch bowl, another with cookies and various types of junk to eat. A line of kids hugged the wall as if glued there, anything to avoid getting on that dance floor and being exposed.

Jack tugged at his collar again, still getting a lay of the land as his vision adjusted to the Valentine-red cast on everything. At this age, most of the girls were taller than the guys, which meant if they *did* dance, the guy'd often enough be stuck staring at the girl's chest. If she had a chest. Which was pretty much nip or tuck with the eleven-twelve age group.

He didn't immediately spot Charlene—not because of the gloom—but because he instinctively searched the crowd for Merry. The instant he located her, he found his attention glued there and his feet hustling in that direction.

Damn went his heart. And his head.

Normally she seemed to dress like...well, he didn't

know what she dressed like. Herself, he guessed. Lots of free-spirited prints with dipping necklines, jewelry that danced around when she moved, pants that cupped her butt. Not tonight. He suspected she was trying to look like a proper chaperone type, and she did. The black turtleneck was plain, the skirt sedately swinging at midcalf. All that rich hair was snugged back with some kind of clip.

She was standing at one of the tables, feeding cookies to a tray. Some woman next to her was asking if she'd participate in a fund-raiser. The meetings were every second Monday. Breakfast. Racquet club. A great cause.

"I'd be happy to," Merry said. "But on Mondays, I'm already at the school for a mentoring thing they asked me to do—"

"But this is early. Really early. Before school starts."

"Well, I don't mind getting up, but the thing is, I drive Charlene to school, and—" And then she saw him. Damn woman. Her face tilted up, lit up. The smile flashed on brighter than straight UV. "No," she said, "you're going right home."

"Huh?" the lady next to her said, but Merry was already winging around the table, aiming straight for him.

"I can't claim I'm not glad you're here. I am. But honestly, Jack, you don't have to do this. I had no idea how bad this was going to be."

"You're saying the cookies are no good?"

"I'm saying that I wouldn't ask my worst enemy to do this with me. Truthfully I was looking forward to your being here—but that was before. Now I get the whole picture. And I may never recover from the guilt if you feel you have to stay."

She was so full of hell, she took his breath. Maybe she didn't have the free-spirit clothes on. But her lips were sex-red, her eyes smoky. And he didn't know perfumes, most of the time thought women wore too much of that stuff. But this one was wicked. And she just had a hint of it, around her throat, around her wrists, so that when she moved, he forgot his own name.

"Thanks," he said. "I confess, I'm not sure how long I'll last. But definitely I don't mind staying for a little while—"

"A little while'd be good. Even a few minutes would save me from the next rash of people asking me to do something for their cause. Everybody here has a cause. What is that? Don't women do regular jobs during the day?"

"They all did. But a lot of them dropped out of the workforce to do the parenting thing. Only they can't sit home or they go stir crazy, so they fill up on doing good stuff for the community."

"I *know* it's good stuff. I want to be involved. But if this keeps up, I'm going to be busier in Charlene's school than Charlene is. And I can't…oh my God, oh my God."

"What?" Merry's face had that look—that parent-look like when your toddler gets free from you for the first time and runs out in the road.

"Charlie. She was doing fine, staying over there with a guy friend. One of the boys who slept over, the computer geek with all the cowlicks. Only now she's on the dance floor. *My Charlie.*"

"And that's bad?"

"Bad or good isn't the point. She's with Dougall! Whitmore! The boy she beat up the first week I came here! I thought she couldn't stand him. And he's in eighth grade besides, so he must have come here with someone else, and oh my God—"

He sighed. That was exactly what Cooper coached him about—protecting Charlene from being hovered over. "C'mere."

"C'mere...where?"

"Dance with me."

"What?" She squinted as if he'd spoken in Japanese. "Did you say 'dance with you'? I didn't know you even danced."

He didn't usually. At least not unless he'd been liberally plied with liquor. But he couldn't disappoint the squirt, and God knew, his sons were going to put him through an inquisition on anything he did or failed to do. So he just hooked her hand and led her to the dance floor, then spun her around—an easy way to get her into his arms.

The kids all immediately gawked. Both those on the sidelines and those few on the dance floor. But he fixed it so that he could see Charlene—and she couldn't.

"Um, Jack?"

She looked...bemused. Not reluctant to be on the floor with him, not unwilling to dance. He figured Merry'd always be like that, willing to go with an impulse, happy to take on a dare. He wasn't sure how he knew that. It wasn't as if he knew her that well. But...those big, dark eyes had a natural dare-you devilment in them. The cock of her head, the tilt of her shoulders, hell, even the perkiness of her breasts, all had ample female chutzpah. She wasn't afraid of much, his Merry.

Not that she was *his* Merry. The thought just came to him that way. In the possessive. It wasn't his fault. That was how his brain had spilled it out.

"Jack…" she said again, as if aware of failing to catch his attention the first time. "You do know this is a fast song, not a slow one?"

"Well, yeah," he said. "But I don't do fast songs. You don't care, do you?"

"Um, no. This is just fine."

Maybe it was fine for *her.* But it was damned disturbing for him to be dancing with her at all. Naturally there was a ton of air space between their bodies. There were a bunch of impressionable kids here, for Pete's sake. None of his body touched hers…except for his hands snugged around her waist. And hers snugged around his neck.

Her fingertips were sort of…playing with him. The very tips of her fingertips sneaked under his hairline, tickled his nape, traced patterns in slow, sassy curves and angles.

Her eyes seemed to be playing with him, too. So did the moist, soft texture of her lips. And the tilt of her head. And her scent—that wicked, subtle scent—seemed to go straight as a bolt to his brain. Nothing was getting through but the sensory input from her.

One of her fingertips stopped teasing for a whole millisecond. "You know, I've been here for weeks now, and I still don't know what you do for a living."

"I'm a bureaucrat." The answer was rote. It was always the answer that made people stop asking. Right then, anyway, he was concentrating on keeping those careful inches of separation between their bodies. No body parts had better touch, or God knew what could happen. With all those kids around, he had no choice. He had to be relentlessly disciplined.

"So what does a handsome bureaucrat such as yourself actually do all day?"

"Answer phones. Push paper. Get a paycheck from the government."

"I so believe you," she murmured. Her fingertip resumed its wicked, tickling thing again. Enticing him. Muddling with his mind. "Let's try some easier questions. Do you work with lots of people or just a few? Do you have a good boss or a bad boss? Do you work with more women or more men?"

That finger of hers was going to get her in real trouble. "The office is big. But my stuff, I do alone. Sometimes, on a tough project, I'll add one or two others and form a team. Otherwise…there are people around. People to talk to if I'm bored. But I work independently."

"It must be like project work then."

"Yeah." How'd she figure that out?

"So you work all-out like a house afire…then that project's over and you get a break until the next one."

"Yes." She stopped with the finger for a second. He let out a sigh of relief. And while he was breathing, he caught a look at Charlene over at the far end of the dance floor. Something about the kid looked different. More like a girl. Sweeter. Cuter. A flush of color. And the boy she was dancing with…Jack's eyes narrowed. The kid had his hand on Charlie's back. Where it belonged. But a little low.

He swung his attention back to Merry. "So what did you do? For work or a career. Before you came here."

She hesitated. "I ran."

"Ran?"

"From job to job. I was never fired. I just…left. Any time I felt myself getting attached, getting tied down, I took off."

Alarm shot through his pulse. She hadn't done

anything but answer his question. But it wasn't the kind of answer she'd give a stranger. It was too honest. Too uncomfortable. "So I take it you don't want to be tied down?"

"That's what I told myself for years. But the truth, I think, is that I'd absolutely loved to be tied. I just couldn't let myself be…."

The song ended. She quit talking and dropped her hands from his neck. Talk about heartless. If felt as if the blood was being separated from his veins.

Hell. They hadn't remotely touched any critical body parts. There was just something about that woman that annihilated his previous conceptions about life, rational thinking, sanity—and that wasn't even counting what she did to his hormones. Furthermore, she'd opened a whole box of curious questions that she hadn't even started to answer—but temporarily, there was nothing he could do.

Some mother grabbed him and locked him behind a table, serving punch. She said the kids tended to spill less if the adults poured the cups. Merry took over the Valentine cookie table again, which was clearly an endless job, because kids that age could mainline a dozen at a time.

He assumed he'd get back to Merry quick enough, only things seemed to keep happening. The first was when two snot-nosed squirts tiptoed toward the back exit door—as if even the most brainless adults wouldn't guess they were sneaking out to smoke.

Right after he came back in, he aimed straight for Merry, only to see her hightailing it toward the dance floor. Initially he couldn't see why, but then the sea of bodies parted. Who'd have guessed pipsqueaks that young had a clue how to French kiss? But it was the behavior of Merry, The Morals Police, that completely charmed him. He had a long, lazy vision of her naked, wearing police boots and a holster, talking the criminal youngsters into behaving with her soft-spoken voice and big eyes.

And right after *that,* he heard some kind of scuffle on the side of the bleachers. Boys, after all, would be boys. Once the squabblers were separated, the chaperones all clustered in a frenzy to discuss their punishment, but overall, the two knock heads had only torn a shirt and bruised each other's egos. Add unpredictable hormones to too much sugar—and girls all dressed up—and naturally a few tempers were gonna fray. Jack told both boys to get a brain, keep a low profile and stay away from each other or he'd bash their heads for them.

Their beef was resolved easily enough, but then the chaperones had to get broken up before they talked it to death.

Finally he had a chance to search out Merry again—only to find her bearing down on Charlene. The kid was standing in the open doors, catching the fresh air, talking to the tall guy she'd been dancing with earlier. When Jack realized Merry was going to interrupt them, he finessed the bodies on the dance floor at a fast jog and did his job. Grabbed her. Swung her into his arms again.

"So…" he said. Which was all he could manage, until he'd rearranged her hands around his neck, and his around the flare of her hips again.

"Jack. It's a fast dance again."

He didn't explain, because there was no point in repeating himself, and by then he figured she knew the score. He didn't know how to fast dance and that was that. So he just did the sway thing. And so did she. Who cared what music they were playing anyway? "So why did you quit jobs if you liked them? I didn't understand what you meant, about leaving every time you got attached to something."

"I didn't understand it for a long time, either." She smiled at him. One of those smiles that went woosh to his brain. "You dance so darn well. It makes me think you'd make love the same way. Easy. No performance stress. Just…get into it…with all your senses. Heart, eyes, textures, smells, touches—"

He squinted down at her. "Mer…are you trying to drive me crazy?"

"Maybe a little. I just keep wondering…you must have noticed how this comes up, every time we're together? Pun intended. It's more than your spirit rising. So…are you going to take it the next step, or are you just gonna tease me to death?"

"Ms. *Olson,* there are *children* around here."

"None of whom can hear me. Neither of us are doing anything inappropriate."

"*You* are." Okay, maybe she wasn't physically. But she sure as hell was doing some illegal stuff with her eyes.

"All I did was ask you a question. If you don't want to make love with me, that's totally all right. We can just keep ignoring this…thing between us. I can do denial. There's no real reason we have to *do* anything about it, for heaven's sake—"

Jack would have answered her. He had no idea what he would have said, but he would have answered her. Only a woman's voice said, "Merry!" and suddenly a trio of moms were volunteering her to start the clean-up.

The dance was over?

How the hell could the dance be over? He just *got* there. He'd known from the get-go that every second of this evening was going to drag incessantly, and instead...he glanced at his watch. Three hours had actually passed. His eyes narrowed as he watched Merry blithely clap paper cups together and chuckle with the other women.

Unless he was mistaken, she'd just offered to sleep with him.

It was possible he was mistaken. Every time he was around her, he seemed to be so confused he couldn't see or think straight. But all the same...a guy could generally wake up from a coma, erect and ready, for the promise of sex. At least he could. If he wanted the woman.

And he sure as hell wanted Merry.

WELL, YOU COULD LEAD a horse to water, Merry mused, as she listened to Charlene's chatter on the way home.

And that's all she'd been trying to do. Lead Jack into thinking—about her, about them. A woman couldn't get what she needed or wanted in life by snoozing in the backseat. Not these days. And certain risks, Merry was willing to take. Certain hurts, she was willing to risk.

But at this precise moment, the opportunity to jump Jack seemed as remote as a trip to Tahiti.

"Dougall is so, so stupid," Charlene said, which was a refrain of the same song she'd been singing the whole drive.

"I thought I noticed you dancing with him several times?"

"Yeah, well. What we were mostly doing was arguing. About Space Zest. It's one of those world-building games," she added, as if knowing full well Merry wouldn't have a clue what the context of the name was. "I beat him. But he claims he got to a higher level. Like yeah, right. I know exactly how smart he *isn't* because I see him in math class—"

"I thought Dougall was in eighth grade."

"He is. Come *on*, Merry. You know I'm in the eighth-grade math class. And it's so much better. Because in my class, everybody was calling me a nerd. In the eighth grade, I'm not so far ahead so it isn't so embarrassing. Anyway, Dougall…"

Dougall took up another full fifteen minutes of dialogue—long enough to get them home, to get coats thrown on chairs and shoes shucked at the door and milk poured. The telephone rang just as they were headed back to Charlene's bedroom, annoying Merry no end. Charlene never opened like this, much less chattered like a nonstop magpie, so she hated interrupting it with a phone call.

More annoying yet, there was no one on the other end of the line. Or someone was *there,* but they didn't speak. Merry hung up, vaguely aware that the same thing had happened yesterday—a call where no one talked, just hung up—but it wasn't like it was a heavy breather or porn call. She put it out of her mind, caught up with Charlie in her bedroom, still carrying the glass of milk.

Charlie had already peeled off her dance clothes and pulled on the giant old T-shirt of her dad's that she slept in. Now she bounced on the bed and snuggled up, accepting the milk from Merry. Merry perched at the foot and kept on listening.

"So…like suddenly this girl walks up, all mad and

red in the face. Says, 'Hey, Dougall, you came with me, remember?' As if I were usurping her, you know? And yeah, he had to come with someone because otherwise he wouldn't have been at the sixth-grade dance, but it wasn't *my* fault he was talking to me. He started it!"

"So did you know the girl?"

"Oh, yeah, Tiffany. She isn't in most of my classes, but I still know her. She wears this color, like this blue-aqua. Because it's the Tiffany logo color, you know, like for the jewelry store. Does that tell you enough about her?"

"Oh, yeah." Merry wanted to bounce on the bed a few dozen times. The whole conversation was enough to bring tears to her eyes. They were having a real-life girl conversation. A bonding conversation. It felt better than winning the lottery.

"She has big boobs already. And a Tiffany bracelet. And she puts a lot of junk on her eyes. The guys all call her a slut-in-training." Charlie glanced at her with a pause, as if waiting for a scold on the *slut* word.

"That sounds pretty darn accurate," Merry said instead, but she was thinking how the whole Dougall thing was starting to add up. The fight. The hurt feelings. The denial. The explosion of excitement and conversation. Was there anything more painful than a first crush? And this whole outpouring affirmed that Charlie's style choices had nothing to do with gender issues but were just about her dad.

When she could get a word in, she tried to delicately bring up another girl subject. "Charlie…some of the moms were talking about bras. It seems a lot of girls in your class are wearing those training bras now, so I thought maybe—"

"Not me."

"All right."

"Every time I hear the term 'training bra,' all I can think of is 'what are we training?' Horses? I mean, how do you train boobs? Besides which, I'm not growing breasts. Ever."

Merry didn't say, you already are. But since they were already sneaking into mighty touchy waters, she tried, "Being at that dance reminded me of how I felt in sixth grade. It seemed right around then all my friends were talking a lot about scx...."

"My dad told me everything I ever need to know," Charlie said flatly.

Damn, Merry thought, she'd screwed up again. Charlene shut down faster than a slammed door. She didn't suddenly turn rude. That was never Charlene's way. She just finished her milk and answered any further questions in monosyllables and finally just said that she was "way tired" and wanted to crash.

Merry ambled out, climbed into a robe, washed her face and moisturized, then wandered back into the kitchen. She puttered around for a few minutes, too wired to sleep even though it was almost midnight. After a bit, she tiptoed back to Charlene's room, and found her dead to the world. She really *was* beat. Merry snuggled the blanket closer under her chin, turned off the bedside lamp, and then tiptoed back to the kitchen again.

She should go to sleep herself, she kept thinking. But her mind kept spinning over the night's events. So many things had gone well for Charlene tonight. It seemed she'd finally broken out of her shell, enjoyed the dance and the other kids—whether she realized it herself or not.

But every loving instinct in Merry worried that the child was still buried under her grief. She still hadn't cried. She mentioned her dad often enough, but usually as some kind of defense. There was pain there. Anger, too, Merry mused.

She'd already read a bunch of parenting books, and another bunch on grief and kids coping with grief. Wearily Merry leaned against the counter and closed her eyes. If it were another kid, she'd push harder for the counseling route, but darn it, Charl was one of a kind. She had her own way of thinking through things, and more complicated yet, she was smarter than most books and most people. What she needed...

Was a mom.

And that was the real problem. Merry just wasn't sure what a good mom would do in this situation. Charlie had never had an active mother—and Merry hadn't, either. So between the two of them, it was something like the blind leading the blind. She just wished there was some magic rule book so she could know if she were taking the right steps...or the wrong ones.

A knock on the door made her jump in surprise. Before she could possibly jog over to answer it, Jack bolted in. "Don't you ever lock your door? Ever in this life?"

Well. He was certainly in a fine mood.

"Aren't your boys home?"

"Yeah. They're sleeping like logs. Didn't even wait up to find out what happened tonight. How about Charlene?"

"She dropped like a stone."

"I saw your light on...."

She nodded, not unhappy he'd come over, just unsure what all the attitude was about. He stomped in like a bull who'd been cooped up for a couple of years with no fresh air, had a scowl on big enough to put the *O* in ornery. Something was sure wrong.

He peeled off his jacket, tossed it on the chair. It slumped to the floor. He didn't seem to give a damn.

"So I knew you were awake. And we sure as hell have a conversation to finish."

"We do, huh?"

"Don't you smile at me." A finger pointed at her, royal as a king's. "The only reason in *hell* I haven't jumped you was because I didn't think it was a good idea. For you."

"Oh," she murmured. "So that's what you're here for."

She told herself that she'd lost the mood. It's not as if she'd stopped thinking about Jack, stopped wanting to jump him, stopped wanting to push and see where the relationship could take them. But she'd just assumed there was no way to follow through tonight, after which she'd had absolutely nothing on her mind but Charlene....

She was sure of that. Absolutely sure.

Until she identified the look in his eyes. Even as he strode toward her, looking darker than thunder, crabbier than that cooped-up bull, she knew what he was going to do.

Probably before Jack did.

CHAPTER TWELVE

JACK SURE AS HELL hadn't stormed over here to touch her. Or kiss her. Or anything like that. He'd come home to his boys after that crazy kid dance, anticipating that both his sons would be up and dying to grill him in minute detail about the whole chaperoning thing. Instead, he'd found them snoozing up a storm, Kicker sprawled on the floor, Cooper splayed the length of the couch, the TV still on—as well as every light in the house, or close to it.

So big deal, he'd go to sleep, he told himself. Instead, he'd found himself pacing from room to room, hall to hall, aimless as a summer wind, restless as a storm. Eventually he found himself at the sink, glaring at the light across the yard in Merry's kitchen.

She was there. Moving around. Wide awake like him.

He certainly didn't intend going over there. It was midnight, for Pete's sake. He didn't do impulsive things. His life was as well ordered as a textbook, as mathematically organized as the puzzles he solved.

There was no cupid in his life. He wasn't the kind of guy to give Cupid or Chaos or Fate credit for anything that happened in his life. Responsibility was on him, period, and his goals and choices were crystal clear to him.

Or they had been until the damned woman moved next door. He'd analyzed it until he was blue in the face. Possibly her mouth had some intoxicant genetically ingrained in her lips—a drug, like one of those exotic plants in the rain forest. Only rarer. The kind of thing where you could die if you couldn't have it, even if you'd never wanted it and never heard of it. And it could even look like the weed. It could look like something you *totally* knew better than to touch.

Not that her lips looked like weeds. It was just so difficult for him to understand how or when or why he'd become so addicted to being with her. She was too young for him—maybe not in years, but in maturity. And for that reason alone, Jack knew he couldn't possibly be knocking at her door past midnight for no good reason whatsoever.

Furthermore, once he'd barged in and found her leaning against the counter, in bare feet, wearing some kind of girly, pink fuzzy robe with white cream on her nose, you'd think he'd get some sense, wouldn't you? Wouldn't anyone?

Yet he heard himself say gruffly, "I just don't think it's a good idea. That's why I haven't jumped you. Trust me, that's the *only* reason I haven't jumped you."

And then he jumped her. Walked right in, left the door hanging open—which should have set off some loud internal alarms that he was picking up her bad habits. But the warning just didn't take. Next thing, he framed her face and took her mouth. Hard and completely.

He meant to stop. He'd never pushed himself on a woman, couldn't imagine it, had every intention of backing off and then apologizing up the wazoo…but he kept waiting for her. He intelligently assumed that she'd perk up with a clear *no*—or else have the brains to smack him upside the head.

Instead she made a winsome, yearning sound, as if all this time, she'd needed him desperately. His lips sank in, feeling cushioned by her endless softness. Her arms folded him in, folded him up. His mind…who could explain the inexplicable? Merry just completely sucked him into her vortex. It wasn't his fault. She was the wild one.

"Hey," she murmured. "I'm right here. Take it slow."

That voice of hers…she sounded as if she were nurturing someone, being careful with someone who was coming apart at the seams.

Not him.

That wasn't anyone remotely like him. Jack never had a needy bone in his body and sure as hell didn't plan to take up neediness at this late date.

Her fuzzy robe peeled off. Beneath was nothing but her warm skin, smelling of some kind of warm lotion. The scent reminded him of summer rain, and the texture of her skin under his hands… God. Nothing was this soft. His palms whiskered over her arms, shoulders, back, sides, anywhere, any how he could touch.

And Merry, darn her, didn't have the protective instinct of a goose. He wanted to growl. Even his thoughts came through his head in growls. She just gave and gave and gave, as if she had an inexhaustible well of sensuality and warmth and giving. And heat.

Talk about *heat.*

"Good grief, Jack," she murmured again. "How long since you've done this? Years?"

She had him *so, so* wrong. She was the one broadcasting needs in silk whispers. She was the one who was speeding this up completely out of control. She suddenly loosed free from a kiss, tugged at his hand.

"Not here," she said softly. "Charlene sleeps really deep, but I still don't want to risk her waking up and finding us."

"Your room," he agreed. But his head was so thick he couldn't remember where the master bedroom was, even though he'd been in the house tons of times when Charlie was alive.

"I sleep in the far spare room," she murmured.

Thankfully she was coherent enough to offer that information, because he sure wasn't. She was so hot, so ready. Any place would do, as far as he was concerned— as long as they could get there within the next ten seconds.

A phone rang somewhere. Hers. His mind registered that only emergencies tended to call this late, but the ringing stopped after a couple of peals. Wrong number maybe. Whatever. Wherever the spare room was, he didn't know. He found a room with a door, got her behind the door, closed it, punched the latch, and then focused on what mattered, which sure as hell wasn't doors and phones and life.

It was her.

Damned if he knew where they were. Some place with a floor instead of carpet and a ton of sweet darkness, not a hint of light, nothing to distract his concentration. His mouth leveled hers again, sweeping the texture of her, sailing on the taste of her, drinking her in every which way, his hands just as busy. Her breasts were so nubile, plump, not huge, not small, just so damned perfect. And she sucked in a hoarse breath as if no one had touched them the right way before.

It was hard to work up any performance anxiety when she was this easy to please, this readable. He had no problem understanding what needed to be done. Her body begged to be treated with tenderness and reverence.

Still it was hard to reach where he wanted, with both of them standing up, so he lifted her up. She let out a low squeal of laughter when her fanny plunked down. "You *do* know where we are, right? That's *cold*," she murmured, her whisper full of laughter.

He startled momentarily, trying to decipher what she was talking about, but she wound her arms around him and honed in for another kiss, the greedy woman. "Okay, you," she said possessively. "Speed's okay. Wild's okay. We'll get a little fancier another time."

She made it easy for his mouth to reach her breasts, to find a way to nuzzle, snuzzle, lavish attention on both. Easy to glide his palms up her sides, up, until her hands reached high in the air, and then came down to him yet again, lassoing him softer than petals.

Fingers pulled off his sweatshirt.

He yanked free the snap and zipper of jeans himself, and then the height wasn't right. He needed light to see, but the room was chimney-black and he had no idea where a light was. If he'd thought about it, he'd likely realize where they were, but he just didn't need to think or care about irrelevant issues like that. There was a relevant crucial issue that mattered right then—getting inside her. Initially she was perched too high, so he eased her toward him, slid her down the length of him.

Agony tasted just like that, her earthy groan blending with his, at the sensation of her bare breasts against his bare chest, her tummy against his abdomen, her soft fluff of down against the rougher hair on his upper thighs. Oh, yeah, and Wilbur, weaving around like a thick, drunken pointer gone amok.

It was pretty rude, to be constantly pointing at what it wanted, but Wilbur, for damn sure, never had a problem with indecision. It wanted her. Now. Ten minutes ago. Forever. To be immersed tight inside her.

To do that, though, it seemed he had to lift her up against the wall. Thankfully, there was a wall. Right. There. Right where he could lift her, where she could wrap her legs and arms tight around him, where she could duck her head and let all that silky, lustrous hair sweep around his cheeks as he impaled her deep and slow and completely.

If he could just die this way, he'd never ask for another thing.

Ever.

This was it.

All he wanted.

This was as good as it ever had to get—the feeling of her surrounding him. Her whispered voice, her breath, her vulnerable mouth.

He didn't want this to end, didn't want his body to go into the piston thing, but Wilbur wasn't into savoring frustration the same way he was. Jack had a tearing sensation the roof was coming off his mind altogether, no brain left, now or ever, and he didn't miss it even remotely.

"So beautiful," he said thickly. "So beyond beautiful. Love you, Merry. Love you, love you…"

As if he'd shot her an infusion of power, she tightened around him, her throat bared, a shudder of bliss erupting from her in a low, fierce moan. That was all he could hold back. He let loose in a torrent, pumping out gallons, holding her, owning her—and for damn sure, being owned by her the exact same way.

And then it was over, the rush, the frenzy, that wild climb and claim. He kissed her a dozen times, but could feel his legs start to give out...and awareness start to seep in.

He was too damn old to make love against a wall. Worse yet, he had a horrible feeling they were in a laundry room.

They couldn't be, of course.

He'd never have done that to Merry. Hell, he'd had no finesse when he was nineteen, and he still wouldn't have done that to her back then. At his youngest and brashest, he'd understood—and valued—that a woman needed time, subtlety, tenderness, and maybe even some plain old charm.

Wherever they were, though, he did have to release her, let her stand on her own feet. It was either that, or cave in a puddle somewhere around her ankles. So he freed her, yet still couldn't let her go, holding her close, arms wrapped tight, his head against her head, eyes closed.

"Jack," she whispered.

"I can't talk. And I can't open my eyes. Because if I do and find out I made love to you in a laundry room, I'm going to have to hit myself with a brick."

A gurgle of laughter. "We could have picked a more comfortable place, couldn't we?"

We? It was up to the guy to pick the place, for Pete's sake. To make sure it was good for the woman. To take responsibility.

"Merry." She was already swayed against him, but

now he clutched her tighter than glue. "Tell me you're on the pill."

"I'm on the pill."

"No. I don't mean tell me what I want to hear. I mean tell me for real if you were protected."

"Yes."

Silence. It was still so hard to breathe, to catch his breath, when all he wanted was to be buried inside her for another few years. On a mattress. Not standing up. In a nice warm bed with a pillow. Not in a room with barely a window and no carpet and nothing but sharp, cold edges—except where she was. "Um, I'm trying to think if there's anything else I could possibly have done wrong," he said. "But as far as I can tell, I did everything as wrong as you could get."

"No." There. She reared back her head. All that mussed, tangled sleepy hair. The eyes dark as midnight, the skin white as moonlight. "You did everything perfect. Trust me on that."

He touched her cheek. No matter what she said, he knew perfectly well they'd been on a runaway train and now they were in a crash. He couldn't take her to bed. Couldn't even stay much longer because of the child in her house—and for damn sure, he couldn't take her to his place with the boys sprawled all over the living room. In the meantime they were freezing and naked—or mostly, he still had on socks—in her naked-windowed laundry room past midnight.

Oh, yeah. This could get worse. He just didn't know how.

"I don't want to go home," he said fiercely.

"I know you have to. Just like I couldn't have you

waking up here with Charlene. It wouldn't be right. It's okay, Jack."

No, it wasn't. Nothing was right. Those vulnerable eyes suddenly communicated a little embarrassment, a little shyness. And a few moments before, she didn't have an inhibition in sight, but now she seemed in a hurry to drape a towel around her—a natural enough instinct, with a chill draft shooting under the door—but that wouldn't have been an issue, if he'd just had the prowess, the taste, the sensitivity to make love to her the right way to begin with.

"Thanks for chaperoning with me," she said when he was finally at the door, wearing most of his clothes. He thought.

Chaperoning. Oh, yeah. They'd done such a good job...until they'd gotten home, and then there'd been no one to chaperone him.

THE NEXT MORNING, Merry didn't sing in the shower, because Charlene was still sleeping. But she turned off the faucet, grabbed the towel, boogie-woogied herself dry, danced into the bedroom, and mimed some exceptionally fine moves as she chose what to wear. Life, dag-nabbit, was good.

Okay, beyond good.

No question that she'd been off her feed lately. Not depressed, exactly, but feeling regularly overwhelmed by the problems surrounding her. Charlene, not bonding. Charlene, still not really accepting her dad's death. Herself, not easily finding a way to fit in this alien land of suburbia. Herself, still failing to convince June Innes she was a fit guardian—and not so sure she was besides. Herself, trying to become a sedate house owner and staid community participant and teenage-chaperone overnight.

But some of that stuff was always going to take time to sort out.

She picked out jeans with a heart on the right butt cheek, a pink ruched top, a major push-up bra, then—and just for the hell of it—jumped on the bed to do a few more dance steps as she put it all on. Goofy, yes. But what was wrong with being singing-irrepressible on a fine, fine, sunny morning like this?

He said he'd loved her.

In fact, he'd said it and said it. In the middle of sex, of course. And men, being men, were completely brain dead during sex. But all the same...he'd *conveyed* it—in how he'd made love. In how he'd touched her, in how upset he'd been that he'd failed to remember protection ahead of time, in how he'd failed to set them up in a more romantic environment than the laundry room—which still made her want to laugh.

Romantic wasn't a *place*. Romantic was a man who came apart at the seams for you. A man who wanted you so much he forgot he was one of those fussy-engineering-mind types. A man who just seemed to get lost in being with you. A man who needed, so much, so sweetly, that he made you feel as if you were his whole world.

The phone rang—the land line. And though Charlie could usually sleep through anything—and did—Merry bounced off the bed and charged for it, just in case. She was overdue a call to her dad and sisters, although the time change usually meant it was easier to connect early evening than now.

She grabbed the line in the kitchen and said a breathless, "Hello?" just in time to hear the click of a hang up. What, this was surely the third time in the last two days?

Whatever. A crank caller wasn't likely to spoil her dancing-on-air mood or morning. Whistling silently, she finger brushed her damp hair and debated breakfast choices. The living room was a wee bit trashed, ditto for the kitchen table and counters. Sometime today, she had to turn into Merry Maid again and do the cleaning thing, because June Innes was due for her weekly stop by tomorrow. But right now...

Pancakes.

Decadent pancakes with blueberries and whipped cream.

Yes.

Better served with Jack. In fact, better served on top of Jack and licked off. But that not being an immediate option, she hunted up a bowl and the stuff for a batter and dug in.

Just as she was measuring milk, she heard the knock on the door and yelled out, "Come on in."

She would likely have smiled for anyone, but about the last person in the universe she expected to poke his head in was Jack's son. "Hey," Cooper said awkwardly. "Oh. I see you're in the middle of making breakfast. I don't want to bug you—"

"You're not bugging me, silly. Come on in." She took another careful look at him. She liked both Jack's sons, but it wasn't as if they regularly popped over to visit. The twin thing fascinated her, although there was certainly no challenge telling the two boys apart. As similar as their physical traits, their temperaments affected their expressions and actions. She didn't have a favorite, but knew she had a tiny softer spot for Cooper. It wasn't because she liked him more or less than his brother; Cooper just struck her as more vulnerable. Kicker was so easy in his own skin. Coop reminded her of how miserable it was to be an adolescent. And both boys were so great with Charlene that she'd have loved them to bits for that alone. "If you needed Charlie for something, I'm afraid it was a pretty late night for her, and she's still konked out—"

"Didn't come here to see Charlie. Dad and Kicker are both sleeping, too. And that's why I thought I could maybe find you by yourself for a couple seconds. I just was hoping to talk to you about something."

"Sure." Again, she shot a look at him. Coop had never struck her as shy so much as contained, one of those deep-waters kids. Her dad would have said that he was the kind "who didn't show his cards." But right now he was sure playing a nervous hand.

He was rocking back and forth on his heels, edgy as a hedgehog, meeting her eyes, then shooting his gaze around the room, not coming in, not going out, the worried furrow between his brows deeper than a ditch. She couldn't imagine what was on his mind. "Hey, you know me. At least you know me well enough to be sure I don't bite," she said gently.

"I know, I know. That's why I wanted to talk to you."

"Sometimes when you can't get something out, the only way to do it is just spill."

"I'm trying. Believe it. It's just…"

"You want some coffee or juice or milk?"

"I need this to be between you and me."

"Got it." Or she got "it" enough to recognize swiftly that there was something serious going on for Coop.

She glanced down, saw the first round of pancakes were already black-burned and started to smoke, and turned off the stove.

"I've got a real worry, that's all. A private worry. Something I need to ask a female about." He cleared his throat. "A woman-aged female."

"Okay."

"The thing is…how late is really late?"

"Huh? Oh." Sometimes she needed a slap upside the head to get an innuendo, but this sure wasn't one of them. He meant period-late. As in unprotected sex. As in he obviously had a girlfriend.

She splashed coffee in two mugs, turned off her cell phone and motioned him to the stool across the counter, thinking *eek.* She was honored Coop believed he could come to her with a confidence, but this was such an *ohmygod.* She'd just made love with Cooper's dad, for heaven's sake. Was barely, nominally coping with Charlene. So poking her nose in something as intensely serious as Jack's son's private sex life seemed like a major bad idea…but she couldn't very well *not* help. So there it was.

"Well, flat out, Coop…girls your age," she said tactfully, "aren't always as regular as clocks. What that means is that a period is often not predictable. But it also means that there isn't any totally safe time to have sex without protection."

"It was just the one time." Cooper could have bored holes in the counter, he was staring down so hard.

If he were just a little smaller, she'd have scooped him on her lap and given him a hug. Unfortunately this was a grown-up problem, even if he was still a boy. "I'm afraid it just takes one time."

He lifted worried brown eyes. "We didn't mean for it to happen. I swear. I'd have bought protection if I thought it was going that far. At least this fast. I mean, yeah I hoped. How was I not supposed to hope? I like her. She's hot. It's really going good with us. But I just thought…sometime. Not this fast. But it just seemed to…happen."

Worse and worse, Merry thought. Not that he'd said it, but she was pretty sure this was likely his first time, and the girl's, too. "How late is she, Coop?"

"Six days, four hours, three minutes." He sighed. "She called, just before I came over here. I can't eat. Can't sleep." He wiped a rough hand over his face. "I knew I could ask you. That you wouldn't yell at me."

He had that right. Merry didn't know how Cooper sensed it, but she was incapable of abandoning anyone, come hell or high water. And for damn sure, not a vulnerable kid. "Okay, well, first things first. She needs to buy a pregnancy test. They're about twenty bucks, give or take. She pees on a stick first thing in the morning. At least, that's how I've heard most of them work. It turns color if she's pregnant. Then you two would know what you're dealing with."

"Would she know this quick? Just a week late?"

"It's not by how late. It's by how pregnant. Or not." He looked at her blankly. She tried again. "The test doesn't measure how late her period is. It just measures whether she's pregnant. And Cooper, she needs to do that test. Quickly. Don't wait. No matter what you two decide after that, first you've got to know what's what."

"She isn't as upset as me." Those sick eyes looked at her. "Merry, don't tell my dad."

She could have smelled that coming. Cripes, he might as well have clamped her heart in a corkscrew and twisted. "If she's not pregnant, you won't have to tell your dad. Part of this isn't about your dad, anyway. If you're going to be sexually active, you need to get protection and use it. Every time."

"But if she *is* pregnant…"

Merry squeezed her eyes closed, thinking man, this was not a fun conversation. "Then you'll need to tell your dad yourself."

"But *you* won't say anything to him, right? Promise me?"

Her life had been so much easier when she quit any and everything every time she wanted at the drop of a hat. Hell's bells, there was no way she could keep something this important from Jack. It was dead wrong, even if she hadn't been sleeping with him, even if she hadn't fallen exasperatingly, deeply in love with him. To not share something this important, affecting his son's future? "You won't have to worry about me telling him, because if it comes down to it, *you'll* tell your dad," she said to Cooper. "You know you can. You know he'll be there for you—"

"Hey," said a sleepy voice from the doorway. Both of them whirled around to see Charlene wandering in, her blond hair all cowlicky, eyes still blurry with sleep. "What are you two talking about? What's going on, Coop?"

All right, Merry thought. Clearly she was doing something really, really wrong with her life. It wasn't as if she'd never slept with a man before, but it had never been remotely this complicated. She'd only made love with Jack last night. One time. *One* time. Yet less than twelve hours later, his kid had embroiled her in his life and secrets, and now Charlene had gotten wind of a problem, and her heart was being strangled in confusing loyalties.

What really killed her, though, was that there didn't seem to be a single easy answer in sight.

When she'd moved here a month ago, she'd felt more alone than she ever had in her life. To save Charlene from being abandoned, it seemed as if she was stuck feeling completely alone and abandoned herself.

But there was a difference. Maybe all these problems were new and complex and forcing her to face uncomfortable issues in her own history. But Jack loved her. And no matter how many overwhelming problems life had thrown at her lately…knowing she was loved was incredibly empowering.

She had no idea what she was going to do yet. But it amazed her how much stronger she felt, just from being loved.

CHAPTER THIRTEEN

JACK PUNCHED DOWN a load of sweatshirts and jeans in the washing machine, pressing the cell phone to his ear at the same time. "So," he said. "This is Sunday. Almost noon. And you're just getting around to telling me now that you need me to keep the boys all next week."

Maybe he was talking to Dianne, but he was thinking about Merry. He did *not* love that woman. Every damn dream had been dominated by erotic moments with her. Every damn waking moment seemed consuming with fretting what kind of trouble she was going to cause him now. Possibly guilt was eating him alive for seducing her without protection—a mistake he'd never even made as a brash teenager when his entire brain supply had been located behind his zipper. Never. *Never* had he risked a woman and a pregnancy over his own self-ishness.

It was *her.* She did some kind of spell thing to him. She'd turned him into a stranger to himself. She sneaked under his skin like a sliver. Or an infection. Or a contagious disease.

Worst of all, he couldn't wait to see her again.

Jack knew damn well he needed help. Maybe he needed drugs. Anti-psychotics? Maybe there was some kind of psychologist where a therapist knew how to slap some sense into a man?

"Yeah, yeah," he said to Dianne. "I've heard it all before. Something just came up with your job. Nothing new about that, and you know damn well I want the kids. But you ever heard of a little notice? Yeah, they're already here this weekend, but I'll still have to drive into D.C., get more clothes and stuff for them, get back here, commute 'em to school…it's not as if this is nothing to arrange. Why is it you can never give me some notice?"

He believed in keeping things civil with his ex. Normally it wasn't that hard. He didn't give enough of a damn to argue with her anymore. But he knew better than to play it nice all the time, because that just encouraged her to be more demanding. His time was worth zero. Hers, everything.

"Yeah, well, you could drop their clothes and books here. Instead of expecting me to do it."

Certain kinds of women turned men tough and mean, he thought darkly. But as he walked into the kitchen, he momentarily forgot Dianne when he glanced out the sink window.

Two heads were visible in Merry's kitchen, one blond, one brunette. His attention riveted on Merry, as she reached over, lifting a hand, clearly intending to hug Charlene…but Charlene jerked back. The slim arm with the wild red fingernails just hung there in space, when Charlene darted out of the room.

That damned kid was breaking her heart.

Not that he cared. Not that he loved her. Because he didn't.

"Of course you can talk to the kids. Cooper!" He

traipsed out of the kitchen, through the living room, the
bedrooms. Eventually he located Kicker—who'd been
known to take showers longer than most people
napped—in the bathroom and said "talk to your mother."

Unfortunately it wasn't that easy to relinquish the
phone.

"You've lost Cooper?" Dianne demanded. "You
mean you don't know where our son is?"

Talking to her had a lot in common with dusting.
What was the point? It just came back. It's not as if you
ever solved anything. Besides, by the time he stalked
past the kitchen window again, he saw Cooper.

Coming out of Merry's house, for Pete's sake.

"Hey," he said when the back door opened. "I was
looking for you. Your mom's on the phone. Wants to
talk to you. Kicker's got it in the far bathroom."

"Okay," Cooper said and aimed in that direction, but
not before Jack caught a good look at his face.

Big circles under the eyes. No direct eye contact.
And the kid was rubbing the back of his neck, like a
world of tension was balled between his shoulder
blades. Something was with that boy—the same something that Jack had been trying to get out of him for days
now. A couple weeks even.

And now he'd been over at Merry's house? For what
possible reason?

The kids talked to their mother for a blue moon. He
had ample time to start the dishwasher, heap his brief-
case full of work for the next day, haul clothes from
the washer to the dryer. Kicker wandered in first,
flanked by Coop. Both of them beelined for the fridge,
and came close to emptying it in thirty seconds flat.

"Dad, we gotta go home. Get a bunch of stuff if

we're staying with you this week. Mom said she told you. She's, like, gone already, but I got the number where we can reach her," Kicker said.

So, Jack thought. Same old bullshit. She'd conned the boys into believing it was okay for him to make the long drive to pick up their things. She was so good at that bitch stuff she could give lessons. Come to think of it, she had. To him. He opened his mouth to answer Kicker, but then Cooper interrupted.

"Hey, you didn't tell us how the chaperoning thing went last night."

"I would have, if you two hadn't been sound asleep when I got home."

"Well? 'Fess up. Did you save Merry from the monsters?"

"Monsters?" Jack said.

"Yeah. The other parents."

All right, he had to chuckle. "She did fine. And for the record, she didn't remotely need me there."

"Maybe not *need,* but I'll bet she was glad you were there. You're not still mad we made you go, are you?" Kicker asked, as he leveled the half quart of milk still left—in a single gulp. Then popped the carton on the counter and smashed it, leaving spits of milk all over the counter and wall. Jack sighed. He'd never minded those kinds of messes. Until he had to clean them up himself.

"No. I'm not mad."

"See, Dad." Cooper dug a fist into a cereal box. Jack knew damn well he was going to empty the whole thing. "Do you get what we were trying to tell you now? That there's a difference between Merry and the women you usually go out with."

"Let me guess what the difference is. That I'm not going out with Merry?"

"Very funny. No. The difference is she's nice. And they're not."

"Yeah," Kicker agreed. "Sometimes you pick a babe. But they're all into themselves, you know? They're not looking at *you*, Dad."

Naturally, the boys thought they knew everything. He'd known everything when he was fifteen, too. Listening to their advice on his love life, though, struck him as pretty close to slapstick. Particularly when they could be right. His failure in the love wars was loud enough to be legend.

But where the boys thought he should climb back in the saddle, Jack figured that a guy who was tone-deaf should permanently give up aspiring for a career in music. He'd tried to explain that to them before, but somehow they got confused with the metaphor.

"If we have to drive all the way into D.C. today— you guys better get your butts in gear. And, Coop—"

"What?"

"How come you were over at Merry's?"

"Merry's? Oh. I was trying to talk her into marrying you, Dad." Coop clapped a hand on Kicker's shoulder, inviting him to share the big joke.

All right, Jack thought. Another secret the kid was keeping from him. Of course, no fifteen-year-old told his parents everything; they'd be crazy to expect it. Or to want it, for that matter. Jack figured he'd worm it out of Merry the next time he saw her, anyway.

And one way or another, living next door, of course they'd see each other soon. Unavoidably. He only wished he'd had the intelligence and wisdom to remember that—before he'd slept with her.

MERRY STOOD IN FRONT of her closet, something she'd done a zillion times since she'd reached thirteen. The debate was what to wear for the parent-teacher conferences this afternoon. She cocked her head this way, then that.

Unlike in all the earlier years of her female life, the only choice here was really jeans or…jeans. Sweatshirt or T-shirt.

Dangles and spangles weren't exactly required for a suburban mom. Neither were kicky shoes or glitter cream for her shoulders or pouty lip gloss. In less than two months, she'd gone from actively young and selling-it-vibrant to a life where a push-up underwire bra was optional.

On the other hand, she'd have been happy to revert back to her natural self for Jack…presuming, of course, they ever had two minutes alone together again.

She yanked on jeans and a long-sleeved tee—the blue one—and told herself that enough was enough with the pining. She'd just really wanted to see him yesterday, that was all. Obviously he'd had something he had to do with the boys, because she'd seen his truck pull out around noon and not return until after dark.

Just because they'd made love didn't mean she expected him to dance attention on her.

It was just…that connection had been so special. So not even having the chance to squeeze in a hello really pinched. It was time, though, to get the Sam Hill over it.

"Charlie? I'm leaving for school. It should take a couple hours—"

"I told you you didn't have to go." Charlie yelled the answer from her room, where she was nose deep in

some computer game, thrilled to have no school because of the parent-teacher conference.

"I know I don't *have* to."

"I'm getting As. You know that. So it's a total waste
of your time."

"Uh-huh. You told me." In Charlie's doorway, she
smooshed on some lip gloss and zipped up her jeans
boots. "Hey, maybe you could teach me to play that one
game after I get back."

"Yeah. Like you'd like this."

"Hey, just because I'm not a techie doesn't mean I
don't like games. I—" The land line rang. She chased
it down in the kitchen—so she could grab her keys and
XOXO bag at the same time.

"Hello?" She sighed. "Okay, I've had enough. That's
about the fifth time," she told the silence in the receiver.
"A little of this goes a long way. Quit it or I'm calling
the phone company." She clipped it down hard enough
to convey the message. One or two times could have
been accidental, but now there'd been too many of the
silent calls. It had to be a prank.

"Leaving, Charlie," she sang out, and then zoomed
to the school.

Her Mini Cooper readily found a parking space,
although her baby was completely hidden behind
SUVs. Still, once inside the school, she thought she'd
done a fair job at fitting in. Maybe she was a little
younger and not wearing any alligator labels, but she
had the rest of the uniform right—jeans, boots, tee, ski
jacket.

The parent was supposed to follow their kid's
schedule. Charlene's first class was Mr. Morann's, so
that was where Merry hung out in line first. Dialogue

between the moms covered dinner, cheating husbands, the sale at Kohl's, the best divorce lawyers, how to get your kid into an Ivy League school, and the price of nannies. Most of the faces and personalities were familiar now, or starting to be. The women tried to include her in the chitchat—good thing, since it was a long wait.

Mr. Morann was a tiny little bug of a guy, who wore a checked shirt and glasses that kept slipping down his nose. He taught social studies and history. "And you're here…why?" he asked her in true absentminded professor manner.

"I'm Charlene Ross's guardian. I'm been with her since her dad died. I just wanted to know how she was doing."

"She's gotten all As from the day she walked in. There's nothing new."

Getting any more out of him was like pulling teeth, but Merry had high hopes for the math teacher, because he was Charlene's favorite. And the guy did enthuse. "God, she's smart. You dream of teaching kids like Charlene. She just takes it in like a sieve. I can't challenge her enough. She just saps it up."

"That's great to hear. How does she get along with the rest of the kids?"

He blinked. "Well, fine, I guess."

So…he didn't really know. After that came the gym teacher, Mrs. Butterfield, who bounced a basketball around the gym as she talked. "Charlene's not real athletic, but she never shies away from trying. Good kid. I know she's more brains than muscles, but she always tries."

"The other girls are okay with her?" Merry asked. "Have you noticed the kids she hangs with?"

"Well…she's not in one of the 'in' groups. She tends

to separate herself from groups, in fact. But I've never seen her look real unhappy or anything like that."

Merry thought, maybe the gym teacher had been raised on a different planet than she had, because that sure wasn't reality as she remembered it. Eleven years old, and you *had* to hang tight with someone or have a best friend in the wings, or for darn sure you felt the pain.

The last teacher, finally, sounded tuned to Charlene the way Merry hoped. The subject was English, not Charl's strength. But Merry took one look at the teacher—Jacey Matthews—and felt an instant connection. Jacey was blond, young and dressed in Filene's Basement. The first thing she said was, "I've been worried about her, to tell the truth."

"Tell me," Merry said.

"First, the hair. The whole guy look. Eleven, twelve, they're all doing the sexual identity thing. You can't believe how exhausting it is. And how funny sometimes. The guys doing the swagger, the girls doing the batting-eye thing, the flirting. From one day to the next, the girls are getting boobs; the boys are getting erections. Either one could suddenly cry at the drop of a hat."

Merry said, "A challenge to teach this age?"

"It's why I love them. They're so impossible. But the thing is, they're really *on* Charlie about the guy look. They all love saying 'gay' and 'fag' and 'lesbo.' It's not that they're bad kids. It's just the age, when using a tag like that makes them feel like they're cool, have power. But it's more than meanness. It's also about so much identity. And Charlene…cripes, that hair."

"I know. It's about her dad."

"Yeah, I got that. She talks about him. If there's an

essay to write, she writes about him. She cranks off if the kids call her 'Charlene' instead of 'Charlie.'" Jacey shot her a sympathetic look. "I wouldn't be that age again for all the tea in China."

"I'm struggling. Wanting to be there for her. Wanting to let her get through this her own way. But I admit I'm having a terrible time getting her to talk to me—"

"What? She thinks you're beyond terrific."

Merry stared at her. "That can't be right."

"She says you're only going to be there for a little while, but—"

"What? That's not true, either…"

"I'm just telling you what Charlene says. She thinks you're cool. You let her do stuff the other mothers would never let the girls do. Like that sleepover. Wow. Got her enough status to last six months. But…"

"But what?"

Jacey stood up, went over to the desk and brought back two pages from an essay Charlie had written. Merry read it, then looked up.

"The assignment was to write a short, short story about something you'd never done, but could imagine."

"She wrote about being on a fantasy planet, having to fight everyone," Merry said worriedly.

Jacey nodded soberly. "This isn't her favorite class. She hates writing. She likes math, computers, sciences. But this bothered me. There's nothing worrisome in the content itself, but she's mentioned several times that you're not staying there long. And that if she had to live by herself, she could. She's strong, like her dad. And then there was this. She just seems so…"

"Angry?"

Jacey nodded. "Not on the outside. Not what shows."

"She's still mad that her dad died."

"That's my take, too."

On the drive home, Merry kept thinking, *Okay, take a breath.* She hadn't learned anything she didn't already know. Charlene was still afraid she was going to abandon her, still angry that her dad died—another kind of abandonment.

Neither were problems that could be fixed overnight, any more than grief was something that could be rushed along. But it did hurt—that she'd been trying so hard, and yet still couldn't seem to do the one thing in her life that she absolutely had to get right...and that was being there for Charlene.

Once she got home and peeled off her jacket, she went searching for the kid—not that locating Charlie was ever too hard. With a free couple of hours, she was either going to be huddled over some grease in the garage or messing with a computer game.

This time it was the computer business. "Hey," Merry said from the doorway. "Your teachers seem to think you're pretty darn smart. I guess you can fool some of the people some of the time, huh?"

A rare grin. "I told you that parent-teacher conference'd be boring."

"It wasn't boring. I didn't mind sitting and listening to everybody telling me how bright you are. Speaking of which...if you're so darned smart, don't you think you could teach me one of those games?"

The grin faded. "Look. You don't like this kind of stuff. You don't have to pretend."

"I'm not pretending! I just never learned how to play games like these. You could show me, couldn't you? Like one of those world-building games you like so much?"

Charlie sighed, as if no child in the universe could have enough patience to survive such an outlandish adult request. "We need two computers. I could bring my laptop to the den, and you could use the spare system in there."

For Merry, the whole project was akin to forcing down Brussels sprouts—but man, she tried. She knuckled down, determined to sit in front of the monitor for as long as it took. Smiling. But whatever engaged Charlene about trying to take down Thal's kingdom over Dunphi's—or whatever the purpose was—completely eluded her.

"I think you're finally getting it," Charlene said.

Merry almost gasped. That was high praise. Of course, they'd been at it since three, and it was past six by then. "You getting hungry for dinner?"

"Yeah...when we get done with the game, okay?"

Merry didn't say, what if that's never? What if I'm stuck doing this forever and it never, never ends? But then, out of the blue, the screen went black.

"What'd you do?" Charlie demanded immediately.

"I didn't do anything. That I know of. Your screen went black, too?"

Charlie raised her eyes to the ceiling. "You *must* have done something."

"Well. Maybe I did, but if so, I don't know what. Just tell me what to do—" Merry started to say, only Charlene abruptly shrieked.

"Stop that! Don't push any more buttons! Don't do anything!"

"I won't. I won't. But, Charlie, I couldn't seriously have wrecked a whole computer by touching a wrong button, could I?"

"Just don't touch anything else. Not your computer. Not mine. Nothing. You just—" Charlie pointed the royal finger. "Go. To the kitchen. Out, out, out."

All right. So the new attempt at bonding hadn't exactly worked out, but Merry figured—like any other debacle—that it could be turned around. You just had to keep upbeat, keep trying, find your sense of humor, keep the spirit up.

Right?

"I can help," Merry rushed in. "I'll fix it. Whatever went wrong, I'll fix it. Or get it fixed. Don't worry about a thing! Really, Charlie—"

She didn't mean to touch the computer again. Really. Hers or Charlene's. It was when she bounced out of her chair that she accidentally lost her balance. Her elbow seemed to crash down, which would have been fine if all she'd hit was the desk. But no, her elbow had to collide with the keyboard.

"Merry!" Charlene yelped. "For God's sake, you gave me the blue screen of death now!"

"What's the blue screen of death? What? What?"

Naturally, the phone chose that chaotic moment to ring. Truthfully, the land line might have jangled a couple of times, because it was hard to hear over Charlene's yelling at her. At that precise moment, truth to tell, Merry was kind of happy over the chaos. She realized most normal adults wouldn't consider a temper tantrum in a kid to be a super sign, but Charlene was always so well-behaved, so contained, so quiet. Except for that one fight at school, the girl was darn near perfect, so a little yelling and normal kid behavior seemed reassuring to Merry.

But when Charlene sprang up to answer the phone, Merry abruptly remembered the building number of no-answer calls. She said quickly, "Charlie, let me get that. I'd rather you didn't answer, because lately there'd been some really odd calls—"

Only by then it was too late. Charlie had already yanked the receiver to her ear, and stormed off with the receiver glued to her ear.

Merry hoped it was just a friend who'd called Charl—even though the kids tended to use cells over land lines. But she thought it'd be another sign of normalcy if Charlene whined to her friends about the witless, disgusting grown-up in her life. What good was childhood if you were happy all the time, right?

So she didn't worry when Charlene took off with the phone, just assumed the child wanted some privacy. Only a couple minutes passed before she was back to drop the phone back in its cradle.

Merry, in the kitchen by then, turned around to ask her a question about dinner, and was startled at the sudden change in Charlene's expression. Something was wrong. Her face suddenly looked as if it'd been dusted with chalk and she slumped down in the far kitchen chair. Subdued as a whipped puppy, she said, "Don't sweat the computer stuff, I'll take care of it."

"Who called?"

"Nobody. Just a wrong number." Those soft-fierce eyes suddenly blazed on hers. "I need to concentrate on the computer stuff. I can't talk right now. I'll fix it. Just let me alone for a while."

"I was the one who screwed it up—"

"Shit happens, Merry."

"I know, I know, but I'm the one who—" And then she remembered that she was the guardian. "Hey. No saying 'shit.' Not in this house."

"My dad said the *F* word all the time."

"So'd my dad. But it still doesn't sell well in Peoria."

"Peoria? Huh?"

"Just try not to say the damn *s* or *f* words, all right?"

"Sheesh. All right."

Tarnation. She'd annoyed the kid again. Charlene didn't stomp back to the den in a huff because Charlene didn't do huffs. She just walked back into the den and closed the door.

Merry figured she'd wait her out. In the meantime, she'd scare up something to eat, and hopefully Charlene would be more willing to talk by the time they were sitting together at dinner.

JACK DIPPED THE RAG INTO the can of stain, and then slowly rubbed the color into the naked wood. He'd always loved working with wood. A good piece of wood was a lot like having a lover. Rub her just right, and she glowed. Rub against the grain and you'd get a splinter. Just like with a woman, you always paid if you went too fast. But prepare her carefully, then give her the right rubdown, the right finish, and you could turn a plain-Jane into something gorgeous.

At that point, unfortunately, the whole metaphor broke down.

Wood couldn't talk to you, and for damn sure it couldn't get your rocks off.

Voices raised from the other room, making Jack lift his head. He'd told the boys they could have friends over. Since he was stuck commuting them back and forth to school this week, he didn't mind commuting a few spares. That was the theory…but the minute he'd granted the concession, he knew the theory was a huge, huge mistake.

Four teenage boys could destroy exponentially faster and more destructively than two. And that was when they were getting along.

He cracked open the door to the shop—not just to listen for sounds of destruction and breaking glass. But to eavesdrop on Cooper. There was a long period of fatherhood when Jack felt respecting his kids' privacy was the only ethical and honorable choice. But that was then.

He'd been a father too long to oversweat the ethics business. If eavesdropping netted him information on what was troubling his son, he'd eavesdrop—or whatever else he had to do.

So far the dialogue in the other room, however loud, had been limited to Turbo Miatas, screaming chickens, belly tellies, an argument about whether one lone brain cell could think, Brandy Penny's tit size, NASCAR, and who was getting their drivers' license first.

Jack had just dunked the rag back in the stain when he heard a quiet knock at the back door—almost so quiet he was unsure if he'd imagined it. A moment later, though, he saw Charlene's nose pressed against the glass pane, and quickly motioned her inside.

"Hi, Mr. Mackinnon." Her voice was easy and friendly, as if she visited him every night in her pajamas and her daddy's big navy blue robe past ten. On a school night.

"Hey, Charlene. What's up?"

"I just needed to ask you something, if it's okay."

"Sure it's okay," he said, although just like that, bumblebees started buzzing in his pulse. "Problems next door?"

"Nothing too weird. Merry crashed both our computers. Not a good idea to let her near anything with a plug." Charlie edged forward, located a stool on the far side of the shop, and perched there. "And then last Thursday, it was really cold when I got home from school. You know why?"

"Why?"

"Because. She paid the bill. Only she didn't call the guy to refill the tank. She didn't know that if you didn't refill the tank, there'd be no oil for the furnace, you know?" Charlie sighed.

Jack had to hide a grin. "I just don't think our Merry's going to make a technical or mechanical whiz kid, you know?"

"I know. I try to be patient. She can't help it."

Since that was all the kid said, Jack started to relax, crouched back down to rub stain into the underside of the shelf. But then he realized, she'd shut up. And she was still sitting there like a miniature Green Beret, tense and waiting.

"What was the thing you wanted to ask me?"

"It was a hypothetical."

"Okay."

"It's a pretty scary hypothetical. That's why I needed to ask you. Just you. I wouldn't bother you otherwise, Mr. Mackinnon. Honest."

"It's okay."

"Well…this is the thing. Let's say…I have a hypo-thetical friend. And this hypothetical friend got a phone call, okay?"

Jack kept rubbing, but he'd stopped paying any at-tention to the wood project. The joking look on Char-lene's face had completely disappeared. "Okay."

"And the voice on the other end of that hypothetical

phone call said, 'I don't know who that bitch is that you're living with—' Mr. Mackinnon, I just said 'bitch' because the woman on the phone used that word. Hypothetically. I wasn't trying to be—"

"Honey, I don't care what words the woman used. Just tell me what else was said."

"Hypothetically."

"Okay! Hypothetically!"

"She was pretty…weird. Hypothetically. Kind of angry sounding. I said, 'who is this?' And hypothetically, she said, 'I'm your mother. Not that bitch. She doesn't have any right to live in that house. You're my daughter. Not hers.' And then she hung up. Hypothetically." Hot tears welled in Charlie's eyes, although they didn't fall. "I hated the phone call. I got all scared and shook up. Hypothetically."

Jack tossed down the rag and aimed for the sink and solvent, wanting the stain off his hands lickety split. "It would have shaken me up, too. Did you tell Merry?"

"That's just it. I don't want to tell Merry. She'll get all upset. I don't want her to know. But what if that woman was my mother? Hypothetically. Could she make me go with her? Could she take me away? I mean, she didn't call and say, 'Hi, I'm your mother and I've missed you all these years.' Like she was someone I could want to know. Or could have wanted to be my mother. Instead, she just started out with the bitch talk. And when I got into bed and tried to sleep, I got scared that maybe she'd hurt Merry. Or take me. And then I couldn't sleep. And I have to get back, because Merry might realize I'm gone. But I was hoping you could tell me what to do."

Oh, yeah, Jack thought. He needed this on a Tuesday

night. With four teenagers in the house, he couldn't leave—even for a few minutes, not if he valued his property or his sanity. He also couldn't leave Charlene to cope with this problem alone—even though it was none of his business. And he couldn't get any further involved with Merry, without suffering "guilt times three."

My God. Trying to be a cold-blooded man who minded his own business and quit getting suckered into other peoples' lives was a full-time job. Didn't he learn anything from his ex-wife? When you were nice, women—especially women—took you for a doormat. Stomped all over you. Usually in heels.

But this particular female had fuzzy orange slippers and her daddy's soft dark eyes. He said, "Of course I'll tell you what to do, short stuff. Quit worrying. We'll take care of this."

She brightened up immediately, heaving a sigh of relief that was bigger than she was.

Which was nice, Jack thought. Except the hero hat she'd just given him weighed damn heavy, considering he didn't have a clue how to make this right or what to do. Worse yet, he needed to figure both those things out. Pronto.

CHAPTER FOURTEEN

THE SOUND WAS BARELY audible. If Merry didn't know better, she'd think someone was hurling peppercorns at her bedroom window. She probably wouldn't have heard it at all if she'd been asleep, but since she was lying there, already suffering nail-biting insomnia, she was more than happy to climb out of bed and check it out.

Talk about a reason to wake up fast.

It was almost as good as a fantasy, finding Jack in the moonlight. He was dressed all in black, dark sweatshirt and pants, scowling up a storm—and balancing precariously with one booted foot on the basement sill just below her bedroom window.

When she lifted the window, he started heaving himself up—but not before hissing in a disgruntled tone, "I'm too damned old to be pulling shenanigans like this. Particularly after midnight. At my age."

"Well, then. Why are you?" she asked, although truthfully she was charmed. Whoever got the fairy tale come to life, with the knight climbing heights to save her? Of course she didn't need saving. And this particular knight almost got stuck in the window—his shoulders were uncomfortably wide for a double-hung window. Thankfully, there was some squish room.

"Because…I needed to talk to you. About something that wouldn't wait." He hopped in on one foot, angled the other leg in, closed the window, and then almost got tangled in a trap of lingerie straps on the chair. It wasn't her fault. She'd have vacuumed and dusted and cleaned up if she'd known she was going to entertain a guy after midnight on a weeknight, but as it was, she wasn't apologizing for her lingerie messes. And he was still talking anyway. "I had to wait until the boys were asleep. And then until I was sure Charlene was asleep, too. And I can't believe I'm sneaking around like a kid myself—this is *crazy.* Speaking of which, why in God's name are you sleeping in this crammed, small spare room instead of the master bedroom?"

"Because we're not touching Charles's stuff right now. Until Charlene is ready." Apparently they were going to speak in whispers. And not turn on a light. Still, she could see his tousled hair in the drift of moonlight from the window, see him standing there, tall and hands-on-hips rattled, trying to catch his breath. She'd never seen him rattled before.

"That's silly, Merry. You're entitled to some space, for heaven's sake."

Like he'd come here to talk about her choice of sleeping rooms? Right. She sank on the lumpy couch bed, sitting cross-legged. "It probably is silly. As far as her dad's things, I just want to cater to her. But I could have moved upstairs. I just didn't want her sleeping down on this floor alone. And I didn't care." She wanted to shake her head like a puppy, see if she could clear the muzzy space between her ears. She couldn't seem to stop feeling charmed by his climbing in the window, just like the knight in Rapunzel.

"Well…" Suddenly he seemed to get serious, pushing a hand through his hair. He started pacing, immediately stopped when his foot collided with something silky and feminine. On a new note of panic, he plunked a hip on the foot of her bed. "Look… Merry—"

"Oh, no." She got it suddenly. An unpleasant flash. The obvious reason he must have come over in a panic like this.

"Oh, no—what?"

"Listen, Jack," she said in a rush. "Sometimes kids put impossible demands on you. You know how it is. Didn't you do it when you were little? Ask an adult to keep a secret, to keep a confidence—?"

Even in the shadows, she could see Jack visibly start to relax. "Whew. You already know what I was coming to talk to you about."

She nodded, thinking of Cooper. "But I swear, I was going to tell you as soon as I had a chance. I just haven't caught you alone since the night…" She hesitated.

"The night we made love."

Maybe he'd caught his breath, but suddenly she couldn't catch hers. Her heart had replayed their love-making endless times already. And with him on her bed, in the dark, no matter how fully clothed he was… suddenly those memories were between them softer than stardust and smiles.

"You've had your boys there nonstop. And I couldn't bring up the secret with the boys around," she said.

He suddenly cocked his head and said slowly, "Wait a minute."

"Wait for what?"

"This conversation isn't making any sense. You're

saying exactly what I came to say. That I was going to tell you the so-called 'secret,' but I just hadn't had a chance, because I couldn't talk about it when any of the kids could have overheard." He shoved a hand through his hair again. "My head's going in circles as if I'd had too much to drink. When I haven't had a thing."

"I didn't think you had," she assured him.

But Jack looked even more confused. "I mean it, though. I came to tell *you* that *I'd* felt put on the spot. About keeping the secret. About trying to be honest with the kid, valuing the confidence. But believing you needed to know about the situation."

"Well, I do know the situation, Jack. Because Cooper told me—"

"Huh? How the hell did Cooper know about her mother?"

"Huh? What mother?" Merry had initially felt self-conscious, wearing nothing but an old camisole and underpants. If the atmosphere were romantic, she'd rather be in satin tap pants and a push-up bra with lace. But since it wasn't, she'd just as soon be wearing concealing sweats, like he was. Now, though, she forgot that self-consciousness and started looking as confused as he did. "I feel like we're talking in circles."

"Ditto on the circles. How did Cooper come into this conversation at all?"

"Because I thought that's who we were talking about," Merry said wryly.

"Not me. That isn't who I was talking about." But Jack suddenly scratched his chin. "I think I'm starting to get it. You mean…*Cooper* told you a confidence. Something you didn't tell me."

"Yes. I already said that." Merry's head was beginning to spin. "It was too serious a thing to keep from you, Jack, but just like we were both discussing, neither of us have had a second alone since the night we—"

"Made love."

It was the second time he'd filled in that blank. It seemed easy enough for him. But Merry could feel her body flush with awareness. Her breasts, her thighs, cripes, even her belly button, remembered his touch with exquisite clarity. She wanted again. Wanted him. Jack seemed so alone, so not in touch with his own sense of honor and his giving nature and how wonderful he was.

She had to fight tooth and nail to get her mind tracked to the conversation. "All right, if you didn't come over here to talk about Cooper, then…"

"I came over to tell you about Charlene. She told me something in confidence several hours ago. It was really important to her that I not tell you…but it kept gnawing at me, that this was something you needed to know. And things have been so hectic that I couldn't be sure of finding time to tell you alone, unless I—"

"Climbed in the window," she finished for him.

"Exactly." He sighed. "So have we finally got that straight now?"

She knee-walked over to him on the mattress, thinking that nothing was straight. For that matter, if he knew something serious about Charlene—her whole life was that girl right now. Nothing was more important than Charlene.

But Charlene was asleep. And there were a lot of hours before her alarm clock was going to go off in the morning.

Which meant that right now Merry could freely concentrate on something else that deeply concerned her.

When she first leaned in to a kiss, Jack momentarily stiffened—as if he'd never expected the move. That went for two of them, because she'd never expected to make the move, either. Yet right then, she knew, irrevocably knew, that this was the right thing to do.

She expected to get hurt from inviting more closeness with Jack—but she'd expected that from the start. She couldn't imagine Jack wanting a long-term relationship with someone like her—someone who had to look pretty ditzy and impulsive and unserious, compared to a man like him. But this moment wasn't about the future. It just seemed important to her, right then, to love this man. To appreciate him. To communicate something to him, with him, that neither seemed able to do with words.

When her lips sank on his, she felt him sigh all the way through her fingertips. He didn't want this, all right. He didn't want her kisses…like he didn't want to win the lottery. Like he didn't want a harem-filled dream. Like he didn't want to be loved.

She was above him, for that first kiss, because she was still kneeling on the mattress, leaning over to find his mouth…to take his mouth. But her knees started to buckle. She had to sink back on her heels for balance, but she kept her mouth still softly glued on his, her arms slowly slinking around him.

Even though the room was dark, she closed her eyes, just wanting to savor this extraordinary sensation, the shivery sense of wonder that touching him invoked. Last time they'd come together like a fiery comet, all speed and steam. This time, her fingertips glided over neck, shoulders, arms. Not seeking to hold. Seeking to caress, to rub, to knead and know.

And his skin yielded beneath her hands as if no one had just touched him in forever—not for the joy of touching him. Not for the simple sensual pleasure of enjoying the texture of his flesh, the way it warmed for her. The way it gave for her. The way his breath caught, sharpened, for so little provocation.

She'd fought belonging all her life. She'd fought feeling tied to anything. But it was different, feeling loved. At least feeling loved by a man she had fallen so helplessly in love with herself.

She pushed at his sweatshirt, severed the kiss long enough to peel the fabric over his head, and by then was already aiming for another kiss. This one was deep enough, hard enough, rich enough, to topple his balance.

The couch mattress was thin, its springs mean-sharp, the wall so close that Jack could easily have cracked his head—if she hadn't pulled him onto her, out of harm's way. Her one leg dangled over the side, maybe so did his. But the logistics right then didn't seem to matter.

His chest was bare under the sweatshirt, his heart pounding, hard and fast, making her breasts tighten and swell against him. For another two seconds she was still wearing a camisole. For another three seconds after that, she was still wearing underpants.

Bad mattress or no, one of the few things she'd brought from home was her own pillow and down comforter. Jack didn't seem to appreciate those, either, because they graced the floor along with her clothes faster than silver. Faster than secrets. Faster than he could hook his leg around and twist her beneath him.

As if she minded.

One thing she was far more skilled at than Jack,

though, was sloth. With him, she liked the idea of making laziness a whole art form. She looped her arms loosely around him, tucked her legs up with a little squeeze action, rolled her pelvis in a slinky dance move. He seemed to know that dance, know that rhythm, because he said against her throat, with the groan of a man in pain, "Damn it, Merry. Quit it. What are you trying to do to me?"

How could she quit? Given that kind of appreciation?

No matter what was wrong in her life…being loved mattered. Loving mattered. She believed that, with her heart, with her soul. She didn't *need* anything from Jack. But feeling loved…just changed things. Made her feel stronger.

Made more things seem possible. And one thing that struck her as imminently possible, just then, was turning a traumatic night into a night of softness and love and fierce-hot sensuality. In fact, it struck her as an ideal moment to take her feminine powers out for a long, lazy spin…

"You're so *not* a good woman, Merry," Jack hissed at her.

"Oh, thank you." And yeah, she'd dipped down for a taste. She wasn't normally quite that uninhibited, no matter how much she liked to sell herself outwardly to others, but with Jack…well. It was so much fun. Destroying him. Taking that fine, strong, so serious mind and turning it into a sponge. And it was so easy…

All it took was loving him. Enjoying his body. Taking her time to nip and taste and rub and entice. A kiss here. A tongue there. She gave him a little boob rub…a new idea, one she hadn't thought of before, just pressing her boobs to his chest and then winding her way down, having her breasts guide the way down that long, long torso.

He muttered something harsh and guttural...and for the first time in days, she felt a burst of laughter bubble in her throat. Life definitely hadn't been going too smoothly lately...but damn.

Life wasn't just about problems—or it shouldn't be. It should be about moments like this. When a woman could be with her man. When nothing was going on in the universe but loving. When a woman could vent all the positive psychic energy on her guy that she could possibly conjure up.

Her theory worked just fine until said guy spun her around and leveled her, flat and hard, into the mattress. The face, looming over her in the darkness, looked as sharply carved as a marble statue, but the eyes blazed, dark and hot.

"Hi there, lover," she whispered.

"Don't you try talking nice to me after what you've been doing," he snarled, and then ducked his head.

Well, damn the man, if he didn't abruptly, relentlessly, smother her with tenderness. He offered kisses, softer than secrets. A touch that revered and cherished. And at some point, she felt him sliding, gliding, so naturally inside her. He claimed her slowly at first, but then deeper, much deeper, so deep that he just possibly reached the depth of her womb.

"No one," he whispered. "No one, Merry. Ever. Made me feel the way you do."

And double damn the man if that didn't tip her right off the cliff. Orgasm was such a silly, pale word for the clenching shudders that rippled through her, forcing her eyes closed, her throat to bare for his lips, her hips to cleave tight to him in surrender. Surrender, and triumph both.

Belonging. Who knew it was an emotion? Yet moments later, as they both lay there, spent, she snuggled close with a sweet rush of belonging. "Where'd I ever find you?" he murmured, and she chuckled against his throat—then kissed his throat, right below the chin line. Then snuggled in tighter and fell hopelessly sound asleep.

SHE WOKE UP ALONE, and stretched like a lazy cat. Talk about euphoria. The only way she could feel happier was if Jack was lying next to her—which, naturally, he couldn't be. Thankfully he'd managed to stay awake and get up and go back to his boys. Still. Falling asleep in his arms had felt more luxurious than a present of diamonds, and her body still felt the sated pleasure from being with him.

The clock claimed it was only six-thirty, which meant that Charlene wasn't even close to getting up for school yet. She leaped out of bed, pranced around finding clothes, danced silently out to the coffee-maker...she still wasn't totally friends with the high-tech appliance, but they seemed to reach a fairly regular truce. While waiting for the fancy machine to chug through its cycle, she picked up the phone and dialed Minnesota.

"There's only one person in the solar system who would dare call me at this hour," Lucy said. "It better be Merry."

She chuckled. "And I better not have woken you, but you've said a zillion times that you're up with Laurie at this hour."

"I am. This is a monster baby. She never wants to sleep past four. On the other hand, we get these first two hours of the day together, just ourselves."

"You're still in love? Even after all these days and weeks of no sleep?"

"With the baby and Nick both. You think it's sleep deprivation making me crazy?"

"Nah. I think it's happiness." The light went on the coffee machine. With the phone tucked in her ear, Merry poured the first mug. "I don't want to keep you from the private baby time for long. But I had to call you. Had to share this with someone. Oh, Lucy…"

"What?"

"I am *so, so, so* in love."

On the other end, Lucy let out a soft laugh. "I can hear it in your voice. You're dancing on air. It has to be the neighbor?"

"Yeah, Jack." She couldn't keep the bliss from her voice. "In the beginning, I couldn't believe it could go anywhere…and even now I can't swear where it's headed. For sure there's no way to do this fast. I have Charlene, and he has two teenagers. There's no hurrying anything, but Lucy, I can feel it building. So strong. So real. It's the best thing that ever happened to me."

"Merry…"

"What?"

"I've heard you say this before." Lucy's voice had turned gentle, with a rim of worry now. "You do tend to take on everything at five hundred percent, you know. To throw yourself into a new job. To start a project with all your energy. To love with your whole heart."

Through the east window, the sun was just starting

to peek over the horizon with a flush of pale rose. A bird suddenly started chirping. "But not men," Merry said. "You've never heard me be in any kind of hustle to use the *L* word with a man."

"That's true. It's been hobbies and jobs and projects that you fall head over heels for." Lucy's voice turned thoughtful. "With men, you usually—"

"Drop them. Not stick. Not even think about staying the course," Merry admitted. "But this is completely different. I never wanted to be tied to a job or a place. You said it one time, Lucy, that my mom preyed on my mind. I know you're right now. If there was ever a man who really mattered to me, I didn't want a job or a place or anything else affecting whether I could be with him. I want a relationship where the two of us mattered more than anything else. Because when it comes down to it…if you're not free to love, then you're not really free."

"All right. Now you're starting to scare me." In the distance Merry heard Lucy shifting the baby to her shoulder, heard the creak of an old rocker. "I'm beginning to think this guy is the real thing. Do I need to come there and check him out?"

Merry laughed. "That's exactly what my dad said. And I can't wait for you to meet him. But not quite yet. And that's enough about me— How's Laurie? You said you were going to download some new pictures."

"You mean you actually *want* to see more? Could this be? That someone exists who's willing to see another five hundred pictures of the baby?"

"Hey, you're talking about my godchild." They teased and chatted a little longer, but it *was* early in Minnesota, and Merry hung up after a bit. She sat, still smiling, so easily imagining her old friend rocking the baby. Lucy used to be a fussbudget extraordinaire, a hard-core picture straightener, a complete tidy freak… but that was the thing about old friends—at least the really good old friends. You knew their flaws and they knew yours. No need to pretend.

Lucy knew well how Merry had always presented a flaky image for the world.

Of course, she *had* been flaky in the past. But all her free-spirited attitude and buzzing around from job to job hadn't been exactly what it seemed.

Suddenly she glanced up and noticed Charlene in the doorway. She was wearing a Chicago Bears T-shirt in a man's XXX-large, which meant it trailed almost to the floor. In spite of the budding breasts, she looked so young and vulnerable with the bare feet and sleepy eyes and tousled hair.

"You're up early," Merry said cheerfully, yet immediately noticed that Charlene swiftly ducked away from direct eye contact, and was pulling at her fingers again. And abruptly Merry remembered last night—the time before she and Jack made love—the part he'd been trying to tell her something about a secret of Charlene's.

"Yeah, I woke up when I thought I heard the phone. And then I was just wide awake. So…you have a godchild?"

"Yup. Little baby girl. You've heard me talk about Lucy and the baby before. Lucy was my best friend in school—"

"Yeah, but I didn't know the baby was your godchild."

Merry slipped off the stool, bending down to reach in the cupboard for the granola with almond cereal that Charlene loved. Something in her tone made Merry pause. "Is that a problem?" she asked in confusion.

"Problem? No problem. I'd just guess you'll want to go live back there again. If you've got a godchild and best friend there and all. I mean, whenever."

So it was that old story again. "The only reason I can imagine moving there was if you wanted to. Which would be fine. But as long as you're happy here...one of these days, I want my dad to fly in to meet you. And Lucy can't easily travel yet, just too tough with a baby that age. But a little later, I hope she'll come and bring the baby, give you a chance to meet her."

"Yeah, right."

Merry heard the doubt. Hard to miss, when it had all that preteenager ring of sarcasm attached. It stung. Not for long. She served the cereal, the bowl, the milk, the napkin. Of course a leopard couldn't change *all* her spots. She forgot the spoon.

"So what's on the agenda after school today?" Merry asked. "There has to be a ball game practice of some kind. B-Ball? V-Ball? M-Ball? What?"

Charlene sighed. "Merry, you really don't get the difference in the sports, do you?"

"Hey, I did cheerleading. And dance. It's just the ball games that seem to blur altogether. Anyway, if it's not sports, how about academic challenge? Or the science project—"

"Nothing going on after school today," Charlene jumped in, before she'd run down the complete agenda of after-school activities.

"Good. Your hair's flopping big-time. Wouldn't you like a little cut and style?"

"I don't need a cut and style. I need more wax," Charlie informed her.

They'd see, Merry thought. She had an idea about

the hair. And getting Charlene in a mall or salon environment meant she'd be on Merry's turf. Which meant she'd have a much, much better chance of worming Charlene's secret out of her. The one she'd told Jack.

As soon as the squirt was in school, she intended to call Jack anyway. Then she'd know the secret. And could strategize all day what to do about the problem—whatever it was—before the after-school hair crisis.

It was a good plan, she thought.

Of course everything seemed like a good plan, after having been made love to, thoroughly and fabulously well. Hell's bells. Even looking at the sinkful of dirty dishes that had appeared out of nowhere made her smile.

Love did that to a woman.

WHEN DIANNE CALLED to let him know her business trip had been extended, Jack didn't mind having the boys an extra week. Hell, he wished he had them full time. Even when they were being a pain, he still loved having them, and could usually rearrange his work to accommodate their long school commute. The only trial was getting them up at the crack of dawn.

Root canals had to be easier, and today he had the two extra boys to carpool as well. Once he faced Armageddon and finally got the whole surly crew into the car, though, they immediately quieted down. The three in the back seat even closed their eyes and nodded back to sleep.

Jack had ample time over the long drive to replay the night before with Merry. The climbing in her window, because he'd been so distraught over Charlene's problem. His trying to tactfully start that whole dialogue and getting all muddled. His somehow—and how did those "somehows" keep happening?—ending up in bed with her.

Mostly his mind played and replayed the luxurious sex. That woman gave more in one encounter than he remembered in a dozen years of marriage. She was so…generous. So sensuous, so open, so giving.

So sexy.

Jack kept trying to grasp what was happening to her, to them—to him. He'd never thought he was a terrible lover. At least he'd never heard any complaints. But when Dianne told him she'd wanted a divorce, later, he'd thought he'd have survived the breakup better if she'd left him for another man. Leaving him because of her career just seemed the Ultimate Ego Wilter.

All the women he'd slept with since hadn't helped him recover that lost ego. He just couldn't seem to get that positive feeling about himself as a man back.

He'd stopped expecting it.

Then along came Merry. He'd only seduced her a couple of times—or she'd seduced him; he couldn't tell who got the most credit. But suddenly his ego had flown back home, to hell with Jersey, and was infesting his head with a light-headed euphoric idiot grin.

Real life just wasn't *like* this.

He'd stared in the dark all last night, grinning like a hyena.

She wasn't for *him,* for Pete's sake. Nothing about the relationship or anything else was right. She thought he was a good guy, a hero kind of guy.

The whole thing was a complete mess. Complicated. Confusing. Worrisome. So how come he still couldn't wipe off that idiotic grin?

Maybe he needed a psychiatrist, he told himself, as he pulled up to the school. "Wake up, guys," he told the boys, who obediently started gathering up their gear. "You'll be at Gary's after school until I can pick you up, remember."

"Yeah, yeah." Kicker could not be expected to be civil before 9:00 a.m. And neither boy appreciated having to be pinned down to a friend's house after school. But Jack needed to know where they were, and although the early-morning commute was easy enough to manage, he couldn't always guarantee leaving work at a set time, so arrangements had to be made so they had a safe, sure place to go.

The minute Kicker and the other boys heaved out of the truck, Jack said, "Cooper. Hold up a second."

Cooper shifted his book bag and hung in the passenger window. "What?"

"Nothing really. I just wanted to ask…you okay? Anything up with you?"

"Like what?"

Like the secret Coop had told Merry and failed to tell his own father, Jack wanted to say, but didn't. Some kids could be pushed to talk. Cooper wasn't one of them, but knowing that Coop had spilled a serious problem to Merry worried the hell out of him. He had to try something besides just waiting him out and giving him the opportunity to talk. So he said, "I was thinking…since your mom's going to be gone a while longer, and while I still have you guys at my place, maybe we could hit Best Buy. My laptop's almost three years old now, so I'm thinking I should know what's out there now. And I'd like your advice on a new TV."

Cooper straightened up. "We could skip school and go right now."

"No, not now." But Jack had to grin. When the twins were first born, he'd bought every parenting book under the sun. Those had all gone in the trash. Bribery was the only thing that always worked. One of the toughest parenting problems since the divorce had been getting the boys one-on-one. He always had them together, but a circumstance like now, when he wanted personal time with just Cooper, it was hard to manipulate—even with bribery.

Worrying about Cooper only temporarily distracted him from fretting about Merry. Once his sons disappeared into the school, he drove to work with Merry zooming straight back into his mind and sticking there. It didn't help that he knew he had to talk to her as immediately as possible. Last night, she'd fallen into such a deep sleep that he hadn't wanted to waken her. There also seemed no point, since there was nothing she could do about Charlene in the middle of the night, anyway.

But it was morning now. And she needed to know about the woman who'd called Charlene. Jack had no idea if the woman was really Charlene's mother or not—how could anyone know? But the point was that Merry should know about that call before the stranger could try to contact Charlene again.

At the office, Jack key-coded in his privacy card, hit the elevator, then key-coded in the next set of security keys to the top floor. In his area, it was quiet as twilight. There were other bodies around, who could talk up a storm over lunch, but during the work hours, everyone shared a need for serious concentration and let each other alone.

He zoned straight into his office, closed the glass door, and dialed Merry.

His private space was done up in blues, the same

blend of hues on the carpet, walls, chairs. Windows overlooked noisy traffic and bustling humanity below, but up here, it was soundless. His coworkers tended to dress like undertakers. Not Jack. He only put on a tie when threatened at knifepoint, but otherwise couldn't see a purpose in the formal dress bit when all he did all day was hang in the office and think.

Today, though, was hopelessly a tie day, because there was a big-deal meeting at nine, a team being assembled over a problematic new code. He kept glancing at his watch as he listened to Merry's phone ring and ring. Finally giving up, he left a message on her voice mail with his office number.

Still, he couldn't settle. He got coffee from the back room, shuffled through his mail, booted up his e-mail, and then dialed Merry again.

Still no answer. He left a second message, saying he wouldn't bug her again, knowing she was out, but that he'd be reachable at the office all day. He couldn't risk saying more than that. Who knew if Charlene would get the voice mail messages before Merry? But he couldn't get the problem off his mind. Not just the problem of Charlene's mystery phone call, but the problem of Merry. *His* problem.

Unfortunately, it was nine o'clock by then, and he had to join the team. They'd already started assembling in the old mahogany conference room. The group knew the drill. Laptops, paper, pencils, mugs in place. Shoes heeled off under the table. Everybody got their butts nestled in.

This was a door-locked kind of problem, extra-high security. The whole group of eleven were rarely put together for a single project, because that was too many in the know, but for this particular crisis, they needed all the mind power they could get. Even after all these years, Jack still fired up for the work, the chance to solve what others considered completely unsolvable problems. After all these years, Jack still loved it.

But at nine-forty-five, Mitch—the group's administrative assistant—signaled Jack from the doorway. "You've got a call. I wouldn't normally interrupt, but I got the feeling you might want to take it."

Jack left the table, feeling pulled by sharp teeth. They were seriously right in the middle of a productive analysis.

He picked up the closest phone to the conference room and dialed his number code.

"Am I bothering you?"

He thought wryly, just because she was interrupting a meeting involving national security? But to hell with that. Merry definitely didn't have to identify herself. That voice of hers wrapped around his senses like a velvet rubber band. And yeah, he heard her concern. In fact, she gushed on.

"I didn't want to call you at work and interrupt, Jack. But I had the impression that whatever Charlie told you was pretty serious. I thought that was why you must have called—"

It was. The problem with Charlie was serious enough for him to climb in her window last night.

Not in her bed, though. He'd climbed in her bed totally for him.

And because he realized how true that was, it especially bugged him—that Merry just assumed he'd call about the child. Not about *her.* Not about *them.*

For a moment he felt a gut stab. He just wasn't used

to Merry provoking any memories of his ex-wife—but everything had been more important to her than he was. He never seemed to register on her importance map except as a convenience.

Of course, from the beginning he'd been telling himself that was how he wanted it with Merry. They were so far from a natural pair that it made his head spin. He didn't mind being a convenience for her. He didn't want her thinking he cared too much.

So that annoying little sting could just go to hell and stay there.

"Yeah," he said. "The only reason I called was about Charlene."

CHAPTER FIFTEEN

THE MINUTE MERRY HAD WALKED in the kitchen, she saw the light on the answering machine and caught Jack's message. She was still pulling off her jacket when she dialed his office.

"Tell me what Charlene said," she urged him now.

"Apparently she got a phone call—on your land line over there. I don't know exactly when—early last evening? You were home, but she happened to reach the phone first. She didn't recognize the voice—"

"Oh, God. I've been getting a number of hang-ups lately. I didn't think that much of it, but if this was some crank call or porn or something, I'll—"

"No, Mer. Not like that." From the sound, Jack shifted the phone to his other ear. "Although it's interesting you've been getting other hang-up calls. Maybe this person was just waiting for Charlene to pick up the phone instead of you."

"Okay. You're scaring me good now." Merry sank against the kitchen counter and pressed a hand against her roiling stomach.

"That's why I wouldn't keep this a secret. Because I'm not sure if you should be scared or not—but the caller identified herself to Charlene as her mother."

"What?"

"I can't remember Charlene's exact words. But the caller was a woman, claiming to be her mother. Claiming that 'you'—or whatever woman was living in the house with Charlene—shouldn't be there."

"Oh God. Oh God. I've been worried about this right from the start…." But abruptly Merry put aside her own feelings. She didn't matter in this equation. "How did Charlene react, Jack? She was upset enough to go tell you about this. But was she afraid, excited, happy, worried, what?"

"Well…hell, I don't know. I guess I'd say she was just shaken up. But to tell the truth, she seemed more shaken at the idea of your finding out about this woman than about her mother actually showing up. Because she talked about you. Not the woman."

Merry frowned. "That doesn't make sense."

"She's a girl. She's eleven. Personally, I think they all need to come with interpreters."

She wanted to chuckle, and for a minute, did smile. He was at work; she didn't want to keep him on the line. But just hearing this from him—because it was him, Jack—made digesting any traumatic news easier. It was like knowing she had a bulldozer behind her if a shovel didn't work.

Still, she couldn't smile for long. "Thanks for telling me. This is too serious to sit on."

"I thought it was, too. And I don't know what you want to do, Merry. If you talk directly to Charlene about this, she'll know I broke her confidence. Which is all right, for something this serious, of course, but—"

"I understand. I'll think about how to handle that. I wish she'd told me, but I'm relieved she *did* tell you, that the trust in you is there. I don't want to mess with that if I don't have to." Her mind was whirling at a hundred miles an hour. "I think my first move should be to contact the lawyer."

"Yeah. Completely agree."

She heard voices in the background, someone calling for Jack. She said, "I know you have to go—and again, just sorry I had to interrupt your work day—"

"It's okay. And we'll talk later. Let me know if there's something I can do, love—"

That was it. The connection severed. She thought he'd slipped in that *love* word by accident, the same way a man slipped in an "I love you" under the sheets. It was the kind of context where a woman had to be either naïve or nuts to take it too seriously.

Yet the four letter word wrapped around her like a silk pashmina, not heavy, not hot, just protectively warm and heart-soothing. Maybe Jack did use the *L* word lightly. Or only under stress, unconsciously. But he'd still used it.

And she still felt the emotion of it when they were together. This was nothing like a child's love, or a crush, a teenager-love where every second of the day was smothered by thoughts for the other person. But something different. Something where…she was still living her own life, still struggling with her own problems and choices. But she felt stronger because of him. Her life felt wider. Richer. Safer. More interesting. More wonderful.

It was the kind of love that didn't choke. But freed instead.

Who even knew that was possible?

But this was no time to dwell. After hanging up from Jack, she immediately dialed Lee Oxford's number.

The receptionist gave out her typical, "He's far too busy today, Ms. Olson. There's no chance he can fit anything else into his schedule."

Merry said, "I need to talk to him. I don't have to come see him, but I need to speak with him."

"I can't guarantee—"

Merry understood the woman didn't care for her, but today, she just had no time for petty nonsense. She said, "Get him."

Naturally, she immediately suffered pounds of guilt for being so bitchy. But she did—get him. Lee clicked on the receiver within a few seconds, and maybe the receptionist hadn't been downright mean, he sounded delighted to hear from her.

"How's our gorgeous guardian doing?"

"I have a problem, Lee."

"That's what I'm here for, sweetie. Let 'er rip."

So Merry let it out. That Charlene's mother may have called. That there'd been other calls, hang-ups. That she needed to know, immediately, what her rights were. And Charlene's. If she could stop the woman from seeing Charlene. If she even should. If the caller really was Charlene's mother, could she just show up and legally claim her daughter....

"Let's catch a breath here, honey. No point in you having a heart attack. That's what you've got an expensive lawyer for. You pay me a lot of money so I have your heart attacks. That's how our relationship works."

He was cute. Mercenary, but cute. Only right now, Merry couldn't seem to appreciate cuteness. "What do I do if she shows up? What do I do if she—"

First off, Lee informed her, the woman would have to prove she was Charlene's mother before there'd be any kind of visitation. Someone knocking on the door was hardly proof.

Second of all, if the caller turned out to be the mother, she'd lost custody rights years ago. Because her ex-husband died didn't give her those custody rights back—although she did have a right to ask for a hearing. "She could put her case in front of a judge. That she's a changed woman. Not into drugs or whatever. That she wants to see her daughter, all that."

Without thinking, Merry sank to the floor like a whipped puppy. "So if she proves she's leading a decent life, she'll obviously get the right to see Charlene."

"Yes. But I'd say that's a big *if*. Further, if she's only in it for the money, she's got a big surprise—because I don't care if Superman himself showed up to claim Charlene right now, there's still a trust controlling all funds for the kid. Nobody's just going to get their hands on that money and be able to take off."

"I hear you, Lee. But darn it. I don't care about the money. And maybe she doesn't even know about it—"

"Merry, honey, trust me. She'd know about it. Again, that's why lawyers like me do so well, because there are Pollyannas in life who need us. That's you, if you didn't recognize yourself. A hard-core Pollyanna. And just for the record, even if she did go for a hearing, did win it, it wouldn't take away your guardianship even if she was initially given visitation rights."

"Initially?"

"Hey…you've gotten totally into the kid, haven't you?"

Merry didn't need him to say it. "I love her to bits. I couldn't love her more if she were my own. I don't know how mutual that is, we're sure different as day and night. But I can't think of anything I wouldn't do for her. She's so special. So bright, so unique, so full of character and ideas and she has this funny, quirky sense of humor, and—"

"Okay. We don't have to get too sentimental here. I was just…surprised. I've watched this developing, in the beginning, well, I know how good the money is. I just didn't really think you'd fall so deep into the mom thing."

"Lee—" She pulled an ear. The same ear she always pulled when she was nervous and frustrated.

"Look. This broad doesn't sound like good news, if she's calling the kid out of the blue, no preparation, no going through channels, no thinking how the kid is going to respond. So I wouldn't waste time worrying you're going to lose her."

She was. Going to waste time.

"I won't lie. If she looks reasonable on paper, in person, the judge'll allow visitation."

"And that would only be right," Merry said hollowly. "Charlene needs to see her mother. Needs to know her. I would never stand in her way. It's just…"

"Yeah. I know all about those 'it's justs.' But for right now, this is the deal. If she calls again, you give her my telephone number. If she's serious about seeing Charlene, she'll have to work through me —or through her own lawyer, to get to court. But if she shows up at the house, just close the door and call me."

"I can do that? Even if she shows me proof she's Charlene's mother?"

"Absolutely. Until we know this woman's on the up-and-up— which sure sounds doubtful to me—I'd protect the child. Keep them separate. The law would back you up, so don't worry about that. The law would see this as a matter of protecting the child."

"That's how I felt. But I wasn't sure if the law would see it that way." Merry felt a ton of relief. "I should probably tell the school authorities that this happened. So if this woman tried to get to Charlene through a call at the school, they'd have a reason to be extra watchful."

"Good. In fact, hell. I should have thought to tell you that first. In the meantime, you need any money?"

Cripes, he was always trying to give away Charlie's money, Merry thought wryly. Truthfully, she still hadn't figured out all the finances yet. It was still a steep learning curve for her, figuring out what it took to live in the house, expense and maintenance wise. But she had a ton of money coming in from the trust every month, she knew that.

Right now, she couldn't care less. To a point, talking to Lee this time had been reassuring. But the real crisis wasn't just about legal rights if the mother returned.

It was handling Charlene.

Charlene—who thought she knew nothing about the mother's call. Charlene, who hadn't felt she could confide in her. Charlene, who couldn't very well be protected or counseled or loved about this, if they couldn't openly talk about it.

The problem took major heart-searching. All the projects she'd planned for the day went by the wayside, but she had her head back together by the time she picked Charlene up from school. When they got back in the house, she asked casually, "Do you have a ton of homework?"

Charlene's response was as predictable as snow in

Minnesota. "Huge. And the English assignment is straight torture. Two whole pages I have to write. She had a real edge on in class. And even besides that, she likes to make us suffer."

Thankfully Merry had heard some of this before— if not the exact lyrics, then the same basic refrain, so she didn't immediately fly into a frenzy of help the way she had that first week. Besides, she knew the English teacher now. So she just asked the rest of the relevant questions. "Any math homework? Science?"

"Well, yeah. A little math. But that's not really work. He gave us a problem to see if we could figure it out. It's more like fun than work." After that came more rants on the torture-loving English teacher, who'd never had a fair bone in her body, who probably sat up nights thinking of new ways to torture her students, who was only happy when kids were suffering, etc etc.

When Merry could sneak in a word, she said, "Well, if you can get the work done by dinner, I thought we'd go shopping afterward."

"Weren't you *listening* to me? I'll never get it all done before midnight. It's impossible."

"Oh, darn. Because I wasn't thinking mall shopping." A lie if ever there was one. She was so hungry for a mall hit she could hardly think. But parenting sometimes required lies, Merry was discovering. "I was just wondering if maybe you'd like to go to Best Buy."

"Best Buy? I'll be done with my homework in an hour." Charlie added swiftly, "Of course, I'll have to practically kill myself. But I'm starting right now."

She was done with her homework an hour before dinner, but then Merry couldn't leave that fast. Her dad called. Then her oldest sister. Then a woman from school who was trying to corral field-trip chaperones. Then the newspaper, wanting to know if she wanted to rerun the ad to sell Charlie's car. Then some lawn-care company, who wanted to know if the Rosses wanted to renew their contract for lawn-care service for the coming summer.

For that one, she searched out Charlie in her room. "Do we want Green Leaf to take care of the lawn?" she asked.

"Yeah. Dad did a lot of shopping around. All they do is cut the grass once and week and trim the bushes. So they don't do everything. But it's the best price for the service."

Okay. Par for the course, she took Charlene's word as law. But by then, it was near dinnertime, and she was struggling with fajitas. Actually, fajitas were probably easy for a normal cook, just not for her. Still, what wasn't burned was eaten by six thirty.

"Ready?" she asked Charlie. Foolish question. The kid was already barreling for the passenger seat of the Mini Cooper.

"What are we shopping for?" Charlie asked.

Merry couldn't answer. If they were going to Banana Republic or BCBG, she could have waxed on for a good hour on a potential list, embellishing as she went, but Best Buy wasn't her normal milieu. Shopping, though, was always conducive to talking, at least for females, so she'd picked the place hoping it'd be an environment that would open Charlene up more naturally.

Only she forgot about needing a cover—like an actual reason for being at such a straight place. But then a couple lightbulbs dawned. "Two things," she told

Charlene. "I think we should get a different house phone, one that lists the last number that dialed, you know? Like checks the caller ID. You can buy that kind of thing, can't you?"

Charlie sighed, looked world-weary. "Yes, Merry. Like that technology was probably around before you were born."

"But I'm a dunce at this."

"We know that."

"So I need you to pick it out, okay? And while you're at it, pick out a new cell phone for yourself."

"Me? Why?"

"Because I think it's a good safety measure to change your number now and then. I know it's a pain. But telemarketers and creeps and all kinds of people prey on young teenagers. And I thought maybe you'd like a new phone besides."

"A new phone'd be cool. But I have to tell you, a new phone and a new number aren't necessarily the same thing," Charlie said, in that tone communicating that educating Merry was sometimes an uphill struggle.

"Whatever. And then, since we're stuck in this place...I know you got the computers going after I messed them up the other day. But I thought, maybe you'd like to look at the new laptops out now. Or notebooks. Or whatever they're called."

Oh, yeah. Maybe she didn't have the terminology right, but she knew girls. Charlie clearly picked up the shopping bug, the heart-pounding greed, the excitement, the anticipation, just like Merry might have for a Manolo Blahnik sale.

It wasn't quite the same, though. Because Merry barely walked in the door before enduring a quick, short panic attack. Everywhere she turned there were electronics. The only thing she recognized were the kitchen appliances and the TVs, and likely, she couldn't run half the televisions.

"Don't leave me," she said plaintively to Charlie. Who immediately laughed.

"You're so funny sometimes. Come on. We'll have fun here."

Yeah, right, Merry thought. She suffered through the phone choices, while Charlene took pains to explain the features of each one, apparently to make Merry feel as if she were part of the buying process. The place was crowded—who'd guess, on a school night? But kids and adults and everyone else were jamming up various aisles.

Charlene got into an infernally long conversation with a guy who had Geek Squad on his shirt—Merry wasn't going to let on, but Charlie had the instincts of a flirt, even in military gear.

Still, it wasn't until they got to the new computer area—and Merry had chased off the sales clerks, including one who tried to ask her out—where she could finally initiate a conversation with Charlene. Charlene honed on a Sony laptop as if it were cutest puppy she'd ever seen. Her head never came up again. It was true love. She kept touching keys and letting out little sounds on a par with an eleven-year-old's version of orgasmic sighs. She was in The Zone.

There'd never be a better place or time to start, Merry thought, and started in. "Charlie...I want to tell you something. Something pretty serious."

"I don't know how you found out, but if this is about my slugging Dougall in the hall—"

"No." Merry blinked. Dougall again. But this was no time to get diverted.

"Charl, you've said a zillion times that you think I'm going to leave. That you don't believe I'll stay."

"Yeah, well…" Charlie didn't lift her head from the fancy Sony, but Merry saw her body suddenly go still.

Merry pulled one of the For Sale computer chairs closer to her. "Whenever you say that, I'm not sure what you want me to understand. That you kind of wish I'd leave. Or that you're afraid I'll leave and you'd feel stranded."

Charlene whipped her a look. "I'm not afraid of anything."

"Well, I am. Afraid of lots of things." Merry tried to untense, but it was hard. All day she'd tried to think of a way to get through to Charlene, but this seemed to be the only one. Honesty. And since she never volunteered to bring up old, annoying, worthless baggage from her emotional basement, talking about this was inevitably hard. "In fact, that's kind of why I wanted to tell you this. When I was a girl…just turned eleven, a little younger than you…my mother took off."

"Yeah?" Another quick glance. But this one not so defensive. "Where'd she go?"

"She was really into her career. And she got this big promotion, but she had to move to Argentina to take it. Not for forever. But at least for two years. She and my dad fought about it. But they ended up getting divorced."

"Oh. The divorce thing." Charlie let out a worldly wise sigh, communicating that she knew all about that.

"Yeah. The divorce thing. Anyway. I've known forever that people think…when they first meet me…that I'm kind of fluffy."

"Merry. You *are* fluffy."

Merry tugged on an earlobe. Every once in a while, it'd be nice if Charlie weren't quite so blunt. "Okay, I admit I've had a half-dozen jobs. And that I have a tendency to start things and then quit. And that I'm not on any kind of a career track. But there's a reason for that, Charlie." There was also a reason she never talked about this, because spitting it all out was no fun at all. "I was really angry when my mom left. Really hurt. I felt like I wasn't lovable enough for her to stay. Not important enough for her to stay. So when I grew up, I was just determined not to be like her—the kind of person who let a job become her whole world. The kind of person who'd leave her kids, her husband, everything, just for a job."

Charlie took her fingers off the computer keys. "I wouldn't want to be like that, either."

"I admit, my job history looks like the record of a Mexican jumping bean. But that wasn't because I couldn't commit to something. It was because I never wanted to care that much about any one job. I wanted people to be important to me. Not jobs. Not *things*."

"Sheesh. I get what you mean." Charlie risked another sideways look. "Do you ever see her? Your mom?"

"Every couple years. She sends cards at Christmas, birthdays. I send cards back. Sometimes she flies in. We go out to dinner, talk. But it's like she's a stranger."

"That really sucks," Charlie said.

"It does. At this point, I know that the lousy relationship is partly my fault. But it's just not the same. It's always *there*, that she took off on me. The trust is broken. It's not as if I ever hated her or anything like that. I love her. But I feel really, really violently about not breaking anybody else's trust."

"Yeah, I would, too."

"What I'm trying to tell you…is that I'd never leave a kid. I'd never, ever abandon a child. I'm not asking for your trust, Charl, because trust has to be earned. But I told you that background, so you'd know more about who I am. I can't swear I'm the best guardian for you. I can't swear this'll work out for you. But I can swear that I won't walk out on you. You hear me?"

"Okay, okay." Charlene'd been attentive, but Merry should have known, enough was enough of the adult talk. Still, she stood up, nudged against Merry's shoulder. "You think we could get this sometime?"

"The laptop?" Merry felt a fierce protectiveness nest in her heart. Not about the stupid computer. But because Charlene hadn't done it before. Offered a nudge. A touch. It wasn't as if she avoided every hug—and God knew, Merry was big on affectionate hugs—but Charlene had never volunteered before.

She still hadn't confessed about the mystery call from her mother. But one crisis at a time. It was worth it, spilling all that hurtful history about Merry's own mother, just to feel the squirt snuggle next to her.

"Yeah, of course I mean the laptop."

Back to the ranch. They were talking about computers. Or, at least, Charlene was. "Sure. But not right this minute, okay?"

"I didn't think you'd just let me get it today. But sometime."

"As far as I can tell, Charl, you're more than capable of researching what you need from a computer. If you need something like this, say. The only part I want a vote on is Internet stuff. Parental controls. That kind of thing."

"You think I'd look at porn? Yuck." Charlene ambled

off a foot or two, poking at different computers, peering at their stickers.

Merry ambled after her. "It's not that. Adults prey on kids on the Net."

"I'm smarter than all them," Charlene assured her.

Before Merry could respond, a familiar voice spoke up behind them. "So what are you two shopping for?"

Merry whirled around to see Cooper. Charlene immediately started talking to him about GB and MB and capacity and sound quality. She looked past their heads, hoping to see Jack. He had to be in the store, if his son was in there?

Her pulse was suddenly gamboling like a happy puppy's. Which struck her as annoyingly silly, when sex or any private connection wasn't remotely possible here. No place on the planet could be less conducive to anything intimate or romantic or private. Still, she wanted to tell him how the lawyer's visit had gone, just *be* with him for a few minutes.

But she hadn't forgotten that Jack's son had a serious problem, too. Coop was being so kind, bending his head to talk to Charlene, making Charlene feel like his little sister—cared for, protected.

But the chitchat died after a few more minutes, and Charlene said, "Merry, can I go look at CDs for two minutes? I promise. No more."

"Sure," Merry said, more than happy to grab the opportunity to look closer at Cooper. He looked all cleaned up in a fresh pair of jeans and a logo tee, but his eyes were still tired, and his expression tight and tense. Something in her heart murmured *uh-oh*.

"Any news?" she asked him.

He shook his head.

"Did she take the test?" Merry asked him softly.

He glanced over his shoulder, as if making sure no one else could hear, but then shook his head again. "I could really use your help, Merry."

"How? When? What?"

"I talked her into going to a doctor. The appointment's two days from now, Friday. The appointment's about getting tested. But it's also about her getting some birth control if this is gonna happen again." He heaved a sigh. "I said I'd take her."

Merry cocked her head. "How? You can't drive."

"That's why I need your help. We can get to the doctor on our own. Only it's in D.C. By our school. Which means, because Mom's still gone, that Dad would normally be picking me and Kicker up. So I was kind of hoping that you could pick Kicker and me up from D.C. that afternoon. Like say you were shopping or something, so you were already there? Because otherwise, Dad would want a reason why I was late. And I could invent something for Kicker, like that I just wanted to be with my girl, you know? But that won't work for Dad, so I need a cover."

Her heart didn't murmur an *uh-oh* this time; it thunked like a hammer. The plan sounded mighty convoluted. And sneaky-sticky. Stickier than hot honey, in fact. "Coop, I can find a way to pick you and Kicker up, no problem. I can also take Charlene shopping or somewhere in D.C., so there'd be no reason to lie to your dad. But I think you should tell your dad what's going on. You're not even giving him a chance to help you. I *know* he'd want to be there for you."

Those big brown eyes looked as haunted as ghosts. "I know that, too. That's not the problem."

"So what's the problem with telling him?" Cripes, a half-dozen teenagers suddenly hurled down the aisle. The darn store was teeming with bodies. She urged him over to a quieter spot.

"It's that I don't want to disappoint him. To let him down, you know?"

She hesitated. "I can totally understand that, Coop. But everyone makes mistakes. He wouldn't love you less or be less proud of you just because you made a mistake—"

"Maybe not. But if she isn't pregnant, Mer, he wouldn't have to know. I don't have to risk letting him down. And the thing is, he thinks…"

When Cooper hesitated, Merry said, "He thinks what?"

Those lean shoulders shrugged again. "Dad thinks I'm smart. That I've got good judgment. That I'm not a screwup like Kicker can be." He fumbled. "I like it, Merry, that he doesn't think I'm a screwup, you know?"

"Aw, honey, you're *not*. This is just a human mistake. It's a big one, for sure, but it's something that happens to people."

"Please don't tell him. *Please*. I swear I'll tell him right away if she ends up pregnant. But I want to be able to tell him what we're going to do, so that I can at least show him that I've taken responsibility and stuff. So please don't tell him now, Merry. *Please*."

At that precise moment, she saw Jack and Kicker and Charlene all show up at the far end of the aisle. Her lungs felt strangled for air—or maybe that was guilt strangling her throat. Guilt at all this conspiring. Exhaustion from all this emotional turmoil. She was so darn miserable that the thrill factor at seeing Jack was practically eclipsed.

And that was it, she decided, for Best Buy. Other people loved the store, but for her, it was clearly a road to complete chaos. She was never coming here again if she could help it.

CHAPTER SIXTEEN

JACK COULD HARDLY WAIT to get the boys buckled in the truck before asking, very casually, "So…what were you talking to Merry about, Coop? It looked as if you were having a really serious conversation."

"We were."

Jack waited but his son didn't say anything else. That was Coop. Mr. Talkative. The boys held their Best Buy loot, because the sky was spitting rain, and they didn't want to risk anything getting wet in the truck bed. As they pulled out of the lot and headed home, the spit turned into a messy deluge.

Better than snow, Jack told himself. By the end of February, anything was better than snow. But the roads were winter-cruddy and the downpour just smeared it all around, especially under the glare of night lights and blacktop.

"You can't tell me what was so serious?" Jack finally pushed.

"Sure. It really made me think, in fact," Coop said slowly. He'd claimed the window seat, which meant they were both jammed between Kicker's shoulders—which was even more uncomfortable, because Kicker kept fiddling with the radio. Kicker in motion was all knees, elbows, shoulders and bones. More relevant,

Jack couldn't see through Kicker to catch even one good look at Cooper's expression—assuming he could drop his attention from the road. Which he couldn't.

Coop said, "Merry really had it rough as a kid. She wasn't telling me. She was talking to Charl. It's just…I happened to overhear."

"What happened to her? I've heard her talk about her dad. Seems like they're really close, talk on the phone all the time." Jack thought, this is sick, probing his own son for information about his lover. Not that Merry was his lover exactly…

But, actually, that's exactly what she was.

His lover.

The word stuck in his mind in spangles and sequins, too bright and sassy and noticeable for him to be able to ignore and deny. She really was undeniably his lover. One chance encounter, a guy could call something else. But not two. And not two particularly when there was no end point in sight.

Of course she hadn't had a chance to tell him to take off. If one kid wasn't around, then three were. Even teenagers managed to sneak more free time than they had. Even so, Jack was well aware she could probably have found a way to corner him about those occasions if she wanted to. Instead, she'd neither asked him for anything or implied she wanted any kind of hold on him.

Since the sex had been great—okay, okay, beyond outstanding sex—and she hadn't expressed a single problem or question, Jack knew perfectly well he should be kissing the ground in gratitude. How lucky could a guy get? Except…somehow he seemed to be going around with a continual headache, a continual hard-on, and a continual feeling that his entire life was upside down and no one had gotten around to telling him yet.

Coop was drumming the radio beat on his knee. "I guess her mom jumped ship when she was just a little kid, like Charlene's age. She took off because of a big job promotion."

Kicker suddenly looked at his brother. So did Jack, even though they weren't stopped at a light. Damn it, if that story didn't sound just like his ex-wife. What she'd done to the kids and him.

Cooper volunteered more, now that he had his brother's attention. "You should have heard her, talking to Charl. She was telling the kid she'd never take off on her. Like she knew how bad it felt to be abandoned. She said when her mom left, she felt like she was a throwaway."

Kicker didn't comment, which was probably the first time in history he had nothing to say. Lights flashed in the pouring rain. Jack turned onto their street, and glimpsed Merry and Charlene just pulling in their drive, running into their house, hoods over their heads to protect themselves from the downpour.

Jack wanted to say something brilliant to the boys before they got in the house, because he knew how this would go. They had new CDs. They'd disappear under headphones the minute they got their jackets off. But temporarily, he was at a loss as to what to say.

He tried to never talk down about their mom. Couldn't see the point. Dianne was their mother, would always be their mother, and no matter what she'd done, they needed to get along with her through their lives. His making that harder just never made sense to

Jack…but still. She'd basically walked out on all of them because of her job. It did suck.

Just like it sucked, what Merry's mother had done to her.

"Hey. You coming, Dad?"

Kicker was rapping on the window. Abruptly he realized the boys had immediately pelted outside when he'd parked in the drive, but he was still sitting there. "Sheesh," Jack said. "Lost my mind for a second there."

That was good for a minute of ribbing. But Jack thought, as he locked the door and peeled off his jacket in the back hall, that the lost-mind thing was a little too true.

When he'd started the conversation with the kids, he'd hoped to hear about the secret Cooper had trusted Merry with.

He hadn't found that out.

Instead, he'd uncovered something oddly deeper. How Merry had probably reached his quietest son. And why Coop so instinctively trusted her. Merry understood what Cooper had gone through, because both of them had mothers who'd chosen to spend time with their jobs over time with their kids.

Absently he opened the fridge, pulled out the orange juice, then somehow walked over to the kitchen window and forgot all about the O.J.

As a kid, he'd never remotely imagined a circumstance where his parents would abandon him. He'd had the best parents in the universe—or close enough. Naturally, they'd screwed him up. That's what parents did. But feeling wanted and loved and all that crap—he'd never doubted it for a second of his childhood.

Maybe that was why Dianne's defection had hit him

so hard. All his life, he'd never doubted he was worth loving. And once they hooked up, he'd believed totally that he loved and was loved in their relationship. So when she'd taken off, just for a job, it was as if she'd diminished him to a forgettable dream. Not lovable. Not interesting, not sexy, not appealing, not anything— enough—to matter to her.

His gaze drilled on the kitchen in Merry's house. No lights on in there yet. But he wasn't really looking.

He just couldn't seem to stop the chug of thoughts and memories in his brain. Naturally, he had to fret the boys' response over his own. His first job was to parent them. Not wallow in his own problems.

But the longer Merry was in his life, it seemed the more that personal pot of soup got stirred. Stirred, boiled and bubbled over.

Two months ago, truth to tell, he'd been happy as a clam. Thought his life was damn good. Believed that his kids were thriving, he was thriving, everything was going A-okay.

Then Merry hit.

He'd heard about posttraumatic stress. But he'd never heard of a posttraumatic Cupid attack before. Did a guy recover from this? Could he?

His gaze suddenly narrowed.

The light in Merry's kitchen suddenly went on.

CARRYING A GLASS OF WINE, an old blanket draped around her shoulders, Merry pushed open the glass doors to the backyard deck.

She left the door open a crack, so she'd hear if Charlene called her, and sank down on the steps. It had stopped raining an hour before, and the night was still damp and chilly, but still, a few minutes of sharp, fresh air was just what the doctor ordered.

Charlene had finally crashed extralate tonight. Before that, they'd hung out for ages in the kitchen. Merry made Boston Coolers—vanilla ice cream with Vernor's and cherries—and Charlene had suddenly poured out chitchat like she was a normal preteen talkaholic. She went on about some game she liked. Then about how lame the girls were in her English class. About math. About whether the cosmos could be full of dark galaxies.

En route, Charlene had set up the new phone, and while she'd programmed all that junk, Merry finagled her into talking about phone safety—like not picking up unless Charlene specifically recognized the number. She said everything she could think of to bait the hook. "I've been getting some crank calls, Charlie. That was especially the reason why I thought we should have a different phone. So I'm hoping this'll help, if neither of us pick up unless we recognize the phone number, okay?"

Charlene not only didn't object, she was all about it. Only nothing Merry said seemed to coax Charlene to confess about the call from her mother—or whoever the woman had been.

Now, Merry thought, she should have pressed harder.

Or maybe she should try pressing harder in the morning.

She took a long, slow sip of wine, feeling both tired and wired by the traumatic day. The chilly dampness was hardly warm, but the sky was a glossy black and the whole night shiny, the rain leaving the leaves and grass looking fresh-polished and glistening. The air had a sweet, ripe scent, redolent of green growing things and the promise of spring. The moon was struggling to push past clouds and take center stage.

It was a night for fairy tales, and just like in the best ones, the hero suddenly showed up, walking through the mist, tall and dangerous and handsome. Her heart tripped even before he opened his mouth.

"Aha. I see you've already got a glass." Jack raised an open bottle and two glasses, indicating that he'd not only brought his sexy self, but goodies. Even better, he plunked down on the step beside her, close enough that she could feel the heat coming off his body. Feel the heat coming off his gaze. "I thought you'd need me to bring the wine. Last I knew, you didn't want to drink anything near the kid."

"Yeah, but that was before. Back in that first couple weeks, when I was determined to be the perfect role model."

"And now?" He leaned over, clearly recognized her glass was empty, and poured some nice, warm, red stuff from his bottle. For damn sure, he bought better wine than she did.

"Now I know it's impossible to be a perfect role model. Besides which, I have a ton to do tomorrow. Which means somehow I have to get some sleep. And I was hoping the wine would help."

"Hasn't been the easiest last couple of days, has it?"

When he leaned back, she did, too. The whole world seemed easier with him beside her. No problem seemed as big. No worry as insurmountable. The sky even seemed softer, brighter, silkier. And if all that was silly fairy-tale allusions, the stuff she wanted to share with him was sharply real and had always been real. "Ah, Jack. This raising a kid business is really hard. Three months ago, my toughest problem was whether to wear kicky shoes or clunky heels out on a Friday night. Now…well, now I have to laugh."

"Laugh at what?"

"Just at all the crazy stereotypes I had before." She took another sip, then leaned back her head, letting her hair fall away from her face, floating free in that rich, soft breeze. "I was so positive suburbia was about the matron set, as far as women. That was so off. Maybe most of them are in the PTA, but they're playing soccer, not cleaning their ovens. Volunteering for causes right and left, not sitting home lolling in front of soap operas. They do play golf. Which is unfortunate."

"Ah. Not your game?"

"Let's just say that my favorite sport is trying on shoes. Which, you may not be aware, can be extremely aggressive." They were both leaning back on their elbows, close enough to kiss, she thought. But he hadn't kissed her. For all she knew, he hadn't thought about it. Yet somehow on this rain-drenched night after this impossibly traumatic day, all she could think about was kissing him. Or being kissed.

And he shot her a teasing grin for her "favorite sport" comment. "Are those an example of your shoe-shopping prowess?" He motioned toward her pink bunny slippers. Paired with old yoga pants and an old sweatshirt and an ugly gray blanket, she figured she looked as appealing as a bedraggled cat—which, come to think of it, might be why he hadn't kissed her.

"Well, yes, actually. These slippers were a present to myself for surviving last month. God. Who knew living in the suburbs was so complicated? I had to find out about blue books and titles. How to deal with insurance over the storm damage. Lawn care. Taxes. How a furnace works…or at least, what happens if you don't call up and order fuel before your tank is empty. Who on earth knew there was even a tank! What?"

He wiped a hand over his face.

"What?" she repeated. "You keep giving me a look—"

"Yeah. Because you're doing the fluffy thing." He checked her glass again, noted it was only a sip down, and leaned back. "You can do it well. Act like you're a dingbat who just flew in from ditz land. But it's a little too late for that with me, Mer."

"Hey. I *am* from ditz land."

"No," he said. "You're not."

Whew. It was unnerving…that kind of perception and insight coming from a guy—at least from a guy she loved. So she bumbled into a talk-fest to cover up. When it came down to it, she really had a ton to tell him—what happened that day with the lawyer, what she'd told Charlene about her own past, why she'd bought the new phone, but that she hadn't pressed Charlene about the phone call—so Jack didn't need to worry she'd broken his confidence.

"But I may still have to, Jack. I'm worried the woman's going to show up at our back door, or that there'll be another call. I still feel the best way to handle this is for Charlie to tell me on her own, but if she still hasn't said something after another few days…"

"Hey. If you have to tell her, then you have to tell her," Jack said readily, but then he suddenly hesitated. The easy flow of conversation suffered a hiccup. He looked down, instead of at her, and as if suddenly realizing they were within cuddling closeness of each other, shifted to a sitting position. "Coop mentioned that he'd heard you talking to Charlene about your mother."

"I didn't realize he'd overheard, but yes," Merry admitted.

Jack plunked down his wineglass. "It's easy for me to see why my boys think so much of you. Why Cooper trusts you."

"Thanks. That's a really nice thing to say."

"So…that's what he was talking to you about the other night? The secret? About his mother?" Jack pressed.

Merry felt a short, sharp stab of hurt. It wasn't sensible, to let herself be so vulnerable she could get hurt this easily, but the sting was so quick, so unexpected, that she just couldn't seem to brace against it ahead of time. She forced a light smile. "So that's why you came over, huh? To find out what Cooper told me?"

"No, of course not. I wanted to see you, but…"

Okay, she told herself. It wasn't like she didn't get it. He was a dad. When you were a parent, you worried about your kids. You did whatever you had to do to keep them safe. She hadn't understood that before, but she did since Charlie. So there was no excuse for feeling so darn hurt; Jack wouldn't be Jack if he didn't give a big damn about his sons. It was just…right at that split second…she felt used.

She'd get over it. She just needed a chance to catch her breath, suck it up.

"Hey," Jack said. "I just want to know what was troubling Cooper. What he told you. I told *you* what was going on with Charlene."

"That was different, Jack."

"How?" he asked disbelievingly.

She groped. "It's different because Charlene's so

young. Her mother's a completely unknown quantity. Her safety could be at stake. Where with Cooper…his secret isn't about his safety. It's a serious thing. But he's older than Charlene, and he asked me to keep his confidence."

"So? Charlene asked me to keep her secret—but I told you. I trusted you with it."

The whole magical night suddenly changed. The whiskery breeze suddenly bit. The dampness suddenly sank in at a shiver level. She said softly, "Is it possible for you to trust me with Cooper's secret just a little longer?"

"I want to know. It's about my son. I *need* to know."

"Yeah. You do. But could you trust me until Friday night? In fact…"

"In fact, what?"

Merry thought, it had been a pattern her whole life. She couldn't just dip her toe in mud; she had to jump right in up to the neck. "In fact," she surged on, not looking at him now, "I was thinking of going into D.C. Friday afternoon with Charlie. I was going to take her out of school. There's some kind of exhibit at the Smithsonian. Engines or something. The kind of thing her dad would have taken her to. Anyway…I could pick your boys up from school that afternoon, if you wanted, save you that commute. And maybe we could talk after that. Like after dinner."

He just looked at her, the moonlight making his expression appear silver-cold. "I don't understand why you can't tell me now, if you can tell me a few days from now." When she didn't immediately answer, he said, "You know, trust goes two ways."

"Yes, it does," she agreed, and then hesitated, thinking she was already neck-deep in mud, so why not risk going the whole depth under? Gently, carefully, she whispered, "Do you want me to trust you, Jack?"

It was possible her voice was so soft he hadn't heard her. But then he gathered up the wine bottle and glasses he'd brought.

Maybe he would have answered. Probably he would have answered. But because he had to think so long about it, her heart had already broken, about three times, maybe four.

Until that instant, she hadn't known how completely she'd fallen in love with him. Until that instant, she hadn't known that it was a game, her trying to believe it didn't matter if it went any further. Until that instant, she'd recognized all the huge differences between them; she'd just believed those differences wouldn't matter if the right feelings between them were solid and real.

She said suddenly, swiftly, "Good night, Jack." And disappeared inside the house, closing and latching the deck door before he could say anything else.

SOME BREAKFASTS WENT OKAY, and some were a fight all the way. This morning, nobody could manage to close the refrigerator without slamming it. Nobody could carry toast across the room without dripping jam. Kicker dropped half a quart of OJ. Cooper lost his shoes—which should have been challenging to lose, considering they were a size thirteen. Both boys heaved books and papers onto the kitchen table, threatening the stability of the house foundation.

Jack chugged coffee.

Kicker seemed to wake up talking and never let up.

"So, anyway. I know Mom's supposed to be back on Monday, but this'll happen again. You know it will. And you have to be sick of this long commuting thing, Dad. So I think a real easy way to solve this is to get us a car."

Jack chugged more coffee, trailing after both of them with a towel—sponges were never enough. "What an odd solution, considering neither of you have a driver's license yet. Thank you, God."

"But we will. We will. And one of the great things about us being twins is that we could probably get by with just one car. Two kids, yet we only need one car. Isn't that great? Cooper, speak up, you idiot."

"We need a car, Dad," Cooper immediately concurred.

"Then no one would have to do all this commuting. Which is so unfair on you."

"Thanks for caring," Jack said wryly, in between more gulps, and more swiping the towel after their messes. Somewhere, he had a spring jacket. And he knew there were some bills to go in the mail. "Sometimes it amazes me how unselfish you are, Kicker."

"Hey, me, too." Kicker never turned down a compliment, even in jest, but then he immediately returned to his agenda. "The problem, though, is that this has been two weekends in a row. Now going on three. My sex life is suffering."

Where the hell were those bills? And the damned mug he'd just been drinking from? Who the hell had put it right by the coffeemaker? Still, Jack took the time to remind him, "You're fifteen. You have no sex life."

"The sex life I *want*," Kicker qualified. "Come on. It's pretty hard to cast anchor and throw out a fishing line if you're living too far away to reel one in, you know."

"Huh?"

Kicker dropped the metaphors. "My Friday nights aren't doing so hot."

"Well, I'd take pity on your suffering, but you're gone more weekend nights than you're in. Far as I can tell, you've still got a ton of friends from the neighborhood here. You went out last Friday and Saturday, both times with girls."

"Well, yeah," Kicker admitted. "But I'm trying to keep girls in both cities, Dad. A guy with my charm and sex appeal needs to spread it around, you know?"

Cooper, who managed to be standing wherever Jack was trying to move, made a gesture, mimicking someone digging deep with a shovel. Jack had to crack a smile, even as he impatiently herded both kids to the door. "Well, I don't have an immediate solution for your social life, guys. Normally your mother isn't away this long. If this happens again, we can talk about some other options, but right this second, I don't have any answers. And she's supposed to be back in a couple of days anyway. Speaking of which…"

He locked the door, hiked to the truck, abruptly realized he'd forgotten the truck key and whatever he'd been about to say about his ex-wife and custody schedules as well. His lack-of-sleep headache didn't explain the sudden sinking feeling in his gut, as if he'd lost something real. Not like a key. Something that *mattered*.

His gaze took in every window next door. There was no light or sound emanating from her house.

"Hey, Dad, you go to sleep or something?"

Abruptly he realized that his hand was halfway extended to the truck handle, keys still forgotten in the house, and the minutes ticking by. Hell. A new symptom since Merry had come into his life. A complete suspension of awareness.

Of course, maybe it was just a seizure.

He trotted in and back out with the vehicle key, climbed in. "Anyway," he said, hoping this might be a natural segue from the last conversation, "Friday after school, Merry is going to pick you guys up, all right?"

Cooper, who'd typically installed himself by the window seat and already closed his eyes for a nap, suddenly seemed to wake up. "Say what?"

"That's okay with you two, isn't it? Friday, she's going to take Charlene to some special exhibit at the Smithsonian, so it's not like she'll be right *at* your school—but still close enough to make an easy pickup. She might not be able to get there until fairly late in the afternoon, but I didn't figure you two'd mind hanging with some friends for a short stretch, right?"

"Right. No sweat. That'll be cool."

Kicker was about to wax on, when Cooper suddenly piped up, "When did this all come about?"

"Last night. I was just talking to her, and she mentioned going to D.C. with Charlene. Said she could save me a commute that afternoon, if you guys didn't mind."

"No. Don't mind. But something doesn't seem right here. What'd you do?" Cooper asked.

"What?" Jack made it through the last light before the freeway, but he couldn't make sense out of Coop's comment.

"I thought you two were getting along great. But then you woke up this morning, been grumping around since you walked in the kitchen, then forgot your keys, forgot to get in the truck, no smiles at anybody, no yelling at Kicker when he spilled the juice, either. I mean, obviously something is way off. And now we find out you talked to Merry last night. What'd you do wrong?"

"What do you *mean,* what'd I do wrong? Why would you assume I did anything wrong? She offered to pick you boys up—"

"Yeah, like that's why you were grumping around the house this morning. I just don't know why you'd be mean to her...."

Jack's jaw wanted to drop five shocked feet, but darn it, they were merging into rush hour. Maybe the meek inherited the earth later in the day, but not before 9:00 a.m. The wheel huggers were all gritting their teeth, either drinking coffee or yelling into a phone, their right foot hammered on the accelerator.

Even in a life-threatening situation, though, the injustice of Cooper's accusation bit him to the quick. It was so unfair. So wrong.

And how the hell did Coop know he was suffering pangs of guilt? For Pete's sake, he hadn't done a single thing wrong. Hadn't jumped her. Hadn't dropped her. *He* was the one who should have been good and pissed at her, because she'd refused to tell him Cooper's damned secret.

And he was pissed about that. What was wrong with her that she didn't trust him?

Everybody trusted him. Friends, family. The whole neighborhood. His ex-wife. Hell, the United States government had given him practically every security clearance they'd ever invented.

Everybody knew he was trustworthy.

"I have *nothing* to feel guilty about. And I wasn't

mean to her. I have no idea why you'd even think such a crazy thing—"

"From the bassett-hound look on your face, Dad," Cooper said, which interested Kicker enough to swivel around to get a good look at his face. Not a good idea, to block his view of traffic and create an imminent threat to all their lives.

"You do have a hound look around the eyes, Dad," Kicker affirmed.

"You're both full of malarkey." It bit and kept biting. Not the kids. Merry. How completely, totally unreasonable she'd been. She'd asked if he trusted her.

No, he hadn't answered that right away, because what did his trusting her have to do with anything? She was the one who hadn't trusted him to tell Cooper's secret. She'd twisted everything. That's why he hadn't immediately answered her. Because she'd gotten him completely confused.

And then the damn woman had walked in the house with her eyes welled up as if she were about to cry, leaving him standing there, as if he'd suddenly stumbled into an alternate universe. Where did the welling eyes come from? Insanity? Fluffiness gone amok? He hadn't said anything to hurt her. He hadn't done anything to hurt her.

She had.

"Dad," Cooper remarked lazily, "you missed the turn."

He glanced up. He had. Missed. The. Damn. Turn.

"Look, Dad, you can't let women problems tear you up so bad. Just think of a way to make it up to her, and get it over with." Kicker, the Don Juan of the tenth grade, seemed to see himself as a sage coach.

Hell. Maybe the kid *was* qualified to coach him.

Jack was in the right, all the way, but being in the right couldn't seem to save him from feeling like a heel. A heel with mud stuck to his boots. A miserable heel with mud stuck to his boots.

CHAPTER SEVENTEEN

"I STILL DON'T GET IT. Why you're letting me skip school."

"We're not skipping school. At least not exactly." Merry glanced at Charlene but only for a millisecond. Her hands had a death grip on the steering wheel. Driving 95 veering onto 395 on a Friday was as much fun as, say, welts from poison ivy. All the drivers acted paranoid and manic. Maybe it was the D.C. politics? "You're getting all As. Even some A-pluses. And I wouldn't say spending the day at the Smithsonian is really skipping. It's tons of extra education really…"

A long black limo threatened to cut her off. Frankly, she took it as a personal insult to her Mini Cooper, but what could she do? She could hardly honk at some high-powered somebody.

Her heart was stuck somewhere in her throat, and not because of the crazy traffic. She hated not telling the total truth to Jack, but when she'd thought up this Smithsonian idea, it seemed an honestly super thing to do for Charlene. And if it worked for Cooper, that that was all the better.

Everybody was happy but her.

"You're going to have to help me navigate," she said to Charlene, in a voice showing vibrato talents she'd never had before.

"Merry. You need more than help."

"You're awfully lippy for a kid getting out of school today." She thought it'd all be better when they got off the freeway, but no. Wouldn't you think the Smithsonian was one building? Instead, Charlene's map claimed it was a dozen or more. And that they were all located in that "mall" place between Independence and Constitutional Avenues, only didn't anyone think it'd be nice to provide parking? Somewhere closer than five million miles away?

But the Natural History Museum had an exhibit about mothers. Well, actually it was about some really old dinosaur eggs, and the eggs showed that the unborn little dinosaurs didn't have teeth, and that was supposed to illustrate that the parent dinosaurs must have been caring mothers.

Okay, so Merry fully realized that was the hokiest excuse since boys asked girls out to watch the submarine races. But she needed a fresh way to talk about moms and mom behavior with Charlene.

Besides which, there was some kind of engine exhibit at the Arts and Industry part of the museum, which Charlene was guaranteed to love. Merry didn't have a clue how long either thing would take, but both places opened at ten.

"Merry—you can't fit in that parking place."

"Why not?"

"Because it's about six inches too small."

"So maybe we could go up on the curb just a little bit."

"Maybe you'll get a little hundred-buck ticket if you do that."

A mere detail, Merry thought. Eventually it all came together, the parking, the walking, the fee, getting maps, ignoring the maps, and then, maybe an hour later, getting to the infamous dinosaur egg exhibit. Charlene, thankfully, was all about it, giving Merry a perfect excuse to zoom into her spiel.

"The big deal about this, I guess, is that people had no idea dinosaurs were good mothers before this."

"Yeah." Charlene was sort of listening. She loved the place—no surprise, since she loved anything to do with science. She looked a little rough this morning, a cap pulled tight on her head, hands slugged in her pockets, her khakis fraying at the cuffs. Merry thought she resembled Dakota Fanning trying to look tough.

"You know about the pandas in the D.C. zoo?"

"Sure. Everybody loves our pandas."

"Well, the moms tend to give birth to twins, but they almost never raise both babies. They see if there's one that's thriving. Then if it's doing well, they tend to neglect the second one. Give all the attention to the biggest, strongest baby."

Charlene frowned. "That sucks."

"I guess the idea is that the mom's trying to up the odds of at least one child surviving. So she chooses one to give it every advantage she can. And then there are penguins—" It's not like Merry hadn't been up all night studying this.

"I love that movie," Charlene interrupted.

"Me, too. But with Magellanic penguins, the mom lays two eggs and lets them both hatch, but then she gives all the food to the biggest chick and lets the other one starve. And then there are pigs—"

"How'd pigs get into this conversation?"

By then they were both starved and had settled in a crammed cafeteria-sized place with sandwiches and chips. "The thing is," Merry explained, thrilled to use more of the research she'd looked up, "that pigs are born with these little eyeteeth that stick out sideways. They use the teeth to stick their brothers and sisters, so they can get to the mom's milk better. Unfortunately, that means that the littlest one in the litter tends to get all sliced up, besides which, he can't get enough milk."

"Eeeuuu. Gross. And mean, too."

"That's what I thought. It's weird. I always thought moms were just naturally nurturing and loving. That unless something happened to screw them up, that's how it was. Only that's not always true. Like with chimpanzees…"

"I love chimps."

"Yeah, me, too." She looked around for a waste bin to stash all their paper. "Human moms sometimes abandon their babies—but ape moms never do. Only if a chimp mother is somehow unable to feed her baby— like there isn't enough food because there's a famine or something like that—then she won't hurt her own baby. But she'll kill the baby of another mom chimp."

Charlie screwed up her face. "Ugh. Double ugh."

"Yeah, I know, but it just goes to show…we all seem to count on a mother to be perfect, don't we? But they're not. Nature didn't set up any mom to be perfect. At least not like we'd want them to be."

"Yeah." Charlie chewed on her sandwich, then chewed some more. "Kind of like your mom. And my mom. Right?"

Merry was afraid to breathe. Her baby was getting it. Exactly what she'd hoped. "Right. You and I were both especially stuck with moms who disappointed us. But what are we going to do, let that affect our whole lives? It's just the way it is. We can't fix how other people behave. Cripes, they can't seem to fix themselves, half the time."

She thought, *Now, Charlie. Tell me about the phone call.*

"You know what I think?" Charlene asked.

"No, what?" More not breathing, but Merry kept thinking *now now now.*

"I think I don't want to be a mom. When it comes down to it, I think it'd just be a lot easier to be a boy than a girl altogether."

Eek. That wasn't how this was supposed to go. "Just because we had moms who let us down? But Charlie, think about it. When you're a mom, you can do it the way you believe is right. In fact, maybe because we had absentee mothers, we'll never do the same things they did."

"Yeah, but..." Charlene dusted her hands. "You know what happened on the bus?"

"What bus?" Merry wasn't sure what a bus had to do with the subject—at least with the subject she wanted Charlene to talk about.

"The bus to the spelling bee a few weeks ago."

"Oh, that one. What?"

"This girl in my class. She went down on an eighth grader in the back of the bus."

"Oh, that. Goodness, I hoped that wasn't true."

"Well it was. And if she'd been a guy, she'd never have felt she had to do that. Guys have the power. Guys don't have the same things to be afraid of." She looked at Merry and rolled her eyes. "Come on. Chill. Quit hyperventilating. You had to know stuff like that goes on."

"Not at *eleven,* for Pete's sake!"

Okay, Merry thought, that part of the day had turned into a failure. Not for Charlene—who loved every exhibit and probably could have rented a cot to sleep in the Smithsonian, she was that happy. But Merry couldn't stop being upset about the bus story; she still hadn't heard a confession about the mystery phone call, and she was completely out of ideas how to coax the information out of Charlene now without forcing it.

Still, there was lots of room for the day to get worse, and it did.

Cramming two tall teenage boys in the back of the Mini Cooper was possible, just a lot like squishing sardines in a can. She picked them up at their school before five. She only needed one look at Cooper's face to feel her heart go clunk. He looked waxy pale and stiff as straw.

"Do you guys want to go straight home, or are you hungry?" she asked.

Naturally, all three kids affirmed they were starving.

"Well, how about if we call your dad and tell him we'll be a little late? The thing is that the rush hour traffic's horrendous, so if you guys are hungry anyway and don't mind stopping for a bit..."

Kicker called. Jack gave the okay. Charlene prattled on about the things she'd seen in the museum. Kicker hunched forward and breathed down her neck. Kicker and Charlene navigated.

Cooper didn't say a word.

The vote was for burgers and fries. Merry pulled in to the parking lot, and coaxed Kicker and Charlene to go in to order the food. It was the only way she could think of to corner Cooper, and she did, the instant the other kids piled out of the car. "Okay, Coop. You look miserable. So…she's pregnant."

"No, she's not. That part's okay."

Merry frowned in confusion. She was so certain the pregnancy news was positive, because that was the only thing that could have caused the beaten-up posture, the devastated quiet in Coop's expression. "So what's the deal?"

A dull red seeped up his neck. "I thought I was her first," he said lowly. "Seems not. Seems like she's been all over town and then some. Seems I had to get tested for an STD."

"Oh, *damn,* Coop."

"I won't have the results until Monday. The doctor didn't think it was a problem, but still said I should be tested. I asked him what happens if it's a yes, that I've got this STD. He said I just take a certain antibiotic. It's pretty cut and dried as long as I don't ignore it. That's what he said."

"So that part's good."

"Yeah, that's okay, but that's not the point. She *lied* to me. I thought we were tight, you know? I thought it was a first for both of us. I thought I loved her. I thought she loved me." Cooper thrummed his fingers on a knee. "Well, I'm through with that love crap now. The doctor told me not to mess around until the test comes back. Like I would. I don't need to be around another girl for a long, long, long time."

"Kicker's the one who's usually big on going out, isn't he?"

"Yeah. Exactly. That's how he likes it, seeing a lot of girls. Not me. I never got the big urge before, until I met her. And then finally, I got what all the fuss was about. I couldn't wait to be near her. Couldn't wait to be with her." He rolled his eyes. "Yeah, right. Apparently she couldn't *wait* to be with all those other guys either. I was just one on a really long list."

"Aw, hell, Coop. That so sucks." She'd have wrapped her arms around him, but even if the Mini allowed for that kind of acrobatic move, Kevin and Charlene abruptly bounded out of the fast food place, bearing bags and drinks.

"Forget it. It doesn't matter," Cooper muttered, and then sunk back—as much as he could sink back in the tiny backseat—and stayed quiet the rest of the trip home.

Or most of the way home.

Even wasting almost an hour on dinner and messing around, the traffic around D.C. was still like a major blood clot, impossibly slow going. Being Friday night didn't help. Still, after they finally left the city in the dust, Merry hoped they could zoom the rest of the way home.

They were a short fifteen minutes from home when the car suddenly gave a little…lurch. And then the engine coughed.

"It's okay, baby, we're all tired," she told her car.

The boys cracked up at her talking to the car. Charlene, used to it, just rolled her eyes. But they weren't teasing with quite so much hilarity when the car suddenly just…quit. Right on the freeway. As they were driving. With a zillion and a half vehicles trying to run them down.

"It's okay, it's okay," Merry sang out reassuringly. She managed to pull over to the shoulder, her heart beating louder than a freight train, her stomach pitching panic. "Nothing ever happens to the Mini Cooper. She just probably didn't feel well for a second. She'll be okay. We'll be okay. Just relax, everybody…."

The sun wasn't going down as fast as it did mid-winter, but by then, it was after seven. Dusk hazed the landscape. Car lights were turning on. The temperature was dropping faster than a stone, and when Merry climbed out of the car, the sudden snap of cold made her shiver.

"Merry, what are you doing?" Charlie asked.

"You stay inside!" She didn't have a clue what she was doing, except that she didn't want three kids outside with all the cars zooming by. She searched for some clear problem. The tires all looked fine. The car had a little road grime. There was no smoke or steam or anything horrendous that would give her a clue why the car was so unhappy. The baby had never given her a lick of trouble, so it wasn't as if she had some past pattern to work with.

She wasn't panicking. She wasn't going to freak out.

Cooper and Kevin both started to climb out. "Please stay in. It's not safe!" she insisted, but apparently they'd waited all they could stand.

Kevin reached her first and put a big, friendly big-brother paw around her shoulder, as if he weren't a zillion years younger than her. "Mer," he said. "Do you have Triple A?"

"I think so. I mean, I had it in Minnesota, so I still have it here, right?"

The boys exchanged glances. "I'll tell you what," Cooper said. "Just give me your wallet, okay? We'll find the card. And we'll phone—"

"Of course not," she said. "I'm the adult. I'll do it." She pawed through her purse. Three lipsticks. Two lip glosses. Blush. Mascara. Kleenex. PMS pills. BC pills.

Three nail files—one so old she should have thrown it away ages ago. A teeth cleaner. Two teeny perfume samples. A sample-size hand cream. A cleaner receipt...

"Merry," Kicker said, "Just give over the wallet, okay? We're just going to look for the insurance stuff, like Triple A."

"Hey guys," Charlene said from the front passenger window. "I think it's just that we're out of gas."

Merry whirled around. "I can't be out of gas. I filled up two weeks ago. This car never needs gas."

But it seemed, when the key was put back in the lock and turned, that the gas gauge failed to budge off Empty.

SINCE THE BOYS WERE with him, Jack hadn't stopped once after work for a quick one with the guys. The neighborhood bar was no Cheers. It was just a corner dive with a big-screen TV that served a decent burger. Divorcees of both genders tended to pop in there for a quick drink and dinner, and because it was neighborhood, people could either walk home or get a ride if they needed one.

Since the kids had called about catching dinner on the road, Jack hadn't felt like cooking, and stopped in for a hamburger. The two-pounder had just been handed to him, still steaming and dripping cheese, when his cell phone rang.

He was supposed to see Merry tonight. Supposed to hear the big secret his son had confided in her. But the one thing he absolutely, positively had to do tonight was figure out how he'd hurt her feelings and find a way to make that right. Really right.

He'd gotten a taste of losing her last night.

All day, he'd tried to talk himself out of believing that his whole world had crashed in.

So when the cell phone rang, he jumped, thinking just possibly it could be Merry. Instead, well…he never did get his hamburger. Or a drink. By the time he'd picked up a gas can and located them on the expressway, he was shaking his head at the motley group hovering outside the Mini Cooper. Charlene huddled against Merry's side. His boys framed the girls on both sides like telephone poles, their arms around the girls' shoulders, clearly trying to keep the females warm.

But it was Merry his gaze honed on, like a bee lonesome for its honey. Her cheeks were shiny from the wind. She was wearing a pink jacket, her hair catching a hint of mahogany from the road lights.

"Jack!" She broke free from the group cuddle the minute he pulled the truck up behind them. The night had become too dusky to read her expression, so he couldn't tell if she'd been as miserable all night and day as he had. For darn sure, she was upset now, but it pretty obviously wasn't about the two of them. "I told them I could walk to a gas station! You didn't have to come!"

"I told Mer we'd do it," Cooper interrupted Merry.

"Obviously we wouldn't have let her walk off alone in the night, Dad," Kicker interrupted Coop.

"Man, did we have a good time at the Smithsonian," Charlene informed him.

"I told the kids I had Triple A. At least I think I do. And it couldn't have been that far to an exit. I hated to bother you—"

"I told her you wouldn't mind, Dad," Kicker interrupted her.

"Yeah. We both told her to cool it, that it'd just be safer if you came with the gas, except—" Cooper interrupted his brother.

"Except that I had to pee really bad," Charlene told him, "and that kind of complicated things."

When Cooper got him aside for all of two seconds, he hissed, "Don't say anything mean to Mer. She was really close to crying."

Like they thought he'd beat up on Merry? Ever in this life?

Okay, okay, so possibly under normal circumstances he might have made a *teeny* comment about remembering to read the gas gauge. But not when she was standing there, looking wiped out and fragile and cold.

He figured he'd try to make that up to her, though, too, when he caught up with her later…only "later" slowly became less and less of a possibility.

Naturally, once everybody was finally home, they all split to their respective houses. In the kitchen, Jack honed straight for the breadbox for a hunk of a crust, anything to take the starvation edge off. Even dying of hunger, though, he had to give his sons some solid attaboys. "Looked to me like you took pretty good care of the girls."

"Well, yeah. She'd have been freaked if that happened when she was alone." Kicker glanced at the clock. "Hey. I'm going out in an hour. I gotta get a shower."

"Where are you going and how're you getting there?"

Cooper answered automatically for his twin. "Girl. Her place. Taylor Reed—you know, you play poker with her dad. So it's neighborhood, close enough for him to walk. They're just going to hang, watch a movie, should be home before midnight."

"Sometimes I think you should let your brother answer for himself."

"You had twins. What can I say? It's what we do."

Jack cuffed his son's neck, well aware the kid had dark, wounded eyes tonight. "So you have plans, too?"

"Not tonight. Although I'd like to hit a movie if you got time."

Jack only gulped once. All he wanted from life was to see Merry.

But when a fifteen-year-old was willing to do something with a parent—particularly on a Friday night—Jack figured he'd damn well better jump. Especially because Coop had been so unhappy lately.

"Check the paper. You pick the movie and the time. I just need to climb out of these work clothes and make a phone call, all right?"

It was looking increasingly doubtful that he was ever going to get dinner, but that's the way the cookie was crumbling tonight. He took the stairs two at a time, peeled off his work duds, yanked on old cords and an even older sweater. None of that took more than a minute or two.

He'd just turned off the bedroom light when he hesitated. If he phoned Merry from downstairs, Coop would easily overhear, so he picked up the bedroom receiver by the window and dialed from there.

Her phone rang twice. Then suddenly the light popped in a bedroom upstairs and Jack froze.

It wasn't bedtime. And she normally slept in that downstairs spare room, he knew. So he just didn't expect to see her upstairs. Without clothes.

Well. She was wearing a towel.

"Hello," she said breathlessly...which she undoubtedly was, if she'd just chased out of a shower to get the phone.

Maybe Charlene had just climbed in the downstairs shower. Maybe Merry just wanted to use the upstairs shower for some reason. Who knew? It was just hugely taxing on his heart rate…to see her wet tumble of dark hair. To see the charcoal towel wrapped less than tightly over her breasts, less than modestly over the sweet curve of her fanny.

"Hello?" Merry repeated, this time with tension in her voice.

He got a grip. "Merry, it's just me, Jack." Hell, his hesitation had made her worry it was the damn woman caller, the mom threat. He could have kicked himself. "We were going to try and talk tonight, but nothing seems to be working out here. So I just thought—"

"Yeah, I'm glad you called." The minute she recognized his voice, he saw her shoulders sink in relief.

His window was dirty. He couldn't remember giving a damn in his entire lifetime about dirty windows, only now, when he desperately wanted to see across the yard, when he wanted a crystal-clear view through his window and hers…parts were blurry. She turned around, started walking as she talked. The towel slipped another notch. Her wet hair seemed to leave beads of diamonds on her bare back.

"About Cooper, Jack…"

He caught his breath. He didn't know whether there was a chair or bed by that window, but she suddenly sat down. Almost that quickly she started drying her hair with the towel…which mean she was no longer wearing the towel. Which meant she was sitting there stark naked. The window sill blocked far too much of his view. But he could still see her bare shoulders, the hollow at the base of her neck.

Her voice had turned velvet. "I know, Jack, that you want me to tell you Cooper's secret. But I've turned this around in my heart every which way. I trust you. I'd trust you with my life. But your son asked me to trust him, too. I can't seem to find a way to make this right both ways. So…I *do* want to tell you. The part that I think you want to know as a parent. But for the details, I'd rather leave that for Cooper to share or not."

She fell silent, as if waiting for him to respond to this. And he wanted to. He wanted to focus solely on his son.

But he couldn't seem to stop looking at her. It wasn't knowing she was bare that had his throat going so dry. It wasn't lust. And yeah, of course, lust was an issue. For God's sake, she was gorgeous.

And that's what he'd been telling himself for a while now. That her gorgeousness was the pull. The eternal lust thing. A man was always going to respond to a beautiful woman. And when the woman wanted him and expressly indicated a desire to get naked with him—come on. That lust thing naturally quadrupled.

It's just…he felt the lust thing right now. Only it wasn't causing the yank on his damned heart. It wasn't causing the bluesy song thickening his pulse. It wasn't causing the reason he couldn't move, couldn't break his gaze from the look of her, couldn't think, couldn't breathe.

It was a single drop of moisture, sliding from the back of her hair, down her shoulder, down her arm.

It was the gesture she made with her hand…the fingers in the air, even though no one was there. Her talking with her hands, those slim soft hands. The towel gone. Her hair still wet.

It was feeling how richly he'd fallen in love with her, how much his world had new colors and textures because of her. It was discovering how painfully lonesome he'd been, without even knowing it all these years, because it was her he'd been lonesome for. No one else.

"Jack…what he talked to me about…the part you need to know…is that this girl broke his heart. She really hurt him, in just about every way a girl can hurt a guy. And I know he's just fifteen. That there's always someone who's going to be our first heartache. But he's not like Kevin, you know? Kicker has more…resilience. Cooper really opened his heart to this girl."

It's not as if he wasn't listening. He was. It's not as if his son didn't matter to him. He was going down in minutes to be with Coop, and somehow before or after that movie he'd start some kind of conversation about women and hurts and love. Maybe he liked conversations like that on a par with brussels sprouts, but he'd still do it.

He was the dad. There was no one else to pass that kind of buck to.

But that was a minute or two from now. And right now it was still *this* minute. And in the dark room, his eyes hopelessly locked on her, all he could think of was how in God's name had this happened? At his age? To fall this thick, this deep, this hopelessly crazy in love?

"Jack? Are you there? You haven't said a word."

"I'm here. I—" Abruptly she realized that she'd turned toward the window. And even though she couldn't see him—at least he couldn't imagine how she could see in his dark room—she not only faced his bedroom window but had put her palm, flat, on the glass pane. As if wanting to connect with him. As if wanting, in any way, to touch him.

It wasn't him. It was some madman. A sentimental mad man. A sentimental immature madman who'd lost any sense he'd ever had. Who seemed to be reaching out, and laying his palm, flat, against his glass pane.

He meant to verbally answer her. Tried to answer her. Only somehow he couldn't get any volume out of his voice.

"You need to just…be kind. Take it seriously, okay? I don't care how young he is. He's so miserable. It hurts…to love the wrong person…to love someone who lets you down. It doesn't matter how old you are."

He tried to speak again, but he wasn't sure who she was talking about. Coop? Him?

Her?

Life? Hell, probably everybody ended up loving someone who let them down…but his response had been to put up emotional walls. How come Merry hadn't? How come she was still so giving and generous and open?

How had he not seen that before?

"Um, Jack? Are we done with this conversation?"

The hell they were, he thought. Only right then, he couldn't get a single word to come out of his mouth. Not that made any sense.

"Okay," Merry said suddenly. Her hand print disappeared from the window. She turned around completely, so her back was to him. "I understand what's going on here," she said quietly. "It was about the other night. When you couldn't answer the question about whether you trusted me—"

"Merry—" Finally, he found his voice, only to have her swiftly, immediately interrupt him.

"It's all right. I put you on the spot, and I'm sorry. There's no reason you should trust me, Jack. We've been having an unexpected little…fling. It's been warm and fun, lots of affection involved, some need, some chemistry. But it's not as if we were in over our heads, right? You didn't think I was taking it seriously, did you?"

He cleared his throat, tried, "Merry, I really didn't—"

He heard a short, soft bubble of a laugh. "I'm the original free bird. I never wanted to be nailed down—to anything or anyone. Ever. So if you were even remotely worried about that kind of thing, put your mind at rest. And right now—just go take care of Coop, okay?"

She clicked off the phone and flicked off the lamp.

He clicked off his phone, too. But he stood there longer, staring across the yard at her dark window, because she hadn't moved. She was still sitting there, her back to him, motionless.

And he thought, for God's sake, why the Sam Hill do I have the feeling that I hurt her *again?* When it was her darn fault for not giving me the chance to talk to begin with?

But Jack knew, gut deep, that it was damn well time he opened his mouth and found the right words to say to Merry. Fast.

Or he'd lose her before he even had a chance to win her.

CHAPTER EIGHTEEN

WHEN A WOMAN'S LIFE was falling apart, when people who mattered to her were troubled, when nothing had gone right for four solid days and she was exhausted, don't you think fate could kick in a little break? Just one? Just a little one?

When the doorbell rang midmorning on Monday and Merry saw June Innes on the doorstep, she opened the door with a smile, but what she wanted to do was crawl under a chair and cry.

"I believe I told you that I would be making impromptu visits."

"Yes, I know you did," Merry said cheerfully and stepped aside so the guardian *ad litem* could come in. Mrs. Innes's expression rivaled the friendliness of a Gila monster. She was wearing a skirt in a scaly green, a polyester blouse with a pointy collar, and her hair was curled so tight it could have auditioned as springs.

On the other hand, Merry realized she was hardly in a position to criticize. Her hair was in straggly pigtails, her feet bare, and her old tee and jeans were covered in paint. Pink paint. In fact, the open can and brush were still dripping in the back room, undoubtedly starting to dry out. "I apologize for all the messes. After Charlie left for school this morning, I started painting in the spare room—"

"Yes. Whatever. I'm here because I've been hearing a number of disturbing things that I feel we should discuss."

"Oh? Charlie's doing great in school. Would you like some coffee? Or tea?"

Mrs. Innes wanted tea. With milk. And she was one of those bag dunkers...the kind who dunked and dunked and dunked the bag, instead of just letting the darn thing stew in the hot water.

The kitchen had breakfast dishes heaped in the sink, a dishwasher still loaded up, and a floor that wasn't going to win prizes for sterility—all of which Mrs. Innes made a point of noticing.

Merry had no doubt the situation was going to get worse.

A few days before—in fact, all her life—she'd been an incurable optimist who could find the bright side in a tornado cloud. But these last days, well...Charlene had wakened Saturday morning with a toothache. Finding a dentist on the weekend was a pistol, particularly as Charlene didn't like her dentist and only wanted to go to a dentist who was into "no pain." Fine. Merry had asked half the neighborhood before identifying a name, then got lost driving there—which was nothing compared to how lost she'd gotten coming home. By the time they'd gotten back home, Charlene was sick to her stomach and Merry found two messages from Jack. He was driving the boys back to his ex-wife's, would catch up with her when they could.

It was like that. Phone tag. One crisis after another. Naturally she expected Jack needed some private dad time with Cooper, and that took precedence over anything else. But in the meantime, she was worried about both Cooper and Charlene, and she hadn't slept in an unknown number of nights because of Jack.

That was the Jack who didn't trust her. The Jack who appeared to definitely not want any type of serious relationship, since he contradicted her when she'd tried to tactfully bring it up. And Merry had already told herself, several dozen times, that she'd never believed they had a future together. Her own mother had indelibly ingrained the lesson that she didn't matter enough for people to stay—or specifically, for people to love her enough to stay.

So she didn't expect permanence from anyone, and certainly shouldn't have from a guy she'd probably never have met if they hadn't chanced on living next door to each other. All night, two nights in row, she'd told herself that only an idiot would build a few rolls in the hay and sympathetico conversations into the potential for a lifelong deal. She wasn't an idiot. She was just the kind of person who always did things five hundred percent.

And then paid the price for it.

"I'll be making a formal report to the judge this Friday." June dunked the tea bag a few more times. "As I believe you were informed from the start, you're in a probationary position as guardian. Whether Mr. Ross established you as his choice of guardian or not, the welfare of the child is the court's final responsibility, especially in circumstances as unusual as this."

"I understand that." Merry had poured coffee for herself, but she hadn't taken a sip, couldn't imagine her stomach tolerating anything right now. She was trying to sit across from Mrs. Innes and act as if everything was okay. But it wasn't okay. In fact, darn well nothing was okay.

Not only were dirty dishes heaped in the sink, but laundry was visibly piled on the laundry floor, and the massive canvasses of finger painting draped all the walls instead of Charlie's famous nouveau art. And cripes, none of that stuff mattered. But June Innes's expression did.

Merry felt as fidgety as a child called into the principal's office. She wasn't afraid of June. The woman just always made her feel as if she were absolutely alone, with no one between her and a rotten black abyss.

"Since you made this extra visit," she said, "I assume you want to tell me what you plan to advise the judge."

"Yes. But first let me ask *you*, how you would evaluate how the child is doing."

Merry sensed a trap, but still felt that honesty was the only way to answer the question. "Charlene isn't a run-of-the-mill kid. I don't think any child is. But Charl is…so special. She's ultra-bright, but she's also more self-contained than most other kids. I think overall, her dad's love gave her an incredibly sound foundation, but right now…"

"Right now?" Mrs. Innes pressed.

"Right now, she's doing fine—on the surface. Her grades are terrific. She's become involved with a variety of interests outside school as well. Sports, hobbies, friends. But—" Merry hesitated, thinking maybe she didn't have to be *totally* honest…. Yet to be less just didn't seem right. "I don't believe she's really dealt with her dad's death. She's not the kind of person to easily show emotional feelings, heaven knows, not like me. But I think there's a pocket of hurt deep inside her that she just isn't ready to let up for air yet."

June couldn't have sat up straighter if there was a spear sticking up her behind. "I believe I instructed you several times to take her to a grief counselor."

"I understood that you were advising that. Not forcing it. And I wasn't against the idea, Mrs. Innes, but Charlene was."

Ms. Innes took out a pencil, started thrumming it on the table. "She's the child. You're supposed to be the one who decides what she does and doesn't do. She's in no position to know what she needs."

"To a point I agree with you. But to a point I don't. She's not a baby. She's been raised very independently and has very definite ideas about what she wants and needs—"

"And you'd know this because you raised so many children yourself?" Without giving her a chance to respond, June continued. "The school claims she's still running around in those outlandish clothes. Her father's clothes. Men's clothes."

"She is. Some of the time."

"And she's still wearing her hair in that mannish style—"

"Most of the time. Not always—"

"Yet you still haven't taken her to a counselor. And you're still letting her call herself a boy's name."

"Charlie was her dad's name. The clothes were her dad's clothes. It's not the same thing as a gender issue. It's about her father—"

Mrs. Innes sighed. "You said that before, but you seem to think it's an acceptable excuse. She's doing some very unhealthy, abnormal things."

"Wait a minute. Please." Merry's stomach started churning acid. "I don't know what your definition of 'normal' is. But I'm aware Charlene isn't necessarily doing 'standard' things, but she's not a standard kid. I've been trying to listen to her. To her heart. To her feelings. To respond to what she seems to need—"

"And that sounds very nice," Mrs. Innes said flatly. "But I had questions about your judgment before this. It's not just her hair and appearance. It's not just the lack of grief counseling. But her father seemed to have chosen such a completely inappropriate person to parent his daughter. You're young and single, so you're bound to get involved with someone and shake up her life all over again. You presume to make decisions when you have absolutely no parenting experience or psychology or experience with children. And when I contacted the school—I was told, well, for one thing, there were rumors about your having a pajama party that included boys."

"I was right here. In fact, so was a neighbor. All night. There wasn't a minute that wasn't supervised. I just—"

"Furthermore," Mrs. Innes continued, as if she hadn't spoken at all, "I was informed that you not only *allowed* the child to skip school on Friday, but that you encouraged her. Even that you were frank with the school office about what you were doing."

"Wait. Could you just wait for one second? You're absolutely right that I told the school what I was doing. I had no reason to lie. I was taking her to the Smithsonian. It was an educational day. She probably got more out of it than she possibly could in regular classes—"

"You still took her out of school."

"Because I thought she needed something special. Because I keep trying to find ways to bond with her, to build trust." Merry wanted to go on, but darn it, she felt a brisk stab of guilt. She could defend taking Charl to the Smithsonian forever and a day, but truthfully, she'd originally thought up the outing to help Cooper. And Mrs. Innes didn't have to sense weakness to pounce.

"You think you build trust with a child by breaking the rules? By having her see that an authority figure in her life just arbitrarily ignores the rules? And that *is* the problem, Ms. Olson. You're not an authority figure. You don't appear to have any desire to be in that role, yet a child of that age needs exactly that." Ms. Innes stood up and plucked her purse straps to her shoulder. "I'm not trying to be unkind."

Yeah? That was like saying Attila the Hun didn't mean to rape and pillage.

Merry, flushed and shaken, said, "June, I *love her.*"

"That's very nice. And important. But it's not a magic qualification for being an appropriate guardian."

"I understand that." Merry stood up, too, feeling more desperate by the second. "But I think loving her should matter. I can't think of anything I wouldn't do for her. And I've tried to make up for my inexperience with kids by reading a ton…books on grief, on preteens, on only children. On kids who are especially bright. On—"

Mrs. Innes nodded tiredly. "That reading is very good, too, but books are simply no substitute for experience. Or judgment." She pursed her lips. "I've seen for myself that you're a very nice woman. Pretty. Lots of fun for a young person to be with. But as far as your capacity to provide direction and guidance, to prepare a child for the future, to establish an environment of security…"

Although Mrs. Innes didn't shudder, her opinion on those subjects was clear. As she marched toward the door, she said again, "I am sincerely not trying to be mean. But when I make my report to the judge, I felt it was only fair that you knew ahead where I stood. I believe someone else would be a more appropriate guardian for Charlene."

Once Merry let her out, she sank against the closed door, feeling as paralyzed as a cornered mouse, helpless and frustrated.

They were going to try to take away Charlie?

Her eyes squeezed closed. There was no question that some of June Innes's arrows had hit the target. Hadn't she felt inadequate in this guardian job from the beginning? *Wasn't* she inadequate compared to a bona fide experienced mother?

Her heart whispered a *yes,* because damn it, a heart had to be honest.

Yet an image leaked into her mind of June Innes— or someone like June Innes becoming Charlene's guardian. Someone stiff. Someone who had all the answers. All *their* answers. Not Charlene's.

It was what Charlie Ross had feared all those years ago—that no one would give a damn about his daughter. No one would love her for herself.

But Merry did.

She simply couldn't desert or abandon Charlene to the system—not without a fight. A real fight. A fight to win, whatever it took.

That thought led to another…

Jack.

She may have realized she loved him. But so far she'd run from any kind of painful confrontation with him. It hadn't seemed that way…just the way it never seemed, all her life, that she always had a good excuse for moving on, rather than call a spade a spade. Running away was running away.

To win anything she needed in her life—anything she wanted—anything she loved…she had to quit running. Not talk about it. Do it.

THE TELEPHONE CALL CAME two minutes after Merry had immersed herself in butter-almond bubbles in the bathtub. She couldn't believe it. She was so tired she could barely think. The day had been nonstop, involving painting and then calls to Lee and then more calls to Lee, then dinner and trying to clean up and carpooling Charlene to the library…she just wanted a good long mindless soak.

Instead she grabbed a towel and hustled out. She couldn't ignore the call; she was overdue a return call from both her dad and Lucy. She grabbed the closest receiver, still dripping wet. It was Jack.

His voice rolled over her nerves like velvet on a shiver.

"I haven't been able to catch up with you for love or money," he said. "Cooper and Kevin are back with their mother, so I'm finally free, but I'm guessing you're likely tied up with Charlene—"

"Actually, Charlie's at the library until nine. Her history teacher set the kids up with this terrific project. He's teaching them how to research from a variety of sources, by setting up this treasure hunt kind of thing—" Sheesh, what was wrong with her? Her heart was hanging out like drool just to hear his voice, and here she was, soaking wet and shivering and babbling on like a goose. "Anyway, I don't have to pick her up until nine."

"So…you might have time for a drink? Like over at Wiley's?"

"A drink?"

"Yeah. I was thinking it'd be nice to talk somewhere there weren't kids. Somewhere there weren't interruptions. And I really want to tell you about my conversation with Cooper. You won't believe it."

He wanted to talk about kids, she thought. Not them. Even so…she was determined to stop running away from the chance of being hurt—or of lying. And the truth, very much, was that she wanted to see Jack—for any reason.

She called Charlene on the cell so Charlene would know where to reach her, then dug into her makeup bag. There wasn't dust on it from lack of use, but it came close.

She wasn't about to waste too much time—not when it was already seven. But it only took a few seconds to pull on a loose red sweater that skimmed her shoulders, and jeans with heels, then to swish on some mascara and eyeshadow and a splash of bar-red lip gloss.

After a cooped-up day of worry and hand wringing about June Innes, it felt good to get out in the air, breathe in something different, think something different. Walking into Wiley's was even better. Maybe it was a neighborhood bar, but it wasn't all plump guys with beer bellies glooming on the ESPN screen. With half the world divorced these days, it was clearly a neighborhood place for singles to have an easy conversation. Nothing fancy, but the décor was definitely comfortable—knotted pine walls, plank floor, the ceiling decorated in cartoons and jokes, fat blue cushions in the booths.

Three men glanced up when she walked in, looked her over in a way she'd almost forgotten. She used to do this all the time, but now it seemed like a lifetime since she'd played the game—met a guy for a drink. Indulged in some grown-up flirting. Looked forward to laughing and light conversation and just an excuse to let some chemistry loose on a guy.

Normally she wouldn't have minded the looks of appreciation, either, but not this time. She searched the crowd for Jack. He was the only one she wanted to vent any chemistry on.

She spotted him in a booth by the far window. He was on his feet before she could reach him. There was a snap in his eyes, a kindling when he looked her over. Her heart felt the heady kick. He liked how she looked, was seeing her differently away from a kitchen and a suburban yard.

She'd wanted him to. Needed him to.

"We've had the hardest time getting together," he said wryly. The barkeep ambled over; Jack sprang for a Pinot Noir for her, a draft for himself.

"It's been crazy at our house, too. And today was the worst."

"What happened?"

"The guardian *ad litem* made an impromptu visit this morning. She reports to the judge this Friday. I know she's going to contest my guardianship."

"*What?* That's ridiculous! Is the woman really that stupid?"

Jack's disbelief was like salve for a burn—damn, but she'd needed to hear someone believed in her! And especially Jack. Still, as much as she wanted to tell him the whole story—and scoop up all the sympathy he was willing to give her—it just wasn't the time or the place. She didn't want time with Jack to always be about her or her issues. "I'll tell you more, but just not now. I've worried about it so much my mind's shut down. I honestly need to put it aside for a few hours so I can think about it fresh tomorrow."

"If you want my help, or if there's something I can do—"

"I know, Jack." She *did* know he'd help. Jack was the only one who didn't see himself as a hero. "And I may ask you. But for right now...I'd really like to hear what happened when you talked to Cooper."

He hesitated, clearly concerned about the guardian problem, but then he seemed to honor what she'd asked—which was true enough. Right now all she was bringing to the guardian problem was a sick sense of worry and ten tons of anxiety.

He chugged a few slugs of his draft, and she leveled the Pinot Noir as he spilled the Cooper story. "You told me to be careful, talking to him. That it was a sensitive problem. So thankfully I was prepared, Merry, but damn it, that little hussy really broke his heart."

She knew.

"I'd like to take her apart with my bare hands. Obviously you can't save your kids from the hurts that come from growing up. First loves. Rejections. All that. But, Kicker—hell, he was born loving girls, playing them, being played. He likes everything about the game. Somewhere in there he's got deeper feelings, but overall, what you see is what you get. Where Cooper..."

"Coop is deep waters all the way," Merry murmured.

"Yeah. He doesn't open up at all unless he feels safe, really trusts. So that little..."

"Bitch?"

"I wasn't going to call a fifteen-year-old girl a bitch," Jack assured her.

"Well, in this case the shoe fits. She used and abused him. She knew what she was doing."

"No fifteen-year-old kid knows what they're doing." He suddenly frowned, and when Merry turned around to see what he was frowning at, she saw a woman walking toward them.

She recognized the woman as a neighbor—the one with the house on the west corner, someone she'd seen at the grocer and library and line at the movies. Clearly the woman was stopping to see Jack, because he got a buss on the cheek and a cuff on the neck.

"Hey, stranger, way too long since we had a drink. Hi," she said to Merry, and extended a hand.

The conversation didn't last more than a couple minutes before the woman—Nancy Riker—wandered back to her own table, where she was jammed in with a group of friends. But the short exchange was long enough for Jack to look uncomfortable.

"Sorry about that," he said.

"No reason to be. I could see what was what," Merry said gently, but Jack only looked more awkward.

"She's a nice person," he began.

To help him climb off the hot seat, she filled in, "I'd guess…she was devastated right after a divorce. You did some consoling. You made it clear this wasn't a relationship thing, which wasn't what either of you wanted. So you clicked together a few times and parted ways, no hard feelings." At his astonished expression, she chuckled.

"Someone told you?"

"No. Who would be telling me something like that? It was just…looking at her. And you. She's pretty. And seems genuinely nice. And she greeted you in a way that there'd obviously been something going on sometime, but also…she wasn't hurt. Wasn't worried that you were."

"You got all that out of a one-minute conversation?"

"And maybe a teensy bit more."

"What?"

She finished her last sip of wine. It was one thing, to know in her heart that she needed to quit running, and another to take some real chances with Jack that could be darn tricky. "I suspect she's the kind of woman you hone in on pretty often. I don't mean about her being someone newly divorced when you hooked up. But that you tend to leave relationships with both sides happy. Play the game fair. But also…"

"Also what?"

"Also…you only look for women who don't want a permanent hook up. Who won't have that expectation."

"Why would you say that? Where'd you get it?"

She hesitated. "I don't know. Am I wrong?"

"I didn't say you were wrong. But—"

"I think I got it from your boys, Jack. Kicker wants to be just like you—or like he thinks you are. Free. All about a good time. But, Cooper…he's never said it in exact words, but he seems to want the opposite. He doesn't want to play the game, date, all that. He just wants to find a girl to spend the rest of his life with. He hungers…to be with someone." She hesitated again. "Unlike Kicker, I think Cooper sees your loneliness."

"Me. Lonely?" He looked astonished. "I don't know why Cooper would think that. I've got all kinds of friends. The boys. Good neighbors. Friends at work, work I love…"

Merry thought, for darn sure this wasn't how she'd seen the evening going with Jack. But having started down this side road, she figured she might as well face the road signs she'd failed to before. "She really did a number on you, didn't she?"

"Who?" Jack said, with a look on his face that clearly expressed how ditzy he thought she was being.

"Your ex-wife," she said gently.

"Hell. My divorce was ages ago."

"I understand. But I think…" She groped to find the right words. "When my mom left me, I was Charlene's age. When you're a kid, you just count on your parents as unconditionally loving you. I counted on mattering to her. It never crossed my mind that I wasn't important enough in her life that she could just walk out and really not look back."

"I hate to believe it was that easy for her," Jack said, but she could see something in his eyes. A sharp connection to what she was saying.

"She claims it was hard, that she felt a lot of guilt. And maybe she did. But *my* reality was still that she pretty much left me bleeding—" Merry took a breath "—the same as your ex-wife left you."

"It's not the same thing."

"No, of course it isn't—because you weren't a child. Adults know better than to expect unconditional love from each other. But doesn't everybody want to believe they're irreplaceable? At least to someone? And maybe we're not. But it stings like a knife when we find that out for sure…oh, *damn*." She'd been looking at Jack, not her watch or the far clock on the wall. But a loud burst of laughter from another booth made her glance up, and abruptly she realized it was twenty to nine. If she didn't leave this minute, she'd be late picking up Charlene, and she'd gotten phobic about being late, afraid Charlene would worry that she'd been forgotten.

Jack had already paid for the drinks, but when she stood up, he bolted to his feet as well. The way he looked at her, she doubted he'd noticed the clock or other people any more than she had. His eyes met hers with an intensity that buttered her heart.

"I *have* to go," she said, "but darn it, Jack. I've wanted to tell you for a while that I understood."

"That you understood what?"

She shook her head, wildly, fast, tucked her purse strap on her shoulder and leaned up. Even with only seconds to spare, she closed her eyes before kissing him. It wasn't a bar come-on kiss. It was an I-love-you-and-don't-care-if-the-whole-world-knows-it kind of kiss. Just a tilt of the head. A brush of the lips. An emotion that took flight before it ever turned into a promise.

"That I understood that you weren't going to love me," she murmured. It was probably the only way she could manage to do this—to say what needed saying. In a public place. Where the kids were nowhere around, and all their clothes were on. And where she was in such a hurry that she wouldn't risk getting embarrassingly emotional.

When he didn't immediately contradict her, she gulped back the sharp feeling of loss. "It's all right, Jack. I'm glad we're friends. I'm glad we live next door. But I get it completely, why you weren't looking for more from me. I was hoping for more, I admit it. But that's only because I find you so impossibly easy to love that I couldn't help dipping in those waters, you know? Not because I was looking to be a pain."

She shot him a humorous smile—or a smile that she hoped looked honest and humorous—and then flew.

In less than two hours, the dusky evening had turned

into a glowering night, with clouds fisting overhead and thunder moaning in the west. She could taste the rain in the air, feel the close humidity. The temperature was warmer—crazy warm compared to the first of March in Minnesota—and suddenly she missed home so much she could hardly see.

Or maybe that was tears blinding her vision. Darn it, she'd said what she needed to say, hadn't she? She hadn't run from it. Maybe she hoped he'd contradict her, hoped he'd claimed to have fallen madly in love, that he'd finally found someone who was irreplaceable in his life, namely her. But that was such fairy-tale thinking that she'd never expected it, and she'd tried to be frank so he'd know she wasn't the naïve cock-eyed ditz he'd first thought her.

Now, though, she had to shake the tears before Charlene saw her. Charlene had to be what mattered. She *had* to get perky again.

She would.

She did.

Charlene bounded down the library steps the minute the car pulled up. She heaved in a half-dozen books and climbed in. "So how'd it go, cookie?" Merry asked.

"It was *horrible,*" Charlene said, but clearly she was jazzed. "Talk about a mean assignment. We're talking cru-el. Took us hours and hours. But I worked with Dougall and Mike and Greta and George. Mike actually knows something about computers. But George, he was such an Edsel."

"An Edsel?"

"Yeah, that's what my dad used to say. I think it was a car. You know, a car that tanked? That's George. A lot of ideas, but they all tank. Anyway—"

Buzz, buzz, buzz all the way home. Then cookies

and milk. Then chasing after dirty clothes and glasses and towels that somehow had walked into the living room. Then came a discussion of the next day's schedule of events—who knew an eleven-year-old needed an agenda calendar to keep it all straight?

And the whole time, Merry kept thinking, she was glad she'd gotten that out with Jack. She'd just been building up illusions that he seriously cared, that he was developing the winsome, yearning kind of loving feelings that she had. If he wasn't, it was far better to nip the whole thing in the bud before anybody got hurt.

Like her.

Because right now it felt as if her heart were broken three ways from Sunday and might never recover. Pretty hysterical, considering Jack had never said or implied a single promise, nor hinted at even a vague hope for a future.

Funnier yet, Jack was the first man who'd made her strikingly aware that love and lust were only part of the whole deal. Kids used the "respect" word incessantly these days, yet Merry had never considered how much it mattered to her…that when you really loved a man, his respect counted more than diamonds.

Or else the lust thing, enticing as it might be, was only worth rhinestones.

"So, can I do it?" Charlene asked.

By then, they were both brushing teeth in their respective bathrooms, walking back and forth with toothbrush midmouth to finish their conversations. Only Merry had lost track. Damn it, despair could do that to a girl.

"Run it by me one more time," she said.

"Come on, Merry. You heard me. It's a ropes climbing course."

"You mean like…climbing. As in climbing moun-
tains. As in going up real high so that you could fall real
far. So far you'd risk breaking your ankle. Or your head."

"God, you are such a wimp. It's a *sport,* Mer. Just
like any other sport." When Charlene peered into her
face, she seemed to realize a "no" was coming, because
she abruptly blurted out, "My dad would have let me
do it."

Merry almost dropped the toothbrush. It wasn't as if
Charlene never mentioned her dad, but it was the first
time he'd popped into a conversation, as normal as
sunshine. And how normal was this, for Charlene to try
to guilt her into getting what she wanted? Merry was
so proud of her she wanted to shriek. "I'll tell you what.
I think it's past time we worked with some of your dad's
things—either packed them away or sold them or gave
them away—whatever you want, Charlie. But right now
too much is just sitting there, gathering dust. So…if
you'll give me Saturday morning to deal with some of
that stuff, then you can sign up for the ropes course."

Charlene hesitated. Until now, she'd gotten pretty
freaked at even the idea of touching any of her dad's
belongings. But now she said, "Do you mean it? You'll
put it in ink that I can sign up?"

"Well, I'd need to hear some more. Who teaches the
course. Whether I'd trust him or her. The safety record
and all. But if the details pass muster, then…I think…
okay."

Charlene disappeared into her bathroom to spit.
Merry heard the sound of the water running, then
nothing. She'd started slathering on moisturizer when
Charlene suddenly showed up again in the doorway,
wearing one of her best major scowls.

"All right, we can do that stuff on Saturday," she said.

And that was it. The kid disappeared into her own room, not slamming her door, but closing it with a quiet clip.

Merry thought, *I'm gonna die if I lose that kid.* She had second thoughts about their conversation on the climbing course, because darn it, she knew full well, she might not have power over what Charlene did after the custody hearing.

But that was down the pike. And it was right *now* that Charlene had shown signs, finally, that she was starting to come to terms with her dad's death—which meant that it was right *now* Merry wanted to respond to her. Over the next week, obviously, she'd have to bring up the hearing. But every second they were together wasn't going to be about that, Merry was determined.

She was going to "mom" Charlie with all the love she had. Period. It was an easy choice to make, because love had no timetable.

She only wished that were just as true with Jack....

CHAPTER NINETEEN

JACK HURLED A FISTFUL of gravel at the window, thinking damnation but that woman had messed with his mind for the last time.

A man could take a lot—but there was a limit. That limit, he figured, was what any reasonable male human being could be expected to tolerate in the realm of risking his life, limbs and losing his mind. Not to mention his heart.

He waited, but when there was no sight or sound showing up in the spare bedroom window, he bent over to scoop up another fistful of gravel. Between the cloudy sky and spitting rain, it was impossible to see clearly. If he accidentally gathered up any bigger stones with the gravel, he could well break a window.

A broken window would hardly help his cause. And tonight, that'd just be his luck.

Still, he hurled the second fistful, only to suddenly notice movement from a different room farther to the west. That window suddenly cranked open. "I'm not in the bedroom," she called out.

"Yeah, I had that impression." He also had an inkling where she was, since jasmine-scented steam puffed out the open window.

"You know, if you wanted to see me, you could use the door like normal people."

"Yeah, well, that would have risked waking the squirt. And I needed to see *you*. Merry. *Listen* to me." It'd been spitting rain for the last half hour. Not a deluge. Just enough to drool icicles down his neck, to drizzle from his eyebrows, to make the night truly miserable. "I don't know where you got all that psychological stuff about my ex-wife. But I came over here to tell you that I never heard such nonsense."

"No?"

"I was *trying* to answer you, for Pete's sake. But then you had to run off. And this is like the third time. There's always something to run off for. I can't finish a conversation with you to save my life." When he realized he was throwing his hands around, talking like she did with body movements, it scared him. So he slugged his fists onto his hips in a more normal, tough-guy posture. "So I'm here to tell you, just maybe some of that nonsense was true."

She didn't interrupt. He'd counted on her interrupting, because she always did. Then she'd say the words and he wouldn't have to. It seemed she chose that moment to completely stay quiet and listen, the damn woman. So he was stuck going on.

"I thought we had a pretty darn good marriage," he said. "Perfect, no. But I loved her. I loved our boys. Maybe the fire in the furnace wasn't as hot as it used to be, but she was busy, and I just tried not to care. It seemed to me we'd built too good a life to throw it out. And whether either of us were that thrilled for a period, I know it sounds corny, but I believed in the vows."

"Aw, Jack…"

There she went again. Her heart…man, her heart

was always in her eyes. All that sympathy. All that compassion. All that love, just given so generously.

He flexed his hands. "So when she just took off, it was like she ripped off my ego with her." He scraped a hand through his wet hair, to stop the drips. "I *hate* talking about stuff like this."

"Did you think I was forcing you?"

"No. But I'm just trying to admit…maybe I did take an easy road after that. Not a cold-blooded love 'em and leave 'em track. But maybe I didn't let anybody get too close. Maybe you had that part of things right. I just hadn't put it all in those words before."

She leaned over the sill, crossing her arms. "You're getting soaking wet."

"Sometimes you have to slap a guy upside the head before he thinks, you know? Who wants to think if they don't have to? About stuff like this?"

"Come in out of the rain, Jack."

"But what happened to me isn't the point. What I wanted you to know was that…I wasn't using you. I wasn't playing you. If you thought I didn't care…for all I knew in the beginning, that's what you wanted, someone to sleep with now and then, someone to just be there. For a while. So you wouldn't be so by yourself when you first moved here. That's what I thought we were doing. But I didn't know…that was going to change for me. I didn't know…I was going to feel differently than I had all this time. I—"

Hell and a half.

She disappeared.

Here he was pouring out his heart, standing there in the middle of the night, in the pouring rain, and the woman just disappeared on him.

If that wasn't typical of Merry, he didn't know what was. From the minute she'd moved here, she'd made him think about all this damned crap he didn't want to think about. Made him think and worry about how he was raising his boys, that his sons could get the idea their dad was a man who couldn't commit. She'd made him think about Cooper, and how damn much the boy just wanted to be part of a family and all a family meant.

Hell, a family meant everything to him, too. Or it used to. Once upon a time. All right. *Now.* He fiercely hungered for a woman to wake up to. To share with. To seduce. To argue with over dinner. To just *be* with, for God's sake.

And for someone who valued being with him.

It was pretty dumb, how much that mattered to him. He was no kid seeing life through rose-colored glasses anymore, no idiot who still counted on a woman to *be* there no matter what. But somewhere in his dusty mental attic, apparently he'd locked up that hope that someone'd be there through a little thick and thin. If it wasn't too thick or too thin. And Merry, because she was so infernally upbeat and open, had somehow coaxed him into believing that if a guy was really careful, if he loved her all the way, all the time, if he—

The back door opened. "My God, Jack. You're a mess."

In the silver mist, he could see she was wearing a thin nightgown. Nothing sexy. But here she was barefoot, wearing a pale long nightgown that swooped around her ankles, stepped out on a March night—and no, it wasn't pouring, but it was still coming down in nonstop cold noodles. Proving for all time that she didn't have a single functioning brain—my *God,* she was ditzy—she walked straight toward him with her arms held out.

"Come here," she whispered, as if that made any sense at all. And then the crazy woman wrapped her arms around him, lifted up on tiptoe, and offered her mouth.

And he took it, melding his mouth with hers, aching hard, but he was thinking, this is exactly what was wrong. She was flaky. Witless. Young. Not young in years, but too young for him. She was so beyond him, the way she was open, the way she was so giving.

Way, way, too giving.

He just couldn't give back that way. He clutched her head, feeling the slippery satin of her lips, the heat coming off her body, the roaring thump of her heart against his. Merry was so…Merry. The way she poured out sensuality and emotion. She responded as if she loved the taste of him, the feel of him. That she craved how he made her feel.

She told him that with every kiss, every touch, every volatile response.

She acted…helpless. As if she felt swept away. As if he made her feel swept away.

That was exactly how she loved. As if no one were watching. As if no one existed in the universe but her, but him.

As if they weren't standing in the pouring rain, in a suburb, with her white lawn nightgown getting soaked and her kissing him as if she completely didn't give a damn.

"Merry—"

"Oh, no, buster. You're not getting out of this now. Suck it up and accept your fate."

Maybe she wanted him to laugh. Instead he swooped her up, thinking the damn woman was going to die of pneumonia if he didn't get her out of that dark, mean-wet night. The laundry room was right off the kitchen, the fastest place inside he could peel off that soaking wet nightgown of hers.

He already had fond memories of that dark laundry room—but not fond enough to stall there this time. She was shivering by the time he'd pulled off the gown, either because she was chilled now, or because she wasn't. Once he had his hands all over her, she seemed to heat up faster than a fire for the right kindling. He wanted to be her kindling. Now, tomorrow, and for as long as she let him be.

But right now, just getting her out of that laundry room and near a mattress—quietly, so the squirt didn't wake up—was his immediate primary crisis. He was usually good at logistics. But not when he had his hands all over a wet, warm woman, who was kissing him like she'd die if she couldn't. And he was kissing her back like she was dreaming if she thought he'd ever, ever, let her go.

He knew where her room was, knew that sleeper-couch mattress had springs with teeth and squeaks, but right then he'd have settled for any surface at all. The minute the door was closed and locked, he lifted and leveled her flat. Finally, his hands had the freedom to streak the bare, soft length of her. Her supple skin warmed for his palms. Her breath caught, sucked in as if starved of oxygen. Her breasts changed shape, firmed, swelled, ached for the shape of his palms, the wash of his tongue.

Frenzy. Who knew he could just…lose himself like this? In her? With her? Rain silvering down her windows, the scent of almonds and jasmine on her pillow, on her, the texture of her hair raveling through his hands, the nectar of her kisses, her touch. Tension escalated like an out-of-control fire, too hot, too wild, too dangerous, yet all he could do was take more of her, love more of her, ask more of her.

Need more of her.

He took the bottom this time, thinking it'd force some control on him, force some slow-down, yet when she eased on top of him, her spine arched in a bow, he lost it all over again. He picked up her fever. She picked up his. Even diamonds melted if the temperature was hot enough, and that's how she felt to him, so unbearably willing and vulnerable and sensuous that she could melt even the hard old stone that he could have sworn was his heart.

They rocked together, rolled together, pistoned the same fierce rhythm together, until finally they both exploded...and then crashed.

He didn't want to recover, didn't want to even think about recovering, but eventually he realized that she wasn't covered. God knew where the pillows and blankets had gone, but the only thing warming her cooling skin seemed to be him. She was just lying there in his arms, looking at him, both of them still heaving like noisy freight trains.

"Whew," she whispered.

"That's what I was thinking."

She smiled at him. The rainy windows illuminated her tousled hair, her pale forehead. Her brow momentarily mesmerized him. As far as he could remember—and he was replaying the last half hour in his mind in detail—that was the only spot on her body he'd neglected. Even exhausted as he was, he had to reach over and tenderly kiss that patch of soft skin, right between her brows.

"You're precious," he told her, the words coming out rough, as if they'd been buried deep for a long time and were rusty from misuse. Or from fear. "I didn't know... about precious before."

"Then you—" Whatever she'd been about to say was cut off. They both heard the sound of the telephone. Her body immediately stiffened.

He understood. She didn't want Charlene wakened by a late call—besides which, even though it wasn't midnight yet, it was a little late for the usual friendly call. Only bad news seemed to come this late. She quickly bolted out of bed. "I have to—"

"I understand," he said. "Go."

It was a land-line call, and she didn't have a connection in the back bedroom. He didn't know where she'd gone to answer it, but the phone stopped ringing, and she didn't come back for a minute. Then a couple minutes. Then several.

He wasn't sure what to do. Eventually he had to get up and get dressed and go home, because of Charlene. But he didn't want to leave Merry until he had to. The longer she was tied up on the phone, though, the more he worried that something was wrong.

When another minute passed, he hauled his behind out of bed, shucked on his jeans and sweatshirt—both were damp, but he couldn't very well walk around her house without clothes.

He found her in the kitchen, hunched at the kitchen table with the receiver ironed against her ear, wearing an old shirt she'd apparently tugged from the laundry room for warmth. The expression on her face made his jaw clench. Something was bad wrong. Her face looked bleached of color, her eyes fierce with anxiety. Everything about her posture was tense, as if someone had punched her and she was waiting for the next blow.

"You need to do what you need to do," she said into the receiver and then waited. A moment later she hung up.

"God. What's wrong?" he asked gently.

She came up with a tremulous smile for him, but nothing that eased that look in her eyes. "It was Charlene's birth mother." She closed her eyes momentarily and then heaved a huge sigh. "And I'm fine, Jack—"

"The hell you are."

"No. Really. The thing is, I've been waiting for that call for weeks now. It's not that I wanted it. But it's been like waiting for bad news—it's actually easier when it finally gets there, so the waiting's over. The problem's out in the open."

"What can I do?" he asked.

"Nothing. Honestly."

He didn't want to leave her and go home—and he didn't, for quite a while. But she felt strongly about Charlene not waking up in the morning and finding him there, so eventually he had to hightail it next door. By then, she'd stopped looking so stressed. She didn't relax all the way, didn't fool him that she was really okay. But in the middle of the night, there really didn't seem anything concrete he could do to help her.

But it bugged him, when he left.

He really hadn't done anything for her. Certainly nothing to earn her always treating him like a hero.

Nothing to justify her loving him.

ANYONE WHO WATCHED TV knew the court system moved slower than a turtle in a coma, yet only two weeks had passed since that miserable meeting with

June Innes. Who could imagine the judge would call a hearing this quickly? Merry pawed and repawed through the hangers in her closet—she'd bought an outfit for this, but it wasn't right. Nothing seemed to hit her as right. She told herself she should be happy that reality wasn't like TV. The court system should cater to kids, should resolve things related to kids as quick as it possibly could.

It was just…something was wrong with her.

She seemed to be calm, instead of having an anxiety attack and gasping around like a beached guppy. It wasn't natural. Of course, she still had several hours for a panic attack to emerge. It was only ten. She had a full two hours to get dressed before picking up Charlene from school and driving to the courthouse.

She plucked through hangers one last time, but dagnabbit, no matronly clothes and sedate shoes appeared.

How scary was that? She was going to have to go as herself.

Scarier yet, she even kind of liked the idea. Totally unlike herself, she managed to dress in less than five minutes, pulling on a dark purple flannel skirt, boots and a thick white hand-knit sweater. She was just messing with her hair when the phone rang. It was her dad.

"I knew you'd call," she said warmly. "No, I'm fine, Dad. Seriously fine. Of course I'm worried about the outcome, but at this point, it's almost like waiting for a root canal. I just want it over with. And I know it sounds crazy, but I really want my chance to speak up and say what I feel to the judge…."

She picked out earrings and swooshed on a little blush. Lipstick turned into a problem. The tubes of gloss and stain and stick all seemed to reproduce at night; she must have a good two dozen, but no color ever seemed to be exactly right for purple.

"No, Dad, Charlene's birth mother will be in another room entirely. It's two separate things. My guardianship is one issue, whether Charlene's mother gets visitation rights—or any other rights—is another. From what the attorney researched, she's a real fruitcake, so I have to believe the court will look at the whole history and do the right thing…." Okay, she had to gulp before finishing the sentence. And it could be she really didn't give a damn whether her lipstick matched this morning, but she stuffed three choices of tubes in her purse. "Anyway, all I care about is that Charlie gets what she needs out of this. I'll be fine, promise, Dad. I'll call you tonight. You bet, love you back…"

She hung up, and was just attacking her hair, deciding she'd do a low ponytail, when the phone rang again. This time it was the school nurse, who wanted her to pick up Charlene. Immediately.

That was not an omen, Merry thought, as she ran hell-bent for leather for the car. She could handle anything today. She had to. Because this was about fighting for a little girl who meant the world to her, and damn it, she was going to do it—and do it right.

It was just that there wasn't a lot of spare time built in for extra crises.

Charlene was waiting outside the school, sitting on the cement fence, wrapped in her jacket, her head bowed and her eyes stormier than a cyclone. When Merry drove her to school earlier, she'd looked like a little angel. It was Charlene who'd decided to dress differently that morning, put on jeans, a navy-and-white striped sweater, washed her hair and fluffed it up into a silky little blond nimbus around her face. She still looked as adorable as she had at eight that morning— except for the attitude.

She charged toward the car, hurled open the door and threw her books in the back. "I hate school. I hate my teachers. I hate everybody. And I'm not going back. I'm not going to that stupid hearing, either."

"Ah," Merry said. The school nurse had already told her the problem—that Charlene had started her first period. Merry had been startled—cripes, her baby was only eleven! But she'd expected embarrassment and emotion. Not Armageddon. Silent as a mouse, she eased out of the parking lot.

"Merry, for Pete's *sake,* you've lived here two months now! You turn *left!*"

"I wasn't looking," she admitted.

"It doesn't help when you look! You could get lost in a one-car garage. I think you're darn close to hopeless."

"Hmm. I'd defend myself but it sure seems pointless." She cleared her throat. "Do you want to tell me what happened?"

"No."

"You'll feel better if you talk it out—"

"Like I care what you think."

Merry sucked it in. "Hey. I don't talk to you that way. You don't get to talk to me that way, either."

"So? I don't want to talk anyway. To anyone. Ever. As long as I live."

Merry buttoned it. It's not as if she didn't remember having a tantrum or two at that age. There was still ample time before the hearing to get life calmed down—and hearing or no hearing, Charlene obviously needed some space. Possibly that wasn't going to happen too fast, because the minute they were home, Charl stormed out of the car, stormed into the house, and then disappeared into the bathroom with a slammed door.

Merry heard the sound of the shower. Then the shower went off. Several more minutes passed, but the door didn't open.

When the doorknob finally turned and the door cracked open, enough steam poured out to cook vegetables. By then, Merry was deliberately, slowly flipping through an *Allure* magazine in the living room. Right outside the bathroom door, though, she'd left a small bundle. Clean underpants. Fresh jeans and socks and a pink sweater. Girl products, which she'd picked up the first time she noticed the hint of developing breasts.

She didn't look up, but Charlie eventually made a sound in the kitchen.

"You hungry for lunch?" Merry called out. "It's going to be a long afternoon if we don't have something."

"Maybe," Charlene said irritably. "I can't believe you put out a *pink* sweater for me."

"It's a lucky color."

"For you, maybe." Slowly, though, all that fury started to fade. Charlene watched her put together lunch. Merry might not do the cook thing well or often, but she could do comfort foods. Scrambled eggs. French toast with fresh blueberries. "When this is all over, Merry...when That Woman is gone and we don't have to do this stupid hearing bullshit ever again..."

Charlene waited, clearly waiting for a correction on her language. When Merry didn't say anything, Charl finished her original thought. "I was kind of wondering if I could have a kitten."

"Sure."

"Really?"

"Really. I'd like one, too." Merry could feel the climate in the kitchen changing. Maybe the reason she'd managed to stay so calm and sure this week was because Charlene had been *so, so* tight, poor baby. And this morning sure hadn't helped.

Charlene poked at her food for a while, then dove in. As soon as her mouth was good and full, she started talking. "I was in math class. First hour. Suddenly I felt all this wet crap. Dougall is in that class with me, for Pete's sake! I couldn't get out of the chair. Couldn't move. I just wanted to die."

"Aw, Charl. I'd have felt the same way."

"I *still* want to just die. Dad told me about it all. But I thought a girl would normally be like thirteen. Not *now.* I'm not even close to twelve, for Pete's sake. This totally sucks!"

"You've got that right."

Charlene extended the royal finger. "Don't try giving me that junk about how I should be happy I'm a *woman* now and all that."

"Believe me, I won't. Ticked me off when people told me that, too. And my dad was the one who told me about periods, because my mom was gone by then. All the same, he wasn't exactly informed about the difference in products, like pads and tampons and all that. What to expect. How you'd feel. So you want to ask anything, any time, just pipe up."

"The only thing I want to do is change schools and not have to go back there."

"Can't do that, Charl. But maybe we could take a day off. We can talk about different ways to handle it—"

Just as they'd talked about different ways to handle the hearing, Merry thought, as they drove to the courthouse. Still, she went through it all again.

"There's nothing to be nervous about, honey. Everybody only has your best interests at heart. You just answer whatever the judge asks you and tell him how you feel."

"I don't want to meet her alone. I want you to be in there."

"You won't be alone. Lee Oxford will be in there. So will Judge Burns. And it's only for a few minutes, Charl—"

"I still don't see why I have to see her at all if I don't want to. So far nobody's listening to me. I don't want to go. I don't want to see her. I don't like the whole hearing thing."

"It's not going to be an easy afternoon," Merry said soothingly, "but it's not like a tetanus shot, shortie. Nothing painful's going to happen. It's just about people talking who care about you. We'll be home before dinner."

Charlene was calmer once they finally got settled. They almost ended up in the probation office because of a tiny wrong turn. On the other hand, her getting lost—yet again—finally won a grin and a tease out of Charlene.

"Okay, now. I'll be back in this room to pick you up. I'm just two doors down. Anything goes wrong, you just yell at the top of your lungs and I'll be there."

"Yeah, like you really want me to do that," Charlene said wryly. But the brunette woman with the quiet, warm smile in the office of Judge Burns's chambers was clearly used to taking charge of young people. She'd set up Charlie with a soda and a puzzle book before Merry had to leave her.

She was still doing fine when she walked into the hearing room, which was a surprise. Somehow she'd expected it to look like a courtroom on TV. Instead it was more conference-room size, with tall narrow windows, scarred mahogany woodwork and a long desk on a dais in front. Although the judge obviously sat there, the rest of the room was simply divided in two sections with tables and chairs. There was no space for a jury. At most a dozen could fit in the room as it was.

She was the first one there, except for a female bailiff. Finally Lee Oxford huffed in, his alligator shoes looking spit-shined, his suit pressed sharp. "This is going to go fine, so don't be nervous, Merry," he said.

"I'm not worried," she said, and really meant it. She was cool as a cucumber. Even after June Innes walked in, with her chilly expression and authoritative posture, Merry felt completely collected. Everyone seemed to have a sheaf of papers to pore over but Merry, but that was okay. She closed her eyes and did more of that calm, cool thing. What good would it do to get upset? All she had to do was stand up, project all her feelings and ideas and love for Charlene, do what Charlie would want her to do for his daughter. So she was alone. Big deal. She didn't expect anyone to be there for her.

But then…the judge walked in.

Judges, in her opinion, should look like Santa Claus, kindly and wise and older—just a little thinner. Not this one. Judge Burns looked a young midthirties, and though he was wearing a stereotypical black robe, it was casually open, revealing a GQ tie and tonal shirt. His skin was as tanned as a tennis pro.

Panic started to close her throat, all the more startling because she'd been so positive she was calm.

Suddenly her fingertips froze up and her heart kept hic-cupping, and her lips felt like butter, too slippery to talk. She didn't care if the judge was adorable, for Pete's sake. But she'd counted on being able to talk to him, counted on him wanting to listen, willing to hear how much was at stake for Charlene.

Any other time, she wouldn't have minded looking at a heartthrob—but not *here*. The judge didn't look like anyone who was into kids, and for the first time, Merry felt the terror surface from so carefully buried depths... that she could lose Charlie. Really. Lose her.

The judge took his seat as if he were relaxing for the evening with friends. "There are several issues before the court today, affecting the minor, Charlene Ross. We'll get everyone sworn in, and then start. We all need to be clear that our function here today is to assess the status of the guardianship affecting the minor child, Charlene Ross."

Everyone nodded, including Merry.

"Now, if I understand all this correctly, a few days before this hearing was scheduled, the child's birth mother suddenly appeared in the picture. Mary Ross hasn't seen her daughter since Charlene was two." The judge scrolled through papers and then cocked a glance at Lee, who nodded that the information was correct. "Both Mr. Oxford and Mrs. Innes have raised concerns about the fitness of the birth mother, not just in terms of custody rights but even in terms of visitation. Both parties have provided information that the ex-Mrs. Ross has only been out of rehab two months, after four pre-vious stays. She lost her driver's license related to driving under the influence, has two accidents on record as being drug-related..."

Lee got a quick turn to speak up. "We don't believe there's any question the child should be put in the mother's care, your honor. We all believe that she only showed up because she heard her ex-husband had a sizable financial estate that she had hopes of getting her hands on, through the child."

"Yes." The judge nodded at both Lee and Mrs. Innes. "You both seem in accord on this. But she is the child's mother. And as we discussed prior to this hearing, I believe it is in the minor's best interests—and everyone else's—to have an initial meeting between the two in a controlled, supervised environment in my chambers—with myself, the mother, the child, and the attorneys representing both sides. Ms. Olson, Charlene is in chambers, correct?"

"Yes, sir."

"So we'll get to that shortly. For right now, however, our business is the immediate custody situation with the minor child. Miss Olson, Mrs. Innes has presented a report, that you and your attorneys should have copies of. Have you all read it?"

"Yes, your honor," Lee answered.

"All right then. Miss Olson, would you like to speak on your role as guardian?"

"Yes, sir." Merry stood up. Her heart kept thumping the mantra be strong, be strong, but her hands were slicker than slides. It was the fear.

That she wouldn't have the right words, wouldn't be able to convince the judge that she mattered to Charlene—that Charlene mattered to her.

When had she been able to do that for anyone?

But she clutched her arms and tried. "I *love* that child. I know all the reasons why I must not look like

the best choice of guardian. But you need to understand—I knew Charlie. I knew what he wanted for his
daughter. He wanted someone to value her. To look at
her, not as if she were just a child, but for the unique
and extraordinary person she is.

"Charlene and I both had mothers who left us. I
think that matters, because I know how it affects a
child—how it affects a *girl*. How it affects her feelings
of self-worth, and the kind of woman she wants to grow
up to be. It affects whether she values herself—whether
she even knows how to value herself…"

The judge looked at her, but she wasn't sure if he was
really listening, if he understood, if he cared. She started
stumbling over her words…yet right when she thought
she couldn't hold it together another second, the door
opened.

Jack strode in, banked by Cooper and Kicker, all
three of them dressed in jackets and ties—*ties*. Who
knew her boys even owned any? All three of them
looked out of breath, as if they'd been running.

When Jack's eyes met hers across the room, she felt
a sudden keening deep inside her. She was a softie, she
knew that. But she'd locked up a certain kind of tenderness, knowing it was too easy to rip and tear, that
some things just wouldn't mind if they were broken.

Jack wasn't supposed to be here. Of course he'd known
the hearing was scheduled. She'd told him—and listened
to his advice on preparing for June Innes's comments to
the judge. But she'd specifically insisted he not take off
from work, promising that she'd be fine. If she was ever
to have a chance with him, he had to think of her as an
equal, strong and capable, not the kind of flighty lightweight who couldn't stand up when someone needed her.

JACK MUST HAVE RUN THE LAST quarter mile from the parking lot—damn, they'd started out in plenty of time, but Kicker got gum on his tie, and there'd been a twenty-minute holdup on the freeway because of a traffic accident. He didn't want Merry walking into this hearing alone, didn't want her thinking she was alone.

Because she wasn't.

Right off, from where she was standing and facing the judge, he could see the proud tilt of her chin. He also heard the shaky quaver in her voice. She wasn't crying, but she barely had to turn before he saw the well-up glisten in her eyes.

Merry wasn't used to holding back emotion. She wasn't used to having to wage bureaucratic war, either.

Which is partly why Jack had brought the cavalry.

"And who are you, sir?" Judge Burns didn't look annoyed by the interruption, more curious.

"Jack Mackinnon and my two sons, Cooper and Kevin. We live next door to Charlene Ross, have known her from the time she was a toddler. And we've watched what kind of guardian Miss Olson is for Charlene from the day she got here, as well as how Charlene relates to her."

"They're not scheduled to say anything." Mrs. Innes stood up. "This is supposed to be an informal hearing, your honor, with just- -"

"Informal is correct. But we do want all the information we can ascertain related to the issues. State your names formally for the court, and get sworn in."

The boys went first. Jack paid attention, but mostly... well, Merry hadn't stopped looking at him, any more than he'd stopped looking at her. She so obviously hadn't expected him to come. Hadn't expected his support. But it wasn't surprise in her eyes so much as—

Love.

How much she cared was on display for the whole courtroom to see. The thing was, though, that Jack saw it, and wanted to damn himself from here to Pough-keepsie, for not realizing before. For not understand-ing before. For not valuing her before. Not enough. Not nearly enough.

He was forcibly distracted by the boys—they'd stood up together with the judge's permission. Usually Kicker took the verbal role, because he could usually talk his way out of a high tea with the Queen of England without feeling stress. But for some reason, the two of them had opted for Cooper to speak first.

"She's the kind of mom every kid wishes they had. See, she always listens, but you can trust her not to judge." Coop suddenly looked stricken. "No offense, Judge. I mean, your honor. I mean, I know *you're* supposed to judge. But Merry, Ms. Olson I mean, she'll give you advice. And she'll let you know if she thinks you're doing something stupid, so it's not like she lets you off the hook. But she doesn't make like out like she knows ev-erything, like she's God. She's just there for you."

Kicker had his shot, but kept it short. "We see her with Charlene all the time. The thing is, nothing's more important to her than Charlene, than being her mom. Not a job. Not doing other stuff. And we see her, like, working at it. Not like it's easy for her all the time. But that's the thing. The way she loves the kid, we can all see it. And that's all I have to say."

Damn, Jack thought, looking over at Merry. Tears brimmed in her eyes like crystals. The boys' plan had been to help her, not make it tougher on her. And then it was his turn to stand up.

"I met Merry the day she got here, and I've never known anyone like her. She loves Charlene as much as Charlene's dad did, and believe me, that's saying a ton. The whole move had to be hard on Merry, never having lived in this area before, no friends or family here. But she just knuckled under and took everything one problem at a time, always keeping Charlene's needs on the front line."

Jack shifted on his feet. "Every parent has a learning curve. It doesn't make a first-time parent less effective because they're inexperienced. Maybe Merry didn't give birth to Charlene, but I believe Charlie knew exactly what he was doing when he passed on guardianship to Merry. If it were my kids, I'd do the same. She's that special…."

Hell, he'd intended to go on, but the first tear welled over her eyelid and spilled over in a big, fat single crystal. If she got emotional…well, the judge didn't realize who he was dealing with.

Mrs. Innes, being Mrs. Innes, chose that moment to interrupt. "This testimony is very heartwarming, but we've never doubted Miss Olson's kind heart. It's her youth and inexperience that are our concern, also the fact that she's a young and very attractive woman, so undoubtedly she's going to become involved or marry—"

Aw, hell, Jack thought, and heaved an annoyed sigh as he jerked to his feet again. This sure as beans was not how he'd planned on doing this. Still, there was little he and Merry had managed to hide from the kids so far, so Jack figured it was probably crazy to think this could possibly go any differently.

"Sir, it's not your turn," Mrs. Innes said when she saw him standing up again—making Judge Burns raise his eyebrows.

"Actually, I believe I can decide that," the judge remarked.

Jack was looking only at Merry. "Mrs. Innes implied there was an additional uncertainty factor because of Merry's single status. And I understand why she'd think that, because Charlene's life would be thrown into another major change if Merry took up with some man out of the blue. Since she's so beautiful and fantastic, it'd be crazy not to believe some guys aren't going to be coming around."

Jack, Merry mouthed. *What are you doing?*

"I love you, Merry," he said.

Judge Burns frowned. "Excuse me? I didn't hear—"

Jack turned back to the judge. "I don't know that she'll have me. But it's my intention to ask her to marry me. Not for Charlene's sake. Not for my sons' sake, either—although I believe all the kids will stand up and shout if we do it. But I'm just talking about us. That I love her. That she's changed my life, rattled my heart. She loves, bigger than most people even dream of loving. She gives, more than most people imagine they have to give. Judge?"

"I'm listening." The judge also had a hand over his mouth, as if to hide his expression.

"You'd be a damn fool to give full and complete guardianship to anyone but Merry."

"Thanks for your opinion," the Judge said. "I don't suppose there's a chance you'll sit down now?"

ALTHOUGH THE HEARING WAS adjourned quickly after
that, there was still another half hour of waiting in the
judge's side chambers for Charlene to finish the meeting with her mother. Merry was wedged on a thin-
cushioned bench between Jack and the boys. If they
hugged her any tighter, she was going end up like the
jelly in a pb and j—but they were trying to be good to
her. Or, at least the boys were.

She kept shooting glances at Jack, silently promising him they'd be having a good long discussion about
all these surprises, the very minute the two of them
could beg, borrow or steal a moment alone.

Suddenly Charlene bolted out the far door.

Merry surged to her feet, but didn't have to take a
single step before Charlie flew, like she'd never flown
before, straight into her arms. Holy kamoly. The kid
zoomed toward her like a heat-seeking missile, almost
knocking her over…and then just hung on. Tight, like
glue. Strong, like steel.

She didn't cry. Merry could feel tears in her own
eyes, but Charlie, being Charlie, was strong like her
dad. Just possibly she wasn't all that strong this instant,
though, because those scrawny little arms squeezed in
a fiercely tight hug. Merry soothed the downy fluff on
her hair, kissed the top of her head. She didn't say
anything. Probably couldn't have talked for the lump
in her throat anyway, but that was just as well.

Holding Charlene was all she wanted or needed to
do at that moment.

Eventually, though, Charlene lifted her head. She
looked up at Merry, then suddenly realized that Jack
and the boys were right there, too.

"What's going on? What's everybody doing here?"

she demanded. "Cripes, this has been close to the worst day of my life and you're all grinning like hyenas."

"Yeah," Merry said, "I guess we are. You're okay." She didn't have to phrase it like a question.

Charlene remembered to cop a little attitude. "After she left, the judge talked to me by myself. He said I didn't have to see her again, that I didn't have to worry about custody or anything like that. But that I'd probably regret it if I didn't agree to see her some, because at some time in my life, I'd want to know what made her the way she is. That it'd matter to me."

"That sounds like good sense," Merry said gently.

"Sounds like hogwash to me. But I said if it was that big a deal to him, I'd see her sometime. But I thought it was dumb. I told him I already had all the mom I need. That's you, Merry."

"Yeah?"

Merry thought if she cried any more today she might as well fill up a river. But she put one arm around Charlie and hooked her hand in Jack's, as they walked out into the fresh air.

EPILOGUE

"DON'T TELL ME THIS is how it's going to be," Jack muttered.

Merry lifted her head to grin at him. "You mean, an insane houseful of kids, constant noise and gargantuan messes and the phone ringing all the time?"

"Naw. I don't care about any of that. I just care about the lack of privacy." His mouth found the side of her neck. Because he'd turned off all the lights so they could watch a movie, he kept claiming that it was too dark to see...so his aim was accidental. She couldn't blame him for it or hold him responsible.

She might have bought that ridiculous fairy tale— she'd probably have bought anything Jack wanted to sell her, that night—but as it happened, they weren't watching the movie. And his mouth exhibited no trouble finding her throat in the dark, any more than his hands were challenged to find tender bare skin.

She found herself breathless. "We do need some privacy," she whispered.

"*Soon.*"

"Soon," she agreed. "But you might want to keep in mind that you're responsible for this chaos."

"Some of it."

"*Some?*" He was the one who thought Charlene

needed something special immediately to lighten the stress of yesterday's traumatic day.

Merry had owned up to the kitten idea—but that was kitten, as in a singular model. He was the one who took Charlene to a neighborhood rescue and came back with two.

Charlene had immediately named them Lucky and Buttercup. Possibly it wasn't one of Merry's better ideas to set them up in the master bedroom, but the spur-of-the-moment impulse had been to get Charlie closer to her dad's things, and the kittens would help that. The babies were seven weeks old, fluffy fur balls and wonderful, with claws that could kill you.

Merry had casually suggested that her friends could come over any time to see the kittens. The infamous Dougall was in there now. So was a girl and another boy. So were Cooper and Kevin.

Dougall was the critical issue, Merry had explained to Jack. The major embarrassment of getting her first period in school wouldn't be half as bad a hurdle to Charlie, if it hadn't occurred in the class she had with Dougall. The kittens were proving to be an ideal distracting influence. Both Merry and Jack could hear the kids through the open doorway. No one had mentioned anything embarrassing to Charlene. No one had asked why she'd suddenly, just like that, quit wearing her hair in a brush cut, either.

Jack heard both his sons laughing at the kittens' antics.

"How on *earth* are we going to combine the households? Which house? And *when* is another question."

"Beats me. But my theory is…we should all decide together. Involve the kids." She rested her neck against the arm. "I'm going to be the easiest one to please, because I'll be happy no matter what."

"I *know* that. Because I'm going to work—for the next fifty years—to make you happy no matter what." He took another nip out of her neck.

"It isn't over, you know. We'll have to deal with Charlie's mother. And your ex-wife. And I would really like to go for a formal adoption on Charlie—"

"I think that's a great idea, for us to do together." Clearly he liked the concept, just wanted to change the pronoun. "But the rest of the turmoil just comes with the territory. Nothing's ever easy with kids or life. We'll be stuck rolling with the punches a million times."

She tilted her head again, just so she could see those dark velvet eyes and the way they looked at her. "I didn't say yes, you know."

"Huh?"

Finally, he took his attention off her neck.

"You've been making an awful lot of assumptions ever since you proposed in the courthouse. I mean, I never exactly said yes. In fact, you haven't mentioned a single thing about marriage since yesterday."

"Hey, have we had a single second alone since yesterday? Any possible occasion when I might have been able to spring for champagne, something that sparkles for your finger, a little…wooing?"

"I like all those ideas," she said, "but you could have changed your mind."

"Not in this life."

She poked him, gently, between shirt buttons. "I'm just not sure you know what you're getting into. I've been known to get lost."

"I've heard this," he said gravely.

"I've also been known to leave the dishes in the sink overnight. And I'm into rituals, Jack. Like waxing and mud wraps on Sunday night. I think of shopping on a par with vitamins, necessary for regular health. And inside…" She took a breath. "There's still some anger. Not a lot of it. But what's there has been stored up since my mother left. I didn't realize it until Charlie. But I just have to warn you, it probably won't be pretty when it gets out."

"Is this the worst you can scare me with?" he demanded.

"It's good for starters. The relevant issue, though, is whether you're actually going to ask me that infamous question, when no one else is around, and it's just you and me."

"Ah, Merry…" He eased down beside her on the couch. It was probably not a great idea for the kids to find them prone together, but for that moment, Jack seemed to need—really need—the closeness. To touch as much of her as he could. To be absolutely face to face. "To be honest, I was hoping that it would help if I gave you some time to get used to the idea. That some time might up my odds of your saying yes."

"You were really afraid I'd say no?"

But she could see the answer on his face. Her foolish, foolish man, she mused. In a world with so few heroes, Jack was one of the rare ones. An extraordinarily sexy good man. He was an outstanding dad. The kind of man who stood up for his country, for his kids, for anyone who needed him without expecting thanks or even notice. And he was unquestionably a man who protected those he loved.

Especially the woman he loved.

She knew because that woman happened to be her.

And how much he loved her, she could feel right down to her soul. He'd been hurt, she was well aware…but those wounds and experiences only increased his capacity to love.

She knew what she had. "Yes, Jack," she whispered. "Yes, times ten. Yes, times a thousand." She wound her arms around his neck and pulled him closer for a deep, soft kiss…a kiss full of promise, full of hope, full of love.

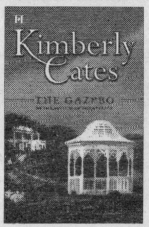

REQUEST YOUR FREE BOOKS!

2 FREE NOVELS FROM THE ROMANCE/SUSPENSE COLLECTION PLUS 2 FREE GIFTS!

JENNIFER GREENE

77145   BLAME IT ON CHOCOLATE___ $5.99 U.S. ___ $6.99 CAN.

(limited quantities available)

TOTAL AMOUNT	$_____
POSTAGE & HANDLING	$_____
($1.00 FOR 1 BOOK, 50¢ for each additional)	
APPLICABLE TAXES*	$_____
TOTAL PAYABLE	$_____

(check or money order—please do not send cash)

To order, complete this form and send it, along with a check or money order for the total above, payable to HQN Books, to: **In the U.S.:** 3010 Walden Avenue, P.O. Box 9077, Buffalo, NY 14269-9077; **In Canada:** P.O. Box 636, Fort Erie, Ontario, L2A 5X3.

Name: _____

Address: _____ City: _____

State/Prov.: _____ Zip/Postal Code: _____

Account Number (if applicable): _____

075 CSAS

*New York residents remit applicable sales taxes.
*Canadian residents remit applicable GST and provincial taxes.

HQN™
We *are* romance™

www.HQNBooks.com   PHJG0107BL